BIG SUR TRILOGY

— Part III —

THE ROAD

In 1923 Lillian Bos Ross and her husband Harry Dicken Ross hiked from the Hearst Castle, where he had worked as a tile setter, to Big Sur for the first time. They were enchanted by this magnificent and rugged land, extolled by Robinson Jeffers, and settled in for good. The photograph above shows Lillian Bos Ross at work in the kitchen of the Livermore Ledge homestead in 1924. She died in 1959, but Harry Dicken still lives in the area. *(Photo by George Challis.)*

THE ROAD

by

LILLIAN BOS ROSS

> *Author of*
>
> THE STRANGER IN BIG SUR
>
> *and* BLAZE ALLAN

and by

GARY M. KOEPPEL

Coast Publishing

LIBRARY OF CONGRESS CATALOGING IN PUBLICATION DATA

ISBN 978-1-467950-08-4
LCCN: 2012905299

Coast Publishing
P.O. Box 223519, Carmel, California 93922
800-875-1757 • www.cstpub.com

DEDICATIONS

This is only a story, true enough. Nothing that happens in this book ever happened in the Big Sur. As far as I know, the people in my books never lived anywhere. Yet, in these Big Sur hills, live the spirits of those who tamed this fierce and awesome land; perhaps their essence could have become infused in mine for, how else could I have written of them with such knowledge of their plain spoken thoughts and feelings? But now three generations of Zande Allans have lived in my heart, walked off my typewriter and gone their own way. I can only hope and believe they have found their way home, far back in the high hills of the Big Sur country where I have lived and loved for almost 25 years.   —Lilian Bos Ross

In 1985 I was humbled when asked by Lillian's husband to rewrite and complete her unfinished manuscript of *The Road*. Now, 27 years later, having at last fulfilled my promise, I am honored to dedicate my efforts to those remarkable American men and women who committed themselves to a hard but self-sustaining life in the wild and lonely mountains of the Big Sur Coast, many of whose descendents I had the personal good fortune to meet, befriend, talk story and learn about the Oldtimers, their lifestyles and their ranches, which they called their Home Place. May this book bestow upon its readers the knowledge from whom and from whence we have come; may it allow us to learn from these courageous homesteaders and their sturdy pioneer ways with the hope that their lives will inspire and improve our own; and, finally, may this book grace us with gratitude toward those hardy generations that built this extraordinary land in which we live freely and are privileged to call our home, America.   *—Gary M. Koeppel*

INTRODUCTION

The Big Sur Trilogy is the story of the last American Pioneer family who lived freely and with self-reliance in that area of the California central coast called after the Spanish, *El Sur de la Grande*, then by the early pioneer homesteaders as the Coast and now known simply as Big Sur.

From Monterey on the north to San Simeon on the south, this 100-mile stretch of rugged and breathtaking coastline was accessible only by foot, mule or horseback until the 1870's when a wagon road was built from Mal Paso Crossing to Bixby Creek. The next 80 miles of the Big Sur coast could be reached only by the Coast Trail high along the mountain ridges until the opening of Highway One in 1937, a remarkable achievement that took eighteen years to build, most of it by convict labor using dynamite and steam shovels.

It is the only highway in America that bypassed an interim wagon road and went directly from a horse trail to an automobile road.

The people who lived in this country earned a plain and hard living by raising cattle, growing stock grasses, fruits and vegetables; they harvested honey from wild hives and picked fresh watercress from the streams; deer were sparse but available; grizzly bears poached the cattle and were slowly killed off, but the mountain lions kept their distance, foraged alone and lived in peace with the pioneers. The eagles and condors soared effortlessly on the updrafts as they circled down from the Santa Lucia mountain tops to the sea.

These were the last American Pioneers. Their lives were forever changed with the building of a road along the cliffs below their mountain homesteads. When the road opened, the "outlanders" began streaming down the narrow and precarious highway in Model A Ford automobiles bringing a flow of change that forever shattered the peace, quietude and independence of the Big Sur homesteaders.

The Big Sur Trilogy tells the story of a way of life, perhaps the ways of the last pioneers in America: their lifestyles, faith, standards and traditions; their plain spoken ways, strong ethics and love of the land on which they struggled which, in turn, gave them the good life of health and happiness, independence and the freedom to feel free.

The old timers scoffed at the idea that a road could be carved into granite escarpments rising some 6,000 feet from the surf, often straight up, unscarred since time began. A Monterey doctor, John Roberts, who photographed the land while making his occasional rounds down the coast, felt that all Americans should have the opportunity to see the beauty he had captured in his camera, so he spent many years petitioning the California legislature to appropriate funds to build a road along such a magnificent coastline that he believed was the most majestic meeting of land and sea in all America.

For eighteen years he was the prime mover of the road as it was being legislated, planned, surveyed and eventually carved out of the cliffs. Just imagine the thoughts and feelings of the pioneers looking down from the high mountains on horseback with rifles slung across their saddles watching, at first the survey teams marking trail, and then the convicts dynamiting their canyons and headlands for a road to carry strangers in auto machines into the land where they lived, loved, flourished and had protected for generations, a road they knew would forever change their lives.

A famous Big Sur stone sculptor, Jim Hunolt, once said about a block of marble: "Every act of destruction becomes an act of creation." I can think of no better description for the building of Highway One in Big Sur, California.   —*Gary M. Koeppel*

FOREWORD

No road leads into that part of California's Coast that is called the Big Sur. A rough wagon road comes only as far as Bixby's Creek and Landing, then goes inland and up the steep west ridges of the Santa Lucias, then bears south through enchanted redwood canyons, wet and impassable in winter, until reaching the flatland at sea level on the Coast known as Rancho El Sur, not far from the Pfeiffer Resort and Big Sur Post Office.

Along 100 miles of sparsely inhabited California coast, the rugged Santa Lucia mountains step down into the ocean's blue-green and brace their boney feet in its mysterious dark. From this shoreless sea the headlands rise to a stark six thousand feet in majestic silence, broken only by the sound of swift streams plunging toward the sea through deep redwood canyons and the steady breaking of surf against the granite rocks far below.

In the spring of 1909 the Coast is less settled with folks than when Portuguese explorer Juan Cabrillo saw it from his ship four hundred years earlier. Now the Indians are long gone, stricken by the white man's ills and mistreatment while building monasteries along the California coast. But in this remote coastal land, the same warm fragrances of pine and sage, of laurel and redwood, of tan-oak and yarrow, still drift down the mountains and out to sea as they did when time began.

And the great eagles and condors still soar on the updrafts from the cool canyons and rise proudly above the clouds to the highest spires of rock. The few families who scrape a hard-earned living from running cattle in these mountains live simple lives, much like herdsmen in the Bible, with faith in the future by steady work and living each day, simply and to its fullest. Years come and go with little to make one year different from the year before or the one to follow. Years are remembered by rainfall, by new grass in the spring, by the size of the calf crop or the good honey years. Now and again, a baby is born and an old man dies.

I

Through that deep notch south of Old Baldy, between two peaks in the Santa Lucia mountains, the sun was already rising in the east window, or Ventana as the Spaniards called it. It was early May of 1919 and, outside the dark redwood walls of the kitchen in the old Allan place, the sloping foothills of the Big Sur country were veiled in wild lilac, and the new morning was as sweet as lilac honey.

Eleven-year old Zande Allan the third tightened his strawberry-stained fingers over the empty milk mug and wished that Gramp would push back from the table and start with him to Buzzard Point. Outside was always the best place to be when anyone felt broody.

His grandfather, the first Zande Allan, tugged at the collar of his faded blue work shirt, impatiently running his thumb between the worn neckband and his weathered neck. He finished his fidgeting by pushing his empty plate toward the center of the bare board table. Not only his voice, but his eyes, too, had an accusing sharpness directed toward his wife's straight back, as Hannah Allan stepped around in her kitchen where every inch of work space was already piled high with fixings for the large family party.

The old man said briskly, "It don't settle anything for you to say forget about the road; that'll never come to be in our time."

She crossed the kitchen, opened the storeroom door and, as she held the swing door open with her back and reached in for the sugar pail and brown crock of fresh butter, both Zande Allans had a look at eight fat young fryers hanging smooth and golden-skinned from the meat hook in front of the screened north window.

From a nail on the redwood wall she took down her one precious new aluminum kettle, almost filled it with sugar, added a half-cup of flour and a pinch of salt. Mixing this together thoroughly, she poured half of it over each of the two large enameled pans of hulled strawberries. As she began to blend this into the berries with a hand carved wooden spoon, her husband said, "Hannah, I spoke to you."

Still stirring the berries, she looked over her shoulder at him, explaining, "I was thinking. I didn't really say, 'forget it.' I only said—"

"I know, you said, 'it wouldn't make any difference in our time.'"

Zande got up slowly and walked toward his wife, looking as though he appreciated her starched blue calico dress, her white bleached flour sack apron with its ties and pockets of the same blue print. He leaned against her worktable, dodged the stirring spoon as he selected one of the largest sugarcoated berries, ate it with a relish and smiled at her teasingly. "Good," he said. "Crisp and sweet; not much like the days when the ranch was just startin'."

He bent toward his wife, his hand half-reaching out toward her. "It's not that I'm again' change, Hannah. God knows I wouldn't go back to the old ranch I brought you to some fifty year ago. I know things change. Folks get born. They die. Our own young ones change and we can't hold 'em back. But we got a way of living worked out here that' good, real good, and it ought to last forever."

"And I can't see why it shouldn't," she said reasonably. "We're up here in the hills on our own land, mindin' our own business. All the road talk is for a road that goes along the shore far below."

Adding half a cup of butter broken into small bits to each pan of strawberries, she set the pans on the back of the stove to warm and deepen their flavor slowly before they became filling for the pie.

As she began gathering the dishes from the table, she asked her grandson, "Why don't you run outside for a bit, Zan? Picking all them berries and hulling them, too, before breakfast, I'd say you've earned some playtime. You're grampa'll excuse you."

The boy looked down, pushing the empty mug back and forth on the redwood table before he said, "Gramp's give me play time already. Him and me's going over to Buzzard Point to look at the young stock."

The old man rapped the worktable with hard knuckles, but he winked as young Zande, startled, looked up at him.

"Come on, Zan. We got marchin' orders. If that wood box's full, let's you and me go calf counting before this place breaks out all over with relations."

Zan, grinning widely, jumped up, pushed the log bench neatly back against the wall, went over and lifted the wood box lid as he stood beside the door.

"It's full, Gramps. Got lilac and sycamore and some redwood limbs, Gramma, so's you can keep the oven like you want it."

Both grandparents looked at the boy fondly. Old Zande saw the Mariana blue eyes, the slender proud nose and long capable hands that were his wife's when he had brought her to the ranch as a mail order bride. Hannah also saw his stubborn chin and the slight build that strongly resembled her husband when she came from the East long ago to be his bride—those same features that had put upon him a need to prove himself as good, or better, than the next fellow. And the same full, wide mouth of the boy's mother, Dulcie Gallo, who had little practical sense, but was packed with love and laughter, now smiled up at them from their grandson's face with Dulcie's own impish zest and relish for life.

Zan let down the wood box lid with one hand, pushed open the screen down with the other, and his grandmother alertly reminded him, "Don't let it slam, Zan. I'm hoping Baby Lara will sleep until I get the pies ready for the oven."

He protested, "I hardly ever forget about the door over here anymore, Gramma. I make myself remember how much slams bother Aunt Margaret. Gram, you go'n keep Mrs. Ramirez' baby for always?"

"We'll see," she evaded.

The door shut softly, and the boy was outside but shouting back cheerfully, "Come on, Gramp. Let's go, huh?"

"In a minute." He turned to his wife, shaking his head as though for once he was bewildered.

"Change?" He asked. "We got enough of it right now to upset a whole county. Margaret's no better," he said bitterly, "Avery's new bride and she's as helpless as a twenty year old baby. You got her on your hands long as she carries on that way. Got Avery, too. But you don't have to saddle yourself with the Ramirez baby when its own mother tries to kill herself."

"You think it would be easier for me to let Lara stay up there with her and starve?" Hannah asked.

"Maybe Mrs. Ramirez will pull through; we'll find out when Dr. Roberts get here. We got to take the day as it comes," Zande said, "get used to what upsets and changes it brings along. I guess if a road come we can get used to it, too!"

Outside the door young Zan stopped shuffling his bare feet, heard his grandfather say, "Any place a road comes it brings its 'here-today-gone-tomorrow' ways along with it. We got troubles enough already. Nobody runs a road across my land long as I live."

He shut the door behind him very gently and the two Zande Allans walked out through the garden together, crossed the barnyard and went up the pasture trail.

The trail was a gentle one for the Big Sur country, and wound among knolls so thickly covered with yellow Johnny-jump-ups that they looked like plump sofa pillows tossed out to rest on the great fields of blue pine. The white forget-me-not, with its almost invisible stems, made a fragrant floating mist above the blue and yellow, flowing over the open slopes until it joined the tile of wild blue lilac that cover even the most perpendicular slopes. The lilac stopped where a narrow strip of bench land broke the mountain's sheer plunge into the sea. Here the benches were so thickly covered with wild golden poppies that, to the boy looking down from the trail's height of about two-thousand feet, the gold band was like a golden light, joining the pale blue lilac to the endless pale blue sea and sky.

He took a deep breath, trying to find some faint salt sea odor mixed with the heady flower perfume, but let out the breath in a rush of laughter as a wood dove from the madrone trees higher up called mournfully, "No tomorrow, No tomorrow."

"Listen to that old dove still bellyaching, Gramp."

His grandfather looked back, his craggy gray eyebrows frowning above the brown scythe of his sharp nose, and said, "Huh?"

Seeing that his grandfather was still studying on something, Zan made a game of trying to keep pace with the spare frame that moved so swiftly ahead of him on gnarled old legs that were tough as Manzanita root. Even at the age of seventy-one, Zande Allan was still able to keep his reputation for covering more mountain trail miles than any man from one end of the Santa Lucia's to the other.

When at last he stopped on a knoll at the top of the climb, Zan was glad to rest silently while his grandfather's eyes roamed over pines high up in the rocky peaks, redwood darkly green, almost black in the windless canyons. They followed a fifty-mile length of wild broken coastline, but always his eyes came back to dwell on the wonder pastureland above Buzzard Point.

The small boy shifted his weight slowly to his other foot, but his grandfather noticed and turned his head quickly. "Be still, boy. I'm thinking on something."

"Yes'r."

Again and again the old man looked over this country he had been born in, looking at the mountains as though he were a stranger to them. Zan felt easier when his grandfather snorted, "If he tried to put his crazy notion through right now, he thought, he'd be bested. "I'm strong enough to fight him and any amount like him."

"Fight who, Gramp?"

"Doc Roberts. Crazy man, he is, with his idea of bringing a road into Big Sur...into country like this. Damn foolishness."

The boy's curiosity was stronger than his respect for his grandfather's testy humor.

"Doctor Roberts?" He asked. "I thought he was bringin' his picture-taking box today and was comin' to take our picture."

"That's what he thinks," Old Zande sniffed. "He should of knowed something was up when I asked him would he come take a picture from all of us."

The old man stamped fretfully, then paced back and forth on top of the knoll. He was so wrapped in his own concerns that he could not hear young Zande's faint protest.

"Walk careful, Grampa. You're stepping right on the flower's faces."

He did hear the last word, "faces," for he glanced quickly down at the crushed flowers and stepped back onto the deeply worn trail, muttering, "Faces." "Any fool should know I've no use for a picture-made set of our faces. I know what us Allans look like, don't I?"

The little boy looked uncertain for a moment and then his face slowly crinkled in a wry Allan smile. "Course you do," he agreed. "I know what you look like too, I guess. But don't you want to see how that black box works on folks' faces? I do. You said yourself that a picture box has a sharp eye for mountains; gets every wrinkle and even the steep of 'em. I bet I'm bug-eyed from holding my breath by the time he clicks it shut on all of us."

"Stuff."

The old man reached down and put his hand on the boy's thin shoulder. He looked down at the blue eyes lifted to his and said slowly, "Never forget you're an Allan, boy. No matter what you're called on to look at as you grow on through this world, face it with your back straight and your head high. You're my namesake, Zande. I look to you to keep up for me when I'm done and have to sit back."

His grandfather was talking to him, man to man. Pride and embarrassment darkened his eyes, flushed his fair skin. He tried to answer, but no word would come so he pulled from his pocket the knife his grandfather had given him on his last birthday, turned it slowly on the braided buckskin cord he had fashioned to keep his treasure safe.

His grandfather smiled, bent down and took the knife and cord into his own lean, knobby hand.

"That's it. That's Allan," he said. "You don't trust it, you won't lost it; you take steps to hang onto what's yours."

For an instant he turned the cord in his fingers and then asked, "Where'd you get the string, boy?"

"Made it."

"Hump. Not bad, not bad. Who helped you?"

Zan straightened his back, lifted his head and drew the cord into his own hand, dropped the knife back into his pocket. "Pa's been showing me how to work leather," he said flatly. "But he never helped me. He shows me. I make my own stuff."

As the old man pursed his lips, nodded, his eyes held a bit of a twinkle. "Thought so," he answered. "Well, your pa never was no great shakes with his handling leather. Take that knot at the end. Now—" he reached for the end of the cord but he boy drew back.

"It's the chain for my knife, Gramp. I made it and I'll keep it like it is."

Very amiably came the answer, "Sure you will. Use what you got. I'd hide ye if you threw it out, 'stead of wore it out, what you got."

He started forward on the trail that led down into the pasture filled with high-tailed young caves, mad with spring. As the old man's eyes took count of all the lusty young stock, his step quickened until it seemed to young Zande that he'd have to run to keep up. But he didn't want to run.

Drawing by Robin Coventry

He'd just been talked to as an Allan man, and he wanted that right, so he broadened his stride grotesquely, trying to will his legs into the length and strength of what was fitting for his grandfather's approving nod.

He fought his labored breath to silence, but the thing his grandma, Hannah Allan, called "growing pains" threatened to betray him. He kept on for a few more steps and his prayers were answered when old Zande stepped off the trail, sank down on the flat stump of the large oak tree.

"Hot for May, boy. Let's sit and cool and take a count of them calves, what you say?"

The boy nodded, not trusting his breath.

After a few minutes the older man asked, "What'd you make of 'em, boy?"

"Thirty-five."

"Wrong! There's thirty-four in sight."

Elated, the boy jumped up, pointing to a small tuft on the edge of Buzzard Creek, half a mile away. "Watch that spot, Gramp, and tell me now, ain't it got ears?"

7

Old Zande's seldom-heard laugh rang out. "You'll do, young'n, you'll do. Sure it's a steer. I was testing you, seeing if I could back you down, wondering if you was sharp enough to pick it out."

Offended, the little boy stood up, "I know how to tally stock." His voice betrayed hurt. "You taught me. An' if I say I see a thing, I seen it, and the devil couldn't make me go back on what my own eyes tells me."

The youngster watched his grandfather's head nod thoughtfully, his thumb rubbing slowly back and forth on his lower lips and chin.

"You got the straight of it, young'n," he said. "Stick up for yourself. Man's got no need to run his self down; the neighbor'll take care of that." He waved his hand toward the log and said, "Sit down, little bantam; get your wind back. You near busted your lungs keepin' up."

With a grin the boy relaxed against the warmth of the stump, pulled out his knife and broke off a piece of splintered oak to whittle. His grandfather sagged a trifle, as though, in the companionable silence, he was delicately telling the boy that the rapid walk had also tired him.

He took off the old felt hat that years had whittled down to a little more that a broken crown and an absurd suggestion of brim, pushed back his thinning hair, then set the seasoned old hat back firmly and looked down to where Buzzard Point stopped being pasture and sheered off into forbidding granite that dropped straight into the sea, eight hundred feet below. There was no beach on any part of Buzzard Point and no man knew how straight or how deep into the ocean that steep gray wall stood.

The minute the older man put his hand on the stump to shove himself to his feet, the boy closed his knife, cached the oak chip against some future time for whittling at this spot, and was carefully on his feet, not a second before but a polite second after the head of the Allan clan stood erect.

"I been thinking on you, Zan," the old man said. "You say you can believe what your own eyes tell you, but I don't know—things ain't always like they look; times when a man needs to stop and touch a thing, and to smell it. Even so, can turn out that what he sees, smells and feels still ain't what he thinks it is."

The boy's eyes widened. He blurted out, "You feel all right, Grampa?"

Laughter shook the old man and to hide it he pulled out a faded, neatly mended blue bandana, snorted solemnly into its crisp folds, and then waved the boy back toward the house with his hand still clutching the kerchief.

"You been spendin' too much time with the women folk, boy; all winter with a woman teacher, your sister a'raisin' you, your Gramma cluckin' over you. You should ought to be throwed to the coyotes to be raised like I was, but by damn, the women's getting too much for us. The world's goin' soft."

"School's all right," the boy protested. "I can read, Gramp, and I'm learning to draw running letters— writing, you know. An' I'm going to have a new reader next year and there's a buffalo's picture in it that tells about buffaloes and about lions with big manes to them, like collie dogs has. Ever seen a lion like that, Gramp?"

"Never did. Never thought about it. Grizzlies, that's what I was thinking about when I was your age. Big fellows, they was; seemed to me they stood nine foot tall and weighed a half ton."

Awed joy, mixed with a trace of doubt, colored young Zan's face. "Honest, Gramp, was they?"

"That's what I'm telling you. They looked to my eyes when I was eight and left alone with an old blunderbuss that I had to lash down and shoot with a string or it'd kicked me into the next county. Corrals and fences my pop and the Coast boys built to save small pigs or young stock from grizzlies looked powerful thick and stout to me till one of them grizzlies reared up and looked over it. That stout corral looked mighty puny then, and my hand, it'd be a-shakin' when I pulled the string. I could see that old b'ar, and I could smell him all right, but I never felt him. Never hit one till I was most a growed man. Never did kill one what was half the size of them I saw as a boy. But I did get a big 'un once, got him with the long knife, though he nearly killed me dead. Gave away the hide to some mountain fellahs just for pushing the carcass off me and took me to their cabin to mend. I'm just telling you not to pay too much heed to what your eyes tell you."

"Nos'r. I'll remember, Gramp. And Gramma says I can go down the trail with a bit of lunch for Doctor Roberts, wait for him by Wild Cow Creek, and walk back with him."

"Well, you go on back and help your Gramma first. Set on feeding the whole tribe today, she is, but you tell her I said there was no call for her to run her cooking clear out to Cow Creek. The ol' doc won't starve till he gets here, and won't do me no harm to have him start out in our talk today by bein' glad for a bellyful of good food he et in my house."

Regretfully, the boy answered, "Gram wants me to take that baby Lara ridin' around the yard in my old wagon, or keep her quiet till some of the girls come over. What we get saddle with Mrs. Ramirez' baby Lara for, anyhow?"

"We didn't get saddled with her," the old man's voice sharpened as he drew his craggy brows together and looked down at his namesake. "Nobody puts anything off on us. Your Gramma's went out her way to fetch the baby up here when Mrs. Ramirez took so bad. The Ramirez' been right good neighbors to all the Coast folk since I was born. You skip on now and help your gram like you said you would."

"Yes'r."

The man looked after the small figure that shrunk as if his legs widened the distance. The too small, faded blue overalls, the outgrown faded blue shirt, blended into the blue of the lupine and the towhead was lost among a wealth of cream-cups and tidy-tips. Thinking of Zan's eager blue eyes, big generous mouth and stubborn chin, he looked down at the barefoot print in the dust of the trail. The print looked as delicate and slim as a girl's; Zan Allan was certainly undersized for any Allan, and yet as his grandfather studied the print he seemed satisfied.

"Good, square toes the young one's got, but he toes out a bit. Plenty stubborn, and God knows he'll need it in the world he's coming up in."

Thinking of the arguments he meant to use in making Doctor Roberts admit that a road through the Big Sur was wasteful, extravagant and useless, Zande Allan strode across his pasture and to the edge of the cliff. Bad Tooth Rock, the black rock pinnacles that stuck sharply out of the sea beyond the breakers striking against the straight cliff, pleased him. He looked at them, and then bent out against the strong upsurge of wind from the heady drop of straight cliff. As long as the Allans held fast to their own coastline and refused to have a road cross their land, there would not be any road. Not Doctor Roberts, or the devil himself, could get a road past Buzzard's Point and, besides, that was his land.

Happily, even if a bit off key, Zan was humming, "Oh, the Big Sur Coast is wild and lonely," as he closed the gate between the barnyard the small, tidy fenced-in garden in the back of his grandparent's house.

The path, which was kept clear of weeds by a thick layer of crushed abalone and mussel shell, suited him. It didn't drive straight for the back porch as if its only business in life was to get a fellow from the barnyard to the door. No sir, not this path. Hannah Allan had laid it out, and it went meandering around a gnarled old lilac tree now covered with heart-shaped leaves and long bunches of grayish purple flowers. Zan stopped humming as he watched a bumblebee roughing up each of the tiny square trumpets of the large clusters. The old bee's had honey for his breakfast and now he's got his pack bags loaded with gold pollen. He's making a lot of buzzing and grumbling; guess it's a heavy load for him to fly with.

The bee launched himself and the youngster's tough bare feet slapped lazily along the shell path. He pulled the screen door open, jumped in, and remembered just in time to put his hand out to stop the screen from slamming.

Hi grandmother was bending over the very same baby cradle Zan's own father, Zande Junior, had swung in more than thirty years ago. With his mind the boy knew that his father, even Gramp Allan himself, had been a baby once upon a time. But the idea of his Uncle Martin or his Aunt Blaze ever swinging and crying in that cradle always made him laugh. Try as he would to think of knitted bootees, it was his Uncle Martin's size twelve boots he always envisioned dangling out of the little cradle.

"You came as square on the minute as if you had a clock in your head, Zan." Hannah Allan lifted a whimpering baby that seemed too small for the tremendous shock of black hair above its crumpled red face.

"It was Gramp's clock in his head," Zan confessed. "He sent me."

The spare old lady and the small boy looked companionably at each other. Secretly she was proud that she had lived to see the mark of her own Martin family dominate the face of one Allan man. But she was pleased that he had the stubborn Allan chin, one that would see him into trouble and out again. A good, stirred-up mixture, the youngster is, she was fond of telling herself. And the Demas' relish for life and laughing had shaped the boy's quick warm mouth.

Her pity was that, only a scarce year ago, so slight a thing as a cold that turned into a fever, had taken little Lara's mother, Dulcie Allan, when she was in her prime and so full of life and laughter. The memory put an added tenderness into Hannah's smile as she handed the squirming baby to the reluctant boy.

"Don't be afraid, she's dry," Hannah promised Zan, and settled the pucker-faced baby Lara in his unwilling arms. "Just hold her for a minute and I'll get a pillow and a blanket for your cart and you can wheel her 'round the yard."

Zan scowled down at the baby who scowled right back at him as he called after Hannah Allan, "When's the aunts or some of the girls getting here? Seems like this young one could stay put till there was women folks to hush her. My gosh, I got things to do, like sharpen my knife, and I ought to be at it."

Zan was still scowling as he trailed outside after the brisk step of his silent grandmother. She settled the pillow to her satisfaction, smoothed her own white afghan for little Lara Ramirez' comfort and, as she took the baby into her own arms with a soothing "there, there, lambie," she also soothed the ruffled boy. "Blaze said she'd come early and she's stopping by at your house for Maria."

"Then we'll get something done, after all. If Aunt Blaze said early, she means early, and Maria was no loafer either, even if she is my sister."

"Nice of you to admit it."

Startled, the boy looked up at his grandmother, but her face was as bland as her tone. "Blaze and Maria are coming to set up the table for dinner and then they're going to fix the parlor pretty so's we can have the picture taken there."

"Aw, stuff. Couldn't one of them look after this baby? Whyn't we get our picture took outdoors? That's where we live, anyhow, not in a parlor!"

Laughing, Hannah ran her fingers into his thick hair, tightened them and gave his head a little shake. "Real Allan man, you are. We work outdoors, honey, but even you must admit a house is a cozy thing when it's night, or raining."

He grinned, but wouldn't answer.

She smiled back, nodding as she went on, "As long as we're getting a picture, I want a rag carpet, the melodeon, the lamp and what comforts we got to show in it. Then the grandchildren and their children won't think they come from savages. A picture lasts a long time." Hannah sighed, but as the baby started to whimper, she turned back toward her kitchen and told the boy, "Roll her along easy, Zan, and be careful when

12

you turn the cart. Don't take her out of the yard."

"No'm."

The baby's whimper had turned into a lusty howl, and Zan impatiently jerked the wagon forward, then found himself feeling important as the crying stopped the moment the cart moved. He turned the cart carefully around the fragrant lilac, at the gate, and again at the porch steps.

Suddenly there was the sound of hooves, the creak of saddles and light voices. Zan stood on tiptoe, peered across the small barranca to the north and jerked the small wagon around so quickly that the baby rolled off the pillow, onto the path, and into his grandmother's prized bed of pansies.

Unaware that Lara and the white afghan were settled among the flowers, Zan pulled the wagon as fast as he dared, reached the porch steps and called in an agitated whisper, "Hi Gramma, take the baby, will you? The girls are coming and Tilli's riding behind Maria. Gosh, if she caught me baby tending she'd never stop jawing about it."

"Nonsense." His grandmother's voice came crisply through the screen door. "Either of you should be pleased to mind that poor baby for a fine neighbor like Mrs. Ramirez."

Zande look chasten but he defended himself, "If Tilli gets a notion to tease, she's worse than a buzz fly."

Hannah pushed open the screen door with the toe of her shoe, dodged through the opening with four bubbling strawberry pies in a rack and set them in the shade to cool as she said, "Run along, then, boy. I'll take the baby in now."

Her glance covered both the retreating Zan and the empty wagon. "Merciful goodness, boy, what did you do with the baby?"

Zan skidded to a stop at the corner of the house, his eyes wide. "I just wheeled her like you said—"

"Where is she, then?"

"She's in the wagon. I never touched her."

Hannah Allan was sixty-seven years old but her grandson had a hard time keeping up with her as she ran down the path. He cut across the yard and they met by the gate where the large syringa bush sheltered the pansy bed.

"Oh, Gramma, your nice pansies, she's smashed them!"

13

Hannah had picked up the afghan-rolled bundle, turned back the fringe that covered the baby's face, and she drew a long breath. "Not hurt. She's fast asleep, and the pansies will straighten up." She sounded pleased as she said softly, "I guess you're almost the only man creature in all these hills would ever give a thought to my flowers!"

Zan looked down bashful as he said, "When I was out with Gramp I wished you was along. Flowers so thick'n great big hunks like crazy quilt patches. Tidy tips, lupines, Johnny-jump-ups, every which color.

"We'll go look together when the house gets quiet again. But if you want to miss Tilli, you'd better get going. They're riding up the hill right now."

"Thanks, Granny. Say, listen—I'm going to meet the doctor. Been aiming to greet him down by Cow Creek. I'll take him a handful of jerky, can I?"

"Yes, you may. But wouldn't you rather take a nice cut of pie?

Loftily the young boy answered, "Naw, he'll want a man's sort of bite. Nothing like jerky to stay a fellow's stomach when he's trail walking."

He had no eye for his grandmother's amused smile, only a fixed purpose, to meet the doctor, maybe even, in return for bringing along venison jerky, he'd get to carry that wonderful picture box, at least part of the way...

He had rifled the small storeroom where the bacon and ham swung from the ceiling, and the shelled yellow corn hung in sacks for the grinding. He had his pocket stuffed with the best pieces of dried venison when he heard the light gay voices of the girls greeting his grandmother.

He heard Tilli's voice sweetly begging, "Oh, do help me down, Aunt blaze. I want to hold the baby for Grandma."

Zande made a face in her direction, quietly opened the narrow back door of the shed, and then slid down the steep bank, putting on brakes for himself by catching at the branches of wild lilac and cascara. One of his favorite games was sliding down canyons standing upright, and he won if he made it to the bottom without once being knocked off his feet.

"I won that time," he told himself, as he slid down a steep bank, landing on the trail over which the women had just ridden. He kicked and cleared the train of the mass of dead leaves, sticks, boulders and dirt that had come down with him. While his feet cleared the trail, his hands

were busy feeling the back of his neck for any wood ticks he might have knocked off the brush. He felt none, took a hasty brush at his sleeves and back, and then struck off down the trail toward the Coast.

At any other time this trip would have given him endless things to loiter over: tracks, birds, their nests, the slight hollow among the redwood needles that told him where a deer had slept. Right now his one idea was to get to the rest log where the trail crossed Cow Creek, and be sitting there waiting when the doctor came.

Breathless, wiping the moisture from his face, he started down the little canyon that held Cow Creek. There were deer tracks, coyote tracks, and a regular crisscross of bird tracks, but no man's track. He could see the whole stretch of the rest log and not one was on it. This really was a day. He'd won again!

He dropped down on the old moss-covered rest log and with a loud "huh," rubbed his face with his arm and ran his hands over his hair.

He knew how shy he would have felt at walking up to the doctor. Not only a town man and a stranger, but a doctor as well, and Zan wondered if the man had also been sitting on the log, claiming it, could he have been able to walk right up to him and act like the man his grandfather was always telling him to act like?

He heard a slight rustle behind a clump of small redwood just beyond the log. Zan felt the same sort of shock all over that he felt whenever the noiseless deerfly suddenly drew blood on his bare leg. He sat as stiffly as the hardened knot on the log beside him and only his eyes moved slowly toward the spot where he had hear that human-sounding rustle.

At first he could see nothing. He waited a few seconds longer, holding his breath, but as nothing happened, he turned his head slightly. Now he saw what he had missed with his first glance. Under the low branches of the redwood saplings, down among the tangle of last year's ferns with their dry brown fronds were two brown shoes resting on the crumpled point of a fern-brown blanket.

Zan sat as quietly as before in spite of himself, an amused smile broke the blankness of the face he held proper for a young Allan man to show strangers. The thing that amused him was that when the doctor woke up, he'd wonder who the fellow sitting on the log might be.

Zan felt that he had the right to be pleased with himself. Of course, he knew this was the doctor because he'd come to meet him. But no Allan had to wonder if anyone was an outsider. They'd know. Say you start with the brown blanket; a Coast man walking home from a far place might have such a thing, but no Coast man would ever have such shoes. It was not the brown hide, though anyone could see that the color was dye. It wasn't the brass rings for the sting to lace through, either. Plenty men that made every shoe worn on their ranch put those rings in. Gramp didn't, but some folks bought all sorts of truck from outside. No. What clinched it, what made those shoes into town stuff, were the machine-stitched soles. Sidewalk stuff, soles like that were.

Suddenly the man behind the sidewalk shoes sat up, put a strong blunt hand on the pointed toe of his shoe, pulled as though he were trying to work his toes back where they'd have more room. Between a thatch of thick brown hair and a brush of thick brown beard, a pair of gray eyes blinked at the boy. A deep voice said, "Hello there, boy. Where'd you drop from?"

Zan jumped to his feet, answered, "From the Allan place, Sir. Come to show you the short cut."

16

The doctor tucked both feet back under himself, put one hand on the log end, used the nearest sapling as a lever and still he groaned as he pulled himself to his feet. He hobbled around the end of the log, sat down yawning as he brushed dry brown redwood needles out of his hair and beard.

He said, "You been growing too fast, Zan. I didn't know you. Short cut, huh? Well, that's a thought. Shouldn't have started here in these toothpick shoes, but it was like this—"

The doctor broke off to yawn and stretch, and Zan nodded to show he was interested and the doctor went on. "I been trying to get here all spring. Always too busy. But when I had to come as far as the Garrapata to bring in the Ramgate baby, I got the job done and lit out for the South Coast before I got caught by another measles case or another baby."

Zan's eyes were anxious as he asked, "But your picture box? Didn't you bring that?"

"Sure, sure. Never come onto the Coast at all without old Betsy. There she sits, under the top of the blanket." The doctor flexed his spine, muttered a word in his beard, and asked, "Fetch her around, will you, son? And fold up the blanket, too. I'm stiff as the log over there and as lank as a she-wolf."

Zan made no sign that he had brought anything along that was good for hunger. He picked up the large camera, carried it over to the log and chose the broadest, flattest surface before he cautiously put it down. Then he went back, shook out the blanket, folded it and made a pack sling of the rope he found at the blanket's edge. As he put the roll alongside the camera, the doctor said, "You're a good woodsman, Zan."

Zan felt it was true. He was as handy as most, maybe a mite better than some boys when it came to pack gear. He answered, complacently, "Pop and Gramp Allan both helped learn me. They know how."

He caught a smile vanishing from this bearded man's face and stiffened a bit. But he offered the handful of jerky he pulled from his pocket. "A string of meat and a drink of creek water helps a lot when a man's tuckered from the trail," he said.

The doctor chose the largest piece of dried venison, chewed busily for a long time, and then held out his hand for more. There were four more pieces. Zan put three of them into the doctor's hand, the last one into his own mouth.

As they chewed jerky, the stream sang to them. A quail cock warned his hens and chicks that something strange was going on down by the creek. A stubby-tailed brown wren, not much bigger than an acorn, worked busily over branches and twigs not two feet away from the rest log, and on a dead oak tree a bright flicker's sharp bill vibrated his own roll of forest drums.

After the last of the doctor's jerky was eaten, the man and boy still sat quietly together watching the shadow of the wide woodwardia ferns shift and change as the sun moved slowly ahead on its own sky business. When a shaft of light struck across the brightly pebbled water close to their feet, the doctor stood up.

He felt for the rope on the blanket roll, and Zan reached an uncertain hand toward the camera. "I'm sure-footed," he said.

"It's pretty heavy to carry," said the doctor as he nodded and Zan lifted the camera. "She's heavy, Betsy is, but she's worth carrying." He waved a hand, pointing about the silent little canyon. "This canyon is the real magic, but Betsy's got her own magic. Helps me see all this while I'm rusting in towns."

"What 'magic' mean?"

The doctor considered a moment. "There's all kinds of magic, all sorts of meanings to it, depends on who is thinking about magic."

Zan's confused eyes met the doctor's glance. The bearded man let go of the blanket rope and leaned forward. "The easiest sort to understand is something like—something like, ahh—" and his eyes sparkled triumphantly as he said, "like me picking that silver two-bit piece out of your ear, for instance."

The boy's hand lifted quickly to his ear, felt it curiously. The empty hand dropped. "My Gramp thinks fooling talk and lies is both cut off the same stick."

The doctor cocked his head, pursed his mouth. "Does he now? I wouldn't wonder but he's right, in a way. But I was talking about magic, not lies. Look here, boy. And watch me closely, look at my hands."

He put both stubby hands out in front of him, held them quietly as the boy looked at the strong short fingers, saw the fern-like patterns of shining brown hairs that started back of his wrists, were hidden by his shirt sleeves.

The doctor's drawl was light, teasing. "You've looked carefully?

Anything on the back of these hands except hands?"

Puzzled, Zan shook his head.

"Well, keep watching. Don't take your eyes off my hands. I want you to catch me if I'm up to any tricks."

Uncertain of what this might be about, but fascinated, Zan watched the doctor's hands turn palms up. The hands then turned rapidly under his gaze, first the backs, then the palms.

"Anything in my hands?"

Zan shook his head.

Triumphantly the doctor called, "All right, sir. Now for the magic."

His right hand shot out suddenly, Zan felt the blunt fingers very gently touching his ear, and then, with a shout of "I thought so!" The doctor held his right hand out before the boy, a silver quarter shining between the tips of his first two fingers.

"That's magic," he said. "The simple kind. What do you think your grandfather would call it?"

"A silver two-bit piece," the youngster answered. "How'd you get it into my ear?"

"I took it out of your ear, didn't I?" The doctor asked teasingly. "And now I'll take that gold watch out of your pocket. Watch me!"

Startled, the boy clapped his hand to his pocket, felt it thoroughly before he faltered. "No watch in there to take out. Nothing but my knife and some leather string."

"That's what you think," the doctor chided gently. "Might take quite a bit of magic to do it, but I bet I can pull a gold watch out of that pocket. Watch me close, now."

With a muttered "Hocus pocus humm-i-mocus" the large man rapidly waved his hands in front of Zan's blue eyes, showing first the palms, then the backs, moving his big square palms so rapidly that Zan could scarcely keep track of them. Suddenly the doctor's left hand shot out, his fingers dived into the youngster's pocket and drew out the knife, the leather string— and a gold, open-faced watch. The watch was ticking loudly and the hands point to ten minutes of eleven.

"Well, sir," the doctor observed cheerfully, "Just what I expected, a real gold watch. What do you think of that?"

Zan looked frightened. He swallowed and whispered, "You fooled me someway, didn't you, huh?"

The doctor hastily sat down on the rest log, reached out and put an arm around the boy, drew him down to sit close beside him. "Sure, I did. That was just make-believe magic—a trick. Would you like me to show you how I took that two-bits out of your ear?"

Eagerness lighted the boy's blue eyes. He leaned forward excitedly. "Could you learn me to do that, honest? Could I do it without I had two-bits?"

"You got the money, that's yours. I took it out of your ear, didn't I?"

"No sir. You was too quick for me. But I know you put it there. I didn't have any money so it's not mine."

The doctor agreed, "You're right, boy. Your mind is quicker than your eye—and that's a good thing. Allow me to present you with this magic two-bit piece, and then, let me see—" he looked at his watch. "We could take ten minutes now for you to practice this trick and still get up to your place before noon. I suppose your grandfather knows I'm on my way, doesn't he?"

"Yes'r. Arvis Demas rode by day before and left word you was driving into the Coast. Said you'd maybe leave your rig at the Captain's place and walk in to Gramp's place. Gramma's getting dinner for you and the whole Allan clan and hopin' you're going to take a picture of us all."

"Can't think of a thing I'd like better than to eat one of your Gramma's dinner and then take a picture of the whole contented kit and kaboodle of you. How many you your Allan folks will be there?"

Zan looked vague. "Oh, I d'no. Guess fifteen or twenty, maybe."

The doctor whistled. "Make old Betsy sweat to catch 'em all smiling at the same time."

"Yes'r. But could you start showing me how to magic a quarter now?"

"We've started."

By the end of ten minutes young Zan had gotten the idea that the hand can be quicker than the eye. He knew how to make magic, but his hand was no help in creating illusion.

Suddenly the doctor, who had been as absorbed as the child, jumped up and said guiltily, "We got to start traveling, Zan, or we'll catch hell from your Grandpa. Bad manners to come late to a meal, you know."

The boy stood up, pocketed the quarter, and carefully took up the camera. The doctor slung the blanket over his shoulder and they started up the steep castle trail that was young Zan's idea of a short cut. He

chattered eagerly, laying out a plan for secretly performing the two-bit trick, shaking with laughter as he told how he would fool Tilli, then his sister Maria, working up to trying it on his father as he got better and quicker and, finally, when he was certain sure that he was good almost as Doctor Roberts, he'd fool Gramp.

"I bet I could fool Cousin Tilli right now, she's a regular fraidy cat. Maybe fool Maria, too; she doesn't know nothing about Magic. I guess girls is easier fooled than boys and men, don't you think, Doctor Roberts?"

The doctor stopped, his breathing labored. His eyes danced as he answered, as soon's he'd got his breath, "I believe that is a question every man has to answer for himself, Zan. And you may have different ideas about it at different times in your life."

"Well, maybe. But wait till you see Tilli. I can come up behind her and say, 'there a snake in your apron pocket,' and she'll run screaming every time."

"Will she now? I'd say she'll get along all right as she grows up. Smart girl, would be my guess."

For a moment a small doubt of the doctor's own smartness clouded Zan's loyalty for his new hero. Then he decided that the doctor was so short of breath that it must have bothered his thinking. He asked, "Would you want to sit down a bit to rest here?"

The doctor took a deep breath. "Better keep on. We'll get there sooner."

Young Zande kept ahead, trying to slow his own gait to match the heavier step of his new friend. He wasted none of the doctor's breath by talk as they drew themselves up the ladder-steep trail.

When at last they came to where the cattle track joined the main trail, the boy stopped, pointed up the cliff down which he had slid from the smoke house.

"That's a short cut. Real short, but it's pretty steep," recalling how he'd "won" when sliding all the way down and standing up without falling.

The doctor looked up at the cliff, wiped his face with his handkerchief, and shook his hear. "Not for me, young man."

Zan nodded back. "Not a very good place to take the picture machine, either," he agreed. "Anyways, it's close enough going by the main trail. We're almost to Gramp's home place now."

The doctor drew a long breath. "Do I smell baked ham?"

Zan laughed. "Me, too. An' I smell the light bread biscuits and fried chicken, too."

The doctor whistled softly and began stepping out so briskly that Zan was able to travel along at his regular rate without having to remember to wait for the doctor to catch up.

II

There was a flash of light-colored dresses in the garden among the sweet alyssum, pansies and lilac. The dresses disappeared as the doctor came through the last gate and into Hannah Allan's herb and flower garden. The chatter inside quieted down as Zan and the doctor walked toward the back porch and came upon the erect and tall but silent figure of Zande Allan. Zan saw that Gramp had on his clean checked shirt, his second best pair of blue denim pants and a dandy clean red bandanna peeking out of his back pocket.

The youngster had always thought his grandfather the best, the smartest and the wisest man in the world, but now he found himself irritated when his grandfather gave no sign of knowing that an old friend was at the door to his house. Gramp always had one like that; waited for folks to name themselves before he would even let on he knew they were there. Zan had admired this trick, tried to school himself to imitate it. Now he glanced up to see the doctor's friendly smile and outstretched hand.

"Glad to see you again, Mr. Allan, and to find you looking so well."

It took one more step before the doctor was within touching distance and old Zande waited until that last step was taken.

But once the hands touched, the spell was broken.

The boy felt it was very fine, the way his grandfather spoke so heartily. "See you carry yourself well, too, Doc. About to have a bit and would be please to have you join up with us for some supper."

"It'd take a shot gun to keep me from doing just that," Doctor Roberts laughed. "I never smelled anything so good in my life as right now."

"Yes, yes," Old Zande drawled. "Garden truck and flowers do smell pretty good along in June. Best month, I think."

He turned his head and called over his shoulder, "Wife, here's com-

23

pany. Think you can find an extra plate?"

The small boy chuckled. Gramp was teasing just like the doctor did. But he kept that discovery to himself. A lifetime of hearing that children should be seen and not heard kept the Allan young folk quiet in the presence of their elders. Even Tilli heeded that to some extent, at least when she was visiting and around her grandparents.

The screen door opened. Hannah stepped out and quietly closed the door behind herself and Zan figured little Lara was upstairs sleeping. She hurried forward, a smile brightening her rather faded blue eyes, both hands held out in that welcome, giving way that made a friend of every person who came to the home place.

"So nice to see you here again, Doctor Roberts. Arvis let us know you were coming. Such a good neighbor, Arvis. Rode out of his way to tell me so I could do up a little something to make you feel welcome."

"Good to be here. A lovely day, fine world. And you look as bright as the day, Mrs. Allan."

A brief meeting of eyes, a slight flush sprang from Hannah's weathered cheek, and acknowledged his words, but spoke to her grandson.

"The doctor will want to wash, Zan. I've put out clean towels. Go get some warm water for him, will you? And don't forget to do your own cleaning up!"

She started back to her kitchen but paused at the door, saying, "And put Doctor Robert's camera up on the lamp shelf in the parlor where it'll be safe from the little ones. We're ready to dish up now and so when you're washed up, help the other boys find enough boxes for seats at the children's table."

With his hand importantly on the camera, the boy's happy "Yes'm" caroled through the closing door. Never before had there been such a wonderful day. The doctor was in his charge, he had the magic two-bit piece in his pocket and the children's table was set on the pergola porch just outside the dining room. While the spreading grape vine let in the right amount of shade and sun, the open dining room windows would let out most of the grown-up talk.

With patient courtesy he saw the doctor through two pans of warm washing water, one pan of cold rinse, before he took a quick splash of cold for himself and rushed off to put in his claim for a seat close to the window where he could hear the talk.

24

On the porch under the pergola, and within sight of the three women folk putting food on the main dining table inside, a subdued but lively wrestling bout was going on between the five boy cousins for the very seat Zan had hoped to get. Eric and Isaac, in alternate hisses, kept whispering, "We're twins and that's special, so's we ought to get first pick for place."

Ephraim, the twins' brother, had what seemed to the rest of the boys, the last word. "It's my B.B. gun and I'm the best shot and nobody gets dibs on it unless I get first pick."

Zan's big brother, Tony, said he didn't care where he sat, that there'd be food all over the table, enough for all.

But the squabble grew noisier and Tony finally put in his word. "What you talk so much for, anyway? You twins, and Eph and Zan; why don't you fight it out?

Before the fracas went further, authority appeared, though it was not Blaze, but her sister-in-law, Tena, wife of Martin Allan and mother of the five children, Ephraim, Eric, Isaac, Cedric and Tilli. She set down all the platters and said sternly, "That's enough nonsense! All of you sit down and behave."

Without turning her head to see if her orders were obeyed, Tena went back to the kitchen.

Without fuss or further comment, each boy took the place nearest to himself. Cedric couldn't climb into the high, unsteady box that fell to him and Stephen got up to lift him up. He was blocking up one corner of the teetery box as Grandmother Hannah and Blaze Allan Janson, followed by Maria and Kari, came carrying bowls heaped with liberal mounts of ham, chicken, peas, potatoes and all the good things.

Zan asked coaxingly, "Aunt Blaze, can't Allan sit with us? He's going on three and I'd watch out for him."

Blaze laughed. "I wish he could, at that, Zan, but I think Allan will act more like a proper Allan if he's sitting between me and his father—and straight across from his grandfather!"

Kari set down her burden of creamed peas and smiled up at her mother as she said, "Allan feels his Grampa's eyes, alright. He never throws cups, hardly spills anything even, as long as Gramp's got an eye on him."

Blaze nodded. "There's never been any ifs or ands about your grandfather. He says what he means and he says it only once."

25

"Once is enough for me," muttered Tony under his breath as he pulled a big platter of chicken toward himself, saying in a loud but cheerful voice, "Let's eat! I'm starved!"

Inside the dining room, while her son-in-law Stephen Janson was settling down, Hannah comfortably sat at one end of the long table, and as Doctor Roberts gallantly escorted the pretty young Tena to a place at the right side of Old Zande Allan, the young child began fussing to sit beside her grandfather.

Zande just looked at the youngster, then cleared his throat and bowed his head.

Allan's head bobbed down with more haste than reverence but it stayed down and quiet through a rather lengthy blessing.

His Grandfather's blessing took note of the increase in family, field, flock and fold; he returned thanks for health, peace and plenty. But his real eloquence he reserved for the close: "You have set us Allans upon Thy footstool, letting our feet not trace the paths of wickedness but walk always in the green and gold of Thy mountain pastures. I will lift up mine eyes unto the hills from whence cometh our strength and covenant with Thee that I will let no serpent, in any guise, including a road on the coast, crawl evilly into this earthly paradise to which Thy servant has been led. Amen."

The doctor's hearty "Amen" boomed above the rest of the murmured responses. Young Allan tagged along with a timid "amen," followed by, "Drumstick's my best, Gramp."

The head of the House of Allan heaped chicken and ham rapidly on plates, passed them to Tena who added vegetables and sent the plates speeding around the table. The ninth plate passed to her held one chicken leg in solitary splendor. She said, "This is for little Allan," and set in front of the child without any vegetable hampering the plate.

As Allan grabbed the chicken leg, Tena caught the amused glance of Blaze and winked.

Talk stayed small and sketchy as everyone first took the keen edge off their appetites, and then savoured the subtle flavors that Hannah Allan seemed able to develop in the simplest country fare.

Blaze made another trip to the kitchen for cotton-light hot rolls, Tena refilled the two empty bowls with giblet gravy, and Hannah saw to it

26

that the pickle, jelly and mashed potato supplies were served a jump ahead of every ones' appetites.

While the table was being cleared to make way for the strawberry pies and bowls of cream as thick as muffin dough, to be spooned over the ruby juice slowly oozing out from under the rich pie crust, the men talked of crops, stock and hunting. But when Doctor Roberts tested the full flavor of Hannah's strawberry pie, he put down his fork, sighed and looked at old Zande with a quizzical twist to his head and a pursed mouth.

"Earthly paradise?" He asked. "You didn't put it strong enough, Mr. Allan. In my judgment, this pie came straight from heaven."

"Heaven's no joking matter, Doctor. Not to me. I think maybe your taste for pie oversteps your judgment."

The doctor smiles, "I was only trying to say that it is like no pie I ever expected to find on this earth."

Zande agreed and nodded. "Yes, Mrs. Allan's a prime cook. So's my daughter and the granddaughters are not bad, for children. They'll do all right by the time they've growed up."

"You've done well for yourself and your family, in every way, Mr. Allan. And you are quite right to call this place an earthly paradise. But I wonder what you mean by an evil serpent crawling into the Coast."

Zande looked silently at the doctor for a noticeable moment, and then said flatly, "You don't wonder at all what I mean by the evil serpent? You know well enough I was meaning that road you're doing your level best to push in here."

The doctor finished his pie, broke off a small crust of bread from what was left of the last roll beside his plate, wiped up every trace of pie juice and cream, ate it thoughtfully before he said, "You got me again. I knew what you meant, that's true. But I thought we ought to bring it out in the open, talk it over, man to man. It'll be no serpent, but a real blessing to all of you when the road finally links you up with the world of today."

"Telling me I'm an old mossback don't scratch my hide none, Doctor. I get a look at this world of today that you're talking about ever time I take out cattle to town. Young men old enough to know better: high white collars, and over 'em a pimply face with a cigarette hanging out of it. And them swinging doors to saloons that they push open, lets out a stink of stale liquor and dirty spittoons. Yes, a fine world out there that your road would bring into the Coast. Big Sur. A fine world!"

"A fine world, indeed," the doctor said calmly, "only you're taking a wrongful look at it. What about paved roadways, automobiles, telephones, schools and theatres? We're on the edge of a new world," Mr. Allan, "a world of discovery and new inventions the twentieth century that no one has ever dreamed of before."

"New contraptions and new ways on original sin have always kept about nick and nick since Adam and Eve, I reckon. But I'm telling you that right here where you're setting right now is a good today. It was a good yesterday, too, and it'll be a good tomorrow—without no road. What we got right here grows good crops and good steers. Grain and children both grows straight and strong and good. What we brought in from outside ain't added much to crow about."

Avery, who had been sitting beside his brother, Zande Junior, looked hurt and angry, pushed back his chair and murmured, "Excuse me, please, I'll go sit a spell with Margaret if you don't mind.

His feet clumped down the bare hall toward the room that Blaze had when she was the daughter of the house. Now the room that had meant independence and refuge for young Blaze Allan was a prison cage for Avery's invalid bride, Margaret Allan. Married to Avery for more than a year now, she was still a virgin bride, destined—as far as the doctors could tell, to remain so for the rest of her life.

Avery, beginning at thirty to be pointed out as an old bachelor who probably would never marry, had made a trip down to the Ocean school to fix a pump and saw Margaret Edwards, fresh out of Normal School. Before the pump was fixed, he'd asked her to marry him. And before the term was out, he'd persuaded her to go to San Francisco with him on the Easter vacation to get married and finish her school term as Mrs. Avery Allan.

But the San Francisco Fire, referred to by unknowing, non-Californians as The San Francisco Earthquake, had burst out and interrupted his wooing of his bride on their very wedding night. Avery had two broken legs and a wrenched shoulder when the hotel collapsed and he was dug out from it all. His bride, Margaret, when she was dug out, was paralyzed from head to toe. Her mind was still alive, but her body was so froze up she couldn't even feed herself.

Doctor Roberts looked thoughtfully as Avery left the table until he heard the sound of the bedroom door shut, then turned to Avery's father, Zande, and asked "Any change in Margaret, Mr. Allan?"

Old Zande shook his head. "No. She eats some, not much. If only she'd get better— or something. Makes life plain hell for my boy, that's all there is to it."

"I'd like to examine her, if I could?"

Hannah came in from the kitchen, interrupted her husband who was angrily telling the doctor that the girl didn't want to get better, so it wouldn't do any good 'cause she's not going to get any better. "Won't see anyone but Avery or his mother, and won't even talk to them most of the time," Zande said.

Hannah said, "Margaret will get well, I know she will."

"Your faith in that can't help but aid her, Mrs. Allan," said the doctor, "Even though she may appear to resent it, it's good for her to know that you feel that way.

Hannah turned her head away for a moment but when she looked back at the doctor, she only asked, "Did you see Mrs. Ramirez on your way here?"

"Yes. Yes, I saw her. Poor woman. It's only a matter of days with her, maybe only hours now. How's the baby?"

"Lara? She's pretty. Healthy and good. I'd like to take her to keep but, well—I don't know. Do you think," doctor, "that it's fair to the baby to have a couple of old grand folks bring her up?"

With a convincing lack of hesitation, Dr. Roberts said, "It would be a fine thing for the baby," Mrs. Allan. "But would it be too hard for you? That's the main thing to think about. And what about the Ramirez family? Would one of them want to take the child, or wouldn't they?"

Zande put in, "Not that bunch. When Mrs. Ramirez left her husband, and though I don't hold with such goin's on, I got to admit that she had plenty of reasons to part ways. But once she left him, them Ramirez family folks left her flat, 'though they all knowed that she had a baby comin.'"

The doctor's voice sharpened. "Well, how about the husband, Larry Ramirez? He could be made by the law to take care of his own child."

Zande's lip curled. "Him? He stays so drunk he don't know if'en its summer or winter. Can't take care of his own skin, much less a young'n. If Hannah don't know enough to take things a mite easy now, she sure

29

can take care of the child, and I guess there's nothing again' us having the baby here at the home place to raise like our own."

The three girls, Maria, Kari and Tilli, came in, cleared off and brushed up the table, and then shut the kitchen door behind them to dim the sound of their dish washing.

The doctor leaned back, felt in his pocket for his pipe.

"Mind if I smoke, Mr. Allan?"

"I do," he looked at his wife, and winked, "but Hannah don't. It's her room, built so's she could gather all the kin, or do what she wanted with it."

Hannah's smile had the brilliance of redwoods at sunset. "Go right ahead and smoke your pipe, Doctor. I enjoy seeing a man comfortable."

"Thank you, both of you."

The doctor struck a match, savored his first puffs, and then leaned back, relaxed, as he turned the talk back to the road.

"I'll admit I'm puzzled, Mr. Allan. I know you as a man of good sense. You're a proud man, and you want the best for your family. What ever could be had in such an isolated place, you've gotten for your folks, and the biggest and best of whatever it was. The road will do so much to make life better—"

Zan pounced, his lean, knotted hand striking the plank table for emphasis as he said, "Easier? Maybe yes, some ways. Better? All the talk in the world would never change me about that. People been living alongside roads for a lot of years now in America and damned if the whole lot of 'em ain't running to seed. Take these here Ramirez folks. You knowed 'em 'most as many years as I done. Long as they lived here in the hills on their ranches they held themselves together, even if they was a trifle on the lazy side. But then they sell their holdings, move to town, and what happens?"

Zande looked challengingly, but the doctor tapped his pipe, held another lit match over the bowl, and waited for the old man to have his say.

Zande made a wry face.

"You know when to keep still, Doc. 'Cause you know what happened. They emptied their pockets, didn't fill their heads with one thought as far away as tomorrow. That good solid piece of money was all gone, and not a bit of land or a stick of a house bought with any of it. And when a man's broke in town, he's poor folks—he's trash."

Zande paused, and then continued, "In the Big Sur the Ramirez was sort of poor ranchers, but they was good neighbors. Outside, the old lady Ramirez died in the poorhouse; the rest of 'em took to drink and fighting and divorcing, and they scattered out like last year's tumbleweed. People riding out on trails can get into enough hell if they're minded to, but roads make it too easy for the hell-raisers to get in an' foul a fair place. I'm again' roads, on principle."

Martin Allan said, "I don't want any road in here either, Father; spoils the hunting. But you're making pretty broad statements, seems to me. My family is growing up in town—"

His father sniffed. "Yup. An' you're too busy makin' money to throw the fear of God into them, so you turn your father job over to Tena."

Tena flushed, said stiffly, "Women understand children."

Her father-in-law laughed. "Children understand women is more like it, my girl. Women is all right if there's a head of the house to back 'em up. You'll see what I mean, eight or ten years from now."

Old Zande caught the amused glance between Martin and Blaze, his own twin children; his first-born who had called forth all his pride and tenderness but who had felt only his sternness as they grew up. But he ignored this subtle flouting of his pronouncement and waited pointedly for Doctor Roberts to defend the world's right to build a highway into the Big Sur Coast.

"I know what you mean, Mr. Allan. But I don't think that one man's personal, and if you'll forgive me— selfish—point of view, should be allowed to carry any weight when the good for so many people is involved."

Hannah took advantage of shrieking and laughter outside the window at the children's table to try and switch talk on to safer matters. She called, "Tilli! Zan! Stop that nonsense. Tilli, you know very well Zan would not put a snake in your pocket, and Zan you're not to tease Tilli in that silly way."

Excited voices pelted words back.

"Zan's showing a magic trick."

"Make Tilli shut up, Mamma, she's just putting on."

"It ain't fair; Zan's got two-bits and he hides it in his hand so's we can't see him."

Hannah said, "Well, I can see all of you are making too much noise. Clear the table nicely and then go play out in the orchard."

Old Zande's mouth remained stubbornly set, and as the children's voices faded, he turned to the doctor. "Call it selfish, or any other hard name you're minded to, Doc. I know what I'm talking about. That wagon road part way into the Sur has already played hob with marketing my stock."

The doctor's politely attentive face couldn't hide from any one at the table his amused unbelief as he asked, "How's that, Mr. Allan?"

Zande put his hands on the table, leaned forward as he said softly, "You'd laugh out the other side of your mouth, Doc, if you was trying to drive stock out. The road takes the easy grade; wagons have the right of way. Now my cattle has to scramble over places no sane man would ever think of using. Picks the meat right off their bones and every mile of them bypass trails costs me money. The road touches all the good water holes, crosses the only feeding grounds we had. All closed to us now, the wagon road's for the outsiders; teams and rigs first, if you please. Takes no note of the folks that got a living to make off these hills."

"Well, yes, I see what you mean." The doctor pondered a moment, and then asked, "You ship your beef out of Monterey by train, Mr. Allan?"

"No, never ship 'em at all; never intend to. I'm not dealing with any of them city buyers. Don't trust 'em, don't know 'em, don't want to. I always took my beef straight to the slaughterhouse. Got the best prices in Salinas, but now I can't get my stock there at all, much less in prime market shape. They got a couple of them gas wagons running along that road now and damned if a man can drive hill stock on it even at night!'

Zande Junior, who had not spoken all through the meal, suddenly said, "I saw an auto car one time, didn't see it too good because I was helping Pa with the drive, and I reckoned it went all of ten or twelve mile an hour and the cattle went fair crazy. Brass shining, folks bouncing up and down from the ruts, and a fellow with black glass spectacles was squeezin' a rubber bulb and a horn kept mooing right back at the steers who was all bellowing at the sight of 'em all. Sure was a strange thing to see, I'll tell you."

Martin jeered, "Mossback." But his voice held affection as he urged his brother, "You come up to San Francisco this fall, Zande, and bring along young Zan. I've got a new automobile ordered and I'd like to take you for a spin."

The doctor was smiling broadly as he spoke to Zande Junior. "For a man in the middle of a cattle stampede, I'd say you didn't miss much about that auto." He turned to the head of the house and went on, "No horseless carriage I've seen yet would ever tempt me to swap my good wagon team for it. Cars break down all the time. I expect they'll get better as time goes on, but I'd be willing to bet good money they never improve them to a place where they could be counted on to climb the Serra Grade."

The idea of an automobile climbing Serra Grade seemed so absurd that the women laughed. Tena said, "Martin gets so provoked. I always get out and walk at the worst places. I guess I always will, no matter how much he tells me that the team is steady and the brakes good. I know he's right, but I can't do it. I shudder even when I'm walking; those steep turns are horrible, that's all, just horrible."

Her father-in-law nodded understandingly, but he was smiling as he said, "Matter of fact, I'd rather be afoot or on my good horse myself, about the time I hit the top of Serra—or even Mud Hill—with a wagon. Tryin' to take one of them horseless cars either up or down the grade'd

33

be like askin' a cat to swim the ocean!"

Hannah barely waited for appreciation of her husband's joke to be over before she cut in with, "Shouldn't we get the children together and have the picture made while the light is at its best, Doctor Roberts?"

"Better ask how much it costs, Wife, afore you get any further," said Zande.

Hannah raised an untroubled face, though the rest of the family—particularly the younger women—seemed embarrassed at Zande's bluntness.

The doctor wasted no time hedging. "I'd like to make you and Mrs. Allan a present of the portrait of your family, but I've known you long enough to be sure you wouldn't have it that way. I'll say ten dollars, and give you five prints. How's that?"

Martin put in eagerly. "Let me pay for them, Pa. I'd like to buy something for Mother that would really please her."

"So would I, thank you just the same, Son. Seems a pretty steep price, but if you want it, Hannah, get yourself and the children ready. I'll just look on."

Hannah's voice was sharp with hurt as she asked, "And make a widow out of me before my time? I wouldn't thank you for such a slight, Mr. Allan."

Zande looked puzzled as he muttered, "Slight you, woman? What's wrong with you? I was trying to do you a favor. Pictures is women's foolishness. Never had one took and don't mean to; but I'm not stopping you. Get your picture and I'll pay for it. What more'd any sensible woman want?"

"A sensible husband," sniffed Hannah. "And lacking that, a picture of the one she's got." She left her place at the end of the table and walked slowly around it, her fingers touching lovingly back of their chairs as she passed Blaze and her son Zande. She motioned Zande Junior to move over and sit on the edge of his bench between her son and her husband. Looking around at the others seated at the table, she murmured, "Please excuse this but it means so much to me, and we've got the Doctor and the camera here now—"

Her voice trailed away and, for a moment, she looked as uncertain as she had sounded. Then she plunged in, "I haven't asked you for much in the way of presents, husband. I haven't wanted much. But the few

34

things I do want, I want badly, so I can't give up. It took me twenty-five years to convince you I had to have the China set."

"You got it, didn't you?" He asked, making a great show of his impatience in order to hide his uneasiness. He cocked his head, listened, and his face brightened as he said urgently, "Hannah the Ramirez baby Lara is yelling for you. Best fetch it."

She looked around, called to the first youngster her glance found. "Zan! Go pick up Lara and bring her here. Right now."

Her husband put his hands on the table, started to push himself up from his chair, but she leaned over and caught both his hands in hers.

She was laughing as she bent toward him, but there was a little catch in her voice as she said, "Oh, no, you don't, Zande Allan. You'd be out of the door and down the trail quick as a lizard if I didn't hold on to you. I want a family picture. It wouldn't mean a thing to me, having it with you not there in it."

He shook his head stubbornly, but his voice was gentle as he protested, "I'd feel a fool, sittin' there froze stiff and staring into that dumb box."

"I want you standing close by me; all our kin around us." She bent over and whispered, her back to her son Zande. "He give a lot for a picture with Dulcie in it, but that's already too late with her passed an' all."

"Hush that kind of talk, Hannah. Alright, alright, I'll do it. Get 'em together and let's get it over with."

Young Zan, looking almost as irritated as his grandfather, came in from the hall carrying Lara, stumbling over her long dress. Its tatting edge ruffle dragged the floor and the frill around the small yoke and shoulders dabbed at his eyes, threatened to get into his mouth.

"For gosh sake, someone, here— take her, will you?"

His Aunt Blaze hurried over from the group of giggling children she had been trying to impress with the need of sitting very still while the picture was made, lifted the contented Lara from Zan's arms.

He darted away, intent on getting as close as possible to see the large black cloth under which most of Doctor Roberts had disappeared.

Immediately the baby set up a banshee wailing and Grandfather Allan barked at his daughter, "What's the matter, Blaze? Can't you keep the young'n quiet??"

"There's nothing wrong with her, she's just mad at something. I

35

think it's me she doesn't like. Mother, please—you take her, will you? I'll go help with the children." She leaned over and whispered in Hannah's ear, "Tena's putting all her children right across the front. I think each family should be grouped by age, don't you, Mother?"

Just so they all get in, I don't care. You and Tena work it out between yourselves. What in the world ails this baby?"

Lara's fists were doubled up, and she was arching her back as though trying her best to squirm out of Hannah's arms. She shifted the baby to her shoulder, petted her back, whispering soothingly, "There, there, Lambie, never mind, never mind," but all to no avail.

The strain of the big day had tolled on Hannah. It didn't help to have her husband scowl, or for Doctor Roberts to withdraw his head from the shelter of the black cloth to look inquiringly at the baby. The little girls broke from the picture group that had been formed by so many orders and counter orders that he clustered around their grandmother, full of advice about how other babies had been quieted. But Lara continued to howl. Hannah began to look utterly confused.

"I had hoped for a moment to straightened up my hair and dress," she muttered aloud, her eye following the children that her husband was now sternly shepherding to places of Doctor Robert's choice.

She noticed Zan still standing by the camera, apparently absorbed by the doctor's muted directions to the sitting and the ghostly convulsions of the black cloth as the doctor raised or lowered his head.

"Lara wasn't crying when you brought her in, Zan," She called, holding out the baby meaning. The boy looked around, pretending he didn't hear, and then as though hoping to hide, but his grandmother was firm.

She handed over the small fury in its rumpled christening robe and Zan grudgingly took the baby.

Lara settled her head against the boy's reluctant shoulder, the shrieks immediately changing into broken sound, and then with one last half-sob, half-gasp, Lara relaxed into a peaceful sleep.

The faces of the children already in the group froze into rigid fright as Doctor Roberts picked up his hold of flashlight powder.

"Over there, right between your grandfather and your father," Doctor Roberts said, moving the camera a fraction of an inch and then waved the reluctant Zan forward into the derisive faces of his cousins.

"Oh my gosh."

As Ephraim whispered, "Zan is a sugar-tit, a baby-calmer," the quick-witted Tilli began chanting, "Zande chases girls with snakes and teases them with fire."

The rest of the youngsters shook with suppressed giggles as Zan, red-faced, moved blindly forward as Doctor Roberts said, "You take the center of the back row, Mr. Allan. Your wife on your right, Mr. Zande to the left of you, and the boy—let's see, young Zan you stand between your father and grandfather and a little in front. Now we've got the three Zande Allans together, all in one group!"

Hannah stepped into her place. The doctor took the rubber bulb into his hand, disappeared under the black cloth.

"Everyone here now? All of you ready?"

Old Zande muttered, "Not me. I don't want my picture took."

Hannah took firm hold of his hand, bent her arm until the two clasped hands rested between the senior Allan's shirt pocket and shoulder. She counted heads quickly then, satisfied, called out, "We're all here, Doctor, go ahead."

Young Zan pleaded miserably, "Please, Gramp, make one of the girls take Lara, please!"

The craggy old face of the grandfather frowned like a black thundercloud as he looked down on his young namesake, and as baby Lara yawned magnificently, Doctor Roberts press the bulb and dropped a match in the flashlight powder.

The doctor stood up straight, began folding up the cloth, and looked pleased as he said, "If only I got what I saw in there, it ought to be a real good picture."

"I'm so afraid I moved," Lamented Tena.

"I'm afraid I didn't." Old Zande looked amused for a minute, now that the ordeal was over. Then he turned commandingly to the young group. "All you young fry scatter out of here now."

The rest of the children surged toward the door but young Zande hung back, silently offering the baby to his grandmother. She smiled down at him. "I'm real proud you did such a nice thing for all of us, Zan. In another second Lara would of broke up the whole thing and your Grampa would have had his chance to run off on me."

She wrinkled her face at her husband with the derisive confidence of a young girl, and then left the room, calling back, "All that ailed the poor little thing was hunger. It's her bottle time but I was so fussed I didn't even think of that."

Her husband shrugged, reached over and gave the boy's shoulder a kindly shake, "Go play with the rest of 'em, sonny."

Zan held his place for an instant, started to obey and then turned back. "Doctor Roberts give me a magic two-bit piece," he said. "He showed me how to work it, but I can't quite get it. If I could wait, maybe he'd show me again."

"Later—if he has the time. I told you I want you to go outside now."

The children were at the back of the house, running and shouting. Very softly the boy let himself out the seldom-opened front door and used a long line of berry bushes as a shield between himself and the cousins who seemed to him like a wolf pack waiting to tear him apart with teasing about having to hold baby Lara.

Inside the parlor Doctor Roberts was gathering together his blanket roll and camera. "Yes, I got to get started. I'll stay the night with young Mrs. Ramirez; do what I can for her. May I take her word that you and Mrs. Allan will look after the baby until some of her own folks want her?"

Zande looked thoughtful. "Best say we'll keep her till my wife feels sure she's in a place as good, or better."

"That will bring her great comfort, and that's about all I can do for her, I'm afraid. I'll either come back or send the picture down with some-one about the time fall hunting gets good. And now I must look in and see Margaret for a minute, then go and tell the rest goodbye."

The farewells took some time, as the women were out gathering up their families for the trip back to their own ranches. By the time Doctor Roberts had made his round and was passing the barnyard, he found Old Zande Allan waiting, with the gate to the lane unlatched. At the end of the steep lane, guarded by a split redwood fence and bordered with elderberry and wild roses, the last Allan gate opened on the Coast Trail.

Old Zande closed the barnyard gate after himself and said, "Ill walk a few steps with you, Doc. Maybe you'll admit what you must know is the truth; that there's no practical way to get a road built along the Sur Coast.

The doctor looked at him shrewdly. "That means that you think it's not only possible, but probable, doesn't it?"

Zande's voice was a harsh as the creak of the wood hinges on the gate he'd closed behind them.

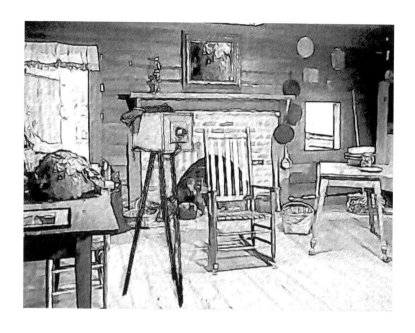

"It means I think the fool-killers are overworked. Fools keep shouting for all kinds of stuff to be built out of tax money; don't ever seem to know they're paying for it themselves. That being so, any agitating for a road down here is bound to stir up a lot of contractors and government plum-pickers. Looks bad for a respected man like you to be sticking up for it."

They had reached the end of the land and old Zande stood with his hand on the gate latch, not lifting it. Neither man seemed to notice young Zan leaning against the gnarled madrone tree where the Allan lane and Coast Trail cornered.

After a moment the doctor put his hand warmly upon the veined and corded hand that held the gate latch. "We're friends, Mr. Allan, with respect for each other for the same reason: neither of us is wishy-washy. If we believe a thing, we believe it. I hope it doesn't make any difference between us that we have found something upon which we will never agree. You don't believe a road here is any good. I do."

The doctor lifted his hand. Old Zande lifted the latch, stood aside for the doctor to pass through. The older man called after his friend. "I always like a fellow that says what he means. Come see us again, soon as you can, Doc."

The doctor lifted his hand in farewell, stepped forward briskly for a couple of paces and then stopped, faced his lean opponent, draped against the gate.

"I better tell you that petitions for this road have been before the legislature for some time.

Zande nodded. "Knew it. Heard it over to King City. Bought a newspaper and the talk was all set out in it. Just talk. Been goin' on for years."

"Yes. And the talk's been growing for years. Now there's a petition with plenty of signers, going to be presented to the Transportation Department. It asks for $300,000 to be appropriated for a survey."

"Yeah?" Zande laughed. "Set their sights a might high, didn't they? If they started asking for $3,000 I might be worried they'd get it and come pesterin' around. Guess I been stewin' a lot for nothin.'"

Young Zan's bare feet carried him silently toward the doctor, who was still facing the Allan gate. The doctor looked down, startled, when a small brown fist suddenly appeared in front of him, opened to show a silver quarter. "Would you take the minute to show me just once more?"

"Yes, but just once. I'll do it very slowly—" He put the coin between his fingers, started through his routine. Old Zande crowded in as close as his grandson, looking even more puzzled than the boy, who at least knew how the trick was done.

When the lesson was finished, the doctor gave back the coin. "Plenty of practice now, and when I get back here you'll be as good a magician as I am."

He picked up his camera and said, "Well, goodbye again. And it may be early winter before I get back because I'm going up to Sacramento. I might as well tell you, Mr. Allan, I think this Coast road may cost a lot of money before it's done and I think it'll be worth every cent it costs the citizens."

Old Zande smiled sourly. "Suppose you're going to the Capitol to talk road. Well, I hope you have a good trip. $300,000, eh? That's so foolish, it's funny! But I hope you enjoy the trip."

"I will," said the doctor briskly. "And so will the legislators. I'm taking all the pictures of the Coast I've been recording for the last twenty years; every bay, every stream and waterfall, every view that proves this section

40

is like no other place in America. With my camera I'm able to show them that instead of only a few ranchers benefiting from this road, it will bring beauty lovers from all over the world."

Old Zande's hands tightened on the gate, the cords on his neck stood out, but he kept most of the contempt out of his voice as he said, "Beauty lovers my foot! Just another high-flown name for the generation of locusts that's breeding so fast they'll eat up and destroy the whole country. They'll not set foot on Allan land while I live."

The doctor looked troubled as he said softly, "You'll live longer and happier if you can learn to move with the times, my friend. This is a bigger thing than your few acres. No matter how you fight it, there will come a day when money will be appropriated. The road will come."

Zande Allan fairly vibrated with sardonic energy, his tense voice cracked as he said, "my land is my land, and no road will cross it. I won't give a ridaway. That settles that."

Young Zan had followed the controversy with fascinated attention. His Gramp was the strongest, smartest man in the world—or was he? He didn't have a camera. He didn't know nothing about magic. Zan suddenly found himself disloyally wondering if his grandfather knew everything about roads.

Almost as though he felt his disciple straining at the family tie, the grandfather spoke. "Go back to the barn and start the chores, Zan."

The doctor said, "There's only one more thing I feel I must say. This lad belongs to the world that's coming and he has a right to know what's going on. Believe me, Mr. Allan, you cannot refuse to grant a right of way—"

"I told you I would do just that!"

"Yes, I heard you. But didn't you know that when money is set aside for the road and work begins on it, land for the roadbed can be acquired by seizure, under the law? You'll be paid a reasonable price—"

"Paid, hell!" The old man bellowed. "I've never sold an inch of my land. I never will. I'm the law on my land, and if the need comes, I got a gun that can talk straight. Zan, go on up to the barn like I told you!"

He stepped angrily toward Zan, who drew back, then dodged behind the doctor. His eyes filled with angry tears and his voice was shaken as he defied his grandfather. "I'm not going back to the barn. My pop said for me to come home when the party was over, so I'm going. An' I'm going to walk with the doc till I have to branch off."

With icy detachment the old man spoke to the child, the one person beside his wife that he had ever completely loved and, as though he were speaking to an adult. "Do that and you needn't hurry back—either of you."

Very quietly the doctor did his best. "Please, Mr. Allan, the boy's excited. It's been a big day. He spoke without thinking. Why don't you two Zandes walk up to the barn together?"

The boy shook his head. "Gramp won't walk with me no more. He's again' the road. I'm for it now, and I got some magic right in my hand."

The boy cut across country, scorning the trail. The doctor walked slowly into the deeply worn Coast Trail, and old Zande Allan stood alone, straight as a gun barrel, his bleak eyes staring unseeingly out over the lovely wild land that he possessed and that possessed him.

III

Nineteen-twenty-nine was a different year for the Big Sur Coast. Doc Roberts prophesy seemed to be coming true and old Zande Allan's resolve became stronger that no road would ever cross his land.

This year a crew of outlanders who called themselves surveyors were again trying to blaze out a track for what they boasted would one day be a road along the Coast. But the old timers knew that no one could ever build a road along the Big Sur Coast. It would have been a fine joke for everyone were it not that those survey men were getting paid with our tax money.

And this same year the Allan family was having their annual roundup come July. For over fifty year they'd been branding and dividing up their stock on the first day of May.

So when Gramp, who was old Zande Allan the first, sent out word he didn't want the stock brought into the corrals until July 18th, his family felt like the sky was about to fall. Everyone on the Coast set their calendars—and almost their clocks—on the Allan work habits.

The same thought come to all the Allans. Zande the third, who everyone called "Zan" to keep all the Zandes straight, was coming into his twenty-first birthday on the 19th, the day after the roundup.

Up to now, Gramp had always been strict but just when splitting up either his land or cattle. Every Allan boy who stayed with the homeplace and worked for Gramp had always been given his own hundred-and-sixty acres as he come twenty-one and was a man. And after that he got his man's share of the cattle increase every year. But young Zan, whose mother had died when he was seven, had lived a lot of the time in his Gramp's own cabin, and was closer to him than any of Gramp's blood sons had ever been. All this was something to think about as spring turned slowly into summer.

43

Now, in the grove where the barbecue would be held, the shadows were already shortening toward noon. The bright July day was scented with smoke from the deep bed of oak bark coals glowing in the barbecue pit. The mournful lowing of penned wild cattle and the light chatter of Allan women folk, who had shed off hard work for this day, were enjoying visiting together, and their talkin' broke the grove's usual silence.

Far down the mountain a young girl stood alone on a high point of Allan land, calling over and over, like a wild dove, "Zan, Zan Allan, where are you?"

Old Zande's three sons and one daughter were all doing things as the Allans had always done them, getting everything ready for the branding of the new stock and the barbecue. Not one of the four had commented on the absence of Old Zande and his grandson, Zan.

Martin, the oldest son, was not as busy as his two younger brothers, Zande the second, and Avery or his twin sister, Blaze. Martin had turned against ranching, refused his land when he was twenty-one. Now he was forty-nine and the owner of a big chain of grocery shops. He was balding, rotund and sentimental about the hardships of his youth. He lived in San Francisco and his children went to private schools.

Zande Allan Junior, now forty-seven, was busy with the branding fire and sorting out the branding irons. If his light hair had thinned a bit, he was still as slim-hipped as his own sons. He always had been one for keeping his mouth shut and eyes open. Though his eyes seemed to be on the branding irons, he noticed how gently his youngest brother Avery put a cushion under the shoulders of Margaret, Avery's invalid wife. Avery look so thin, so old for his years. Zande turned away thinking how full of laughter, how in love with loving his own wife, Dulcie, had been for the short twelve years she had been with him before she passed.

Only Zan, the youngest of their children, seemed like her. Both Marie and Tony seem to favor the dark Indian strain that had missed showing in their mother and came out in her first two children.

Zande Junior was sure that his sister Blaze had been watching him when she left the barbecue table, came over and squatted on her heels beside the branding fire and began examining the irons as carefully as though they were new to her, not something that she knows as well as she knows her own face. Zan liked the silent companionship, but it gave him a twist to notice for the first time that her madrone-colored hair was beginning to show a few touches of gray above her ears.

Out of the corner of his eye he was watching his own daughter Maria. Her hair was as black and bright as a crow's wing, but her mouth looked sullen, her eyes angry. She stirred and tasted the pot of wild pigeon stew she had brought to the barbecue. Nodding her head as if pleased with the seasoning, she put the lid back on the kettle and went over to sit on the ground beside Margaret Allan and adjusted her pillow.

As the call, "Zan, where are you?" Again came drifting faintly from the high point toward the Coast, Maria said gruffly, "If no one else does, I'm certainly going to give that Lara a piece of my mind. Why, she's getting to be a big girl, almost 13 now. The idea of her mooing after young Zan like a calf! I don't care if her mother did die when she was born and left her an orphan to grow up in an Allan house. The child was still a Ramirez. Grandma Hannah should never have took her in and I bet no good comes from it. And now Gramp makes a pet of her like he never did for none of us blood kin."

Margaret sighed as though very tired but said nothing. Maria sniffed, but changed the subject. "I don't care if Zan is my own brother. That's no good reason why he should get extra from Gramp, being his namesake and all. So's my papa, Zande the second, and what'd he get? You know well enough he got the worst old no good piece of land Gramp had to give."

This time there was nothing Margaret could say. All the Allans knew it was because of Zande Junior marriage to the daughter of Maria Gallo— old Zande's worst enemy—that his first namesake got the short end when Grampa had the first division of Allan land. But he still got his hundred sixty acres, even if a goat could hardly stand up on most of it, and he had to build his cabin on the flat piece his wife Dulcie Gallo had inherited from her mother.

Marie kept looking at Margaret. She wanted to hear what Margaret had to say about any favoritism that might be shown to the youngest Allan, Zan. She had no mind to let Margaret get away with any of her lady schoolteacher airs. She prodded her, "You're thinking Zan's my own brother, ain't you? That's no difference. All alike and no pet is what I say. You think it's fair if Zan gets extra?"

Margaret hesitated, and then said, "Mr. Allan is such a good man. I'm sure he always tries to do what he thinks is right."

Maria Shrugged. "Of course. Thirteen years he's done plenty

enough for you and Uncle Avery, and you being hardly an Allan even, only by name."

Margaret turned away from Maria's sharp eyes and sharper tongue. What she said was true. Margaret, shy, young and pretty, had come to the little school six miles from the old Allan place on her first teaching venture. That's where Avery had first seen her. She and Avery had been married in San Francisco the very evening of the big earthquake and fire. Avery had been only slightly injured, but Margaret was still paralyzed. Although no longer in much pain, she suffered constantly that Avery had never had a wife, in the Biblical sense, much less a child. Avery was so patient, always so good, even though all doctors said the same thing, that they could find no physical cause for her paralysis.

Lara Ramirez came breathlessly running up to where her Aunt Blaze Janson and Martin Allan's wife, Tena, were busy making the salad. Both women stopped when Lara said, "Why isn't Zan to his birthday party?"

Martin, Avery, Zande Junior and their brother-in-law Stephen Janson had all been sitting around the branding fire. Now they all got to their feet and started looking around at all they could see of the ranch. Martin said, "I'd just started wondering about that. I hadn't missed him, but just got to thinking it was strange father wasn't here either, bossing things as usual."

Tilli, the Martin Allan's eighteen-year old daughter, who most of the family thought she was far more ornamental than useful, put down her mandolin and called sweetly, "I saw Grampa about half an hour ago. He was walking out on the Trail toward Buzzard pasture."

Her father laughed. "He was checking up on us, I bet. Taking a last look to see if we missed getting in any stock. I remember there always used to be a few yearlings hanging around Buzzard, just over the edge they'd hide. Makes Pa feel good if he can turn up one or two head that younger had eyes missed."

There was a minute's silence, broken by the polite, unhurried voice of Stephen Janson. "You'd got better than the usual average this year, didn't you, Zande?"

Zande Junior answered, "that's right. We did. And we got some new blood in the herd, too. You notice those four big black calves, Stephen?"

Stephen smiled apologetically. "No, can't say I did. Black calves? Didn't think Mr. Allan ever had any cattle but white faced ones."

As Avery and Martin pushed forward to get their share of the gossip,

the women began to make a clatter with tin plates and cups as they set the long plank table.

Avery said, "Pa never did have. Not till Graves bought that big black bull. Was sure a fence breaker. Made Pa mad as hops when he had to fix our fences. He and Graves had some hard words before Graves got around to putting hobbles on the brute bull. Come too late, though. Pa was boiling when he found them four black drops suckling our cows. He was for killing all four right then but I talked him into waiting and driving them out with the rest."

The men went off together to take a good look at the four black strangers. Maria began arguing that it was time to start cooking the steaks if they were to be ready at noon.

Blaze protested, "We ought to wait until Pa and Zan get here. A steak goes bad if it has to wait to go on the plate."

Maria shrugged. "Grampa said dinner at straight noon."

Tilli asked if she should go up to the Buzzard pasture to see if he was still there.

"Certainly not. He'll be here when he said," Maria said and asked Margaret "You got your watch on?"

Margaret nodded and pulled on a slender chain that went around her throat and drew out a tiny watch. "Twenty-two minutes of twelve."

Blaze looked pleased. "There's plenty of time." She thought for a minute, and then asked Maria, "Do you think Tony will be here for the dinner?"

Maria said, "No, my brother Tony's out for trouble. He took the Jolon Trail after that girl, that's what."

Tilli Allan's face betrayed amusement as she said, "But what could he do, Cousin Maria? Since Lola Ramirez has already eloped and married that cigar drummer? Won't he have to forget her, find someone else?"

Maria tossed her head scornfully. "City-girl talk. Easy come, easy go. Us mountain Allans don't change like weather. Lola is Tony's girl. He's gone after her. He'll get her, too."

Blaze said softly, "Tony's a good boy. He won't do anything foolish."

"Won't he? What you call wanting to marry one of them Ramirez? We got too much Ramirez around here already. Granma's little pet, that Lara Ramirez. Don't tell me she isn't already hunting after our Zan. You tell her to stay away from him, Aunt Blaze."

Blaze waited, took a deep breath, and said, "Maria, you know Lara and Zan were raised like brother and sister. Besides, Lara's only eleven, ten years behind Zan." She smiled, went on, "And she's going away to school this fall to become a teacher."

Maria said stubbornly, "I'd never trust no Ramirez. Tony's got luck, but not the sense to know it." She started straightening the knives and forks beside the platters, muttering, "That fog's comin' higher. Gramp and Zan aren't here. Tony's gone after that girl. Looks like there's no luck in this day for no one."

Old Zande Allan was down at the edge of Buzzard Point, cursing the fog. It wouldn't let him see more that a few hundred feet down over the cliff's edge and hid the shoreline from his sight.

Born in these Santa Lucia mountains in 1835, Zande had never known any other world than the Big Sur Coast and it suited him fine, just as it was. For almost forty years he had laughed at rumors that outsiders were laying plans to build a road down the entire Coast. But today he was not laughing.

Somewhere down in that fog, a survey crew was at work again, scarring his own land with a rough trail, hanging bits of red cloth to brush and branches, making marks on Allan cliffs. For all he could tell, his own namesake, young Zan, might be down there taking a look at what was going on.

He turned his head, held his breath to listen once more, but no sound of voice or axe came to his ears. He straightened up, rubbed his back for a minute. Then, spare, erect and sure-footed, he made his way across Buzzard pasture and down the Trail to the grove where the barbecue steaks were now starting to brown.

Old Zande made straight for the table, took his place at the head, picked up the knife beside his plate and rapped sharply on the bare board. Come on, all of you," he ordered, "I'm hungry."

No smell in the world as good as steak roasting over oak bark.

"Flip 'em over, said Zande, and come on. I aim to start the blessing at square noon. By the time I'm done, the steak'll be ready."

"I'll help you flip 'em, Zande," Martin called, lumbering his weighted body over to the pit and picking up one of the pointed willow sticks the Allans' used to turn barbecued meat. "I'm so hungry, I could eat a mule."

Old Zande sniffed, "And you may have to, if you stay in town selling them groceries long enough, and eatin' your fair share of 'em. But any time you want good meat, you come on home, my boy, and you'll get the best beef on the Coast."

A ripple of laughter greeted this sally, but Martin, who was providing for a very extravagant family in town, said nothing.

Lara came running down from the point and went over to the old man. Out of breath, she leaned on his arm, her pale, pointed face coloring slightly, as she asked, "Mr. Allan, can't we wait for Zan? Where is he?"

"He'll be here. No nonsense about that boy." He craned his neck forward, his high, thin nose giving him an eagle's look, and he snapped, "Where's Tony? He's the one that's always late."

Maria answered, "He rode off. To Jolon, I think."

Her grandfather answered, "Very well. If he's not here he forfeits his share this year. If it's worth that to him to chase a fifteen-year old hussy who's jilted him, he deserves no better than to get her." The drawn skin on his lean face tightened some as he turn to young Lara and said, "Sit down, child. It's time for the blessing."

He squinted at the sun, and then nodded his head, giving to all

49

notice that it was not quite noon. Just then Zan ran up from the Creek, his hair, face and hands dripping from the cold Creek water.

"Made it Gramp", he called cheerfully, "had to run, though. Didn't want to be late…"

Zan's voice Trailed off as he saw his grandfather's folded hands and bent head. He sat down at the other end of the table, got his own head bowed just as his grandfather began, "Almighty God, we give Thee thanks that these, our generations of Allans…"

As always, old Zande first gave thanks for the goodness, the modesty and the spotless reputations of the generations of Allan women. The long, detailed and friendly discourse was held directly with the Almighty. The younger ones became restive but the four who were his first generation children, Blaze, Martin, Zande Junior and Avery all looked relieved and happy that, for the minute, their father seemed to have no quarrel with either the world of here or the world of the here-after.

They joined in a chorus of fervent "Amens."

The women left the table to fill hot plates at the fire and set the savory meal swiftly before the waiting men.

Old Zande's fork hovered over his steak and the pigeon pie, and chose the pie to test first, then nodded and smiled at Maria, "Tastes like your gramma's pie, girl," he said. "Isn't a Allan woman yet that ain't a prime cook. Now stop looking sour enough to ruin milk, Maria. You done right well for yourself."

Maria mumbled, "Thank you, Grandfather."

She and Blaze got up to refill plates and bent over the hot fire, Maria whispered angrily, "I ain't got nothing. No chance to get anything, either. Gramp never gave a thing to any of the Allan women except a warning to behave themselves. Huh."

"You know your grandfather's old-fashioned, Marie. He's too old to change now. But we all do have everything we need."

Maria answered sullenly, "That's all right for you to say. You got a rich husband. I got nothing of my own but my work."

Blaze put her free arm around Maria and gave her a hug but said nothing. After every one had second helpings, the women sat down to their own dinner. The younger girls, Lara and Tilli, made a proud ceremony of serving everyone the pies, cakes and custards as well as fresh summer fruit and berries picked from the homeplace.

As the women cleared the table, the men talked of cattle and crops, of weather and hunting. But as soon as the last dish was dried, packed in the large rawhide pack-bags, an uneasy silence spread among the Allans, except for the oldest and youngest Zande Allan.

The old Zande sat easy at the head of the long table, his eyes looking over what he could see of his land. His dominion had grown from one stony claim he had jumped when he left home at sixteen. Now it was a widespread kingdom that took in five great Canyons and ridges stretching for miles along the Big Sur Coast. He owned a bountiful supply of mountain water; many canyons covered with redwood, pine and oak trees; and enough wild pastureland to feed more cattle than the Allans would ever need to run.

He thought of the first four runty calves that he had traded old Demas for a whole year of backbreaking work. They were the seed that had grown to the fine large herd of sleek calves now waiting to be divided. And his own seed, the generations of Allans, were a godly crop. He took pleasure in looking at his children, and the children of his children. Already the third generation was growing up and would soon strike out for themselves. He nodded his head. Yes. The Allan strain was being steadily diluted, but the old blood was strong.

The lot of them was whispering together and they might as well have all spoken out. He knows what they were saying. He stood up and answered what they had not asked.

"I'll settle about the land first," he said, "and then we'll divide the calves. Zan?"

Zan had been lounging, his back comfortable, and clinking something in his pocket. The instant he heard his grandfather call his name, he answered, "Yes'r."

"I'm giving you the hundred-sixty that lies this side of May Creek".

The old man watched the startled look on the faces of the rest. He noted with satisfaction that his grandson's face show no change at all.

"Thank you, Gramp", Zan said, "I'll try to work as hard on it as you could when you was twenty-one."

Blaze protested. "But, Father, that May Creek piece is nothing but rocks. You must have forgotten what it's like."

"Nope. Rode over there last week. The shack's still there. And, the feed shed. Fence pretty well down, but the timber is right there. I give it to Zan because I think he's got the gumption to make something out of it. And don't forget it's a lot more'n I started with when I was five years younger than him. And I managed to do right well."

Zan said, "I'm suited, Gramp. You got the paper for it ready?"

"Got it. And the pencil to sign with. Here you are."

Zan came over, reached for the brown stub of pencil his grandfather had placed beside the bit of ruled tablet paper he took from his shirt pocket.

His grandfather snatched back the paper, said sternly, "What's the matter with you? You going to sign something without you read'n it first?"

Zan colored, took the paper and read it careful. Then he grinned at his grandfather.

"Served me right if you'd a pulled a trick on me. But this is fine. That's the right description of May Creek place. All else it says is that I'm to live on it starting tomorrow. Fellow ought to live on his land, not waste time going and coming to it."

"All right, all right," his grandfather answered shortly. "Sign it. You witness it, Avery, and we'll give it to Maria to put in the strong box."

It was quickly done.

The rest had already strolled toward the coral where the new calves were shared, then branded. Zan asked his grandfather if he had seen Zan's pack mule, Buster, lately.

"Sure. Fat and sassy. In the upper pasture."

"Good. I'll get him early tomorrow, then. Seems like all the stock's in extra fine shape this year."

"Yep. They'll do. There's ninety head of our good stock. I'm not counting them four black critters."

The old man looked carefully at his whole family. They were looking at him. He said, "I don't count Tony this year, either. If he don't think enough of his share of the stock to be here to look out for himself, he's old enough to start learning."

Maria said, "Tony earned them calves. All year he worked. They're his all right."

Without looking at Maria, the grandfather went on. "I'll take Tony's share. Let's see now, I'm pen one. You're pen two, Zande. Avery gets number three and Zan takes four. Let the black ones alone. Besides that, it's every man for himself."

Lara plucked softly at the old man's sleeve. "What are you going to do with the pretty black calves, Grandy?"

He didn't answer the child. But rushed through the gate and was among the calves before any of his sons, or even his grandson, could beat him to his first choice.

His sons wasted no time admiring the oldest Allan's ability to look out for number one as they crowded in and set about cornering a share of the largest and strongest calves for their own pens.

Dust flew and swirled in a yellow fog about the corral. Calves bellowed and butted. Allans fell in the dust and roared out angrily at calves and at each other. The women stood on logs and tried to see through the dust clouds. It was a tense struggle and seemed that neither the calf hunters nor spectators could tell who was besting the others.

The women's anxious faces relaxed when Zan called through the dust cloud, "Them irons ready? We are, or just about."

Lara ran over to the small fire of deep red coals that bristle with branding irons. She touched her finger to her tong, and then tried an iron well up the shaft. It sizzled.

Her face, always pale, seemed whiter than usual and her eyes looked frightened, but her voice was steady as she called out, "Irons are right. I'll tend 'em for you this year, Zan. You got stock of your own now."

Tena, Martin's wife, said, "Nonsense, child. You hate branding. Let Martin do it."

Lara laughed. "It's a boy's job. Uncle Martin's too big. I won't watch, Aunt Tena, just hand the irons and keep 'em hot."

There was now less stir inside the corral, and as the dust began to settle, the women could see bright bandannas wiping off dusty faces, and hear a jumble of counting as the men stood still, checking up the number of calves still out in the corral.

The four black calves were un-penned and there were seventeen of the red calves in old Zande's pen.

"You got nineteen head in number three pen, Avery. Get one of them out."

"I didn't know it, Pa." Avery opened his pen's gate and the first calf that slipped out completed old Zande's second string of eighteen.

"Scrawny critter," commented his father. "Not worth yer trying to add it to your share."

He looked at the eighteen calves that was the stock Tony would not get. "We ought to hold this bunch together," he commented. "Tony could see he didn't lose much. You fellows are pretty fair pickers, I'll say that for you."

The Allan men joined in a hearty laugh and young Zan asked, "You ready to start branding, Gramp?"

"I'm not holding back. You and your father start throwing and holding. I'll mark and brand 'em faster'n you fellows can catch 'em."

There was some confusion while the first lot was branded, but the work went smoothly. Gramp's brand, a simple A, was quickly burned on the stock he had taken away from Tony. But he refused the calf Avery had let out, and one more small red calf. These two, and the four black outlaws, he ordered the other men to run into Tony's unused pen.

Maria's scowl faded a trifle as she watched this happen. She ran forward to open the corral gate for the branded sixteen. Roaring with pain and fright, these calves rushed out to their mothers. They crowded against the pasture fence and went on bawling.

Lara took in the cool irons and handed out the hot ones with speed, and always had the right iron waiting. Young Zan and his father threw and held the calves. Old Zande did the branding. By four o'clock the job was done. All the calves except the four black and two scrawny red calves had joined their mothers. The pasture gates had been opened and the stock were making their way up to the highest pasture land.

Lara's big dark eyes followed their trails up the mount for a minute, then said to no one in particular, "Funny how they always go back to just where they were grazing when the drive started. Maybe they want to play like it never happened. Guess I will, too."

She went down to the Creek that flowed along the edge of the grove, stepped across on a couple of stones and was out of sight among the big redwoods.

As soon as the dust had settled from the branding, the women, Blaze, Tena and Maria, unpacked what was left of the layer cakes, got out the cups and a big jug of milk that Maria carried up from the Creek where it had been chilling.

By the time the food was on the table, Zande and Avery had cleaned up the mess left from the ear marking of all the calves. They went down to the Creek to wash up just as Tilli, cool and pretty, strolled in from where she had hidden herself away from sight and sound of the branding.

Before Maria could say anything, Tena spoke sharply to her daughter. "You haven't done one thing to help us today, Tilli. Now put down that silly mandolin and cut some cake. And you can wash the dishes afterward, too."

Tilli looked up, surprised, with a look of innocence in her blue eyes. "Of course, Mama. I'm sorry. I just didn't think."

Her mother's voice softened. "All right, dear. But you must start thinking of practical things. You're growing up." She sighed, and then asked curiously, "What on earth do you think about, Tilli?"

Tilli carefully put her mandolin on the edge of the table before she turned to answer her mother. She had an amused smile as she said softly, "Oh...moonlight, and love songs...beaus and pretty clothes. You know, the important things. Like how I can get out of having to go back to Miss Kraft's school this fall."

Tena asked, "Would you rather stay here on the ranch and help Grampa and Maria?"

"Yes, Mama. If you and Papa want me to."

Tena said, "What I want you to do right now is cut up those cakes."

"Yes, Mama. Oh!" Tilli's eyes widened. "Aunt Blaze has it all cut up already."

She picked up her mandolin, sat down on the bench and, holding it tenderly as she plucked the strings, began to sing, "By the light of the silvery moon, I want to spoon...."

Blaze called out, "Father! Boys! Here's a little sweet'ns. Come rest yourselves."

Zan and Avery came back from the Creek. Old Zande took his place as headman of the clan and the others found places. After a piece of cream cake, a slice of chocolate loaf cake, Mr. Allan pushed aside his plate, saying, "I've been thinking. Maybe Zan did get a bit the short end on the land." He turned his sharp eyes from one face to another but saw only respectful interest. He fastened his attention on his grandson and, after a minute, began to speak.

"Those two little calves, now. I don't feel much for taking the extra care they're going to need to make 'em amount to anything. And the four black ones. We could butcher 'em for meat come winter, but I ain't got no stomach for such. And I don't aim to give calves born from my own cows to the neighbor Graves. Let him keep up his fences and his black bull inside. So. Anyone here that feels Zan shouldn't get 'em for his birthday, speak up."

No one spoke up.

Zan looked both embarrassed and pleased. He murmured, "That extra nice of you, Gramp. I'd like to raise them four blacks, sell 'em, and put the money in a good white-face bull."

Old Zande nodded his head. "Not a bad idea. Sort of along the line I was thinking. But see here, young fellow," he said, pointing his gnarled finger at his grandson, "you get this extra stock on one condition. You fix up that fence and get a pasture ready for 'em. I'll hold 'em in the home lot, feed 'em for one month. If the pasture is fenced and ready by then, you get 'em for your own. If not, they belong to me, and I'll do what I please with 'em."

"Sure, Gramp. But you won't get 'em, for sure. I'll have that fence stock-proof long before the month's done. Can I come get 'em as soon as the fence's ready?"

"Sooner you take 'em off my hand, better I like it. I'm doing you a favor to keep 'em around my place at all."

Twenty-one year old Zan still wasn't as tall as his grandfather. But his shoulders were broader, his muscles flat and strong. He was pleasantly sure of himself, having never known fear of hunger, or felt anything but love and kindness. There were things never spoken of but taken for granted. Now at twenty-one he felt himself ready for anything. The world outside the Santa Lucia's was completely strange to him. Zan was about as fit to cope with its problems as a young mountain lion.

He clinked the silver in his pocket, took out three silver dollars, put them in his hand and showed them around. "What do you think of that for fifteen minutes work?" He asked.

He grinned at the looks of amazement of the women, then the look of doubt on the men's faces.

His grandfather asked loudly, "What sort of foolishness is this?"

"Pretty solid foolishness, Gramp. Well, I'll tell you. It was like this. I felt like seeing what the survey gang was up to, so I rode down to the water hole by the willows. It's where that trail they're blazin' come out. Seems to me if'en they can't build a road better than they can build a trail, no need ever worry they'll ever be puttin' a road through the Coast. Seen by their track they was working north of the water hole, so I rode along till I found 'em working with a sort of windlass they'd rigged up right above the nose of Buzzard Point."

"That's my land. Didn't you run 'em off," bellowed old Zande.

"Nope. Nothing they can do down there, Gramp. No grass, not even brush for feed. No. I set a bit and watched. The fog was terrible thick. And one of the fellows, Jim Short, they call him, was supposed to get into that rope harness and go down over the cliff. They was goin' to let him down with the windlass. But he wouldn't go. None of 'em was willing to go over. Fraid of the fog. Well, I laughed right out. I told the boss, Beeson's his name, that if the rope would hold when the sun was shining, it would sure hold when the fog was there. Make no difference to the rope, I told him."

Blaze asked, "What in the world were they doing? It sounds crazed like."

Zan looked a bit superior as he answered. "They think they'll be blasting there one day. The boss wanted this Short fellow to go down on

57

this rope sling, bring him up some samples of whatever rock and stuff the cliff was made of, so he could write it all down in a notebook he carries. I thought it'd be fun to take a trip six or seven hundred feet down there, and get a close look at the Black Tooth rocks, so I told him I'd go down."

He waited a second for this announcement to take effect. Then he went on, "You'd never guess what this Beeson told me."
No one tried to guess. They waited eagerly to learn what the outlander had said.

Zan was a natural storyteller. He sat for a minute making the money clink in his hand before he shoved the three silver dollars aback into his pocket. Then he said solemnly, "That fellow told me he didn't know enough about rocks of this country to do the job he wanted done, done right, that is."

Zan's father said, "Well, I hope you told him it was you that'd been stubbin' your toes on this country's rocks for twenty years, not him!"

Zan laughed. "Didn't think of that, Pa. But he got my dander up. He said he wanted samples from every ten feet or so. I grabbed up a grain sack that was laying there with some rope, tied it so as a fellow could sling it over his shoulder. Guess they had fixed it for this Jim Short to use. Then I got a bunch of papers they must have been bringing their dinners wrapped up in, and I shoved them papers in the sack.

'You lower me down', I says to Beeson, ' and when I get to the end of the rope I'll start puttin' in whatever stuff I can pry loose. I'll put paper between 'em so as it'll be like you was down there, looked at it yourself.'"

"I guess you thought you were pretty smart," Maria said. "Looks to me you were. You know Gram, or none of us, want a road."

Gramp said, "No need for you to be tellin' what I want, Maria. Maybe you got the notion I'm in my dotage, but don't fool yourself. I'm able to speak out when there's need." He turned to his grandson, asking, "What did he say to that?"

Zan laughed. "Something that got me pretty hot. He looks at me like I'm a kid and asks me how old I am. Well, I told him. And I told him I was on my way to my birthday doings and, if he wants, I better get down the cliff or I'd be late. And I said right out I wasn't fixin' to be late."

"And you went down on the rope?"

"Sure did. Was fun. And easy for me. Wasn't more than ten or fifteen minutes, at most. I could tell by the way they paid out rope them fellows

running the windlass was scared even to do that. But I got what this Beeson wanted, and he was satisfied. So was I, when he hands me three dollars. Don't know what ails him, but that's what I got for fifteen minutes.

His grandfather was thoughtful, silent for a few minutes. Then he said, "It's your birthday, Zan. And twenty-one isn't half as old as you think it is. But I remember feeling fine to be a man grown, all of twenty-one. A man can always use three dollars, and I ain't holding you to fault about it. But now you got your place, your work. Keep away from them fellows, that whole crew. The Allans stand together, and you know how we feel about that road business. There'll be no road 'long this Coast while I'm breathin.'"

"Sure Gramp. Just like I feel. The same. But I was curious to see what they were up to. Well, I saw. And I made a good thing of it. So I'm through with it. I'll be moved and working my own ranch tomorrow. My own ranch. Sounds good, don't it?

Maria spoke in a toneless voice but her eyes were filled with bitterness. "It sounds good. Sure. Like Aunt Carmen Gallo's letter says, she's got stuff, too. She writes bragging they got so many cows, sell so much butter, and milk, and cream. She gets a share. And all the egg money, that's hers. She's crazy with money, I guess. Say, she's throwing out all them good brass beds, buying some new style ones. I ain't even got a real bed. Just the old frame with rawhide nailed on. Maybe it's better for women if they live closer to towns."

"Stuff," said her father, Zande Junior. "Carmen is all Gallo. Got no sense about money. If you want a brass bed, write her to throw one of 'em your way."

Maria's black eyes lighted angrily. "I got my pride. I'm as much Gallo as Carmen is. You think I take in what she throws out? I'd sleep in the dirt first."

Her father said, "There, now, child. I was only trying to fun you a bit. But you got a good bed. Made it myself."

Marie answered, "Sure. Like I said. Got nothing of my own but work." A tear dropped on her hand as she started to turn away.

Zan was beside her in an instant, whispering coaxingly, "Look here, Maria. I'll see you get something of your own. Something you want. I got money. You pick any bed you like from the catalogue. I'll be proud to buy it for you, Sis."

She looked at him doubtingly. "Then what you whispering for? So's you can forget it? Like when Pa forgot to send for my white dress for graduating? Three other girls, all in white, and me in my old faded calico. Men forget. I remember."

Half angrily Zan caught her arm, swung her around so she was facing the whole family. "Listen. I told Maria I'd get her a new brass bed. I want you all to know she's going to get it. To have something of her own."

Maria swallowed, blinked her eyes. "You'll really do it, Zan? I'm so happy. So silly. I feel to cry."

She brushed her eyes, then urged, "And the blue bedspread, too. It's on the bed, in the picture." Her eyes were softly alive as she half-whispered, "I'll make the blue cross-stitch on bleached flour sacks for curtains. Yes. And I'll crochet a blue rug from overall strips. Then I'll write Aunt Carmen to come see me."

She drew a long, shaken breath, her worn fingers covering her lips as she said, "It's got five knobs on each post, that bed. Or is it seven? And brass wires, twisted like a picture frame."

The family joined in an animated discussion of things they had seen in the catalogue. Avery laughed as he warned Zan. "You better watch out or all these Allan girls will be camping on your Trail with them catalogues in their hands."

Zan raised one shoulder, made a wry face. "I'll write the catalogue company, tell 'em to stop sending the wish book to us. But not till Marie gets her wish. She's earned it."

Maria started busily packing the cups, put what was left of the milk, back in to the pack bags.

Zan stretched. "I tied Misty down by the Creek when I rode in. Guess I'll saddle up. Got to get my stuff together, get ready to move by daylight tomorrow."

"That's so," said Grampa Allan.

The rest of the Allan men sauntered over to the rail where the riding and pack stock were tied and began putting on saddle and packs. The women looked around carefully to see that no cup or fork had been overlooked.

Zan stood beside the little Creek in the redwood grove. He liked this place, so full of happy memories of his grandmother, Hannah Allan, now passed. For years she had brought slips of willow, tiny sycamore trees, seeds of Canyon-loving wild flowers. She was long gone, but the beauty she had planned for and planted, deepened and sweetened with the passing years.

Zan did not even start as he felt a small, slim hand slide into his. His hand closed around Lara's as she whispered, "Grandma likes how the columbines look this year. I think she sees them, don't you?"

Zan nodded and together they stood silently watching the fire-throat of a humming bird as it gathered wild honey along the stream.

Bits of July's blue-white sky were visible through inter-laced branches of giant redwoods. The branches were so far overhead that they lay like huge black fern fronds against the sky's pale ceiling. Close to their feet the small stream pushed quietly through a lush growth of the strange brown-green chatter-chin orchids, thorough tiger and leopard lilies and columbine.

Zan broke the silence with an inclusive wave of his hand that took in the Creek, trees and flowers, the rock wall of the Canyon beyond the Creek and the gentle spot where the barbecue table had been spread. "It's all like Granma wanted. I'll make a place like this on my ranch."

Lara nodded. "Granma'd like that. I'll help. You can spade. I'll

61

gather seeds during vacation time, and I'll plant."

Zan said, "Funny to think of you being off in a city, earning your keep, Chicken. Going to school, when you're already through school."

"Zan?" Lara looked around quickly and then drew from the pocket of her faded dress a small packet bound with string.

He looked at her affectionately as she raised her thin, pointed face, whispering, "I got a present for you, Zan. For your birthday. It's my lucky piece. First two bits I ever earned. Got it just for washing dishes for Aunt Blaze and I kept it three years for your big birthday. Here. It's yours."

"Ah, Lara," he said, for a minute tempted to try and make her keep the coin for herself. But some bit of wise sweetness, probably gathered from his grandmother, as well as from Lara herself, changed his mind.

"I'll keep it forever, Lara. It'll be my luck piece, always."

She looked doubtful. "Well, maybe, but if Maria picks the best bed, and she will, maybe you'd better think it's lucky to add that two-bits to what you got. The luck won't leave you if you spend it for some happy thing."

"Maria'll get her bed. I promised her. And I'll keep my lucky piece in my pocket—always!"

IV

Zan had ridden a mile and there were still streaks of sunrise lingering, but it was full daylight when he pulled up abruptly. A mount quail mother and her still unsteady brood had been using the Trail as a highway until Zan suddenly rounded the curve.

The quail chirped sharply at the approaching horse, and then with desperate but gentle urgency, she led her covey of seven tiny newborns into the underbrush for safety. The mother quail returned to the Trail and ruffled her feathers, stretched her neck to its utmost length and stalked forward, as if ready to do battle with the large horse in her path.

Zan had been holding Misty steady, leaning over to see that the Trail was free of the baby quail. He had been amused until the tiny mother got ready for battle. Her courage so touched him that he pulled up Misty sharply to the right and headed for the bank, which was solid, but Misty was a nimble as a deer, so they road above and cleared the trail for the mother quail and her family.

Zan glanced back as he swung Misty on to the Trail again. The quail mother was still watching and scolding the little ones, but her tone now seemed to have the note of a conqueror's pride. Zan smiled, thinking he'd feel proud himself, if he might be sure he could always face danger that way himself.

He rode through stretches of mescal and black brush, liking the spicy scent of bruised pennyroyal, sage and southernwood with its feather soft silver branches. The air was already promising a hot day in the high hills, though now it seemed tempered by the luminous fog that again lay thick over the Coastline far below. He was so busy making plans for this first day when he would be on his own ranch, and for all the days and years to follow, that Misty brought him almost to the barbecue grove before he realized where he was.

A sound of voices brought Misty's ears forward and Zan, too, listened with quickly growing interest. Men, at least two of them, were having hot words. One voice was Gramp's.

Zan slackened rein and Misty lengthened his soft-footed stride until the big table, branding corral and holding pens were right before him. So were the quarreling men. They didn't look around, not even when Zan swung down and walked up beside them. Zan was surprised to see the other man was Beeson, the engineer in charge of the road survey team. He wondered what he was doing way up here.

"—Shovel good money into the sea and be done with it," old Zande was saying. "Better than wasting men's time and money for years. We pay the taxes, and we don't want a road, I tell you."

When the engineer answered his voice was not as loud as Gramp's, but it had the curt sharpness of a man thoroughly out of patience.

"The tax money that will pay for this road, Mr. Allan, is coming from every part of California. Your share of it each year will scarcely buy a loaf of bread."

"That's the first truth you've uttered. It won't buy a loaf of bread. Never bought a loaf of bread in my life. Don't mean to start. Bought bread's like your road. Good for nothing."

Mr. Beeson said sharply, "Come, now. I find it hard to believe you're as selfish as you make yourself out."

Zan stepped forward, stood very close to Mr. Beeson and felt himself taut with anger as he said, "Seems you're a bad judge of me. This is my grandfather's land. If he ain't got the say over what goes onto it, or what don't go onto it. I'd like to know who has?"

Mr. Beeson looked curiously at Zan. He answered soberly. "When the road is finished and you get to be part of the world, you'll be able to answer that for yourself. A man who opposes the common good is not thought of as a good citizen. The best men see other people's rights, as well as their own, and that makes them fine citizens."

Zan answered stiffly, "I don't take it kindly that you run down my grandfather, or the Allan family, Mr. Beeson. We got work to do so I'll bid you a good day."

He turned to his grandfather. "I'm riding up to rope Buster, Gramp. You want to ride along?"

"Far as the home barn."

Mr. Grandpa Allan went over to the corral tie rail, undid the knot that held his big red horse, Ranger, and mounted as nimbly as any of his grandsons could. Then he raised his hat slightly and said, "Good day, Mr. Beeson."

Mr. Beeson answered, "Good day, gentlemen," and began walking rapidly down the trail as the two Allan men began riding side by side up the trail to the large gable-roofed, hand split lumber barn.

They rode with no words between them until they were inside the barnyard and then Zan's grandfather said, "Buster's here, boy. Avery and I drove him in last evening when we went up to see the stock was all back and settle down."

Zan gave his grandfather a warm look but said nothing except, "Then I'll pick up that old shingling hatchet you gave me for my first axe, and be off. Might as well get it now, so I'll have it when I fix the roof for the winter."

"I'll get the hatchet. Know right where it is. You get Buster ready while I get the axe."

"Yes'r."

Buster, the mule, had been out on pasture for some time and tried to act as though a bridle and packsaddle might be some strange, dangerous thing. Zan laughed. He talked softly to the animal and Buster decided to behave.

Zan was already in Misty's saddle when his grandfather Zande Allan came down from the tool house with the old hatchet. Like every tool on all the Allan ranches, the hatchet was oiled, clean and sharp. Zan leaned over, took it from his grandfather's hand and dropped it into Buster's empty packsack.

He gathered up the reins and said, "Be seeing you, Gramp," and rode out through the open gate, turning to latch it after Buster had come through.

His grandfather was still watching him and, for a minute, Zan was tempted to try to put something of his feeling into words. But he couldn't. He shouted, "Come on, you lazy Buster, you."

He wished he could have said it. The thought stayed with him. He said it to himself, "You started empty-handed, Gramp, but you fixed it so I had land ready waiting. You had nothing at all, not a thing. But you put an axe in my hand."

Mentally checking over his stuff, how he was to pack it, Zan was at his father's home before he gave the trip a thought. As he tied up his stock, he saw that Yip, Tony's black and white pinto, was under the shed. Yip's saddle and bridle had been taken off, but the horse had not been curried. Zan got the brush, shaking his head at the dust and dried lather. Seemed strange that a snip of a girl like Lola should be able to stir up Tony so bad that he'd forget to take care of his horse.

Zan loosened Misty's cinch, dropped the reins and then led Buster up to the kitchen gate and tied him to the tie post.

The small, gray, weather-beaten house with its orchard, kitchen garden, flowers and vines looked very bright and friendly to Zan as he went up through the garden to the kitchen's door. Well, one day he'd have a wife, children, a garden and a house that was warm when he come to it tired by a day's work. Meanwhile, complete independence on his own ranch was all he wanted.

Maria was washing up the cook stove as he opened the door. Tony was sitting on the lid of the wood box. From the way he was hunched up like a knot of wood, Zan judged that Tony was still out of sorts with the world.

Maria said, "I got all your stuff together so's it won't take you long to pack. You can bring your socks over and again and I'll see they're mended."

Zan smiled. "There's something I never thought of. Socks! Guess I wouldn't be too handy with them darning needles. Thank you, Maria." Tony looked up, said, "Better watch out, Zan. Find out how much furniture she's fixin' to stick you for, before you start being thankful."

Maria turned on him. "You keep out of this, Tony. I never asked for a thing. Zan offered."

Zan was folding what few clothes he owned so they would roll smoothly inside the blanket that he had already lined up carefully on the tarpaulin resting on his pack rope.

He looked up at Maria, saying half-teasingly, "Don't you get riled up, Maria, or you won't be able to sleep in your new bed when you get it."

She sniffed, dabbed at her nose and said mournfully, "Guess if I wait for that bed to sleep on, I'll be dead. But you hadn't ought to promise things if you don't mean it. I already wrote Carmen and told her to come over to see me." She sighed. "But, anyways, I didn't have no chance to send the letter. That's one good thing, I guess.

Zan said angrily, "What ails you, Sis? I said I'd buy you any bed you could pick out, didn't I? Here. Give me a hand with this rope. That's right. Hold it tight. Thanks."

He stood the neat bedroll upright against the wall and started packing odds and ends in the two leather pack bags. "Get the postal order made out and give it to me. I'll ride down to the survey camp right soon and leave the envelope there. They send out their mail every week."

Her eyes brightened but her voice was still full of doubt as she said, "I made out the order, Zan. I did believe you. But maybe it's too much money for you to spend now when you're starting for yourself."

He had started for his room but he stopped, patted her shoulder and urged, "Give me the order and let me do the worrying about the money. And give me Carmen's letter, too. It might as well go out when the order goes."

Maria turned, jerked open the drawer of the kitchen work-table, and

67

took out the mail order envelope. She started to pick up another envelope but took her hand back empty and closed the drawer. She handed the envelope to Zan.

He took it, absently tucked it into the deep pocket of his overall jacket without looking at it, and asked, "Where's Carmen's letter?"

Maria swallowed, shook her head. She said doubtfully, "Maybe it's better I send her the letter after the bed gets here."

Zan looked irritated, but he shut his lips firmly, took a long breath, and said, "Well, I'll get my gun, then I guess I'm off."

Tony stood up, picked up the bedroll and one pack bag.

"I'll give you a hand with Buster. Like me to ride down with you, help you settle in?"

Zan shook his head. "Nope. You don't know how it is. I've always been the kid of the family. I got a hankerin' to be top dog on my own place for a spell."

Tony lifted his shoulder, made a mouth. "I know. I tried it. Remember? But I soon felt lucky my place was so close to home and a good cook."

Maria had pulled out a basket of long strips of faded blue overall material, was busy at them with a crochet hook. She looked up at her little brother and said, "You got enough cooked stuff in that square box to last a few meals. And the gunnysack's full of potatoes, beans, and onions. Smoked meat and a couple cooking pots."

Zan said ruefully, "I never thought about food. Only about getting the fencing done. You spoil your men folks, Sis."

He leaned over, rested his cheek on her hair for a second and then, with the gun and the other pack bag, he walked out the door.

The packs were on, balanced. The gun was in Zan's saddle boot. He swung on. "So long Tony. Tel Pa I'll be over in a few days, will you?"

"Sure, kid. Well don't take no wooden money. And keep off the women. They're all poison."

Zan let that slide. He touched Misty with his heel and as he turned to see that Buster was following, called, "Don't forget to tell Pa I'll be up to see him, will you?"

"All right. Now take care yourself, Zan."

The orchard, the barn and the shed, were all behind him. The last

gate was closed. As soon as that was done, Zan felt his spirits lift. He hated good-bys, just like his father did. Pa was smart to light out to the wood lot, or wherever he was. But once a gate closed behind a man, he was no longer riding away from something. He was riding toward something else.

Zan whistled himself a tuneless tune and no July day ever looked brighter, more full of promise. Even if he did have to waste part of this day getting the shack so he could camp in it, he had till the 20th of August to get the fence stock built tight. He'd have that done long before Gramp would be expecting him to have it ready. And he'd do it so good that not even Gramp could find fault with his work.

After he left the well-traveled Coast Trail and turned steeply down May Creek Trail, he had to work his way around slides and downed timber. He forced a way for his stock through overgrown lilac thickets. One of his first jobs, after fencing, would be the trail building.

He was sweating. The inside of his shirt was full of dried leaves and small twigs. A couple of ticks seemed to be crawling up his back but he had no time to look into small irritations like that. When his own bit of clearing suddenly came into sight, he reined in Misty and sat looking at it contentedly for a few seconds. His own land!

The ancient board house was about seven by nine feet, but there was a narrow back porch, boarded in on two sides. A snug place to stack things, sheltered as it was against the south wind that brought heavy rain-storms. The roof had lost some of its shakes and those left were moss grown. There was one very small window that once had wooden shutters. Part of leather hinges was still hanging to the frame. The home-split shutters must have blown away. Then he saw the edge of one sticking out from a tangle of sage and cascara. By October he'd have a new roof, and new shutters.

There was a large flat stone for a front doorstop and the plank door was solid. The stone chimney looked solid, too. The ground was so steep that while the house rested on a six-inch sill on the north side, to the south, a square timber seven foot tall held the floor sill level. He'd dig out the whole thing, lay up a stonewall. Then he'd have a stone walled outdoor room just as big as the house above it. Could certainly make a fine place out of this with work and time.

He got off his horse, unpacked Buster and leaned the pack bags against a small tree north of the house so they would not roll down the mountain. He decided to stand the gun against the house until he got the right place picked out for it.

Having unsaddled, he hobbled both animals so he wouldn't have to watch out for them. The pasture, a thick mat of dried golden grass, rich with oily seed, would keep a lot of stock well fed.

He walked through the golden grass toward where he remembered there was once a bucket that ran over a pulley on a rope and brought water up out of the Canyon to where it was almost level with the house. He found the pulley and rigging, then went back to his packsaddle to get his pick and shovel. First job ought to be to clear the spring, he thought. The day was hot enough so that he was already thinking about water.

He returned to the pulley and leaned out to see if there was any sign of water. The spring had been cleaned out and a pool all of three feet across reflected the sky and the sycamore tree beside it. The bucket was clean and the pulley had been oiled.

He lowered the bucket, jiggled the roped until the bucket tipped and began to fill.

As he tested the sweet, cold water he thought, "Good old Gramp. I heard him tell Aunt Blaze he'd been over here."

Back at the house, he pushed the dragging back door open and looked inside. There was a thick layer of old rotted leaves covering that part of the floor that was not covered with scores of heaped up, trade rat nests. Having cleared off the worst of the litter with his shovel, he then cut a rough broom from the cascara bush at the edge of the field, binding it together with a buckskin thong from his saddle.

Once he cleaned the floorboard so they showed and swept the fireplace hearth, Zan thought the room looked orderly. On either side of the hearth was a wood bench, rat gnawed but otherwise sturdy. A square table sat in the middle of the room and some boxes were nailed on the wall for cupboards. The bed was a large, homemade wooden box on four legs, which completed the cabin furnishing.

Zan nodded to himself, well pleased. Everything a man needed to do was here. No fancy stuff to get in a fellow's way.

He carried in the boxes and sack of food and kitchen stuff that Maria had packed for him. Those went on the empty table. He saw some nails on the wall beside the fireplace to hang up kettles. He opened the sack and took out two stew pots, a heavy skillet and a tin wash basin. From the other box he took a thick roast beef sandwich and went outside, munching it as he made his way along the fence line that he must start mending.

As he scrambled up steep rocky slopes and along the edge where the field dropped away into May Creek Canyon, Zan saw that there was not much fence left. A fire had run through here some years ago and the land had been brushy enough so that plenty of pickets had been turned to charcoal by the hot blaze.

It seemed a pretty big twenty acres by the time Zan had been around the pasture. But here were quite a lot of pickets left that were not too charred for use. And there was plenty of stuff down in the Canyon to be had for the splitting.

He went back to the house, got another sandwich and his axe and was starting for the Canyon when Misty nickered. Buster's ears pointed up the Trail. Zan's eyes, too, were alert as he wondered if it was a horse grazing, or a horse with a rider.

Ranger's head came in sight among the brush and scrub oak. Gramp called gaily, "Hello, the cabin! Does the dogs bite?"

"I got both my dogs hobbled," Zan said playfully, referring to his horse and mule. "But they were on the job; let me know you were near."

As soon as old Zande had his feet on the ground, Bottle, his old shepherd dog, left his position as rear guard and came leaping forward to greet Zan.

"Don't let me keep you from your work, boy. I only dropped by to see if you was here."

I was just starting for the Canyon, after pickets. Get me good splittin' log, and they won't take long. Could you eat a bite, Gramp? Got bread and meat all cut."

"Nope. I'll be up to the house before suppertime. Never eat between meals."

Zan looked around at his new holdings, then at his grandfather. "Got everything here a man starting in could want," he said.

The old man nodded. "I've seen worse." He started back to his horse, stood for a minute beside Ranger as he said, "Better get your trail brushed out. Ain't fit for a dog trace, way it is." He swung into the saddle and turned Ranger up the hill.

Zan started for the Canyon but his grandfather's voice stopped him. "Say, forgot to tell you. That Beeson fellow was lookin' for you, when he asked me where he could find Zande Allan. He looked surprised all right when I told him that was me. Guess he thought that trip down the cliff on the rope had aged you considerable."

Zan and old Zande looked at each other for a second and what they each saw struck both of them as uproariously funny. They laughed with an abandon seldom heard among the Allans. Every time Zan started to say something he went off into another burst of laughter. He was wiping tears from his face when he finally managed to ask, "What did he want of me, Gramp?"

"Said he had a job for you. Was how we got started jawing about the road."

"So that's how it was. Tell you the truth, I been to busy thinking about my ranch to wonder what Beeson was doing way up to the home place."

His grandfather smiled. "Guess that's a hint for me to get moving. Well, come up and get your stock when you're ready for 'em."

"I'll do that, Gramp."

Zan followed a deer trail over the Canyon rim and came out close to the sycamore that leaned over the spring. He looked for a minute at the deer and cattle tracks around the water. Then he looked around for enough stout poles to fence the pool, and the source of the water, away from the animals. With a sharp limb he dug a temporary stock pool outside the fence. Not even taking time to stay and watch the water clear, he made his way alongside the Canyon slope over to a good sized redwood that had broken in three pieces and shattered as it fell.

The tree was dead and dry, just what he wanted. It took some time to get it trimmed up, free of bark and limbs. It was not until his axe was making ringing echoes filling the air that Zan felt he was really at work.

The birds were flying homeward and the dusk of early evening was beginning to darken the Canyon before he suddenly realized it was a long time since he had eaten a couple of Maria's sandwiches.

He put his axe in the curve of the log, sheltered it with a piece of bark. Then he took up all the pickets he could carry and made his way up to the house.

He'd been thinking of cooking up a slice of ham and a couple of eggs, but when he looked in the grub box, changed his mind. There were more sandwiches, some fresh tomatoes and young onions.

He took the grub box with him out to the front of the house and sat on the cool stone step looking out at the ocean and enjoying his food.

After the first of his hunger was dulled, he thought of Maria's thoughtfulness at putting up the sandwiches, and then wondered about her catalogue order for a bed. It was no more than two miles, for sure less than three, down to the survey camp. He'd ride down this evening, leave the order and what money it took, with Jim Short. It was Jim that had said he went out of Big Sur every week for mail and supplies that come in on the stage.

The big cut of cold strawberry pie was almost finished as Zan drew out the envelope from his jumper pocket. Leisurely he opened it, looked to see how much money he'd have to leave to be changed into a postal office money order.

He looked carelessly at the bottom of the order. Then he stared at it. He felt his heart beat; his mouth got dry.

Hastily he added the two items, bed and spread, then the amount needed for shipping. There was no mistake. Maria had ordered thirty-two dollars and fifteen cents worth of stuff. The goldarn bed must be gold instead of brass! Where did she think he was going to get that kind of money?

He didn't want the rest of the pie. He put it down on the tin plate, brushed his overalls and pulled his wallet from his pocket. One five-dollar gold piece. Three silver dollars. And a twenty-five cent good luck piece from Lara that he wasn't going to part with. He was short twenty-four dollars and fifteen cents. But he'd promised Maria. And it was his own fault.

It was nobody but him that had told her to go ahead, pick out what she wanted, he'd buy it. But who in God's name would ever think anyone would make a bed that cost as much as even five dollars?

He tried to feel anger at Maria because she'd known how much the bed would cost. She had spent her evenings all winter long looking at everything in the wish book. All he ever looked at was saddles, knives, overalls—important things a man had use for.

Soberly he reflected that it was Maria who kept saying that he wouldn't get it for her. But he was the one who shot off his mouth in front of the whole family, feeling so big with his easy-made three dollars.

But he had wanted to get her something, felt he owed it to her, something special. Maria'd done a powerful amount of patching and cooking for him ever since his mother died when he was seven. Hadn't she, this very day, looked ahead for him? Sure. She foresaw him tired, a bit strange in a new place, and she had gone ahead and fixed him a bait of ready cooked grub to carry him past dinnertime, and supper, too. Take that berry pie, now. He picked up the bit that was left and looked at it curiously. How in hell did a fellow go about making a pie? Be a long spell before there was another one in his house unless Maria gave him one.

He nodded solemnly to himself. Yes'r. Maria was going to get her bed, and the new spread, no matter what. But he couldn't take the order down to the camp. Too bad. It would have to wait a spell until he figured out how to get the money.

The more he thought about money, the bigger the amount seemed. He couldn't get it. He had to. He'd made her not one promise, but several, over and over. An Allan's promise was strong no soft thing like Maria's piecrust, easy broken. An Allan man kept his word.

He sat staring out to sea, thinking of money, of land and cattle, of fences and piecrust.

When the first bat flittered by his head, he stood up, picked up the box of food and went into the house. Then he went out to the water pulley, found the piece of hollowed log that was the old watering trough, and cleaned out the dead leaves.

It took a lot of water and a long time to fill the trough. It was stumbling dark when he led Misty and Buster down to drink. The trough was strange to the animals that washed out their mouths, took a few sips and would have no more.

He hobbled them again and went inside to make himself a bed on the frame. He doubled his canvas, spread the blankets, put his jumper over the pillow and lay down.

He was falling into an uneasy sleep when he suddenly sat up, excited and happy.

"Sure. I can borrow the money from Gramp. I'll give him a note on my calves. Pay it when I sell this fall. Should have thought of that sooner."

The bed was soft to him, the house friendly. His sleep was deep and untroubled.

When Zan rode up to the kitchen door of the old Home Place at about eight o'clock in the morning, Margaret was sitting in her wheel chair beside the table. Her bible was open and her hand busy with knitting as she read. She glanced up and looked at him.

"Oh, Zan. It's you. I thought it was either Mr. Allan or Avery. They should be back about now, I think."

"Which way did they go?" Zan asked. "Maybe I'll go out and meet them."

"They went down to the beach for abalone. The tide was low and the sea smooth. They meant to try for some of the big red abalone out on the rocks where they can seldom get to."

"Abalone, huh? Guess I'll ask myself to supper."

Margaret looked pleased but Zan went on, "Here. I forgot for a minute that I'm a rancher with a job to get done. Abalone hunting and family suppers'll have to wait for a while. I'll get along, Aunt Margaret. Wait for Gramp where my trail turns off the Coast Trail. Might be he'd come up past my place, though he was growling about my brushy trail. But if I wait there, I'll catch 'em either way they come."

Margaret answered, "You come up for supper the minute you feel you can spare the time, Zan."

He said cheerfully, "That's a bribe to get me to work hard. Soon as my fencing's done, you'll be seeing me often. I learned this morning that cookin's quite a trick."

She laughed. "I used to think it was harder than teaching school, but now I like to cook."

He called back, "I think I'll start looking around. If you see a pretty cook, let me know."

He chuckled at the gaiety of her answer. "I shan't worry about you. A man desperate for food doesn't make conditions but would be glad to have a cross-eyed cook!"

Gramp's fences looked wonderful to Zan this morning. Although he had seen them all his life, now he was seeing these miles of sturdy picket fence with a new interest. He stopped at the pasture just below the barn for a minute to look over his own stock. A likely looking lot, he thought. It was a pity to have to wait a couple of work hours, wait that much longer before he felt like a rancher with a growing ranch. But he must get Maria's mail order off his mind. He hurried Misty along the steep trail, and at his own trail, got off and started clearing out some of the overhanging brush with the machete he carried on his saddle.

Soon he heard the clatter of rock out on the main trail. He hurried back and was waiting by the time the two men rode in sight.

"Any luck?" He called. "You get that big red fellow you been wanting, Uncle Avery?"

Avery grinned. "Might hurry him to span ten inches, but I'm suited. Biggest abalone I remember getting."

Zan laughed. "You better save the shell. There's some will want to see it to believe a fellow could get one that size, from shore."

His grandfather pulled alongside Avery. "Didn't do bad for an old man, myself. But what you larking around over the hills about. Got your fence done?"

"There was some business I wanted to see you about, Gramp. I was up to the house and Aunt Margaret told me where you were, and so I cleared trail while I was waiting."

Avery said, "If you're going to talk a bit, I'll ride on up and see how Margaret is, Pa. Come up when you can, Zan."

He rode off and Gramp sat looking at his grandson, waiting to hear what he had to say.

Zan felt suddenly, under those piercing eyes, foolish and tongue-tied. Then he blurted out, "I wanted to borrow twenty-five dollars from you. With my calves for security."

"I don't lend money."

The old man tightened Ranger's reins, was about to ride after Avery.

Zan stood in the middle of the trail and did not move aside. "But I got to have it, Gramp. I promised Maria I'd buy her a brass bed. You heard me—at the roundup."

"Nonsense. Twenty-five dollars? For a bed? The girl's got a bed, hasn't she?"

Zan said, ""She wants a brass bed. I don't see why she shouldn't have it. And I promised to get her one."

The old man shrugged. "Well, go ahead and get her one if'en you're that foolish."

Zan set his teeth, took a deep breath. "I didn't know how much a bed like that cost. I haven't got the money."

Gramp looked amused and a trifle discouraged. "I always knew Maria was all Gallo. But I fooled myself that she'd become an Allan. Pride and vanity, boy. Pride and vanity. That's the Gallo of it. Let it be a lesson to you, and to Maria."

Zan said stiffly, "If the calves are not enough security for you, I'll put up the rest of my stuff: Buster, Misty and the ranch. But I got to have that twenty-five dollars."

His grandfather said, "I told you I don't lend money. You know that. And I never borrow, either. You'll have to swallow your pride. It's all a lot of foolishness, anyway. The girl's got all she needs. Forget it and get along to your work."

"That's your last word, Grandfather?"

"Last word on the money. And you'll be out a lot more than twenty-five dollars if that fence isn't ready in time. Remember, I told you I'd hold that extra six head for a month. You're using up time jawing me. No hard feelings, Zan. But I feel you're lucky that you ain't got the money.

It's no good for a young man just staring out to get big ideas. And it's ruin to start borrowing and run up something owed.

He spoke to Ranger. Zan stepped aside, his face white, and his throat dry. The old man rode by calling cheerful, "We'll look to see you up to the house soon's you're ready to take care of your own stock, Zan."

"Yes'r."

Zan was startled that he had been able to force his dry mouth and throat to say the word he spoke. He felt as though a rock from the cliff had fallen on him. All his life Gramp had gone out of his way to see that his youngest grandson had what he needed; even things like store-bought shoes to go to school in, and a pencil-box.

He couldn't believe that now, when he really needed help, when he had offered security, man to man, that Gramp would fail him.

He stood at the corner of the two trails, shaking his head, trying to get rid of the cottony feeling in his mouth and throat. Maybe Gramp was right about the pride and vanity. Maybe the best thing to do was ride over, tell Maria he didn't have the money, and couldn't send for the catalogue bed.

But he couldn't do it. Not with the picture of Maria bent over her basket of rags, so hopefully making herself a blue rug to go with the blue bed cover on the bright brass bed.

But he had to tell her. He had nothing to use for money. He took Misty's reins in his hand and plodded blindly down the brushed trail toward his new ranch.

V

Back at his own house, Zan got his axe and a mattock to start building a rough trail into the Canyon. Down this trail both animals could come to water and Buster could pack out pickets.

There was no music in the ring of his axe, no satisfaction to him in seeing how quickly he could make the trail.

The money. The goldarn money. What to do about it? How to get such a sum as twenty-five dollars? Uncle Stephen would hand it to him, not even asking what he wanted it for. But all the Allan men, though deeply fond of Stephen Janson, had too much pride in themselves to lean on Stephen for even a nickel. Zan knew his own father would feel exactly as his grandfather felt—that Maria had a bed, that he was positively stupid to encourage a woman's extravagant nonsense.

Zan grunted as he rolled a big rock over the edge. He waited to hear it crash on the floor of the Canyon. He could only think that both Pa and Gramp had good sense. It was like Gramp said about signing a paper before looking at it. If he'd had any idea a brass bed cost so much… No! Darn it all, that wasn't the idea. Maria wanted that bed as much as he wanted a ranch of his own. She had a right to something of her own, and he guessed that all women wanted something just pretty and useless now and then. Look how long Grandma Hannah had kept trying to get her a set of China dishes. She never gave up. Zan thought that Gramp must be glad now that he finally gave in and got them for her so she had use of them for a few years before she died.

Maria was going to have her bed. He was going to get it for her. But how?

The Trail clearing was finished; two loads of pickets had been packed out of the Canyon and spread along the fence line before an amazing thought struck Zan.

Could get the money by working for Mr. Beeson. He could earn it and be beholden to no one. Didn't Gramp say that Beeson had come looking for Zande Allan to offer him a job?

Zan got the packsaddle off Buster, turned him out as soon as he was hobbled. He slung Misty's saddle on, led him down to the house and tied him while he quickly washed up.

Making sure he had Maria's mail order in his pocket, he rode down to the Coast.

Beeson's men were working only about a quarter of a mile north of where his trail met the new trail the survey crew was blazing.

He stopped to swap a few words with the Short boys and Will Hubbard who seemed glad to give their axes a rest. As soon as it seemed polite, he excused himself, saying, "I came to see Mr. Beeson, so I'll get along."

Zan felt he was in luck to find Beeson out of hearing from his men. He rode Misty along the sliding shale until he found a solid place for the horse to stand and then left him with the reins hanging.

Zan picked his way up the slide carefully so as not to start a loose rock. It was not much of a climb but he felt shame that he was both sweating and breathless when he drew even with Beeson.

Knowing the longer he held off, the harder it was going to be to speak out, so Zan plunged right in. "My grandfather said you come up the other day looking for me. Said you spoke of having some work for me."

"Yes, that's right."

Zan felt his face burn as he said, "I need to earn some money. I'd like the chance to work a bit."

Mr. Beeson looked at him. "Part of my job is to make friends with the landowners down here. Your grandfather seemed pretty certain you wouldn't want a job with me. I wouldn't like to do anything that would stir up the old gentleman."

Zan said, "It's me that wants the job, not my grandfather. I'm past twenty-one and on my own. You still got the job?"

Mr. Beeson thought a minute, and then said, "Yes. I'd like to use you. It's the same sort of job you did before. Could you start tomorrow?"

"Yes'r. If you got enough work so's I could earn twenty-five dollars, and if you'll give me that much money right now."

Beeson smiled. "We pay once a week. I expect that will be all right with you."

"No, it won't. I got to have that money straight off. Is why I come for the job."

Mr. Beeson said, "It's rather unusual."

Zan's face was red but his eyes met Mr. Beeson's very steadily as he said, "Yes'r. I never been pressed for money before. But right now I am. I can put my ranch and stock for security. You're running no risk."

Mr. Beeson reached into his pocket, took out a flat wallet and opened it. He took out two ten-dollar bills, one five, and handed them to Zan, saying, "From all I've heard of the Allan family, Zan, your word is as good as gold, any day. You start work tomorrow morning at eight. We work an eight-hour day. You come and go on your own time card and, for this job, which involves considerable risk, we pay three dollars a day. All right?"

"Yes, thank you Mr. Beeson. I'll be here. Do you mind telling me when the man goes out for mail?"

"Tomorrow, I think. No. It's Friday he goes. Day after tomorrow."

"Much obliged. And you'll hold the money till I get it earned, will you?"

Mr. Beeson shook his head. "No. I wouldn't think of doing that. This money, this borrowed twenty-five dollars, is something between you and me. You'll get your money every week, just like the other men. When you pay me back is up to you."

Zan muttered, "Thanks, Mr. Beeson," and hurried away.

He was shocked, as well as touched, by this stranger's treatment of him. It was mighty different from Gramp's way. It was confusing to think that his own grandfather would treat him as a child while Mr. Beeson, who only knew him by hearsay, treated him as a man. And Mr. Beeson was one of them men from outside the Coast that Gramp was always runnin' down, saying they'd corrupt and ruin the country. Seemed queer.

He stopped for a few minutes to take up with Jim Short about the matter of getting the postal order, the stamp, and sending Maria's letter out on the mail stage.

The men in the crew seemed willing to stop work and talk about the country for a while, but it made Zan uneasy to be using up time that Mr. Beeson's company was paying for. He said, "I got a big job of fencing waiting at my place. So I'll just get along."

He heard Mr. Beeson calling him and rode Misty north to meet the engineer.

Mr. Beeson waited until Zan was up to him before he said, "One thing I almost forgot to tell you, this job you're getting now only lasts three weeks."

Smiling, Zan said, "Oh, that's all right. I only mean to work seven, eight days, long enough to pay you back."

Mr. Beeson looked grave. "Then I couldn't use you at all, Zan. I got three weeks of work at cliff scaling, going down over places like Buzzard Point. If you can't see that job through, I'll have to send out for a man that will."

Zan felt trapped. He thought of the pickets to be cut, packed out, and driven in by the end of this month. He thought of Maria's mail order already in the pocket of Jim Short and almost on its way to the post office.

He'd found a way to keep his word to his sister. Maria was going to get that brass bed, get it right away, and not be waiting half her life for something to call her own.

He said, "I didn't know you had as much as three week's work, Mr. Beeson. I'll be glad to have the job."

"That's fine. I'll see you at the bunkhouse at eight tomorrow morning, then."

"I'll be there."

Misty, restive under lack of exercise, danced along the cliff trail, tossing his head, and made all possible speed up the mount and get back to Buster and to work.

Zan ate a hasty snack from his grub box, and then hurried down the Canyon to split pickets. As he split, he sharpened and stacked them, and was busy figuring how he could manage his two jobs.

Nine and a half hours of his day was all it would take him on Beeson's job. Daylight came early enough so that he could be working on his fence by four each morning. Work till seven and eat breakfast as he rode down the Coast to work with the surveyors. Only working an eight-hour day, he could be back at his own place and building fence by six. But that would only give him six hours of daylight each day for his own ranch work. Sundays he could get in fifteen, near sixteen hours. Might gaunt him down some, but he could do it easy. Not only that, he'd have about thirty dollars left over in his pocket after paying for Maria's present.

The pickets piled up in encouraging number and Zan felt good about it all. Queer how things work out. He'd never in his life been in such a stew as he'd been in over how to get the money he needed. A fellow had to be pushed real hard sometimes to make him learn what he could do when he had to. Anyway, he'd found out one thing. He couldn't go back on his past world. He couldn't even feel if it was right for Gramp to have advised him to do that. Gramp was a good man all right. No one could say different. But he was a bit old fashioned. If Gramp had treated him as much like a man as Mr. Beeson did... Oh, well, no use to fool around with them "ifs."

At dark Zan cooked himself a slice of ham and four eggs, filled out with Maria's bread and the last of the tomatoes. He set a kettle of beans and ham to cook in the Dutch oven, covered with the coals and ashes of his supper fire. Then he moved his bed outside where the first hint of daylight would wake him.

He woke up so startled that he was standing beside his bed before he realized he was awake. Somehow in his waking, the idea that his grandfather might come down to see how he was getting along, hit him. By the time he was really awake he was eagerly on the way to wash his face, build a bit more fire around the beans in the fireplace, and eat a bite. That his grandfather "might" come 'round was just another way of hunting trouble with an "if."

He put the thought out of his mind and chewed happily on chunks of bread and ham, which he finished eating after he pack-saddled Buster and was leading him down into the Canyon to pack out pickets.

He kept a wary eye on the quality of light, trying to work on the fencing job as long as he could, and still be down to the Coast by the time the survey crew was ready to work.

When the sun came in sight through a notch in the mountains, he made a deep mark on the ground where the shadow first touched. Five minutes later he was riding down the Trail.

The men were finishing up breakfast, picking up their bags of lunch. The cook shack smelled good. Zan was hungry already. It was going to be all of ten hours before he could get back to his own place and he had not thought to bring anything to eat.

While the other men were rolling cigarettes and picking up their tools, Zan made what was a tremendous decision for an Allan. He would ask the cook if he could buy some dinner in a bag.

Walking back to the cook shack he found the cook sitting over a cup of coffee and plate of doughnuts.

"Good morning. I'm Zan Allan and I've got a short job with the crew. I forgot my dinner. Could I buy some from you?" Zan asked.

The cook said, "Well, sit down and have some coffee. Help yourself to the doughnuts. My name's Lester Berryman. Call me Les. Nope. I can't sell you anything."

Zan put down the doughnut he was lifting from the plate. Red-faced, he stammered, "I'm sorry. I don't know any of the camp rules yet. This is my first job. Got a lot to learn."

The cook laughed. "Don't get all lathered up. I was just having fun. I don't sell anything, that's true. The company charges for board. Lunch is two bits, and I'll fix you up in a jiffy. Wade into the doughnuts, them's free, and don't be bashful."

The doughnuts were light, crisp and had been sprinkled with sugar and cinnamon. While Zan watched the cook put four sandwiches, a cut of pie, hard-boiled eggs and an orange into a stout paper, he had a terrible thought. The only two-bit piece he had was the lucky piece Lara had given him. He'd go hungry a long time before he'd let goof that birthday present.

The cook put the sack down in front of Zan but he didn't pick it up. He asked, "You got change for a dollar, so's I can pay for this?"

"Where you been all your life, son? You think the company's goin' to trust a cook to collect? That'd be crazy. I write it down, and it's took out of your wages before you get your hands on your pay."

Zan said slowly, "That suits me. But it seems queer this company would hire folks if they didn't trust 'em."

The cook looked at him for a minute with a startled light in his eyes. Then he said, "Ya. Well, you'll find out there's a lot of queer things going on, once you start living."

Zan ignored this. He'd been turning over what seemed a good idea, even if an extravagant one. With his hand above his lunch bag, he

hesitated, and then said, "Could I get two of these dinner bags a day, after this? I mean to get them every day while I'm workin' here."

The cook shrugged. "Well, the other guys grouse because they have to carry one. But if you want an extra, it's no skin off my back. Cost you an extra quarter, that's all."

Zan heard the men leaving the clearing, picked up his lunch sack and hurried after the gang, calling back, "I'd be obliged to you if you'd fix me an extra one, starting tomorrow."

He felt things were working out good. The sun came up a few minutes earlier each morning. The clock in the cook shack had said it was fifteen minutes before eight when he'd walked in to get a word with Mr. Berryman about the food. So he could move the line of his shadow clock a bit more toward the west, get him an extra quarter hour of work on his fence. Minutes would count up to a lot of pickets set, when you figured the time saved in a month.

Mr. Beeson came out of the small drafting shack as the two Short boys, Will Hubbard and Zan were passing it.

"Take a pick, and a brush hook from the shed, Zan," he called.

"Won't be anything but Trail work for you until we get up to Gray Head. The boys will get you started. I'll be along in time to build the coffee fire."

Will Hubbard dropped back with Zan, said, "I'll show you where to get your stuff."

From the warehouse behind the cook shack Zan took an axe and a brush hook instead of the pick. "Guess I can get the use of a pick from one of the men, happen I need it."

"You're welcome to mine any time, and don't hurry to give it back." Will Hubbard had a slow voice, a slow walk, and a look of mild amusement.

Zan hurried to catch up with the men ahead and was astonished that while Hubbard seemed to loaf along, he kept ahead with no effort. Zan had thought that he could cover trail as good as the next one. It nettled him to have this city man be loafing along a trail while he, an Allan, hurried.

A thought struck him.

"You born in the mountains, Will?"

"No. Born in New York City, New York State.

"You grow up in the mountains?"

"No. Grew up in New York. Finished high school there. Wanted to get to a college out west, so I went out to Oregon. Great state. So's Washington. I did road work my first summer vacation in Oregon. Next two, I signed on with a crew-cutting trail in Washington, the Olympic Mountains. This year I'm seeing the backwoods of California."

Zan studied over all this before he said, "You seen a lot of country already. And got through high school. And you know about towns. Walk like you learned some about mountains, too. What you going to do when you finish your college?"

"Me? Oh, I've finished. Got my Bachelor level degree. I'll stay with Dariel Beeson till this job's done. That's November. I'll go home for Christmas. Plan to work in one of the automobile factories for a year. Then I'm going to get into airplane manufacturing. That's what I'm keen about."

Zan said nothing. He was too amazed. Cities, mountains, schoolin', automobiles and flying machines. This man seemed to have already lived a couple of lifetimes, and he wasn't even old.

They were almost up to the other men when Zan asked, "How old are you Hubbard?"

"Getting along. I'll be twenty two in December."

Zan made no comment.

During the morning's work the three outsiders did a lot of joking, stopped now and again for a smoke. But Zan admitted to himself they were all doing a good day's work, and were as handy with tools as he was.

When Mr. Beeson came along, the morning was pretty well gone. He set Jim Short to building a fire and making coffee. Zan noticed that while Short kept up the fire and watched the coffee so it didn't boil over, he'd also take a file out of his pocket and was sharpening his brush hook.

Zan felt faintly disloyal to his grandfather as he wondered why Gramp said all outsiders were a lazy, drunken lot. They were not all lazy. This bunch sure wasn't. Maybe Dariel Beeson was extra careful who he picked for his crew. That was why these fellows weren't like most town men.

The day went quickly and it was not until Zan was walking back to camp next to Jim Short that he found out there was yet another way that city boys were just like the men in the Santa Lucias of Big Sur.

Jim said, "You married, Zan?"

Zan was halfway between flattered and frightened. It was flattering that this fellow should think he was already married. But it was more than a little frightening to have a city man of his own age most likely fixing to pry into how he felt about girls. This fellow must know all about women, but Zan knew less about women than he did of towns.

He answered, "No. All I got yet is a ranch. Not even a fit house to live in."

Jim said, "I wondered. There's a pretty blond, name's Tilli Allan. She rides down and talks with us once in a while. Never did know if she was Miss Allan or Mrs. Allan. Thought she was about the right age to be married to you."

Tilli? Down here alone? Talking to strange men? She knew better than that.

Zan hid his shock as best he could, answered a trifle stiffly, "Tilli's my cousin. She's visiting with her folks."

Jim persisted eagerly. "Any chance there's a dance or something I could take her to?"

Zan said, "She'd go with her folks if there was anything to go to. But Fourth of July's past now. There'll may be a big barbecue at fall roundup. I was out to the dance near Jolon a year ago the Fourth. Didn't do no dancing, just watched from the door."

"My God. What a life. These mountains must be full of sour old bachelors."

Zan laughed. "Nope. Seems like when the time comes right, the girl comes along from somewhere. I got too much to do to think about girls for a long time yet."

Jim said, "Cheerful liar." But he was grinning in a friendly way and Zan decided no offense was intended.

Anyone told this morning that a man would call him a liar and not find himself in a fight, Zan would have thought that person was telling a lie. Allans spoke plainly, carefully, said what they meant. It was a new idea that a man could say such a word as "liar," and make a compliment out of the saying.

Jim said nothing for some time and then, "I'm riding in to the post office tomorrow. Got a letter with "Miss Maria Allan" on the address return. Another cousin of yours?"

"My sister."

"Sister, huh?" How about taking me up to call on her?"

Zan laughed, shook his head. "Maria's the oldest one in our family. Guess she's almost thirty. And she's never been the dancin' kind. She'd be rattled to have a young rooster come crowing at her door."

The thought of Maria's startled, disapproving face, sent Zan off into explosive laughter.

Jim didn't seem to mind, though he was being laughed at, and said, "I'll cross Miss Maria off my list. And since Miss Tilli Allan isn't Mrs. Allan, I'll settle for her as my number one girl. You say she goes to dances with her folks? But she goes out riding without them, so I think I'll ask if I can come sit on her porch."

Zan said nothing. The idea of Tilli flouncing around the country by herself, visiting with a crew of men all by herself angered him. That's no way for a girl to act. It was hard to believe that Tilli would make such a show of herself. She must be man-crazy, that's what. He wondered if his Uncle Martin was so old he didn't take notice of it. Gramp wasn't too old.

He'd noticed Tilli rolling her eyes around. Told Aunt Tena she'd better keep an eye on her girl. Made Aunt Tena mad as hops. But she was polite. Thanked Gramp for his advice, but her voice was cold and drawed in when she spoke.

Zan decided he'd have a word with Tilli if she came down to the Coast again. When he got through telling her a few things, she'd be done with making a show of herself.

He said good night to the crew, rode quickly up to his ranch to fix supper and got to work on the pickets.

The next day he had his supper in the extra bag he had asked the cook to put up for him. That saved him almost a half-hour's time. Also fed him better than he could spare time to feed himself. Already he knew that the long hours were beginning to tell on him. The first three days he worked steadily with the crew at cutting brush, making trail. Then Mr. Beeson asked him, "Feel like going down over Gray Head tomorrow, Zan?"

"Sure. That's another of the places I've never been. Don't think anyone else every did, either."

Mr. Beeson said, "If I was as sure footed as you are, you wouldn't get the chance."

Gray Head was not as high as Buzzard Point. As he was lowered on the windlass, he saw there was more solid rock, fewer layers of clay and broken stuff. Zan liked the excitement of his small journey over the edge, in space, and for the first time in his life he wondered how it would feel to go flying through the air in a flying machine. Before he had talked with Will Hubbard, airplanes seemed completely unreal. He'd heard them talked of, but never by anyone who had seen one up close. But Will had been in them plenty of times, he'd said. His brother had been a flier in the war and was now flying airplanes for a living. It sure was something to know a man like Hubbard.

He jerked on the hang rope, his signal he was ready to come up the cliff, and in a few minutes, he was back on top of old Gray Head, ready to hand the bag of samples to Mr. Beeson.

"Just put the sack over there between those two big rocks, Zan. I'd like you to come up the Coast a short way. Got another place to look over," said Mr. Beeson.

He told the rest of the crew to take down the windlass rigging, stack it and cover it with canvass. When done, finish the day working trail toward Gray Head.

Mr. Beeson started climbing along the steep rocky face of the cliff that followed around a small bay in the sea below. Every step was a risk, but both men made it over shale patches, leaping to safety when, what looked like a solid rock, fell away from the touch of a foot.

As soon as they came to the mouth of the bay, Mr. Beeson sat down on a log beside the small Creek that came down into a waterfall almost at the sea's edge.

"No name for this Creek, or this bay, on my map, Zan. You got a name for it?"

Zan looked way up to where the rough cliffs gentled off into brush and scrub trees. "I'm not sure," he said. "Never been down here before. He looked again at the shore, then up at the mountains. Then said, "it's Old Man Creek. Sure, it'd have to be, since it comes in alongside Gray Head."

Mr. Beeson smiled. "Old Man Creek. Of course. Now I wonder who thought of all the names along this Coast. Most of them seem so right, the minute I hear them."

Zan said, "My great-grandfather called most of them. He come here in about 1830, I think. The Indians must of called them all something, but no one remembers what, any more."

They sat resting, not saying anything for some time. Then Mr. Beeson stood up, saying, "The world's like that. Nations, people, place names. A hundred years—a thousand years go by, then no one remembers."

Zan said, "Gramp says all America is changing. Too much easy money. Too much runnin' around, not puttin' down roots. He's dead set against change. Guess old men are always that way."

Mr. Beeson sat down again. "I don't think they are. Not if they live where they get new ideas, watch new things make life easier, and better. There was a man, a grandfather, up in Washington State where we were putting a road back into the mountains last summer. He didn't want a road, either. He was pretty down, when we got there. All he had left of his family was a married daughter, and he wanted a grandson as bad as most men want money."

"Married daughter?" Zan asked. "Was she a widow?"

"No. She couldn't give birth to living children. There were three little graves on the ranch already. All boys. All dead by the time they were delivered with the help of a local woman. When I told Mr. Larson we'd get in extra men, get the road open in time to get his daughter out to a hospital where she'd have a chance, he picked up his tools and went to work for me."

Zan was leaning forward, listening. "What happened?"

"We got the road cut and opened. His daughter's time came. 'Cause of the road, we got her to a good hospital, a good doctor and especially in good time. He operated on the old man's daughter, took the baby. Liveliest little rascal as ever I saw. Named it for his grand pappy, too. There's a case when one old man that didn't want a road, but he can't say enough good for it now. When we first got there, the children were so shy they ran and hid under the beds. Now they all climb into the District school bus, get driven to school to learn things, and get to play with other children. Bright lot of youngsters, once they got a chance. All because of a road."

Zan shifted uneasily on the log. Between a stubborn loyalty to his grandfather, and a feeling that Mr. Beeson was a sound man, and because his growing sense of a wider world than the one he had always known, made him feel confused. But he was too tired to think straight.

Mr. Beeson yawned, stretched. "Getting old," he said. "I was up till my lamp went dry last night. Studying a new catalogue of better road-building machines. Another few years and men will be peeling roads off the sides of mountains almost as easy as peeling an orange."

Zan said defensively, "Couldn't get that road machine in here, even if there was such a one."

"Not now," Mr. Beeson agreed, "but one day it will, and not too far off." He stood up and Zan did the same. "We got to get back and get those samples you brought up checked, or the day will be gone."

Zan following him across the cliff to Gray Head where the windlass hoist had been taken down and covered with canvass. The two men bent their heads over the various pieces of rock. Finally Zan asked, "What good's this stuff to you, Mr. Beeson?"

"Part of my job is to get it. It's not for me that I'm having you do this, but for the power man who'll have to blast a roadbed here, some time.

The road's going right along the edge of the Coast, you know."

Zan didn't answer. He couldn't. He wondered if Mr. Beeson actually believed anything as crazy as that?

On his way riding up to his ranch that night, Zan found what seemed to be a reasonable answer for Mr. Beeson. Some boss higher up told him to go survey a track for a road along the Coast. It was a job Beeson was paid for. It wasn't his job to tell the boss it couldn't be done. His job was to survey the track and let the next man higher up figure out what to do next. Was as simple as Gramp telling him to plow a field. Gramp was the boss of his land. Zan told himself he never asked Gramp any questions. He just went ahead and plowed the land. Mr. Beeson didn't have to believe the road was possible. He just went ahead and did what he was told.

He ate his supper from the paper bag as he rode along. The minute Misty was unsaddled; he put the packsaddle on Buster and started packing pickets. He had made three trips into and out of the Canyon, when he heard Misty nicker.

Zan stood watching the entrance to the Trail, his whole body tense. He didn't want anyone to come and take up his time. What scared him was the visitor might be Gramp. He didn't have enough done to have Gramp come poking around, sizing up things.

Gramp, on Ranger, rode into the clearing.

Zan led Buster over to where he had been stacking the pickets, and began to unload.

Gram rode right over. He looked cheerful as he said, "So you're hard at it, are you?"

Zan said cautiously, "Well, I ain't been wastin' my time. Can't say though I got as much done as I'd like."

Gramp was in fine humor. He said, "No man every does, Boy. Not if he's a real man and working his own land. It's like I remember. I felt I was just slaving for my Pa, but when I broke away and started working for myself, I drove myself harder and longer that my Pa every thought of driving me—and he was not easy going man, I tell you."

Zan relaxed, laughed. "I'm up before daylight and don't eat supper till after pitch dark."

"Then I won't stay for supper, thank you." He swung around in his saddle, looked over what he could see of the place.

"Well, you got that first piece of fence patched good, but I don't see where you been doing much fencing, Zan."

Zan took a quick breath. Then he said, "I figured out that I'd make time by first gettin' all the pickets rived out and sharpened, then packing them along the fence line where I'll use 'em. Wastes time to drive in one load, then go back for anther."

"That's right. What you doing? Getting out what you need for this first stretch from May Creek, and planning on cutting the ones for the upper field from Little Canyon?"

Zan said, "No. I hadn't thought of that. But it's a good notion. I'll do that, Gramp. You say you can't stay for supper?"

The old man said, "Not the hours you keep. I'll be abed before you've et."

Zan said, "Then I'll not waste time standing here gabbin'. I got a field to fence."

"That's the stuff. I guess you'll do all right."

He gave Ranger a nudge and turned him, started up the Trail. Zan was half way back to his Canyon when his grandfather called, "You're looking a bit peaked. Better come up for a meal soon."

Zan called back, "I'll do that, Gramp, when I got the fence done. The day I come for my stock."

The days flew by, that first week. But the long hours, the short sleep and the monotony of eating cold food from paper bags began to tell on Zan. The first long Sunday of steady work on the ranch had been a joy. He got such a lot done, felt confident he could do both jobs and do them both well. The second time Sunday came, Zan felt something had happened to his eyes and arms. The axe didn't seem to hit true. His legs shook as he went up and down the Canyon Trail. He couldn't understand it.

When his splitting mall slipped and hit his shin, he trembled so hard he had to sit down a minute. He thought he must be sick with something. It was Sunday and he had to cook, so he had started a pot of beans when he built his fire at dawn. But at noon he couldn't eat the cold, half done beans. The day was hot, but he felt as cold as the cold, greasy beans.

He went outside into the warm sunshine. He decided not to pack any pickets today but to spend his time on the hot, rocky slope. Driving pickets in the sunshine was a good way for a fellow to sweat off a summer cold. Besides, it was encouraging to see real fence, new and strong, marching along to hold in his steep pasture.

When he rode down to his job with Beeson the next morning, he knew he was going to be able to see the rest of the time through. Only this one-week to go. One more Sunday, then, after Tuesday next, he'd have all his time to give to fencing on his ranch.

The weather turned even hotter. Zan couldn't remember any August that had been so still, so hot. His cabin was like a bake oven when he stumbled to bed. The heavy heat still crowded every corner when he got up before dawn and went to work.

He couldn't escape the heat when he went down to his job with Beeson. In ordinary summers, when it was this hot up in the mountains, the Coast would be cool with fog. But now the survey crew walked sluggishly to work, cursing the glare from the ocean that lay still like a lake.

It was Wednesday when Jim brought in the notice that Maria's bed had arrived at the post office. Jim asked, "How you going to get all that stuff packed up the trail to your sister, Zan?"

Zan's gaunt and haggard face took on a look of desperation. He wet his cracked lips and looked confused. "I don't know. I got to do something about it. She's waitin' for it."

After a minute he said, "I'll bring Buster, my mule, down tomorrow. Go after it tomorrow night."

He put his fingers, full of small cuts and splinters, up over the top of his hair, pressing them down on his buzzing head. Then he said, "Maybe they'd let them stand till the last week in August. I could get them then, easy."

Jim looked at him. "You better lay off a day or two. Looks to me like you're coming down with something. You feel all right?"

Zan looked startled. "Sure. Feel fine. It's the heat, I guess. Tires a man."

Jim thought for a minute, and then offered, "Look here. How would it be if Hubbard and I went after that stuff? Something to do, some place to go. I'd like it and I'm sure he would, too."

Zan said, "No foolin'? I wouldn't want you to put yourselves out, just doing me a favor."

Jim gave him a playful shove. "Truth is, I want to have a look at your sister, Maria. Since Merve Williams started beauing your cousin Tilli

around so steady, I figure I got no chance there. So I want to do a favor for Miss Maria."

Zan only said, "Thanks. It'd be a big help to me to get that stuff up home."

As he went up the trail along the cliff's edge, his head swimming with weariness, his mouth set in a hard line.

Tilli was either a complete fool or a complete hussy. He was inclined to think she was just a vain, silly fool. But if she had to make an idiot of herself with some man, why choose Merve Williams? The William's family and the Allan family had been at outs ever since Aunt Blaze Allan flouted Joe Williams, Merve's father, and married Stephen Janson instead. Tilli, acting this way, was making the whole Allan family look ridiculous.

Funny black spots kept swimming before his eyes and he stumbled as he shook his head to try to clear them away. He felt he should take time to go and have a talk with Tilli, but decided he could not until his job with Beeson was finished.

As he rode home that afternoon he kept telling himself that only four more days, or was it five, couldn't make much difference. The very first day he had the whole day to himself he'd see Tilli and explain how such things looked to outsiders. Tilli was all right. She was still only a schoolgirl. Besides, she was an Allan.

The day Zan's job was finished, his account settled with the boss, he rode home to his ranch with thirty-two dollars in his pocked and a warm word of praise from Dariel Beeson—an invite to come back any time he wanted a job!

The praise carried Zan up most of the mountain, but he was so worn out that, before he was in sight of his own place, he had admitted to himself that this night he would not drive one picket. He would go right to bed, sleep ten hours.

He figured one night's real rest and he'd amount to something again.

He was almost asleep in his saddle when Misty nickered. He straightened up with a start, looked ahead and saw Ranger had been tied there for some time because a complete circle had been trampled around the tree.

Old Zande Allan was standing in front of the house.

Zan took one look at his grandfather and felt a shock strike through his whole body. His grandfather's eyes were fierce as an eagle's. His face was white, his mouth hard.

Zan swung down silently, dropped the reins and stood facing his grandfather.

Old Zande looked at him as though waiting for Zan to say something. Zan looked back at him steadily, silently.

His grandfather said, "Don't try no lies. I know what you been up to. I saw you myself."

Zan said, "I been working on the survey gang. Yes, I had to get some money quick to pay for the brass bed I promised Maria."

His grandfather took a step forward. "You broke your word to me. You neglected your land, your stock. A hell of a man you turned out to be. Let pride and vanity drive you to betray your whole family. For three Judas dollars you spoil the name of Zande Allan. Your house is a mess. Your bed isn't made. Your fence—faugh! Get out of my sight."

Zan reddened, bit back the words he was thinking. This was his own place. If his grandfather couldn't stand the sight of it, let him ride away. His knees sagged. He couldn't seem to keep his mind on anything but sleep and rest. But he moistened his cracked lips, said, "I finished my work with Mr. Beeson today. Now I got all my time for this place. And I'll have the fence all done before August nineteenth."

His grandfather's voice seemed shrill and far off. "Never mind fencing. You think I'll turn any stock over to you after what you've done?"

Zan felt a shock of anger.

"What have you done for me, Grandfather? You refused to help me when I told you I had to have money to keep my word to my sister. Mr. Beeson give me the money right out of his pocket with no other security than that my name was Allan. It's hard to have a stranger trust you when your own kin won't. He advanced the money against my work. Would you have me not work out my debt?"

"Don't put words in my mouth, young man. I told you the right way to settle about that cursed bed. You set your judgment above mine. You sold yourself to my enemy. I'm done with you."

Zan said, "If that's how you want it. I'll not expect the extra stock you promised me. But I'll come up and drive down my regular share as soon as the fence is done."

His grandfather glared at him, his face twisted with anger. His voice was shaking as he said, "You got no cattle of any sort. And I don't want this piece of my land fenced. And I don't want you using on it, either. Be off."

Zan looked at the furious old man for a minute and then, in spite of himself, he laughed. He wanted to stop laughing but he was too tired. Every time he thought of the red-faced old turkey cock ordering him off his own land, Zan started laughing again.

The old man said in a steady, quiet voice, cold as a dip in the Creek, "You'll laugh out the other side of your mouth before we're through. I said for you to take yourself off."

Zan stopped laughing. He took a couple of quick breaths and then said, "This is my land, Grandfather. It's for me to say who stays here—or leaves here. Good day, Sir."

The old man tilted his head sideways, sniffed. "Your land, it? You got no paper to prove that. I say it's mine. Any man that neglects land to earn a quick dollar working for the road I hate gets nothing from me."

Picking up Misty's reins, Zan led him over to the door stoop. "Excuse me, Sir. I got to sit down for a bit. Will you sit down, please?"

"No. I won't. Neither will you. Go on back to your father's house, if he'll take you in after what you done. But get going."

Suddenly Zan was so angry that he was neither tired nor sleepy. He stood up. "I've heard tell of spoiled children Gramp, though I've never seen one. But I'm lookin' right at a spoiled old man. I don't like what I see. You've played cat and mouse with your whole family for fifty years. You're expecting me to plead with you. I been workin' with fair-minded, grown-up men, these last three weeks. And I like it. This is my ranch but you can have it. These cattle are my cattle by all the rules you yourself made for the family. They're mine. But I give 'em back to you. I don't want any part of being treated like a ten year old. Misty's mine. Uncle Stephen gave him to me. Buster's mine. You gave him to me when you thought he was a dying mule colt. I've had him for eight years and he's mine. The axe you give me when I was thirteen means something to me. I'll take it with me. And my bedroll. I'll be gone in ten minutes with what is mine. Goodbye, Grandfather."

The old man walked stiffly over to Ranger, got on, but held him, watching Zan while he put the pack saddle on Buster, then tied on his bed roll.

When Zan came up from the timber with his axe, walked over to Misty and swung into his saddle, he said, "The rest is yours, Gramp. Good bye."

The old man lifted his reins, started up the hill. After a second he saw that his grandson was not riding up toward his father's house. He was heading down the trail toward the Coast.

The old man stopped his horse, yelled, "Where do you think you're going?"

"Back to a place that belongs to me, that I made for myself. I'm going to work for something I believe in. I'm building road."

His grandfather yelled after him, "You'll rue the day."

Zan did not answer and, as the old Zande Allan rode slowly up the mountain, young Zande Allan rode off the Allan kingdom, rode down the steep narrow trail toward all his tomorrows.

VI

Zan was so tense he forgot all about being tired. It seemed a good sign to be riding toward the brightness of sundown. He whistled *Sobre las Olas,* wonder if some day he might even ride over the waves instead of only whistling the tune.

More soberly he began to sing the chorus of the South Coast Song:

> *The Big Sur Coast is a wild Coast, and lonely,*
> *You might win in a game a Jolon,*
> *But the lion still rules the barranca*
> *And a man there is always alone.*

He was a Big Sur man. He, too, was alone. Now, out on his own. He had made a choice. Gramp would have soften if he'd pleaded with him like a boy. If he'd done that, he'd have stayed a boy, under the family thumb for the rest of his life. But he had chosen to take a new road. He drew a deep breath. The road ahead looked toward tomorrow; the trail he was leaving led to the past. He wasn't afraid. He'd build road and he'd make a good life of it, too.

Maybe by the time he had boys of his own they could ride in their own automobile down the Coast road. Life by then might be so easy that when he told his boys how *he* started out on his own, they would think a man who started with an axe, a gun, a horse and mule, yes, a man with money in his pocket and a job promised, was starting with nothing.

Misty was picking solid footing across a gluey blue-clay sump that was a favorite deer-lick when suddenly it seemed to Zan that all hell broke loose. The zing of a bullet, the sound of a shot, and Misty's mad lunge forward, bucking and kicking, sliding in the wet clay, all came so close together that the horse was across the sump, on solid ground and under

99

control before Zan could realize what had happened. Buster was solidly picking himself a trail across the grass as Zan leaped off Misty, grabbed his twenty-two out of the saddle boot.

Someone had taken a shot at him. It was still an instant before amazement gave way to anger. The mark of the bullet across Misty's satiny rump was like a welt made by a savage cut from a whip.

White with fury, Zan sheltered Misty and Buster where the stout trunk of a Allan redwood protected them from being hit.

He felt his knees shaking as he ran across the trail, forced his way through the undergrowth, gun in hand, making for an open spot higher up.

Looking across the Canyon to the open land a couple hundred feet about the clay lick, he saw a man, gun in hand, running toward the trail.

Zan yelled at him. "What the hell you think you're up to?"

The man didn't look up, or give any sign that he had heard. He dashed into the brush, still going toward the trail.

Zan slipped through the tangle of thimbleberry and willow that crowded both sides of the seepage.

He was at the edge of the clay, between the man and the trail down to the Coast, his gun checked and ready, before the man floundered out into the clay.

"Where is it? Where is it?" The man was fighting his pocket, trying to free a big knife. He was out of breath and shaking like a leaf.

Zan said, "I'm right here. I'm what you shot at. But you can't cut my throat yet. You missed me." His fury mounted as he realized his own voice shook.

The man struggled with the big clasp knife, trying with shaking hands to pry out the stiff blade. He let the butt of his gun sink into the wet clay as he leaned it against a willow, fought the knife with both hands, muttering, "Got to bleed 'em right away. Damn such a knife—."

Zan walked across the clay, stood beside the man and shouted, "What the hell's wrong with you? There ain't any deer. Never was. You damn near killed me. You shot my horse!"

The man looked at him as though seeing him for the first time. He asked irritably, "Did you move it? I shot one. It's right here unless you moved it."

Zan gave up. He reached for the hunter's gun, emptied the magazine, letting the shells fall unheeded and sink in the mud. He shoved the empty gun almost into the man's face, saying, "Take this thing and get out of here as fast as God'll let you. Get going."

Now the man saw him, heard him. "What's the idea?" He asked threateningly. "You looking for trouble, kid?"

Zan repeated. "Get going. And keep going. Either you were shooting at me, or else you were shooting without knowin' what you shot at. It's against the law. So is shooting out of season."

"I'll look into this myself," the man threatened. "You can't lay hands on my gun, waste my ammunition, threaten me. I got friends and influence in this state."

"Well, that's fine. You surely need someone to look out for you."

The other man had made no motion to take his gun that was held by Zan so close to him.

Zan let go of the gun, heard it drop in the mud as he turned and walked back to the log, picked up the reins he'd let hang in front of Misty.

Buster ambled along without waiting for any word from Zande. Misty was not hurt but seemed as stirred up by the excitement as was his rider. Zan had to hold him in firmly or he would have arrived at the survey camp far ahead of time. Since Buster had made a few trips down the Coast, it seemed better to Zan to keep him in sight. As long as Buster could see Misty, nothing would make him turn back. No use to move out from a place and then look behind you and find that all you owned was already halfway back there.

There was a lighted lantern in front of the shack Dariel Beeson used for an office, so Zan stopped there.

Beeson came to the door in answer to his knock. "Oh, you, Zan. Come in, glad to see you."

Zan stepped in, suddenly shy and nervous. Perhaps Beeson had only been polite when he'd said he would like to have him on the crew. Well, there's a way to find out.

"If that job you spoke of is still open, Mr. Beeson, I come to take it."

"Fine. When can you report for work?"

Zan's face showed his surprise. "I'm here."

Dariel laughed, a strange, barking sort of, "ha, ha, ha," that held a contagious mirth. Zan listened uncertainly. Dariel must be laughing at him for some reason.

He felt relieved when the boss said, "Then I take it you're working for me. Got a place to keep your animals?"

Zan tightened up all over. He had never before thought of where he was going to keep Allan stock. Anywhere on the miles of Allan acres was a handy place for them. Corrals, tight little grain sheds, hay enough to last through any short need. A man could find such things within a mile of any job he was doing on Allan land.

But he couldn't tell this man that he, Zan Allan, didn't know where he was to put his critters. What could he do with Misty and Buster? Allan land came down to the Coast in plenty of places. Gramp's land. Might be Gramps wouldn't pinch in on him and tell him he'd refused his right to Allan land. But whether Gramp did or did not, the fact remained, he had no place of his own to keep anything.

All this whirled through his mind in the brief instant between the question and the time for an answer. He said carefully, "I'll want 'em somewhere handy, but I haven't fixed on a place yet."

Beeson looked down at the table he used for a desk, his hand covering his mouth for an instant, but there was no smile on his face when he asked, "You'll be boarding at the camp?"

Zan considered the money in his purse and asked, "How much does it cost?"

"Thirty dollars a month."

Zan said, "That's a lot of money."

Beeson answered, "It's the usual charge."

At this rate, in one month he would eat up his fortune, his whole thirty dollars.

Zan said, "Sort of startled me. We never pay out for food on the ranch. We grow it. Don't think we ever paid out thirty dollars in a year for store food."

Beeson offered, "You don't pay for it in advance. We take it out of your pay."

"How about if I put in here for a day or two till I can get me a place to batch?"

"Sure, Zan. Whatever suits you, suits me, as long as you're on the job from eight to six."

"Then I guess that settles things. Only...well, you spoke of wages, and I don't know what you pay, regular."

"You start at three dollars."

"Well, I'll try to earn it."

"I know you will. And you can earn a lot more than that if you want to, working with your head instead of your hands. I believe we're right on the edge of a real revolution in the whole process of road building."

"I don't know as I follow you, Mr. Beeson. I'd like to listen, if you got the time."

"Then sit down, Zan. A listener is what I'm always trying to find. Now what I mean is, take the motorcar. It's getting better and cheaper at the same time. And it's going to get more of both, as well as lighter built. That's half the picture. Now here's where you come in—"

"Me? How you figure that?" Zan leaned forward eagerly.

Mr. Beeson laughed. "You're already in, soon as you scale a cliff, pick up a shovel, or squint through a transit. Cars can't get cheaper and lighter unless we give them longer, wider, smoother, safer and cheaper roads to travel over."

Zan shook his head. "That's a bill of goods you're setting out, Mr. Beeson. An' you bite yourself off a real chew when you talk making roads all that much better, and say you got to do it cheaper, too."

"Well, that's how it has to be. It's up to the road builders. Given the right sort of road, the automobile will prove it can travel fast, be safe, and cheap enough for every man to own one."

Zan grinned. "Mebbe I'll buy one myself, someday."

Beeson didn't seem to think there was anything strange about that. "Of course you'll buy a car."

Beeson shoved back from his desk as though tired, and Zan looked at the clock on the rough board wall behind the desk.

"Past my bed time." He said, "I'll bed down where I'm going to tie my stock tonight, and be here for breakfast. That all right with you?"

"Wouldn't you be more comfortable in the bunkhouse? There are empty beds, with mattresses. You could spread your bedroll on one of them. I think most of the fellows are still up, talking, or playing cards."

Zan said, "I'll stay by my stock till I get 'em settled, thank you just the same."

Zan knew now just where he was going. He rode south on the trail, passing the dark and silent survey camp. He grinned, pleased with himself no matter how tired he felt. He'd be getting settled while softer men lay abed.

Less than half a mile south of the work camp he turned Misty into an overgrown trail that crossed a swampy thicket just above the Coast Trail and then circled a small hill. Zan wondered if anyone, even a hunter, had been over the trail and up to Pete's old cabin since Pete Garcia had drowned trying to save his Aunt Blaze's reputation from Coast talk when they'd gone abalone gathering together and got trapped when the surf came in. That was years ago, way before he was born.

No one ever spoke of the Garcias to the Allan family, so he never knew exactly how Aunt Blaze had been involved in Pete Garcia's death. And about that same time, at least in the same year, Pete's two brothers had got into trouble over killing sea otter that the government protected. The Garcia family had to move to Monterey and none of them ever returned to live on the Coast.

A sturdy little house came faintly into view as he made the last turn up the hill. Zan hobbled the stock, found his matches and went to look inside the place.

One room and a lean-to. But it was a good-sized room and the main house was strongly built of rock and adobe. The shed kitchen was built with thick split redwood. The heavy plank door was unlocked, he learned, after he had politely knocked and waited the decent few seconds for an answer. Those seconds were not wasted. He figured that in an hour he could make the adobe chimney fire proof.

The fair-sized windows facing the ocean did not let in enough of the dim light for Zan to see the room. He lit another match.

The adobe fireplace was in good condition, though water-stained from the cracks he had noticed in the outside chimney. Only one water stain on the floor by the kitchen door said the roof was in good shape. A few shakes would fix that leak.

He found the door into the lean-to had settled, but he worked it open enough to slide past it and into the kitchen.

This room also had a window, one looking down the Coast to the south until a mountain shoulder hid the shoreline. But the thing that made Zan forget his Allan caution and shout, "Oh, man what luck!" was a small, rusty, but still whole stove. A cook stove! What comfort a man could take in his kitchen, back braced against the wall behind the old wooden bench, and his feet warming and the ash-catching apron that stood out in front of the fire box, where it got warm, but not hot.

The table was a trifle rickety, and one pane was cracked on the kitchen window, but there was not a thing wrong with the house that couldn't be fixed in a few hours' time.

Zan carried his pack bags inside, tossed his bedroll on the rawhide-laced wooden bed frame that was between the windows across from the fireplace. The light bedroll went through the rotted leather.

"I'll split out some shakes, make it a solid bottom. Can make it a hide bottom soon as I get leather," he said out loud. He spread his bedroll on the floor, good enough for the first night here.

The first morning light was getting very bright outside as he stooped down and, piling his bedding on the worn bed frame, he reminded himself not to start talking out loud to himself. Lone men often fell into that way, he'd heard tell. Was a thing that could get to be a habit. He'd watch himself.

Going outside, he saw a spring close to the kitchen, choked with leaves and brush that it had been collecting for years. Using a thin, flat stone for a shovel, he soon had it cleared down to where he could see sweet, active water pushing up from the earth.

By the time he had led Misty and Buster over to get a drink, the spring was clear and lively with fresh water. He left the saddles racked on an ancient sawhorse by the back door, put the hobbles back on his horse, and struck off for the surveyor's camp.

Again Zan was fifteen minutes ahead of the breakfast call. Some of the men were still struggling awake, cursing good-naturedly as they shoved their heads into the trough of crackling cold mountain water.

Beeson stretched himself as he came out of his bedroom-office, called cheerfully, "Make out all right last night, young fellow?"

Zan grinned, "I made out." He sniffed the air and said, "Smells good around here."

The breakfast bell rang. Zan followed the young engineer into the cook shack. Three weeks of scant food, eaten on the run, had left him hollow hungry. He sat down in the first empty place, kept his mind on his plate and ate everything that was passed down the table. He couldn't have told if the food was good or bad, raw or cooked. He could only exult that he was part of a real road crew.

What luck he had, getting his chance to learn about roads,

machinery, maybe even a bit about engineering from such a man as Mr. Beeson, a man with faith in the years to come.

His own father, his grandfather, his great grandfather had broken from their homes only to do the very same thing their fathers had done.

Zan finished his breakfast without even tasting it. He was the fist to break the old Allan pattern. Their trail led to his past. But he was starting to build a wide road into the future.

He came out of his dreams with a start as he heard Beeson's voice just behind him, saying, "Find an axe, a brush hook, in the tool rack."

Zan could see Will Hubbard and Jim Short, each with a pick and shovel, going out the door.

He was hurrying toward the tool shed and Beeson called after him, "And pick up our lunches in the mess shack, will you?"

"Yes, Sir"

He kept telling himself that he must not run because he felt he was a few minutes late, and he must not jump at every job as though it was the last minute he had on earth and must get it done; the other men took work as though there was all the time in the world to get things done. They'd get down on him, think he was trying to show off, if he worked the way as Allan men had always worked.

He shoved open the door to the cook shack. The cook was not in sight but at the end of the table there were the two bags.

Zan looked at them. One was marked "Beeson." A grin lit his face as he saw how his own name was on the other bag. He picked it up proudly. This was his place.

The road was not a dream. It was being build right now, every day, and under the eyes of the people who laughed at it as a fantasy scheme. Those people—and he had to admit to himself that he'd had the same feeling—thought of the road as though it was to be there suddenly. Yes, that was his little boy thought, and he had never completely outgrown it. One day he had expected that he would come down the mountain and there, like something unrolled as quickly as a strip of rag carpet, would be the new road, complete, and with horses, people, and automobiles already using it. But a road was first an idea. Ideas have deep roots, and grow slowly.

He looked at the brush hook, feeling a fondness for this demon of tools. Today he would use the brush hook to build a road. A road grew almost as slow as a redwood. The idea had to stay alive, grow thirty years just to bring this survey gang.

But they came.

What they did might not look like much, but it was part of the road. First they squinted through a transit, making what they called "lines." You couldn't tie up a sack with, or hang a washing on, those lines. They were just a look, a look across canyons, from one mountain to another mountain, a few figures set down in a notebook. A stake, held to its place by rocks piled around it, a piece of white rag to make the stake show up, and a few figures in a note book line the surveyor's pocket; that was all the token there was that the look had ever been taken, and the line had been marked. As months and years went by the rag might blow off, or wear to thread and be used to line a linnet's nest. The stake would fall down in some high wind, be kicked loose by wandering cattle. But as long as two rocks stayed near the right spot and the figures taken from the transit were safe somewhere, the engineer who came when Beeson's work was done could look at the figures, find the rocks, and say, "The line was run. The mark is here."

Mr. Beeson has said, "Get ahead. Don't work with your hands, use your head."

Zan considered this as he followed Beeson south on the narrow Coast Trail. If a man told himself, "I'll pick up an axe and cut down a tree," that was an idea. If he cut the tree into lengths and then into wood, burned it to keep himself warm, it was still an idea. But if he cut it into boards and built a house, what then?

To use something for today, to burn up the tree and keep warm, was a good idea, nothing wrong with it. But the man with the house-building idea, if he carried it through and turned the tree into a house, had an idea that would last longer than the man. Great Granpa Allan's first little log shanty, built in 1834, still stood on the home place, and he'd been dead for near fifty years.

Thing for a man to do was to get hold of an idea that meant something to more people than himself. Like this road. Wasn't just for himself he'd wanted the road. Was for everyone, even people that wouldn't be for a hundred years. Gramp always said a fellow has to look out for number one. Maybe that was all he, Zan, was doing. Getting a job, getting earned money, looking out for number one.

Building a schoolhouse, now—or a church house—that was something for more than one. Aunt Blaze had urged him to go to town school when he had gone through with the grades. Said the more you know, the more you can learn. Shoulda' done it, too. Did promise Aunt Blaze I'd read that Emerson book I got from the teacher when I graduated. Seems I never had time, but a man's got to make time, use time, time—something worth three dollars for only eight hours of it. Never thought of time that way before. I'll do it. I'll study that book out no matter what. Looked at it a couple of times, didn't seem to make sense. Law of Compensation. That's enough to close a book right now. What's this compensation and who made it a law? My grandfather makes his own laws and they worked for him, most times. Time's worth three dollars?

Feet following the boss. Mr. Beeson walks straight, never turns his head. Polite man. Knows I'm thinking. Bet he doesn't know an Allan is stepping right back of him using on his footsteps. Mine hid his, blots 'em out. He's taller. I got bigger feet; when I grows up to them feet I'll make a big man.

Big man, big money. Five dollars a day–ten dollars for six hours. Don't be crazy—

Zan came back to the actual world with an abrupt start as he realized that Mr. Beeson had halted in front of him.

"If you'll start here, and brush out a line about two feet wide," he said, indicating a place where a rough trail had been started below the line of the Coast Trail, "and carry on with your brush hook until you meet Ken Short. He's working from the Rat Canyon end."

Zan stacked his other tools beside the main Trail, tucked his lunch bag inside his shirt, and began to swing the brush hook. Beeson watched him for a few minutes, remarked, "Easy does it, Zan. We don't expect you to kill yourself working, you know."

Zan nodded without looking up and went on cutting, his practiced stroke leaving the brushed out area as cleanly cut as a grain row.

The sun got higher and hotter but he worked on, unconscious of the heat or the runnels of sweat that dropped from his nose, his chin and eyebrows, and soaked through his shirt. He was neither hot nor tired. He was building road.

After a few days he got the cook to sell him a small supply of groceries from the camp stock. Then he cooked for himself at Pete Garcia's old place.

Through the rest of July and out into the clear fierce heat of August, Zan built road with a lover's devotion. Nothing resembling a road grew on the ground so he gladly sprinkled it with his sweat. He dreamed of work at night. He lost weight. For the first time in his life he knew what it meant to be completely happy. After his dinner was cooked and his dishes washed, he worked to bring Pete's place up to Allan standards. The rusty old stovepipe in the kitchen was replaced with a pipe made from an empty tin lard pail from the camp kitchen. He got all the broken fence repaired with rails that he'd split from Allan timber in Pete's bit of Canyon land. His twenty-two rifle provided him with both meat and rawhide to make a stout new lacing for the bed frame.

One warm Sunday evening in late August Dariel Beeson came up the Trail, leaned on the stout new rail gate and called up to Zan, who was sitting on his front step, "Thought I'd drop up and see how you're doing."

Zan stood up, surprised and pleased. He said, "Just resting. Braiding on a quirt."

The engineer opened the gated, closed it carefully and strolled closer. Zan took a quick look around. He felt his first pride as a householder. Gramp, or even Maria, would have allowed that things were clean and neat around the place.

It was cooler out on the porch but Zan invited Dariel in, motioned him to the new bench beside the fireplace.

They sat silently while Beeson loaded his pipe, looking slowly around with friendly interest. When the pipe was drawing to suit him, he took it out of his mouth, said, "You've done a nice job on this old place. A nice job."

"Just patched it some, cleaned it up a bit. Take a lot of work to fix it real good, but it'll do for the summer."

He looked around, thinking to see it with Beeson's eyes, and even so, it looked all right. He said, "Glad you come on a Sunday. That's my clean day. Guess you noticed the floors was still wet."

He grinned, "You're my first company, Mr. Beeson."

Beeson looked surprised. "You don't say. Well."

He fooled with his pipe for a minute as though doubtful, then asked slowly, "You mean none of your own folks have been here to see you yet?"

Zan shook his head. "They're not much for visiting."

Beeson stretched his back, stood up. "Suppose we go outside, sit on the porch. You can get ahead with your quirt while I look at the country."

They sat quietly together as the sun dipped down beyond the sea's horizon and the hills glowed rosily, reflecting the sunset's color.

Finally Mr. Beeson said, "This is rather a choice spot, Zan. I was looking up boundaries the last time I was in the surveyor's office in Salinas. I looked at this piece. Surprised me to learn there's almost sixty-four acres in this fraction. It's got some redwood, a bit of stream along Rowdy Creek, and a fine stretch of Coast."

Zan nodded. "Good bit of bench land, too. Old Indian camps, those are. Make fine garden soil. Good spring, that's fed by Sinking Creek, never dries out."

Beeson said, "Someday, maybe another ten years, there'll be a modern highway almost where the trail is now. Be a nice spot to own."

Zan answered, "I guess it belongs to some of the Garcia family. They must have took it over when Pete died. That was a long time ago."

Beeson took the pipe out of his mouth. "They didn't pay any taxes on it, never a cent. It can belong to whoever pays the back taxes."

"You thinking of taking it," Zan asked.

Beeson's head turned toward him, his eyes twinkling. "No. Not me. I was thinking you ought to add it to the rest of your land."

Zan would have like to talk freely; he felt the need of a friend. It wasn't right to tell even the most friendly outsider that there was an old feud between the Allans and the Garcias. But he must say some, 'cause Mr. Beeson was waiting. He stammered, "I'd have no need for—I been trying—thinking maybe you'd keep me on when the crew moves to the Salmon Creek stretch."

Beeson laughed. "Ya, ya, ya. That's what's been driving you, huh? Well, long as I got the say, you got a job with me."

Zan bent his head over the braiding job, hiding his pleasure at being praised. The light was going fast and after a few minutes he let his hands rest idly while his eyes followed the knife-sharp outline of the rugged peaks, black against the fading sky. At last he said, "It is a nice spot."

"Then why don't you grab it?" Beeson urged. "Cost you less than fifty dollars to redeem it."

Zan thought carefully before he answered, "These Mountains are kin to me, sure enough. And I know 'em like I know the look of my

110

Gramp's face. But I'm building road so's I can go see new faces, new places. Long as I got a job with you, I got no need to find a place here."

"Something in that," Beeson agreed. "Long as you got land of your own up on the ridge."

Zan chuckled, then laughed right out as he suddenly realized his own freedom. He could share a confidence with a friend of his own choice, as long as it was about himself, and did not involve any women of the family. "I traded my land for my job," he said. "I couldn't have both, not with Gramp Allan so set against the road."

Beeson looked at him, shook his head. "So, that's it. You went against your grandfather's plans for you? That what you mean?"

Zan smiled. "Yup. That's right."

Dariel stood up, emptied his pipe ashes in the middle of the hard packed trail, ground them out with his toe and dropped the pipe in his pocket. "It was a hard choice you made, boy. I hope you never regret it."

Zan walked down to the gate with his friend. Beeson stood on the other side of the gate as though reluctant to leave. Zan said, "I got what I wanted. If an Allan makes up his mind, it's made up. But I guess I'm some of a kid, at that. I'd feel plain foolish, making a big thing of giving up my land from Gramp, then grabbing up some land. It's like I'm afraid to have too much. I picked that which I wanted most."

Beeson pursed up his face. "You'll change once you get out into the world. Fellow soon learns to grab what he can, while he can. But if you really don't want it, I'll get title to this land myself, before someone else does."

Zan said, "It's a nice place for anyone if they want it. When do you think the job here will be done?"

"I'd hoped sometime in October, but it looks now as though it will be late in November before it's done."

Zan felt elated. "We'll get a lot done by then. And maybe next thing I know I'll be helping build a bridge."

Beeson said, "Well, see you on the job in the morning, Zan."

He took a few steps down the Trail, halted and said, "I'm going to lend you a book on road building. Better find time to read it. You ought to go to school, that's what you really ought to do. But you can learn a lot, if you want to, by reading, and working."

Zan answered, "I got the whole world to learn yet, but I got my foot on the road. I'll get there."

As the summer days slowly shortened and a feel of fall gave a touch of briskness to the early mornings, Zan's shyness wore off. He went to the road camp once or twice a week, gathered up the tools and sat in the mess hall sharpening brush hooks, replacing broken pick handles while listening to the crew joke and squabble over the card games. He liked their laughter. If it got loud enough, he sometimes let go and laughed too. It all seemed an exciting, social sort of life to Zan.

The next time Beeson had to go to Salinas, he was gone four days. When he came back, he called Zan, asked him to come into his office.

"Well, I got title to Pete's place, Zan. I got no real use for it and I wanted to tell you it only cost $53.18. What do you think?"

It was a nice piece of land—but! Zan shook his head. "I think an Allan's got to be one thing or the other. If I get fooling around with land, I'll start slipping into being half-land, half-road. I'm all road, Mr. Beeson, but thank you for the offer."

Dariel said impatiently, "You don't have to marry the road, do you? Damn it, Zan, a man has a life over and above his job."

Zan said, "I got what I want. I'm satisfied."

But he found he wasn't quite satisfied with the work he had done on Pete's place. It was all right for a temporary camp, but now that Mr. Beeson owned it, Zan put in less time visiting at the camp, more time working on the place. He built shutters for the windows against the time when he would move down the Coast with the crew. He made a good watertight housing to cover the stovepipe hole when the day came to take down the lard pail chimney. Even if Mr. Beeson didn't get back for years, he wanted him to find everything still firm and solid.

It was the first week in October that Bud Wilson got a bad gash on his leg from a brush hook. He's the one who usually made the trip out to the Big Sur Post Office, met the stage and packed back the camp supplies.

Mr. Beeson asked Zan to take Bud's place, to make the trip. He said, "I know you're a good packer, and besides, the change will be good for you. You're driving yourself too hard."

Zan said, "I get in a bit of loafing. But I'd like to make the trip. I've seen a couple of automobiles, but not very close. Misty and Buster's never had a look at one. I bet they won't like 'em much." He laughed. "They got an auto stage, that drives on the old county road from Malpaso to Bixby Canyon, the fellows say. Did you see it?"

"I came from Monterey on it, last trip. It's a little faster than the horse stage—though not much. That county road was never meant for anything but horses.

Wondering how long it would be before he'd get a chance to see if riding in an automobile scared him, Zan went to put the packsaddles on Jack and Judy, the camp mules. He already had misty and Buster saddled, though he'd had quite a time catching them after their free and lazy summer.

As Zan rode out of camp, Misty's coat was shining like bright leaves, the string of mules following, and he felt it was the start of a real holiday.

He got to the Pfeiffer family Resort and Post Office before the stage came in, ate his lunch while he waited. He'd tied Misty and Buster up short, put them in between the other two mules. They were both used to the gas-driven stage.

When the auto stage at last came down Cedar Hill, Zan was more excited than the stock. The car was high, tinny, old and wheezy, but to Zan it was more wonderful that a city child's first sight of horses in a bright merry-go-round.

He looked at the stock. They were holding steady. Even Misty, reassured by the more sophisticated mules, was only rolling his eyes.

Zan hurried forward and, when he told the stage driver he was from the road-survey camp, he was allowed to help unpack the stage and sort out the camp's supplies.

Zan had day-dreamed that some strange, lovely young lady would come as a passenger on the stage, but was not too disappointed that there were no passengers at all.

As he finished packing his stock, took one more long look at the automobile stage, he knew this trip would always seem one of the high spots of his life. Then he remembered the camp mail sack, went back to the post office to fetch it.

Misty was as impatient as his master to be on the homeward trail. He wanted to prance up the long Post Hill, and when Zan held him in, Misty sidled along the narrow wagon road sidewise, the three mules close on his heels. But once on the Coast Trail, they settled down to an easy, fast walk. All the familiar Canyons passed, the packs riding securely.

Finally Zan pulled up at the survey camp, tied Misty, unloaded the packs and took the mail sack over to Beeson's cabin.

He knocked on the door and a strange voice said, "Well, come in." Zan opened the door and in the light of a dim and smoking lantern, he stood facing the man who had taken him and Misty for a deer, and shot at him more than three months before.

The man's face had an angry look. He asked, "What do you want?"

He spoke as though he had a right to be there, and Zan made his first attempt to speak cautiously. "I been to the post office and I brought in the mail. I'll put it on Mr. Beeson's desk and push on home."

As he dropped the mail sack and turned to leave, the man growled something Zan couldn't make out. He didn't want any more words with this fellow and he surely did not intend to get into an argument in the camp office. He felt a nagging worry that the man had some right to be in Beeson's office. He didn't seem to be waiting for anyone, but acted as though he had a right to the chair in back of the desk.

Zan stepped out quickly, glad to feel the cool air of late evening on his face. He was down the three wooden steps on the south side of the uncovered porch when a step sounded on the other end, near the door, and Mr. Beeson called, "Wait a minute, Zan. I want to talk to you. Glad to see you back."

Zan waited, hoping Mr. Beeson might follow him over to the tie rack.

He didn't. Instead he went on in his loud, cheerful voice, "Come back and meet our boss, Zan. He's had a word with all the older boys, and he'll want to see you too."

Zan said awkwardly, starting to edge off the last step, "If you mean the man that's in your office, I spoke to him."

"Oh, you did? Well, that's all right, then. Did you get through with your talk?"

"He didn't say much to me." Zan edged away. "I left the mail sack on your desk. Goodnight, Mr. Beeson."

"Wait a minute. There's a letter here for you. A little girl brought it . I'll get the letter."

Beeson opened the door, walk in and Zan could hear him saying, and "I'll be right with you, Murt." Where did I put that envelope?" A desk drawer, fashioned from an empty dynamite box, squeaked open, then shut again.

Mr. Beeson was at the door and, following him, as he walked across the porch to Zan, was the quarrelsome man.

Mr. Beeson was smiling as he said, "Murt Murtagh, this is our newest helper, Zan Allan. He's a good worker."

Murtagh didn't even glance at Zan. He said, "I've been over your work sheet and expense accounts, Beeson. Too much money going out for the result. Cut down on food, or raise the board bills. Ridiculous. Every other camp we got makes money on the kitchen. This once scarcely breaks even."

"Maybe so." Mr. Beeson's voice seemed quite untroubled. "But I've had no labor turnover and this is a pretty remote place to hold these young bucks. You know that."

"You're going to have some labor turnover. I tell you, you're paying out too much for wages. Let the last man you hired go as of today."

Mr. Beeson protested, "Zan Allan's lived here all his life and climbs these cliffs like a cat. He's the last man put on the payroll."
Murtagh answered, "I'll make out his check. He can wait for it."

Zan said, "I'll call for it next time I'm by. You'll be here, Mr. Beeson?"

"Any evening, Zan, and glad to see you. I'm sorry about this."

Zan nodded and went swiftly back to Misty, untied the hitch, and swung on as Beeson called through the growing darkness, "Hey, wait a minute! I forgot to give you your letter."

Misty circled nervously, eager to be off, but stopped when Beeson leaned against him, said, as he handed the letter up to Zan, "Murtagh's got a bee in his bonnet; sore as a boiled owl about something and taking it out on the first man he sees. He cools off. Give him time."

Zan thought it over for an instant, and then made his decision. "He won't cool off about me, Mr. Beeson. He took a shot at me the day I moved down here and I rounded on him. He's gunning for me, and this time he's got a weapon he can handle."

"I don't understand—"

Zan said, "I didn't want to say nothing about it. I was kinda hard-headed about it myself; shot off my mouth more'n maybe I should of to an older man and a stranger. But he was so goldarn aggravating, and just missed killing me. Shot Misty and she ain't no deer."

Quickly Zan told him the details of his first encounter with Mr. Murtagh. Beeson chuckled as Zan told him what he said, what Murtagh said. But he looked serious enough as Zan concluded with, "That's about all, I guess. 'Cept he's an ornery man and conceited, too. I had him in a bad spot, and that's not going to do me any good."

"No, it isn't. Ordinarily Murt's a pretty good fellow. But you hit his weak spot. He can't ever bear to be wrong about anything."

Zan shrugged. "I know the breed. A lot of 'em is named Allan. I tangled with a critter as stubborn as myself, I guess, when I run into Murtagh."

In the wavering light the lantern cast through the window to the south, Zan saw Mr. Beeson's eyes. He said, "I'd hoped this was something that could blow over, that I'd put you back on the payroll as soon as he went back to the head office, but you're right. He's got a stubborn streak, once you cross him. I hate to say it, but—"

"That's all right. I'm through getting paid for working on the road right now, but I'm not through working on it. Not by a jug full."

"That's the stuff, Zan. Stay with it. But Murtagh's the boss on the Salmon Creek section, so you're out of a road job with me for some time. Now you got a reason for having land of your own. You give me only the money I paid out for taxes and I give you the deed to Garcia's place. I'll know where you are, and I'll keep in touch with you. You know I didn't really want the place. Got no use for it."

Zan said, "I know how you said you feel about land here. But you don't know how I feel. That land's worth money. I can't let you almost give it to me."

Beeson gave him a playful push. "I know you're a stiff-necked idiot, young Allan. All right. Pay me a hundred dollars for the land. I figure that ought to about clean you out. If a man pays out his whole fortune for something he's put a real value on it."

Zan drew a long breath. "That makes sense to me. You'll 'bout double your money, so it works out 'bout right."

He dug down in his pocket, drew out his purse and started to open it.

Beeson laughed. "Keep your money tonight. I'll stop in with the deed tomorrow and collect. And don't worry. You'll get plenty of time to work on this road. It may take another ten years before it's finished."

Zan said, "soon's Murtagh's gone, I'll be down swinging a brush hook. I don't have to be paid. I'll be working and learning long as you're here."

Beeson said, "Nonsense. It's foolish to give a big company that's fired you your work for nothing."

Zan answered, "I got my mind set. One thing about an Allan, if he knows what he's after, he knows. Getting paid was fine, sure it was. But my folks been building what they want, back in these mountains for more'n eighty years, giving small need to money. If a man knows what he wants, he don't let nothin' turn him from it, he gets it."

There was an impatient shout from the office and Beeson answered, "Be right with you, Murt."

"So long, Mr. Beeson. Be seeing you."

Beeson called after him, "*Hasta la vista*, Zan."

Up the hill, around the curving fence, in through the gate. Misty rolling in his dusting spot, the gear hung up, a fire crackling in the cook stove and a candle lit, Zan thought he could take a look at his letter while potatoes fried and bacon crisped.

He gave the letter all the respect such an occasion called for.

There was nothing on the outside except his name written in ink. For a minute he felt it would have been even better if there was a stamp on the envelope. The writing was in a strange hand. But he admired Maria's round, carefully drawn letters, knowing the care she had taken to make each one so even. She had erased the lines she had traced to keep the writing straight.

The more he looked at the outside of his letter, the more pleased he felt. Maria had taken as much care with his letter as she thought it was meant for a stranger.

Mr. Zan Allan.

He took out his pocketknife, opened it and with the tip of the blade carefully cut open the end of the envelope, drew out a folded bit of paper. The letter was short.

> *The bed came and the things. They look good as in the picture. Come Saturday for supper. Pa is so quiet. Try to come. He misses you.*
>
> *Maria*

This was Friday. Saturday afternoon he would go up the mountain.

As he ate his meal, Zan read the letter over again. Under and over and around the things that Maria wrote, were all the things she would never think of writing. But he knew his sister. This was a fine letter. Made him welcome home.

117

The moon was up by the time he had his few dishes washed, the stove wiped off with the dishcloth. He opened his own door, went out into his own yard, and walked over to the pasture fence to look at his stock.

At first it seemed a bit discouraging to have for stock only two dark blotches against the gold of the dry moonlight stubble. Sixty-four acres seemed a bit small when held alongside Gramp Allan's land that stretched from mountain to mountain, took in good streams, fine redwoods and fed enough stock so that Gramp would never want, long as he lived.

On sixty-four acres a man could live; could marry, raise a family, enjoy life. But such a man must watch out he didn't get a girl like Tilli. A motor car of her own to drive, white ruffles and green ribbons for an everyday dress....these were not even a beginning of all the things a girl brought up like Tilli would feel she needed.

He wondered why moonlight on golden stubble should make him feel heavy-hearted. A new, nice looking girl should have come in on the stage today. He felt like going courting.

A pretty girl would make any house a mighty sweet place to come home to.

He turned away from the golden moonlit field, went back into the house to go to bed. But even with the candle lit, the house seemed small and dark. He picked up his roll of blanket and carried them outside, put them where he could see the fog, hanging far out over the water, then turn a glistening silver and hear the soft voice of the ocean come whispering up the draw, saying, hush, hush, hush.

Things began to seem very hopeful as Zan found himself listening to the soothing "hush." His eyelids grew heavier and his heart lighter. Sure, he'd lost his job, it is was a happen-so, not because he didn't do good work. And look what he'd got. The furniture for Maria, his own house and land, a look at an automobile stage. He had a house, provisions in it, a pasture and money in his purse. He had leave to go home and a welcome waiting.

But the best of all was knowing what he was going to do with his life. He was going to use it to build something for more than himself. Next ten years he'd build on the road, keep his eyes open and his mouth shut. He would learn about bridges and schools, churches and roads in far-off places like Alaska—or roads to anywhere. Even when he was dead and gone, folks could go right ahead using the new road he would build.

VII

With his saddle polished, his boots oiled, and with his hat at a jaunty angle, in skin-tight Levi's Zan rode up the trail that led home. He felt fine. Disinherited, landless and without any stock but a horse and mule when he left, he was returning as owner of sixty-four acres of good land bought and paid for.

It was the middle of a perfect afternoon and he was pleasantly hungry. Maria's black cake, full of chocolate and whipped cream, was something to look forward to.

He touched the blue silk handkerchief knotted at his throat and decided he would stop in for a few words with Uncle Martin, maybe a glass of cool lemonade and eat a plate of cookies with Tilli, who might have gone back to San Francisco by now. But it was a nice idea that she might be there, and pickin' at her mandolin.

But his mind forgot about mandolins and cookies as he passed the place where he had heard the shot fired by Murtagh, where he felt Misty leap and then found Murtagh looking for the deer he'd been taken for by this strange man.

It was strange to think that if he'd come by this spot ten minutes earlier, or ten minutes later on that July day, he would still have a job. If he hadn't forgotten his axe, gone back for it when he was leaving home, he'd have passed well ahead of that shot. He wondered if things *had* to be. It was frightening to think that no matter how a fellow tried to do his best, no matter how much he meant to keep out of trouble, sometimes he had no choice. Suppose the shot that had been coming toward and had found him and all his twenty-one years of life?

Zan had heard people talking to his grandfather about such things, and some of them believed that a man's whole life was laid out for him;

119

the plate of beans he ate Friday, the woman he married, the instant of his death.

Gramp didn't believe that. He'd listen. But when he got tired of it, he'd say, "Mule's got a choice. He can balk or he can go. Long as I call myself a man, I'll figure I got as much choice as a mule."

Well, he'd had a choice. He could of felt lucky that neither he nor Misty were killed, and they had ridden right on. Or he could go find out who was shooting, what they were up to. Soberly he decided if a bullet tipped his hat in the next second—he'd do the same thing again. He'd track the man down.

He gave Misty a good drink at Cress Creek. The cress was still tall and green, not full of flowers or seedpods, so he got off, gather a good-sized bunch. Maria liked cress, often complained that she had no time to go hunting in the Creeks for it. He dampened some big thimbleberry leaves, tied them around the cress with a bit of string from his pocket.

The sun was well in the west as he rode up out of the Canyon. As he cleared the trees and rode along beside the sheer rock cliff that faced the sun, it seemed, after the cool of the Canyon, like riding straight up inside a mile-long oven. Misty lathered, and foam flecked his chest as he fought to go faster. "You ain't going to fry, little horse, even if you do think so. And you ain't goin' to get wind-broke, either, not while I can hold you down.

Either the heat, the steepness, or the soothing tone had an effect, for Misty stopped trying to get his head free, settle down to the hard, hot climb. But he perked up when they had reached a place where the next turn in the trail would show a glimpse of the cool green of oak and maple, alder and sycamore leaves, and a good stretch of level trail that went through a corner of Martin Allan's land.

Having gotten away from rocky trail bed and rock-reflected heat, Misty showed no more inclination to hurry. He ambled along as silently as a ghost horse on the soft thickness of last year's leaves.

It seemed to Zan that he had been away from home for years instead of months. He thought of the particular and special way each corral was fenced, how the sweet-smelling, satiny oat hay was stacked, the little well-house, and the old Indian grinding rocks made a paving all around it.

With all the exciting new things that had happened to him, he had lived in the minute, scarcely giving a thought to home.

He wondered if his new life had aged him. Must have. He was thinking about old things, as his grandfather, and his father, had a way of doing. When he lived home, not free to choose, those same old things, day after day, had irritated him. He'd been impatient for new ones and, like Maria, wanted to throw out the old stuff.

Yes, he was getting old, all right. He wouldn't want a stone of that wall changed or anything to happen to the slab bench beside it where his father sat silent on summer evenings, swinging his foot and looking off across the hills.

Misty's lunge and the sound of the shot came right together. There was no whine of a rifle bullet this time, but the sound told Zan that whoever fired the gun was not far away.

He quieted the horse as he decided the shot must have come from the incense cedar grove off the Trail about five hundred feet to the northwest.

Zan's face was set, his eyes cold with anger, as he touched up Misty, sent him toward the cedars on a run.

Murtagh. He'd bet that's who. Hadn't learned a thing. Up to his old tricks. Only this time he was trespassing on Martin Allan's land, as well as shooting at anything that moved.

Zan was mentally taking Murtagh's gun away from him, heading him down the Trail and riding behind, hazing him along like a scared calf.

Misty made a slight turn and Zan could see ahead of him the faint outlines of a trail. The trail puzzled him. It was no deer, or other animal Trail. It was a new trail.

Zan's lips curled. Murtagh might be the big boss in his own line but any six-year old Coast boy would know better than to pick a spot for deer hunting that had neither water or forage.

The grim look lightened on Zan's face as he thought it would be amusing to call Mr. Murtagh's attention to the things he didn't know about hunting. He'd tell him that as a hunter, he'd be about in his right place if he stayed in town and threw rocks at tame cats.

As the Trail ducked under the low hanging branches of the cedars and Zan flattened down, leaned to the right so the branch would not scratch his face, he was laughing to himself. He felt he hadn't grown up as much as he'd thought. That sort of talk for sassy ten-year olds. He'd be very cold, very brief, and very firm with Mr. Murtagh.

He straightened himself in the saddle and Misty came to a dead stop.

Tilli Allan was right in front of him. She looked dazed. She was shaking.

Damn that Murtagh man. The shot must have come close, to scare her into such a state.

"Where is he, Tilli?"

"I don't know."

"Which way did the shot come from?"

"Out of the gun."

He looked at the terrified girl with pity. Her face looked dead, the gray color of the bank beyond Clay Creek. Her mouth was almost the same color. And her eyes were as dull as dry pebbles.

He said, as though he spoke to a small child, "I'll get rid of him for you, Tilli." He swung down to stand beside her, urging her to get calm.

"You get on Misty and ride home. There's nothing to be scared of now, honey. I'll get him out of here in a hurry."

She lifted her face to look at him, a faint flicker of life coming back into her eyes.

"Oh, Zan," she said, "Could you do that?"

She made no move toward getting into the saddle and he had a confused feeling that she had already forgotten what he had told her.

"You'll need to tuck your skirt around you tight," he reminded her. "Misty isn't used to having fluttering stuff around him, you know."

He held out his hand to help her but she didn't seem to notice. Her lips moved stiffly, her voice was harsh and despairing, as she said, "No you can't. Nobody can."

He didn't understand, but didn't question her, and let her words pass. He gave up the idea of getting her on Misty. She was in no condition to ride anywhere by herself.

"I'll tie Misty. You sit down here and pull yourself together. Everything's all right, Tilli."

She stood as stiffly as though she had been baked out of the gray clay. He urged, "Stop it, Tilli. You're not hurt. Sit down and I'll go find him. Did you see him at all?"

"Yes."

"Which way?"

"There." She didn't make any motion with her hands, but her eyes, with a look of terror in them, shifted toward a clump of cedar not twenty feet away.

Misty was pulling back, acting strangely. Zan didn't trust the dropped reins to hold him, so he tied him short to a slim cedar within reach of his head.

"Sit down, Tilli, that's a good girl," he said. Grandma Allan used to say that to Tilli in a comforting way when they were both children when he had dropped a small garter snake close beside her, after threatening to put it in her apron pocket.

He took off for the direction she'd looked toward, but he didn't look to see if she'd obeyed him the way she used to obey her grandmother. He rounded the dark clump of cedars and halted, then froze up into the same rigidness as had held Tilli.

He turned his head toward her to take a quick look to make sure she was staying put. But she wasn't sitting down. Her eyes were watching him.

"It's Mervin Williams," he said out loud.

Tilli only looked at Zan.

Zan stooped quickly, lifted Mervin's arm. The arm was warm, but the ugly hole through his head told it; no need to feel for his pulse. But he did. There was none.

Zan put William's arm down, stood up, feeling sick.

Murtagh must have seen what he had done and ran off like a thorough coward.

Listening intently for any sound of a breaking twig, a misplaced stone, Zan looked as far as he could through all the opening in the cedar thicket, but there was no sign to indicate that anyone had left hurriedly.

Then he saw the gun. A rifle was lying in the shadow of a log not more than thirty feet from him. He walked over, pit it up, and saw the initials, "M.W." engraved on the small silver plate a the side of the stock.

Carrying the gun he went back to where Tilli was still standing watching his approach with that same unnatural stillness.

"This is Mervin's gun," he said.

She said nothing.

"Did you see the man?" He asked patiently.

She whispered, "Yes," in a sound as faint as a sigh.

"Which way did he go, Tilli?"

Her lips tightened until they were almost folded from sight and she covered her mouth with shaking hands.

"He fell. He fell." She gasped for breath over a sound, half moan, and half scream. Suddenly she grabbed at Zan and he could feel her whole body trembling through the fingers that closed so fiercely on his arms. Then she sagged against him, sobbing, "He never moved at all. He fell, he fell, he just fell. He's dead and what can I do now?"

Zan felt his knees sag, a sick trembling his own spine. He looked down at the slight girl clinging to him, so soft and small, so frightened and despairing. He couldn't believe the horrible thought that was hammering in his head, shaking his nerves like a thunder in a storm.

He made himself speak. "Did you do it?"

She pushed back fiercely from his steadying arms. Her eyes lighted with an insane look and she said rapidly, "He made me. I love him so. I love him, Zan."

Zan stiffened, his voice stern as he asked, "How could he make you shoot him?"

"Don't look at me like that. How could I help it? I loved him so and...and...

She broke down, gasping for breath. She turned her head away, whispered brokenly, "He was too strong. I was so crazy. I thought I could stop but I couldn't. I loved him too much."

"For Christ's sake, talk sense. What made you shoot?"

She turned on him furiously. "You fool, you stupid fool. What could I do? I told him why he had to marry me and he... he...."

Her face, her voice, held the amazed unbelief of a child. "He said he was going back to France. He laughed at me." Large tears dropped slowly down her face as she said, "He said I wasn't the first Allan girl that took her men into the woods."

Zan's head spun with a sickening realization that she meant it. It couldn't be. But it was. His mouth and throat felt like an old rusty tin. This fool gird had wrecked her own life. She'd ruined the whole Allan family name. Caused permanent damage to the family. This would kill Gramp. It must be hushed up, some how.

Tilli went on in hysterical anger. "He meant Aunt Blaze and, it's a dirty lie. He's a dirty liar. He wants French girls, that's what."

Zan forced his dry throat to swallow, tried to moisten his lips with his tongue, and said, "He's dead, Tilli."

"You said you'd fix it, Zan."

"I'd fix it? How could I? I didn't know anything about it."

Tilli panted, "You did. You did say so. You told me you'd get rid of him."

Zan stared at her. Then he remembered. "I thought it was Murtagh shooting at a deer."

"Murtagh?"

He brushed this aside. "Never mind Murtagh. A new man, down on the Coast. I thought he was trespassing on your father's land."

Her eyes widened with horror. "Father," she said. "He'll be here. I set a trap for Marvin.... She slowly folded up, sat on the ground, her head dropped almost to her knees as she went into hysterical laughter, gasping, "I forgot, Father. I set the trap but I caught myself..."

Feeling that she was on the verge of insanity, Zan shook her, and her head wobbled. A rag doll with the sawdust running out couldn't have been any more limp. He took hold of her hair, lifted her head, and slapped her face.

She stopped her sobbing laughter, looked at him helplessly, murmuring, "I'm going crazy. I wish I was dead."

He squatted down beside her. "Take it easy, Tilli. What about Uncle Martin?"

"I was a fool. Everything I did. Crazy. I tried to feel so proud and sure. But I had no pride. He sang, and he laughed, and he teased me and he kissed me, and he kept me waiting, didn't come when he said he'd come. He never said anything about marrying. Oh God, what a fool I was…

Zan interrupted. "Your father? Is he coming here?"

"Yes, yes. Didn't I say he was? I did. Why don't you listen?"

He's got that friend of his, Andy Greub, of the Special Police, down for some hunting." She looked at Zan, her eyes shamed, her young face haggard and haunted. "I was afraid all the time about Mervin, that's he'd just go away and leave me. I tried to make sure he'd stand by me by having him fess up to father. Why was I so crazy?"

Her shaking hands hid her face as she muttered, "Me. Tilli Alan. I'll kill him! I'll kill him!" She slumped. Her hands fell as of their own weight. "But I did kill him. I already did. My God, what will I do now?"

Zan's head was spinning, his thoughts as broken as Tilli's. He wouldn't put it past his Uncle Martin to hurt Tilli if he knew Tilli had been acting like a strumpet with a son of Joe Williams. It was Joe Williams himself that, more than twenty-five years ago, made up a slimy story about being in the woods with Aunt Blaze Allan—just because she wouldn't marry him. Gramp had gone after Joe with a gun, made him sign a paper that he had lied about Aunt Blaze. So the Allan's had been able to go on proudly thanking God that no scandal had ever touched any of their women. How could Gramp ever—how could any Allan, ever hold up their head again if the truth about Tilli and Joe William's son Mervin was made a public show?

He thought of asking Tilli how she got a hold of Merv's gun, and then changed his mind. Didn't matter. She had got it. She had fired the shot.

He wondered if it would it do any good if he hide the gun?

It seemed a good idea. Maybe Murtagh might have been out hunting close by. What about trying to lay the shot to Murtagh's crazy way of handling a gun?

"You get out of here quick, Tilli. I'll meet your father and the officer."

"I won't go. I can't. You'll tell them."

"It's better for me to talk to them. Uncle Martin won't listen patiently. You know that."

She drew back, her eyes holding a new terror, and then she turned, started to walk toward the main trail. In a minute, she came running back, grabbed his arm. "It doesn't matter what you tell him. I'll still be having a baby. I can't hide that. Not for long. Father would rather push me over a cliff than have that happen to me, an Allan."

"Oh, God, Tilli. I don't know. It's like being in a corral with ropes swingin' at every post."

Her body shook until it seemed she would fall down. Zan put his arm around her, steadied her and walked her down the faint track out of the cedars, across the regular trail, and fifty feet into the undergrowth beyond.

"Wait here," he said. "Don't move, Tilli. I'll bring Misty. I'll try to work it out."

He made his way back as quickly and quietly as he could, feeling his scalp and spine sending shock over him. He had heard faint noises from up the trail and doubted any animal made it. He must get Misty out of that clump of cedars before his uncle got there.

Misty was the only living thing he could see as he untied the horse, started to lead him away. Then he stopped dead still.

He could get Misty away, but the horse's tracks were marked clearly where he had pawed and stamped around the tree.

"God damn, such a mess," he muttered as he started feverishly trying to cover the tracks. They were the first things Uncle Martin would look for, if he came into the clearing, found a man dead. Allans read tracks as easy as town people read newspapers.

He was so intent on clearing Misty of having been at this spot that he heard nothing more until a faint voice said, "Go away from here quick, Zan."

Lara, looking almost as white and frightened as had Tilli, was peering at him from back in the thicket beyond Mervin's body. Had she seen it? He didn't dare ask her.

He tried to sound natural as he said, "You startled me, Chicken. I didn't want anyone to know I'd been here"

She motioned frantically. Uncle Martin and Mr. Grueb, they're riding this way. Misty'll nicker. Go quick. I could fix the tracks, Zan."

What did she know? Had she seen Mervin's body?

"I'm going to home, Lara. Maria asked me to supper. You skip ahead and tell her I'm coming, will you?"

She nodded her head that she would, but made no move to start. Then she whispered, "Go as soon as you can. I'll tell Maria I saw you on the trail. Is Tilli gone?"

Lara knew something was wrong. Whatever she knew, she wouldn't tell anyone if he asked her not to. The log was between her and Mervin's body, but he knew she could see the gun from where she stood.

"It's not right for me to do this, Lara" he said, "but I have to. Don't tell anyone you were here. No matter what happens, don't say you saw me here…"

"I won't say it. But if they ask me, Zan what'll I do?"

"Something terrible has happened, honey. Promise you'll not say anything no matter who asks you. And go away. Quick. Don't let anyone see you near here."

"I promise, Zan. Kiss up to God. And I'll cut across, not go the trail."

"That's a brave girl. Remember now. You promised."

She gave him a long look, and then slipped back out of sight as quietly as an owl in the night.

"They that touch pitch shall be defiled!"

Trying to get out of his mind the remembered sound of Gramp's stern voice reading those words aloud, he worked furiously at the tracks, looking to make sure no hair from Misty's mane or tail was clinging to the trees. He said over again, "Goldarn such a mess." It got worse all the time. Now Lara was touched with the pitch. Asking Lara to start lying was like asking a bird to stop singing. The small triangle of white face, the dark frightened eyes framed in thick black bangs, the straight black hair hanging to her shoulders haunted him.

Leaf shadows across her face, across her faded light dress, had made Lara seem as much part of the forest as the trees themselves. The silent way she had slipped out of sight when he asked her to go, and had agreed to say nothing, added to his shame.

Lara had grown up in an Allan house, but nothing had made an Allan of her. Allans loved the land, but they used it; fenced it; cleared and

128

broke it; cut the great redwoods and watched them fall, thinking only of the use they would make of the tree.

Lara never picked a wild flower, or broke a branch. She went so lightly through forest or pasture she scarcely left a footprint, loving the land for itself, not for what it could give her.

Tough pitch—dust—ugly—death—murder...

"Stop it, you fool," he charged himself roughly. "You're into this now. Keep your head."

The gun? He eyed it with the loathing he would feel for a rattlesnake of the same length, but he went over to it, picked it up.

The gun was under his arm as he led Misty away and rejoined Tilli.

He whispered to her, "I'll hide the gun. Maybe your father won't find Mervin. But someone will find him soon enough."

"What of it?" Her face looked hopeless, her voice sounded dead.

Zan explained, "No gun, there's a chance it will be thought an accident, a stray shot."

She drew a deep breath, let it out in a long sigh, her shoulders slumped. Then she said, as though she were scarcely interested, "Yes, they might think that's how it happened. Mervin didn't fight, had no enemies." Her mouth twisted, looked ugly. "He didn't have to fight. He got what he wanted other ways."

She sat down, her hand muffling her mouth as she said, "It's no use. I don't care what they think. Mervin's dead and I wish I was."

"Quit that. You should wait for your father and tell him what you've done."

She jumped up, her fists tight, her jaw set. "I won't. No one can make me. No one. She looked at him pleadingly. "And anyway, no one will ever believe I did it. My father would pull anyone apart that tried to say I shot—" She shuddered, would not say it. "But I can't have a baby with no husband. If that happens then people will believe any bad thing about me. Father told me not to see Mervin. He thinks I minded him. I told Mervin not to come to the house, that I'd meet him in the cedars. Men are so easy to fool. Papa thinks I always do what he says."

Zan looked at her. "Never mind how smart you've been. You've been too handy at fooling men and you're not as smart as you thought. Here you are. Here's the gun. Now what?"

"Don't speak to me like that, Zan. I can't bear it. I've been bad, but

I didn't plan to be. It happened. I couldn't help it. How can you be mad at me when I'm in such trouble? I thought you liked me—"

He made no answer.

Her eyes filled with tears. " I can't bear it, Zan. I'm just the same as I always was. I talk ugly because I'm so unhappy."

He said, "I suppose so. I—Oh, never mind. You can't stay here. What do you want to do now?"

She turned away for a minute, her head bent as though she were listening. When she faced him again her bearing was resolute, confident. "I want you to marry me, Zan. Will you?"

"You're crazy."

She said, "Yes. You marry me. I'll live at your place till my trouble is over. Then I'll go away and divorce you. That won't hurt you none. It'll save me. You got to, Zan. You got to do it."

He stared at her. She looked little and helpless. But she was hard as an axe handle, thinking only of herself. He said again, "I won't marry you. Get that in your head. Anyhow, it's against the law for cousins to marry."

She struck her hands together impatiently, raised her voice. "What do I care for the law? Do you think I'm going to have a baby and not be married?"

"I don't know. Just leave me out of it. Right now. You got to get out of here—and quick."

She started to argue but he said, "Shut up, Tilli. You do what I tell you. Go home fast. Keep off the trail. Don't let anyone see you. Saddle up and ride as far as you can and still get back before dark."

"Why?" She whispered, "What for? I'm so tired I could die."

He said again, "Ride as far as you can. Summer Creek? Yes, you could get that far. Drop something there that belongs to you: a belt, handkerchief, anything you can prove is yours. Then you can prove you were over there. See what I mean?"

She said, shakily, "but that's over by the old Indian graveyard. It's haunted. You know it is. You told me it was."

He said patiently, "We were children then. I was being smart, teasing and trying to scare you. You go to Summer Creek. Get back by dark or sooner if you can. Don't let anyone see you. Mention what you lost. I'll try to take care of the rest of it."

She started to cry softly, whispering, "I'm so afraid. I hate all this. What can I do?"

He didn't answer. After a minute she began to work her way out of the thicket toward where she could cut across fairly open country and still come into the barnyard and pasture without being in sight of the house. Zan picked up Mervin's gun, trying to think what to do with it. If there was a search for the gun every one would look in the dry hollows of trees and logs first. And all such hiding places almost as well know as ranch houses.

Suddenly he knew what to do with the gun. His own saddle boot was empty. That was the place for it. Even if he met anyone, his uncle or the officer, why should they think he had a gun that was not his own. Unless they started talking guns. That thought turned him cold. Talking guns; stock, bore, charge, sights, all those things went on endlessly in making talk, getting acquainted.

He wiped sweat from his forehead with the sleeve of his shirt, put the gun in his saddle boot.

He rode Misty out on to the trail, went up the mountain toward his home, trying to whistle a careless tune. He had to give it up. His mouth was fuzzy as a milkweed pod.

The gun was longer than his own gun. It stuck out like a bandaged thumb, asking people to look. He had to get rid of it, but the bare rocks he was riding past offered no help.

His nervous state seemed to be catching. Misty was starting, shying, and then a rock moved under his feet and the horse jumped edgily, though he'd been walking on rock all his days.

Zan pulled up, swung off and dropped the reins. His finger felt cold as he undid the straps, pulled the gun free. He stepped to the edge of the Trail, then drew back, rubbed his wet forehead with his sleeve. He'd suddenly remembered the gun must be loaded. A man going against the law must keep his wits. If uncle Martin had already found Mervin, a chance shot would bring him on the run.

Zan took out the cartridges, dropped them in his pocket. Then he looked to see what cover there might be for a gun. It was a rough cliff, very straight down and a good growth of black brush crowding right up to the cliff. He felt sure no one had ever set foot in the place; seemed no reason anyone ever would. The brush looked to be all of ten feet high.

He dropped the gun, watched it disappear into the brush.

Getting into the saddle again, Zan remembered to check the trail for his own footprints. The trail bed was deep with small rock, the edge where he had stood, was covered with bits of dried brush and rock.

Satisfied, he rode on up the mountain, wondering if he should stop at Tilli's house. He didn't want to, but still it might be better. When he hadn't seen any of the folks for so long, it would look queer to ride right by.

He was in sight of the house when Misty nickered. He looked back.

Zan turned his head to see. Behind him on the trail, a man riding Uncle Martin's leggy old black stallion was riding up pretty fast.

He called to Zan, "I'd like a word with you…"

Zan waited, trying to size up his uncle's friend. The man was as tall and thin as Ray, the black horse. Underneath a neat moustache, his mouth looked full and good-natured. Zan saw lively gray eyes beneath heavy grizzled eyebrows. But his chin jutted out like one of the Coast ridges.

The man pulled up, saying, "I'm Andy Greub. Visiting here with Martin Allan. I want to ask if you heard a shot while back, and where you was when you heard it—that is, if you did hear it."

Zan said, "I noticed a shot, yes. Don't know as I remember where I was. Why. Was it you or Uncle Martin shooting?"

Mr. Greub said, "No."

The man certainly had a close tongue. Zan wanted to act easy, natural. But it seemed hard to say anything, so he said, "I'm Zan Allan."

Mr. Greub didn't offer his hand. He just looked thoughtful. Finally he said, "Martin went on, down the trail. If you were on your way to see him, better ride along with me, and wait."

It made Zan uneasy that Greub said nothing about a hunting accident. He felt sure Greub had been in the cedars, found Mervin. What he wanted to do was ride away as quickly as he could be he managed a smile, saying, "I'll do that. Aunt Tena always has coffeecake or cookies about this time, too."

Greub spoke to the black horse. Zan tightened his reins and they rode ahead, not talking.

As they drew near the gate, Zan sniffed the air, turned his head and called, "I was right. I do smell coffee."

Greub nodded. "Yes. And there's Mrs. Allan on the porch." He

rubbed at his moustache, drew his eyebrows together, and said, "She'll wonder why Martin isn't with me. Would you take care of my horse so I can go right up to the house?"

Zan swung off, took the black's reins. He tied both horses, unloosed the saddles and followed Mr. Greub up the trail to the house.

Aunt Tena sounded a terrible uneasy as she called down to him, "Zan, did you see Tilli anywhere?"

He evaded the truth, answering, "and haven't seen her for quite a time, or you either Aunt Tena. How you been?"

She shrugged. "I should be polite and say we are all fine. The boys are fine, I hear. We got them off to school, but that Tilli, she didn't want to go back to school. Tilli's been edgy, and your uncle so moody. And now this awful thing's happened. I wish we'd all left when the boys went."

Zan asked, "What do you mean, Aunt Tena? What's happened?"

Tena turned to Greub, amazement in her voice as she said, "But you came together. Didn't you tell Zan about Mervin?"

Zan put in, "Nobody tells me anything. What is it?"

At that instant a look of fright crossed Tena's face. She spoke to Greub as though reluctant to put the question. "Was Martin with you all the time till you found him?"

"Yes, he was. Every minute. Martin thinks it was an accidental hit by a stray shot. It looks that way, but a Coroner's jury has to be called in on all such cases, you know. Martin is only going as far as the survey camp. One of the boys from there can go out for the Coroner. Someone else will let Mr. Williams know about his son. Don't worry, Martin will be along soon."

Tena's hand went across her mouth as she whispered, "How dreadful for him. His only child."

Zan asked Greub, "That the shot you were asking if I'd heard?"

Mr. Greub nodded. "Yes. It seems likely. I wish you'd try again to remember just about where you were when you heard the shot, or noticed the sound. It could help in fixing the time of death."

Zan said, "Didn't you and Uncle Martin hear it? You must have been as close, even closer than I was."

Greub said that they dropped down into Bent Canyon to check the amount of water in that spring. The noise of the creek, and the canyon wall both shut out sound. Beside, we were shouting to each other across the Creek most of the time. We didn't hear a thing."

Zan studied on this a minute, then asked, "Couldn't you judge fairly well how long he'd been dead before you found him? And where did you find Merve?

Greub's shrewd eyes studied space for so long that Zan felt panic. He half expected the man would turn on him, and say, "The same place you found him."

But Greub finally shook his head, saying, "We fooled around awhile, fixing the dam, looking for one of Martin's corner stakes that comes in close there. Might have been there ten minutes, or thirty."

He drew his brows together as though puzzled by something. "We found young Williams in a cedar grove, found him just a short way from the main Trail."

He turned to Tena. "I remember now that we turned in there because Martin said something about planning to meet Tilli there. She must have meant to ride down that way. She didn't mention it to you?"

Tena said, "No. I had no idea where she went. And her father said nothing to me about meeting her anywhere. Oh, dear. Tilli's a lot better off in school than she is running around these mountains by herself. I wish they'd both come home so we could pack right up and leave for San Francisco."

Greub could be kind, Zan noted. He said, "What were you going to do with that coffee we smelled? I could certainly use a cup and this young nephew of yours was sniffing the air, too. Martin will be along any minute. He lit right out for help and he's got a good horse. Now, how about pouring some of that coffee?"

Tena became all housewife. She got cups, cakes and coffee. In her interest in seeing the men comfortable, she forgot her worry.

Second cups were being poured when there was a clatter from the trail, both of their tied horses neighed shrilly and Martin Allan rode in sight, his stout palomino lathered, tossing his head fretfully.

Martin shouted as he rode closer, "Did Andy tell you? Young Williams had his head near blown off. No gun with him. We got to find out who did it."

Tena got up hastily, and clutched Zan's shoulder as he pushed back his chair, stood beside her. She whispered, "He was accidentally shot." She looked at Mr. Greub. "You said it was an accident."

Greub seemed not to hear. His eyes were almost closed and Zan got an idea the man was trying to picture to himself exactly what had happened. Then Greub pushed back from the table, stood up, and asked him, "Did you see William's horse anywhere as you rode up?"

This time Zan had no need to pretend astonishment. Mervin must have had a horse. He never walked a step outside his own dooryard.

Where was Mervin's horse?

He answered, "If I'd of seen the horse, without Mervin, I'd of known right then that something was wrong. He don't go any place without his horse."

Martin scowled. "If I'd seen it, I'd have it along with me. I know all the Williams' stock. Never mind the horse. Let's get something done about this business. Act first, talk when the job's done, is my way. Pick up a gun Zan. Come on, both of you. We'll do some tracking while there's light."

Tena put it. "Its already late. Eat your suppers and get to bed early. Tracks will keep, if there are any. But if Tilli isn't home in two more minutes you can start tracking her. Honestly, Martin, I am worried about her. I want you to absolutely forbid her to ever ride off this ranch alone again."

135

Martin said, "Where in hell is she? Why do you let her gallivant all over the country for, anyway. What a family I got. Nothing but jaw, jaw, jaw; trouble every minute."

For a minute there was silence and then Tena turned to Zan as though nothing had happened, put her hand on his shoulder, and said fondly, "I've missed you a lot, Zan. And you're looking peaked, really you are. Better come back home. I guess they work you pretty hard down there, don't they?"

"Not what I call hard," he answered. "Maybe I've had too much of my own cooking."

You stay right here, have supper with us," Tena insisted. "It's ready and you should eat. Come on all of you. Tilli can get her own supper if she comes home after we're done. And don't you help her, Martin Allan."

Martin put his hand on Zan's other shoulder, said, "Come on, boy. Let Tena feed you up. And that little minx will be along any minute now, Wife. She'll be all right."

Zan murmured, "Well, thanks a lot, all of you. But Maria sent me down a letter, asked me to eat to home tonight. I'll drop down right after supper, see if I can help any."

"Tilli might be up to your place. If she is, you tell her to come right home."

Zan said, "Yes, Ma'am."

Martin stretched, shook his legs for saddle kinks, saying, "Gosh, I'm tired. Hungry, too. Guess we better had grab a bite, Andy. Get back as soon as you can, Zan, but send my girl straight home if she's there. I've a mind to shake her teeth out. Been telling her I'd start teaching her to hear her elders, and by God, I guess the time's come to do it."

Tena said sharply, "Don't be silly, Martin. She never means to disobey. Just absent-minded. Girls always are, at her age. She's day-dreaming some place."

Zan somehow made his mouth stretch into a broad grin. He said, "If I see her I'll tell her to go home. Bet that will hurry her up." To the company he said, "So long. Be back as soon as I can."

Zan closed the gate behind him, turned east on the trail. Misty wanted to hurry. So did Zan, but he held the horse back. If Greub was still standing on the porch, he'd take note of a man's hurry. He was certainly a noticing man.

136

VIII

The inquest was being held in the dining room of the road camp, and as Zan and Mr. Greub rode up, closely followed by the rest of the Allan family, he heard Lara say wistfully, "When it looks so much like going to a barbecue, why can't it be a party?"

No one answered.

Blaze had opposed Lara's coming but had not prevailed against Mr. Greub's insistence. Always the argument came back to his quiet voice saying, "Children see everything. They also tell the truth. Before the day is over you may all be glad that she, or anyone else, knows something that we have haven't heard anything about."

It looked to Zan as though everyone in the county must be sitting either around the fire that had been built, or were in the crowd perched on logs around the Creek. But it was no barbecue. Heads turned for a quick look as the Allans rode up, but no greetings were called, no one came forward. Two long tie-poles were left conspicuously empty, waiting. As the Allans turned their horses and rode toward the tie-up, the crowd sitting around behind them became absolutely silent, and the voice of the creek became alarmingly loud.

Blaze was equal to it. She turned her head to say, "I'm going to be lazy and ask you to take care of our stock since Stephen isn't here, Zan. There's nothing like having work for your hands when you're facing something new."

He nodded, helped her down as Lara pull up by a stump, stepped off her horse and led him up, murmuring, "Take mine, too, Zan, I'll hold him till you're ready."

Zan said, "Thanks, Chicken," and edged forward with the mare that Blaze had ridden. He saw that Maria was watching him.

137

Her round face was the glassy white of newly rendered lard. Shock, anger and humiliation showed plainly on her set white face. Their father moved in a confused way, his usually deft hand fumbling as though the unloosening of cinches was an unfamiliar task.

Zan turned his head away, unable to bear the deepened sadness on his father's face, or his own sudden conviction that both his sister and father thought him guilty of murder.

He wished he could feel sure, since he had not shot Mervin, that there was no possible chance that anyone could prove he had. But as he tied up Lara's horse, he found his own hands fumbling.

Mr. Greub was right behind him, waiting for him, and, while he tried to tell himself that this was no more than ordinary politeness, the patient stillness of the waiting added to his feeling of being caught in something too big for him to deal with.

But if he surrendered to panic, he told the straight truth, his whole family would be destroyed. All but Tilli. Even if she went to prison for a time, when she was free again, she would go away. She was different stuff, not made of the Big Sur hills as the rest of them. She'd go east or to Europe. She could fling an Allan disgrace behind her like an old coat. There was no escape for the rest of the family. They would wear Tilli's disgrace to the end of their lives.

He took a couple of deep breaths, let his arms go limp to ease the tightness before he turned to face Mr. Greub, and found his Uncle Martin has come up, was standing beside his friend.

Martin said, "The Coroner's a young fellow named Alred. Ricco just rode in from the Post place and he says the hearse got there last night and that Alred was finishing breakfast when he left. Should be along soon."

Mr. Greub looked thoughtful, turning his lower lip in over his teeth, shoving the lip forward with his tongue run between teeth and cheek, before he said, "Young fellow, is he?"

Without waiting for an answer he asked, "You want to wait out here, Zan? Can't be very long before things start. Or if you'd rather, go ahead into the mess hall and be out of the crowd."

"Thanks. I'll go inside, I guess."

He wanted to get away. His uncle had not spoken, seemed not to see him. But as Zan left the horses and started across the open space before the cookhouse door, he was conscious of many eyes regarding him with fixed attention. He wouldn't let himself hurry and the trip to the door seemed endless as he tried to move naturally but felt that he was as awkward as a wooden sawhorse trying to walk.

At last the steps were in front of him and he was reaching for the door knob, when a friendly voice said, " guess there's nothing against your coming through the kitchen and having a drop of coffee with me, Zan. I ain't on the jury."

The heavy set cook was looking at him as though he were a human being and Zan felt a rush of gratitude for his kindness.

The easy, cheerful way that the cook poured two cups of coffee, pulled up another chair before he sat down, eased Zan's tension. The cook said, "Yup, we'll be pulling out of here in about ten days. It's always like that. Just when I get a kitchen fixed to suit me, it's time to pack up and go start all over again."

"Where's the camp to be, or do you know, yet?

"Yup. Setting up down by Salmon Creek, the boss says. Did ya see him before you come in here?"

Zan shook his head.

The cook rolled a cigarette, lit it and took a deep drag, blew out the smoke before he said, "Just as well. Looks better, I guess. Beeson and our boys are making up the Coroner's jury. Seems like they was about the only ones in the county that wasn't related, or mixed up in this some way. Say, that old Williams is a regular hell raiser, ain't he?"

Zan warmed his cold fingers on the thick hot cup, found himself smiling as he answered, "I guess I'd be smart to keep my ideas about Joe to myself right now."

"Oh, sure, sure. I was only gassing. Wish they'd get started and have it over."

"Me, too."

The cook poured second cups of coffee as he said, "And me too, brother. Did you know they got the corpse out in my cold room by the Creek? Once this is over, they'll get him out, and I'll have a place to hang up my beef without feeling spooky."

Zan set down his cup of coffee, pushed it away and stood up. "Guess I'll wait out in the dining hall. I don't want anyone to have to come lookin' for me. Thanks for the coffee."

Zan opened the kitchen door, went through the storeroom but paused a minute, his hand on the latch of the door to the mess hall. A faint buzz of voices and the heavy sound of nailed boots trying to walk softly, told him the dining room was already filling up. He lifted the latch and went in.

One section of the long dining table had been pushed back into the far corner. The other section has been moved so that it was crosswise to the long room. It held only a few pencils and a block of writing paper. Dariel Beeson's old wooden armchair was directly behind the pencils and paper, but the chair was empty.

The bench next to the armchair held Mr. Beeson, Bud Wilson, Will Hubbard, Jim and Ken Short. Ken was leaning forward, tossing his tobacco sack and papers down to Bud Wilson as Zan crossed to aisle that had been made between two blocks of benches. It was easier to be facing a confused blur of faces than his friends from the survey gang, while they were serving as his jury.

He made for the back of the room, found an empty place on the aisle and sat down. It was a minute before he realized who else was on this bench. He was glad that chance had put him among his own people. Blaze, Lara, his father and Maria had the rest of the bench. He was grateful that none of them paid any attention to him. It was good to have a chance to get his bearings.

Looking around, he realized that it was his own shyness that had filled the room with staring faces. Most of the benches were empty.

Tilli, her mother and father, were sitting with Mr. Greub on the second bench, and directly in front of the survey gang. His grandfather, looking very fierce and lonely, was all by himself on the bench across from Zan.

Leaning against the back wall were Willy Post and Rojallio Castro. Zan guessed they must have come down to pack Mervin's body out to the road for burial in Monterey.

There was also a small sprinkling of strangers in the clothes of summer campers or city folks.

The door opened. Joe Williams and Mr. Murtagh came in together, sat down on an empty front bench. They got as close to the wall as they could crowd, put their heads together and began a whispering talk.

Zan suddenly found his hands damp as well as cold.

Murtagh? What was he doing here?

Then he remembered the cook had said the camp was breaking up and moving south. It seemed likely that all accounts would be checked before the crew moved on and his being with Joe was no more like seeking like kind. But to him they looked like a couple of old she buzzards sitting with their bald heads and red faces together, whispering over dead meat.

Zan noticed that Tilli was watching Joe Williams and that she turned and murmured something to Mr. Greub who glanced quickly at Murtagh and Williams, then shook his head.

A stranger in a dark suit and squeaking new black shoes went up the aisle and was instantly the center of all interest. This was evidently Mr. Alred, the Coroner. A very young and slim fellow who wore gold-rimmed glasses and carried two notebooks and a handful of pencils followed him.

After he put the books and pencils down on the table, he kept fussing with them until they were all neatly in line, all spaced just so far apart and the sharpened ends pointing toward the door.

Then he saw that there was only one chair behind the table and looked around helplessly until he noticed a crude redwood stool in the dark corner beside the door that led to the storeroom. He brought it to the table as though he were carrying a dead cat, put it down and dusted his fingers with his handkerchief.

Mr. Greub had gotten up as soon as the man in the dark suit came up the aisle. He stepped up and the two men shook hands. They stood in front of the table talking together while the pencil straightening went on.

As soon as the young fellow stopped pushing the stool about and dusting his fingers, the other man turned his head, asked, "Ready now, Wilbur?"

With a muttered, "I suppose so," the clerk sat down on the stool, opened a note book and picked up the first pencil in the line. Mr. Greub went back to his place while the other man walked around the end of the table, pulled back the chair, and sat down.

Zan sat back, certain now that this man was Mr. Alred, the Coroner.

Mr. Alred looked out over the room then down at a piece of paper he took from his pocket and unfolded. After a minute, he pushed the paper aside, looked up and said, "Will those of you who have no knowledge of the facts leading to the death of Mervin Williams, leave the room and remain outside during the hearing."

Mr. Alred's sharp eyes moved from face to face and the room slowly emptied of all the outsiders except Mr. Murtagh.

When the door had closed behind the last outsider, the Coroner took a paper that the clerk handed him and called off a list of names. Murtagh's name was one of those called.

After the roll call was finished, Mr. Alred again pulled back in front of him, the first paper he had been looking at. Every now and then he put a pencil mark against something on the paper.

With every minute that went by, Zan became more uneasy about Murtagh's being present.

Blaze leaned close to him, whispered, "I wish he'd hurry. This waiting gets me so nervous I feel that he means to find me guilty of something."

Zan whispered back, feeling comforted, "Guess that's what he wants; think he'll scare the truth out of someone."

Blaze put her hand on his and he was startled to find her fingers were even colder than his own.

At last Mr. Alred leaned forward and spoke very pleasantly. "I'm sure that you all understand that this is in no way a trial. When you are called, feel perfectly free to tell anything, even a trifling thing that might help clear up what led to the death of your neighbor, Mervin Williams. I just want plain facts, not what you think, or have been told. Just tell what you know."

Mr. Alred leaned back, looked at his paper again, and then down toward the end of the room as he said, "Mr. Zande Allan, please.

Zan stood up quickly but the Coroner said, smiling, "No, it's your grandfather I'd like to hear from.

Gramp Allan unfolded himself slowly, stood waiting with an air of conscious dignity. After he was recognized, he took his own time about answering. But when he was ready, he spoke very clearly.

"The boy Mervin had been dead for some time before I heard of his death. The only thing I know that might have anything to do with the son's death is what everyone knows: Joe Williams was never a good neighbor to nobody."

Williams sprang to his feet as though to start for the back of the room, but Murtagh caught the end of his coat, pulled him back and he sat down reluctantly.

Mr. Alred spoke patiently. "Possibly you are too far back in the room to hear clearly when I spoke that I am looking for what you know, not what you think. Since you learned of Mervin Williams' death so late, I take it that you have no fact that would be of help. We will excuse you for now and if you'd rather, you can wait outside"

Old Zande said stiffly, "Thank you, Sir," and made his way outside, closing the door firmly behind him.

The Coroner turned to his clerk and said, "Just strike all that out, or start with a new page, will you Wilbur? Make a new start, that's the best way."

The clerk looked annoyed. "Well, really—"

Alred said nothing more and, after a minute, the clerk tore off the sheet, crumpled it and placed it accusingly in front of his battery of pencils.

"I think we'll start with you, Mr. Allan. Zan, isn't it?"

"Yes, Sir." Zan stood up, asking, "Shall I stay here or do you want me to come up there?"

"Come forward, please." He looked at Joe Williams and Murtagh, suggested that they move to the bench just in back of the one on which they had been sitting. He asked to have the front bench moved up, even with the table.

Zan stayed where he was until the bench was placed, and Murtagh and Joe were seated where Alred had said.

Then Zan walk forward, stood for a minute and asked hesitantly, "Do I raise my right hand? I never saw any court before and I'm not sure what to do."

Mr. Alred smiled. "No, you are not under oath. I hope this matter can be cleared up without coming to trial. You'd all be under oath there, of course. We don't usually make a record of this sort of hearing, but you all live so far away that I thought it would be easier for the sheriff if he had it down in black and white."

Fighting an almost overpowering temptation to tell the whole truth, Zan eyed Mr. Alred with outward composure and said nothing. He kept reminding himself that it was better for him to tell lies and smear his own sense of decency, than that all the Allans in the family should suffer for the shame Tilli's exposure would bring on them.

"What can you tell me that might be of help, Mr. Allan?"

Zan shook his head. "Not much, I'm afraid. I'd been working down on the Coast and my sister sent a note asking me to come upon home to supper on Saturday. I left sort of early and I'm pretty sure I heard the shot that killed Mervin. But I thought the shot was some hunter after squirrels or rabbits, and I didn't think much about it."

"I see." Mr. Alred hesitated a minute, then asked, "Had you been aware for some time that Mervin Williams was spending quite a lot of time with Miss Tilli Allan?"

Zan looked at his inquiringly, frankly puzzled as to what this could be leading to, then said, "Yes, sure I knew it. Wasn't a man in the hills that didn't try to court her."

The clerk scribbled furiously and Zan loathed the sound of that flying pencil. He was reminding himself that now was his chance to say he knew nothing else that would be of any help, but before he could make up his mind to break in on the sound of that busy pencil, Mr. Alred was speaking.

"Would the fact that you had quarreled with your grandfather recently, been disinherited, have anything to do with your trip up the mountain?"

Zan said, "I didn't quarrel with my grandfather. I told him I was taking a job with the survey gang, working to bring in the road. Gramp doesn't take to the idea of the road, so he was a bit riled."

Mr. Alred made no comment on that but asked, "Is it a fact that on the day you quarreled—let me change that. On the same day you had this difference with your grandfather, you quarreled with a Mr. Murtagh, took his gun from him?"

Zan looked bewildered. "Maybe we don't have the same idea of quarreling," he said. "This Murtagh fellow had a gun and took a shot at something moving that he could hear but couldn't see. It was me, with my horse and mule. He hit my horse. I jumped off and when I found him I asked what he thought he was up to. He had buck fever so bad he didn't know what he was up to; waving his gun around so crazy he was apt to shoot himself or me. I did take his gun away from him, that's a fact."

Murtagh was on his feet but before he could break in, the Coroner warningly motioned for him to sit down.

144

Alred asked, "Did you later return the gun to Mr. Murtagh?"

Remembering the scene, Zan managed to keep his face grave, his voice mild, as he answered, "No. He knew where the gun was. I didn't take it away from there at all."

"Mr. Murtagh has made a charge that you destroyed his gun."

Zan felt a slow anger starting to burn deep in himself. All these little pin pricks about quarrels and guns seemed to have nothing to do with the reason he was here, sitting in front of a Coroner's court. The whole talk seemed as unreasonable as the cloud of small black flies that pester a fellow in muggy weather. But caution warned him to hide his annoyance. It could be that these little pricks were calculated to prove that he was a quarrelsome fellow, quick to anger.

Mr. Alred spoke a bit sharply. "I'm waiting, Mr. Allan. Where is this gun you admit taking from Mr. Murtagh?"

Zan answered carefully. "I haven't seen the gun since it fell and sunk in the mud. Murtagh dropped the gun, not me. I let it stay where it was figuring that by the time he'd fished it out, cleaned it up, he'd be over the shakes and able to handle a gun so it was safe"

"You didn't throw the gun in the mud?"

"No, sir. I let it fall. I could have caught it easy enough, but I didn't."

From his bench Murtagh shouted, "That's a lie!"

Alred looked down at him sternly. "Please do not interrupt. You'll have your chance to talk later"

Mr. Beeson leaned over toward the Coroner, said something in a very low voice. Alred considered a minute, and then said, "Well it might have some bearing on this. Under the circumstances, I can't see that it makes any difference that you are part of the jury. Suppose you go ahead and then if the sheriff thinks it's irregular, he can leave it out of the notes." He turned to the clerk, "Take down Mr. Beeson's remarks on a separate page, will you, Wilbur?"

Wilbur looked as affronted as though he had suddenly smelled a dead whale, but he drew the second book toward him, took a fresh pencil, and resigned himself.

"Go ahead, Mr. Beeson."

"Thank you. I'll be brief. I work for Mr. Murtagh. Mr. Allan has worked for me. I find him intelligent, ambitious, hard working and agreeable to work with. I never heard a word from young Allan about Mr.

Murtagh's shot having grazed his horse until in August, when Mr. Murtagh came back to the Coast.

"As soon as he saw Zan Allan, he ordered him removed from the payroll with no notice. I didn't want to lose a man whose service I'd found so valuable to the work it was my job to see done. In my own interest I protested this discharge and, through Mr. Murtagh's reactions, it became very evident to me that the boss had a personal grudge he was nursing. I've also worked with Mr. Murtagh for years and get along with him fine. He's a good executive. But through the years I've noticed that he cannot stand being put in the wrong over the slightest thing, and that time does nothing to lessen his resentment. That's what I wanted to say"

Mr. Alred said, "Thank you," but as Beeson slid back to his place against the rest of the jury, Alred said, "I think that would be regarded only as opinion, personal opinion, Mr. Beeson. In a courtroom it could be admitted from a character witness, but I'm doubtful of its value here."

Wilbur snatched at the page to tear it out, but Alred made him keep it. "Won't do any harm, Wilbur. Let it stand."

He looked at Zan and said, "I think that is all for right now, Mr. Allan, but please stay in the room."

Zan, thankful to have gotten through so easily, made his way back to his place and sat down.

Mr. Greub was called next and when he was seated on the bench Zan had just left, Wilbur briskly noted down in his book the name, address and occupation of the witness.

Then Mr. Alred said, "Now, Mr. Greub, will you please state what you were able to observe at the place where Mervin Williams met his death?"

Mr. Greub said slowly, almost reluctantly, "It seemed to me that there were many details pointing to death by intent instead of by accident. When Martin Allan and I found the body, there was still a smell of gun powder lingering about the woods and on the clothing. About thirty feet from the body, which plainly had not been moved but lay where it had fallen, I was able to find a faint imprint, rather blurred, as though a gun had been thrown there. The body could not have had that gunpowder scent if the shot had been fired from thirty feet away. There was no gun anywhere in the clearing."

Mr. Alred said, "I see." After a minute's thought, he leaned forward and asked, "Has the gun been found?"

146

Zan felt a shock from his scalp to his heels and back again as he listened to the answer.

"Yes. As Martin Allan was riding down the trail to the survey camp for help, I rode up the trail. About a mile from the place where the shooting had taken place I caught up with Zan Allan. He told me he had heard a shot while he was riding up from the Coast. It struck me, then, that he had been on the trail, and within hearing range of that shot, for more time than just the riding distance would take. Also it seemed rather unusual that he did not remember where he had been when he heard the shot. Also, shortly before I caught up with him, I had stopped to rest my horse. There I notice that someone else had recently stopped, been off his horse, gone to the edge of the trail."

He paused, hesitated a minute, took out his handkerchief and brushed it over his moustache.

Mr. Alred prompted him. "Did you think those tracks might have any bearing on this case?"

Mr. Greub answered, "No. Not at that time. But Mervin Williams' gun was not any place in the cedars, where he was shot. It was not at his home. That brought me back to what young Zan Allan had been doing in the time between his hearing the shot fired and my overtaking him on the trail. After supper at Martin Allan's house, I took my flashlight, rode back to where I'd noticed that a horse had been stopped, and that by the trail's edge a dry stick or two had been slightly moved by some weight pressed on them; a couple of dry leaves were freshly powdered under some weight but still whole as to shape. At that spot, turning my flashlight beam down into the brush at the foot of the cliff, I pick up a glint of metal. I managed to get to the spot and recovered a gun. It was Mervin Williams' gun. It was also the gun that had fired the shot that killed him."

Mr. Alred looked slightly skeptical. "What makes you feel certain of that Mr. Greub?"

Zan's hands, tightening over each other, pinched flesh until he had to relax his grip.

Mr. Greub answered almost apologetically. "Well, crime is my hobby as well as my business. I'm interested in ballistics, fingerprints, and everything that helps in crime detection. I'd just gotten a new camera and materials to work with fingerprints and brought it along to show my friend, Martin Allan."

147

"And you used this knowledge and these materials in experiments with Marvin Williams' gun?"

"Yes. I did."

"With what results?"

Mr. Greub reached into his pocket, took out an envelope and held it up as he said, "A ballistic test proved that the bullet removed by me in the presence of witnesses from Mervin Williams' head was fired from his own gun. The fingerprint tests show that two men besides myself had recently handled the gun."

Watching Mr. Greub settle back as though he were through with his remarks, Zan felt limp with relief. He'd been tight as a fiddle string with fear that the fingerprint talk might lead to Tilli being mentioned. But it looked as though there was not as much to this fingerprint business as Mr. Greub thought. Two men, beside Greub. That would be himself and Mervin.

Mr. Alred said, "Anything further to add, Mr. Greub" If not, I believe that will be—"

Greub interrupted, his voice very low, "A woman had also recently handled the gun." He bent around, half way stood up, and placed the envelope he had been holding on the desk so that it was directly in front of Alred. "These are the prints, each identified by name. Those number "One" are the ones developed from the gun; the others are the comparison tests and you'll see that the source is noted on each print."

Mr. Alred felt in his breast pocket, brought out a pair of glasses, put them on and studied the small, glossy slips as he spread them out in four rows. After a few seconds, he slipped off the glasses, looked at Greub, as though startled.

He said, "That will be all for now, Mr. Greub. I'll want to talk with you again, later."

Mr. Greub said almost testily, "I would just as soon finish what I have got to say before I step down. Only two small observations but I believe they are both pertinent. First, the horses. Mervin Williams' horse was found tied to a tree about a quarter of a mile from where Mervin was killed. It was very evident that his horse had been tied there fairly often and over some time. A silvery gray, or sort of roan, had been tied just inside the clearing where Mr. Williams was shot, and a great deal of trouble had been taken to conceal that fact. He had been there long enough to paw a circle around the tree and this had been carefully covered with leaves and brush, and a very good job it was, too. But I noticed a slight bruise on the tree bark from the tie rope and had also picked up enough hair to identify the color of the animal."

There was a stir in the room but it subsided into absolute stillness as the police officer continued in a low grave voice. "The other thing was some prints of a woman's shoe heels quite close to the place where I found the imprint of the gun"

Without any word from Mr. Alred, he stood up and walked down the narrow aisle, not rejoining Tilli and her parents but sitting on the first empty bench he came to.

Zan felt sure that this stuff about the gun, the fingerprints and Misty being tied to the tree would certainly cause Mr. Alred to call him back to answer some questions. He tried to relax his tense muscles by assuring himself that he had expected it to happen. Ever since he had found Tilli in the clearing and Mervin dead, he had been preparing himself to face this minute.

Over and over in his mind he had almost constantly working at what he could say that would save Tilli, and perhaps save himself. But his talk of a woman's fingerprints, a woman's heel marks, had shaken him.

Zan recalled that Aunt Blaze had warned him that Mr. Greub had talked about finding Tilli's heel prints, that the bullet had come from Mervin's own gun and that someone had tried to cover up their horse tracks. Zan had figured Greub was just guessing. But now he talked proof, and the proof told no lies.

Mr. Alred looked down at him, called his name.

Zan stood up, his face expressionless, his feet moving him forward without any conscious help from him.

His body seemed in a trance but his mind was furiously alert, cautioning him over and over again only to tell the false story he had decided on as a last resort. He had faced this instant many times since he first heard that shot, learned who fired it.

He was sitting down on the witness bench, Mr. Alred was saying, "After hearing of these fingerprints and Mr. Greub's other observations, is there anything further that comes to your mind that you would like to say, Mr. Allan?"

In a very low voice Zan answered, "No."

He wanted to leave it at that but Mr. Alred kept looking at him, not moving his eyes, waiting. Zan found his mouth open, heard himself blurt our, "I've handled Merv's gun. No reason why my fingers wouldn't show up on it."

Mr. Alred said, "Your horse is a silver and blue roan, isn't it?"

"Misty? Sure. He's been tied in the cedar grove plenty of times."

"I see no reason to doubt that," Mr. Alred said. "What interests me is that Mr. Greub is certain that the horse was in that clearing during the time Mervin Williams was shot. What answer have you got to that?"

Zan kept his head. There was nothing in this, so far, close enough to the truth to make him fear for Tilli. He'd go on hoping that time would not come. If it did, when it did, he had a story ready and could tell it straight, not let them get him mixed up.

He answered Alred's question carefully. "I'm sure that Mr. Greub wouldn't say anything he didn't think was so. I don't hold it against him. But I was riding Misty out on the main trail when I heard the shot. No matter what Mr. Greub thinks, or why he thinks it, that is the truth. I told you before how I was riding home and heard it."

"Yes. That's what you said. Well, I guess that will be all. I'll excuse you for now, Mr. Allan."

Zan stood up and Mr. Alred said hurriedly, "Tilli Allan, will you come up here, please."

Zan saw Tilli's nervous start, his Aunt Tena's hand placed on her arm as though to hold Tilli back. She shook off her Mother's clasp, started to get up, then sank back onto the bench, her voice sounding small and scared as she asked, "You mean you want me to come up there in front?"

Tilli's eyes and voice held sheer panic. Zan decided instantly that for her sake, as well as for the rest of the family, Tilli must be kept from talking. He turned abruptly to face Mr. Alred, said, "No need for her to come up here at all, once I tell you what I been holding back.

Mr. Alred snapped, "Holding back, were you? That's a new name for it, seems to me." He looked down at Tilli, still sheltered under Tena's arm, saying, "Just stay where you are Miss Allan."

Then he faced Zan, said, "All right. What were you holding back?"

Almost as though he were talking in his sleep, Zan said: "When my sister Maria asked me to supper, I sent word to Tilli Allan, my cousin, to meet me on the trail. I asked her to meet me by Half Barrel Spring, but she was not there so I kept on riding up the trail thinking I was early and I'd meet her on the trail further up. I hadn't met her by the time I got even with the cedar grove on my Uncle Martin's place. Mervin Williams was courting Tilli, and I knew she'd met him there once. Come to me she might be there saying goodbye, so I turned in off the trail, rode into the cedars. She wasn't there, but Mervin was. I told him he was wasting his time, that Tilli wasn't going to marry him. He said I was a liar. I didn't have no gun and when I told him I'd knock them words down his gullet, I thought we'd mix with our fists.

"But he had his gun. And as I went in to hit him, he grabbed up his gun, pulled down on me. I ducked, come close to him and hit him in the stomach with my shoulder.

"I grabbed at the gun and tore it away, but he grabbed the barrel and hung on to it, then tried pulling it back. It went off when he was trying to pull it loose from me by the barrel.

"I didn't want to kill him. The gun went off. But he was dead. I was afraid. I was so rattled that I took the gun, meaning to hide it. I had the gun in my saddle boot when I met Tilli a few hundred yards up the trail, coming down to meet me. She'd heard the shot and I told her I'd heard it, too, thought it must be someone hunting. She was sort of rattled 'cause she knew her father and his friend Mr. Greub were riding somewhere over the ranch and she didn't want them to come on to her near the cedars. So we fixed it up quick that she was to ride down to Summer Creek and I'd meet her there as soon as I could, after I'd had supper with my folks.

"I hid Mervin's gun. Mr. Greub rode up and almost caught me at it. I was scared and I was rattled. I lied. Told old 'em I'd scarcely heard the gun shot. I et supper at home, rode out and met Tilli. We talked, and then we came home. That's the way it was."

As Zan stopped speaking, Joe Williams stood up and said in a loud, angry voice, said, "I knew he killed my boy. I said it all along."

Murtagh added meaningfully, "When he threatened me I felt he had a dangerous temper—might do anything."

The Coroner said, "I'll have to ask you all to be quiet, please, unless you are being questioned."

The whispering and shuffling in the room quieted. After a minute,

Mr. Alred asked Zan, "You did not, then, at any time while you were in this cedar clearing see Tilli Allan there?"

Zan hesitated, his mind racing furiously. The woman's prints on the gun, the heel tracks—they were Tilli's.

He glanced over at Tilli, noting, without thinking about it, how very golden her hair looked under a small black hat. She was all in black except for a frosty looking thing at her neck. Her face looked white above the white lace. She really looked scared. Could she keep her head, and remember to say she'd made the tracks some other time?

The Coroner said, "I'm waiting, Mr. Allan."

But his eyes shifted from Zan's face and he looked warningly down the room to where Martin Allan and Tena were both whispering violently, leaning in front of the girl to keep their voice low.

Tilli stood up, ignoring their whispered warnings to stay where she was. She edged herself out into the aisle, walked up as calmly as though she were going to take her place in a game of whist, and said, "I'd like to answer that. You must have my fingerprints, and those were my heel marks. I was there, talking with Mervin before Zan came."

Zan didn't know if he was to go or to stay where he was, and he sat stolidly watching how the Coroner's sharp eyes softened to a look of sympathy as Tilli lifted to his view a lovely pale face and wide, wistful eyes.

Then he noticed Zan, dismissed him from the bench with a nod and an abrupt motion of his hand.

When Tilli had seated herself and straightened her skirt, drawn her feet back under the bench and folded her hands like a polite school child, the Coroner asked gently, "Can you explain how your fingerprints came to be on the gun, Miss Allan?"

Joe Williams broke in furiously, "They was in cahoots. They killed my boy together. She was running after Merv all summer."

Martin Allan jumped up. The Coroner stood up. "One more word out of you, Mr. Williams," he glanced around sternly, "or interruption from anyone, and I'll ask you all to wait outside until I send for you." He slowly sat down, saying, "I want that thoroughly understood. No more interruptions."

When no protest came from any one, he turned again to Tilli.

"And now, if you please, Miss Allan, I think we can hear what you have to say."

Tilli said in a clear, unhurried voice, "My fingerprints were on Mervin's gun because my hands were on the gun."

Zan, as well as everyone else in the room, suddenly became as still and fixed as figures in a drama.

Tilli sat with an air of innocent attention as though she were completely unaware of the effect of her words on her kin and neighbors.

Her eyes met those of the Coroner and he looked at her appreciatively for a second before he said, "Yes. Go ahead, please."

She looked down at her hands folded over the black purse on her lap, and then raised her eyes again to meet those of the Coroner.

"It happened, I mean the shooting, almost as Zan told you. Only I was there before Zan came." She let her head drop forward and shook it as though she were trying to drive away something she remembered. Her voice dropped lower as she said, "I'd been there quite a while. Mervin and I had made up our quarrel and—and I was engaged to him again. Mervin was holding his gun, showing me the nameplate on it when Zan rode in. We hadn't heard him coming."

She started to go on, faltered, and put her folded hand against her lips, looked up at the Coroner. He waited with an air of sympathetic understanding and, as though she had nerved herself to it, Tilli went on.

"Zan told Mervin to go away, and Mervin told him we were engaged, and they began to quarrel horridly. Zan hit Mervin and then he started trying to take the gun from him, and they both were angry I was frightened and tried to get between them, make them stop fighting."

She looked down at her hands tightening together over the purse, and shivered.

The Coroner waited patiently until Tilli looked up, murmured, "I'm sorry. But it was all so horrible. The sound of the gun and how they both let go it when it went off and I had both my hands on it, and was holding it. I was almost crazy when I saw Merv lying there, his head so—" she shuddered, hid her face in her hands, before she whispered, "Then I saw I still had the gun and made me so sick I threw it away, as far as I could."

She opened her purse, took out a tiny handkerchief and hid her face in it, her shoulders shaking.

Zan didn't shudder. The tale Tilli was telling did not seem like anything she could be seriously telling about him; it was unreal, as though she were telling a bad dream she remembered.

The Coroner fiddled around with the few papers on his desk for a few minutes, but when the golden head remained bowed in an attitude of hopeless sorrow, he cleared his throat and spoke to her.

"I know this must be hard for you," he said, "But you are here to give whatever information you have and I must ask you to go ahead with it, please."

She put the handkerchief in her purse, murmuring, "You're very kind. I know that I must do what I can. I'll try."

She sat quietly for what seemed a noticeable time, and then she raised her head, looked up at the Coroner. "My cousin ran and picked up the gun. He was still very excited. I tried to get him to go get help for Mervin and he acted so strange he terrified me."

She wet her lips with the tip of her tongue, patted at them nervously with her fingers, and went on. "He grabbed me, and he held on to me, shaking me. Perhaps he didn't realize how strong his is or how much he frightened me. He wouldn't let go of me until I'd promised to meet him at Summer Creek. I didn't know what else to do, along there with him, and no one to help me. I promised."

"And you kept that promise?" Mr. Alred asked.

Tilli's eyes widened, as though in astonishment. "I had made the promise. I kept it."

Then she lowered her eyelids, let her head droop forward and said faintly, "He let go of me as soon as I made the promise. I went to Summer Creek. He did meet me there. All I wanted was to get home. I thought that if I could get back to my parents before—before anything else happened—"

She clutched her handkerchief until it tore with a sound that could be heard in the silence of the big room before she began to sob.

Zan watched tears splash down on her clenched hands. This wasn't an act. She really was crying and he wondered why. She'd done a great job for herself this far; backed up his story, accounted for her footprints and finger marks in a way that he never could have thought up. She'd got herself out of it as smart as a lawyer could have done but, while doing that, at the same time, she made him look guilty as hell. What was she crying for?

Tilli started dabbing at her eyes with the torn handkerchief, tugging at her little hat and giving a push at her hair before she said, "All I wanted was to get to my parents before anything else happened. My father won't ever let anything hurt me."

Mr. Alred said, "I can't understand why you felt you must go on with this plan once you got away...or why you didn't appeal to someone to help you."

She half whispered, "I was afraid, ashamed to cause talk. All I could think of was to pray I'd get safely home. The instant I was in sight of my parents, I—"

Tena called out, "She did. She was still on her horse when she said, I didn't want to, Mama. I swear I didn't want to. I swear I didn't want to. That's what my poor child said."

Mr. Alred motioned Tena to sit down and she did, hiding her face against her husband's shoulder as she said, "My little girl, my poor little girl."

The Coroner looked over the people in the room and then asked Tilli, "Aside from your parents, were any of the other people in this room at your home when you got home?"

Tilli looked thoughtful, then said slowly, "I think Mr. Greub, my Uncle Stephen, and Aunt Blaze Allan were there. I was confused, didn't notice much, only that I was home, and safe."

"I see." He looked at Mr. Greub, who stood up as his name was called. "Did you hear Tilli Allan's words to her mother when she came home?"

"No. I realized that someone had arrived but I was inside the house and did not come out.

The Coroner said, "Very well, thank you. That will be all, right now."

Zan watched Mr. Alred's eyes glancing around the room once more and decided that he was looking for Stephen Janson, maybe wanting a man to back up what Aunt Tena had said. He still seemed to have no feeling at all over what had happened except a wish that it would be over soon, and he thought that if a man's say-so was what the Coroner wanted, Zan Allan was in a good spot to tell him that Tilli had said exactly what her mother claimed.

But he found himself tense when he heard the Coroner say, "Mrs. Stephen Janson."

His Aunt Blaze shouldn't get mixed into this mess in any way. Zan was glad she didn't stand up. She raised her head, said, "Yes," in an even, pleasant sort of way, but Zan noticed that her face looked greenish-white above the clear brown plaid of her coat.

"Did you hear your niece say the words her mother told us Tilli Allan said?"

"Yes. I recognized the words as something I've been hearing my niece say every since she was a little girl. It seemed natural to hear Tilli say, "I didn't want to do it, Mamma."

The Coroner pursed his lips, frowned slightly. "Please repeat the exact words you heard Tilli Allan say to her mother when she returned home."

Her voice seemed a trifle less firm, but Blaze answered, "She said, 'I didn't want to do it, Mamma.'"

"Thank you, Mrs. Janson."

He looked down at Tilli and said, "I'm sorry, but it will be necessary for you to remain here with your parents until the jury agree on a verdict."

Tilli answered, "I want very much to go home, I feel tired and ill. But I'll wait as long as I'm needed. You've been most kind. Thank you."

Tilli's slender, black-clad figured moved slowly away from the Coroner's desk.

Mr. Alred looked at his watch, put it back in his vest pocket, and looked down the room. As his glance met that of Zan, he said, "I'd like another word with you, Mr. Allan."

As Zan got up, the room, the people in it, the Coroner's jury suddenly became as unreal as a dream. He knew he was walking. He could hear the sound of his boots against the split board floor. When he got to that wide board with the knothole that was in the center of the room it moved under his step. The board was loose. It always had moved under his foot like that when he was at the camp. Dreams could be like that, full of crazy things, but with the little everyday things mixed in so they fooled a man.

Trying to wake up, he moved steadily toward the waiting Coroner. He longed to feel sure that he would never reach the bench that was coming closer with every step, but rather, would wake up and find he was standing barefoot beside his rawhide bedspring, starting to walk to the door to greet the dawn and see Misty and Buster waiting to nicker a greeting across the pasture fence bars.

Pasture bars. Prison bars. He couldn't wake himself up. He had reached the bench. The Coroner was much too solid and real for a dream as he leaned forward, asking, "Can you think of anything you would like to add to what you have said?"

"No, sir."

Mr. Alred seemed to consider this for a few seconds. He looked very serious and it seemed to Zan that his voice had a note of warning in it as he said, "Would you care to change what you have said in any way?"

This time it took longer for Zan to answer. He hesitated, wondering if he had gotten it wrong, if Tilli was no longer in such desperate need of help. Who was she planning to put the baby off on? Did she think it would serve her better to blame him for getting in a fix?

Tilli was too much for him to figure out. The one thing he somehow must do was to keep her, as well as the rest of his kinfolks, from being smeared with the dirt of a public scandal.

He looked at Mr. Alred, said, "I don't want to change what I said."

Mr. Alred said, "Very well, Mr. Allan. You can wait with the rest until the jury decide upon their recommendation."

Mr. Greub said, "Pardon me, Mr. Alred, I'd like a word with you."

He went up front, bent over the table and said something in a very low voice. The Coroner answered in the same way.

As Greub took his seat again, the Coroner said, "I would like to have Lara Ramirez up her, please."

Lara sat unmoving, staring at the far wall.

Blaze nudged her, whispered something.

Lara still did not move.

Blaze said, "I'll go up there with you, stand beside you, Lara. There's nothing to be frightened of."

Mr. Alred said, "Yes, you come right along with the young lady, Mrs. Janson."

Lara screamed, "I won't go! I won't."

Zan knew he would rather be hung that listen another second to Lara being tortured because of him. He leaned across Blaze, took one of Lara's small, clenched hands in his and said, "It's all right, Lara. You needn't be afraid. Go ahead. It's all right, Chicken."

In a shrill, hysterical voice, Lara cried out. "I won't. I won't go. I won't go up there. I don't know anything."

Mr. Alred looked distressed as he said, "That's all I wanted to know right now, my dear. As long as you don't know anything you think you should tell us, there isn't any reason for you to come up here."

Lara hid her face in Blaze Janson's lap, began to sob heart-brokenly.

As soon as Lara was quieted, the Coroner gave the five jurors their instructions. Then he told the clerk to go with them into the kitchen, fasten the back door from the inside. He also asked that the cook be told to come sit in the mess hall so that no one should be able to disturb the jurors until they were ready to hand their verdict.

Presently the clerk returned. The cook waddled in wearing his apron and still carrying a long handled spoon. A nervously humorous whispering lasted only a few seconds, died away and the dreary waiting began.

It was long after the lunch hour when a smell of meat barbecuing and coffee boiling drifted in from the fire pit down beside the Creek. Evidently the crowd outside had given up hope of having their curiosity appeased and had decided to satisfy their own hunger.

Trying to keep his mind away from his five friends out in the kitchen trying to sort the truth from the false, Zan tried desperately to think of future plans for his ranch. Mentally he got a start of cattle. They increased too fast for the size of his place and it was overgrazed. He gave up as five horrible minutes dragged by. So he tried again, this time splitting timber into rails, making a fence around the whole place.

The jury was still out. He worked so hard to hypnotize himself into forgetting how many hours some minutes can hold, that he married some woman whose face he didn't try to see, filled the little cabin with children, and after the woman nagged at him for a time, he cut logs and built his daydream family a large, two-story cabin of squared logs.

One quick glance at reality showed him the cook nodding sleepily, the clerk fussing with his pencils, Mr. Alred once more looking at the papers that were still flat on the table, close by his hand.

Zan's shoulders sagged. He was sure that if the door didn't open soon, and the jury come out, that nothing could hold him there in that unnatural stillness. He felt he was drowning in sticky seconds, that he had strangled time and killed it dead, made each instant into a forever.

He broke into a sweat when the door actually opened and the five men came slowly into the room, took their places on the bench they had left a short time before.

Mr. Alred turned to them. "Well, gentlemen, have you agreed on a verdict?"

Mr. Beeson stood up. "Yes sir, we have. "I've written it down but I forget if I was to read it out, or just hand the paper to you."

Mr. Alred answered, "Read it, please, then give the paper to me."

Mr. Beeson acted nervous as he unfolded the paper and read in a low voice:

"We, the jury, unanimously agree that the deceased, Mervin Williams, came to his death by a bullet fired from a gun. This verdict is returned without recommendation of any sort."

Mr. Alred took the paper from Mr. Beeson and thanked the jury.

Zan kept tumbling the words he had just heard, around and around in his mind, looking for their real meaning. "Death from a bullet by a gun." That didn't even rule out a stray shot meant not to kill. Could "returned without recommendation" mean that even after all the stuff they'd heard, and they still had no idea of who was mixed up in the shooting? Had they turned in a mixed up sounding thing like that because they were his friends and didn't want to come out square against him? No. Beeson wouldn't do a thing like that.

Zan felt more bewildered, more frightened, that if the jury had returned a straight verdict of murder against him. Didn't he tell them he'd shot Merv? Why wouldn't they take his word for it and have the whole thing over?

He felt hollow as he began to realize that this hearing was only a beginning. Every thing said here today was written down. When the real trial came, lawyers would rake up, scrape over and poke at every word, trying to prove who lied, find the one so guilty that no lie could be of any use.

Zan looked up from his nervously tightened hands as Mr. Alred cleared his throat, pulled the two papers on his desk over in front of him, and said, "I have here a complaint sworn to by Mr. Joe Williams charging Zan Allan with the murder of his son Mervin Williams. Also a complaint issued at the demand of Martin Allan, charging Zan Allan with threat, intimidation and duress, in an attempt to secure marriage with his daughter, Tilli Allan."

The room broke into a confusion of rustlings and whispering. Zan was glad the noise covered his shock that Tilli could do such a thing; his worse shock in learning that his Uncle Martin had set the law against him without even asking for his side of the story.

The Coroner hushed the excited whispers, leaned forward and said, "These complaints will be put on the calendar of the Superior Court in Salinas and will be called for trial as soon as they come up on the docket. I expect that you all know that a subpoena is as binding as any court order and that there is a penalty for failure to appear. Subpoenas will be issued for all of you who have taken part in this action today. You will get them in ample time to be in Salinas for the trial."

This caused another quick whispering but it stopped when Mr. Alred said politely, "I want to thank you all for appearing here today. Thank you very much. You are excused now until your subpoenas come in the mail."

People started pushing back benches, standing up.

The Coroner raised his voice slightly, said, "You will please remain here, Mr. Allan."

Blaze whispered, "We'll be waiting for you outside, Zan."

He nodded, got to his feet and stepped into the aisle so that Lara, his father, and Maria could follow Blaze.

They went up the aisle silently and he stood watching the door open for them. He saw them walk out into the sunlight.

Then the shut door closed him in and he sat down alone on the bench with nothing to do but wait.

IX

The jury filed out, the clerk picked up his pencils, his books, and then followed them. Mr. Greub went to the Coroner's table, sat beside Mr. Alred and began talking earnestly.

Finally they both nodded. Mr. Greub called, "Come up here, will you, Zan? You'll need time to pick up what you'll want in town, and you'll have to make some arrangement for the care of your stock, too."

Zan started to say he could be ready in a half hour, but hesitated.

He asked, "How much time did you figure would be right?"

The Coroner answered, "A reasonable amount. I'll leave as soon as the boys have the body ready to pack out. Mr. Greub has agreed to take you to Salinas."

"Doesn't seem right to put Mr. Greub to so much trouble," Zan said. "I could ride Misty in tomorrow, leave him at the Monterey livery barn. One of my folks could lead him back. I'd take the first train to Salinas."

Mr. Greub said, "I know you'd do that, Zan. But I'll go along with you."

"That's very neighborly of you, Mr. Greub. I appreciate it.

Mr. Alred said, "then that's settled. I'll be off." He shook hands with Greub, hesitated a second, then offered his hand, saying, "Always remember that your best course is to tell the plain truth, and all of it. Perjury is a criminal offense, you know, and the prosecutor is as sharp as they come."

Touched by the unexpected kindness, Zan said, "Thank you for trying to help me. I'm not sure I know just what perjury is."

"Lying on the witness stand when you are under oath to tell the truth: that is perjury. And let me add that whole truth will serve you better than half-truths." He hurried down the aisle and out of the building without waiting for any comment.

Zan stared after him, thinking of the power and rightness of law. A lie was always a nasty thing. He had been filled with shame today for dealing in half-truths and untruths, no matter how urgent the need. He faced the fact that he still intended to stick by what he had already said, no matter what happened to him. He wondered what Tilli would do. If she was warned about perjury, would she take the warning seriously? This hearing had been hard, but he felt now that a real court trial would make today's hearing seem like a box supper. Smart people, trained in law, would be laying for all of them, trying to trip them up.

He looked down the room, thinking he'd better drop a warning word to Tilli. Then he remembered she was gone. The room was empty except for himself and Mr. Greub.

Zan turned to him. "I'd like to have a word with my father, and my Aunt Blaze. Is that all right?"

"Certainly," Mr. Greub answered. "I expect they're waiting outside."

Blaze was waiting by the door, looking anxiously after Lara, who was running toward a group of people crowding around some men who were arguing with Joe Williams. Running after Lara was a carrot-topped, freckled boy of about fourteen.

Blaze grabbed Zan as he came through the door, urging, "Make that Murtagh boy leave Lara alone, Zan. He's chasing here with a big snake, but she's terrified of the boy, not the snake. She's going to run right into Mervin Williams' corpse in another minute and that'll be a frightful shock to the child. Don't stand there. Go get her."

"I'll put a stop to it," Mr. Greub said. "You wait here for me, Zan."

Blaze whispered to her nephew, "Zan. You're under arrest already?"

He nodded. "I guess that's about it. Damn that boy! Lara has started crying. I'm not going to stand here and—"

He cut across the open ground to where Lara was trying to break past the boy who had her cornered between two big boulders at the Creek's edge.

Zan and Greub arrived at almost the same instant. Lara flung herself into Zan's arms as Greub's hand closed on the other boy's shoulder.

Zan said sternly. "You're too big a fellow to be playing such tricks. Throw that damn snake away and go behave yourself."

The boy made an impudent nose at Zan. "Go chase yourself," he said. "She's too big to be fooled by a rubber snake. She wanted me to chase her." He turned to Lara, asked fiercely, "Did you? You did, didn't you?"

Lara rubbed her eyes, her mouth quivered, but she nodded, "I guess so. I knew it was a pretend snake." She looked at the boy and said, "I wanted to play, but you got too close and scared me."

Her eyes filled with tears again and Zan said, disgustedly, "Good Lord, what next? You get back to Aunt Blaze and stay right by her until you get home."

As Mr. Greub let go of the boy, Lara turned from Zan, saying in a heart-broken voice, "You scolded me, Zan. You scolded me."

She ran back to Blaze.

The Murtagh boy joined the group crowded around the packhorses. Zan turned to Greub with a look of startled chagrin. "There she was, screaming like a filly with a lion after her, me breaking the law to go save her, and now she turns on me."

Mr. Greub laughed. "Feminine to her finger tips, I'd say."

Zan said nothing. He'd suddenly remembered his Uncle Stephen saying Tilli acted like a clever little girl when she'd been screaming and carrying on about a snake that she know hadn't been put in her pocket.

He'd scarcely been aware of walking across the clearing until the mess hall door was just a step away and both Lara and Blaze were smiling cheerfully at him.

Blaze spoke to Mr. Greub. "Would it be all right if Zan and I walked over to that log on the edge of the Canyon, sat down and decided how best to handle his ranch and the stock until he is back?"

"Certainly it would. And take your time. I'm not a bit ambitious to catch up with the Coroner, have to drive in with him. He's got a name for getting stuck on every mountain road in the county. We'll take the stage out tomorrow."

Zan touched his aunt's elbow, asking, "Couldn't Uncle Stephen bring our horses home then, if he's coming back tomorrow on the stage?"

She slipped her arm through Zan's. "That's right, he is. It would work out fine." She turned to Mr. Greub. "We'll not feel we have to hurry, then, but we won't leave the log until you come back here." She asked Lara, "Would you like to sit with us, dear?"

163

With a sudden shy and secretive look on her face, Lara drew back, shaking her head. "I'll just sit here on the step, Aunt Blaze, stay right here until you come back."

Zan noticed that Blaze didn't look at the child, only murmured comfortingly, "We won't be long, Lara," and walked toward the log, telling him that his father and Maria had started home.

When they were seated on the log, Zan could not think of anything to say. Blaze was silent for enough time to make a courtesy of the silence. Then she said slowly, "When you write to us, Zan, it would be nice for you to put a note in for Lara. She's so fond of you, and though you may not have noticed it, she's pretty disturbed about this trial."

"I'm not going to write anyone. Do you think I'd have my folks getting letters from a prison? And I don't want none of you to write to me, either, no matter how long I'm gone."

"For heaven's sake, Zan," Blaze protested. "Don't be so Allan! You sound exactly like your grandfather."

"That's all right with me. Can't you hear the stage driver shouting, 'Here's a letter from the jail for the Allans.' I'm not blaming him. He's human. It would be news. I've made plenty of trouble already without keeping it stirred up and fresh in folks' mind every time a letter passed between us. I won't have it."

Blaze sighed. Then she said, "We'll leave it that way. Until you write us."

He managed a smile. "We'll leave it that way."

They sat together silently for some minutes, and then Zan said, "The stock will be all right in the pasture. Good spring, plenty of water."

"I'll see to it that Misty and Buster have everything that any other Allan animal gets, Zan. You know I will."

He said, "Sure," a bit unevenly, and then nerved himself to say, "I don't like to ask Pa if he'd send me his copy of the family picture, but it would be good company. You think he'd loan it?"

Old Doc Roberts, with the camera machine he called 'Betsy', had taken that picture way back in 1909 when Gramp's whole family had been together: himself, Gramma Hannah Allan, Aunt Blaze and her twin Martin, Uncle Avery and Zan's father, the second Zande Allan. Doc Roberts always said it was the best picture he'd ever made and the whole Coast agreed with him. Gramma Allan looked like an angel in it and Gramp was looking at her, real tender and proud like.

Blaze answered, "Yes, of course he would. But you should have one of your own. I've been meaning for a long time to get some copies so my youngsters could have them. There will be extras, so you can have one of your very own."

He stood up. "Then I guess that settles things."

Blaze laughed. "You men, all alike. I suppose you think one family picture will cover everything." She turned to him seriously. "You'll have to wait weeks, maybe months, before the trial is called, Zan. I'm going down to your cabin and see that you pack what you need. You'll need money, too, for laundry, haircuts, all sorts of things."

"I've got some money. And I can shave myself. Just had a haircut."

"We'll see. But you sit down again, Zan, and I'm going to pry some. First, is your land paid for?"

"Yes. Says so in the paper I give you at your place. Could you look after them for me?"

"Yes. And I'll keep up the taxes, and the fences. Don't worry, it'll be in good order when you get back."

He looked at her curiously. "You figure I'm bound for state's prison? Maybe for a long spell?"

Her eyes filled. As Blaze tried to blink away the tears she hid her feelings by saying crossly, "You didn't say anything today that would keep you from it. And the complaint Martin swore to won't help any jury feel that you're a nice, misunderstood young man. Why did you let Tilli say such things, Zan?"

He said morosely, "A part of what Tilli said was true. But she really didn't want to marry me."

"Oh, good heavens! Don't say such things, not even to me. There's no reason for you to help send yourself to prison. Haven't you thought what misery this will mean for the family?"

He looked at her soberly. "Sure, I'm thinking of it, but I can't see any way out. Too many people saw too much stuff."

Blaze brightened. "As long as you want to find a way out, it can be found. Stephen is out now getting you the best defense lawyer he can find. Tell the lawyer everything, Zan, every scrap you can remember, whether it seems to have any bearing on Merv's death or not. Stephen says legal law is full of something called technicalities. They make such difference in trials."

Zan stood up again, pulled Blaze to her feet, smiling a bit sourly as he said, "That's what Gramp says. He says it's why 'lawyer' is a polite way to say 'liar'."

Blaze shrugged. "Father still loves the ideas he got in 1850. The world changes, the law changes, but not Papa."

"Well, I should hope not," Zan said. "I'd as soon think of the Santa Lucias flattening out to prairies, as to find Gramp going soft about what he thinks is right."

Blaze looked startled. "Why, Zan! Watch out! You're like him already!"

He said, "We got different ideas about some things, me and Gramp. But both of us, when we get ideas, hold on to 'em; and we both work at them about the same way, I guess."

His aunt made no answer to that. She stood up, changed the subject, saying, "I want to get Lara home early, so we better both ride down with you now and I can help you pack for town."

As they started back to the mess hall, Zan was surprised to see his grandfather walk into sight from the far side of the building. Their eyes

166

met for an instant and Zan thought the old man was going to speak to him. But as he took one quick step forward, his grandfather turned stiffly, walked back the way he had come, and the wall of the building hid him from sight.

Blaze said softly, "Don't blame him, Zan. This is hard on Father. He's so proud."

Zan wanted to let her know that he understood his grandfather's feelings, but his mouth felt too dry. He managed to mutter, "I know. It's a sorry business."

Mr. Greub had been busy with the saddles and so it took only a few minutes to be on their way. The ride was short. Getting the few things he owned packed took only a few minutes. So when Lara asked for a little time to see Zan's ranch, Blaze agreed, saying she'd like to go along.

Zan followed them. Lara slipped her hand into his as the three stood together on the edge of the canyon above Rowdy Creek.

Lara looked slowly from mountaintop to meadow, from broken Canyon land to the bit of bench land where breakers foamed against the rocks. She said, "Some vacation I'll come here and stay the whole summer, maybe the whole year. The sea sings so nice here. It's even prettier here than way up high, Zan."

He swung her hand, managed to smile as he said, "Don't tell that to Gramp, or to my Pa. Allans have always like to look down at the Coast fog from their high lands, you know. But I sort of like this place, myself."

He felt that this bit of land was his first love.

Lara tugged at his hand, looking up at him anxiously. He said, smiling down at her, "I was just thinking on plans I got for this place, Lara. Lots to do here, when I get the time."

Blaze glanced first at the sun, then at the watch she wore on a thin gold chain. "It's time for us to go. You'll see Stephen getting off the motor stage at Big Sur tomorrow. There'll be time for you to have a long talk with him."

He answered, "Yes. Sure."

Blaze motioned to Lara and she followed Mr. Greub who was walking over to the fence where their horses were tied. When Lara caught up with Greub, she started talking to him, and Blaze turned to Zan, urging, "Promise me, Zan you'll talk freely to Stephen. Tell him whatever it is you're holding back. You must do that. No one can help you unless you will help yourself."

He answered with an evasive, "I'll do my best, Aunt Blaze. I know I must, for all of us."

She looked more cheerful. "And Stephen and I will be in Salinas soon, to see you there."

He said, "I don't want to see you there. And Uncle Stephen won't want you going in that place where I'll be. No place for a nice woman at all."

She snapped, "Oh, for heaven's sake!" Then she took a breath, said patiently, "You're not to think of it as jail, Zan. It's only the place where you stay so you'll be handy to the court where they will prove you innocent, and send you back home to us."

He turned away quickly, called to Lara, "I'll boost you into the saddle, Chicken." His eyes rested for a second on the little sidesaddle that had once belonged to his Aunt Blaze Allan. The forty-year old saddle was oiled and polished as proudly as though the mail order house had just sent it, brand new. He knew how upset Lara felt about keeping her word to Zan about what had happened, and he wanted to speak of it, but couldn't. It was too close to his heart to trust his voice.

Silently he cupped his hands as Lara reached up for the horn and he got ready to boost her up.

She stepped lightly into his waiting hands, and as he took her weight, she suddenly let go of the horn and was clinging to him. Her thin arms wrapped tightly around his neck and held with the tenacity of despair. She whispered brokenly, "I won't let them do it, Zan. I won't. I'll never let you tell lies for Tilli and go to jail. I got to say what's true. I got to."

She felt as thin and cold as a baby Allan bird from its nest.

Blaze called over, "That's enough, Lara. Say good by. Let Zan go so he can come over and help me up, too."

Zan gave Lara a quick kiss above her ear, and patted her back. Then he put a hand on either side of her waist, set her in her sidesaddle. He said, "It'll be all right, Chicken. Don't you fret yourself none. It'll be all right."

She turned away her head, was looking up at the mountain, tearing, as Zan walked over to Blaze and helped her into the saddle. As he raised his face to say good by, he was shocked to see how white she was. He put her hand against his cheek, pressed it, and said gruffly, "*Adios*, then."

She didn't look at him but her voice had a loud and cheerful ring as she called back, *"Hasta la vista, muchacho,"* meaning little boy.

Lara began laughing after hearing a grown man called *muchacho* and Zan knew his aunt had managed the parting and had done it well. It would be a pretty mangy man who wouldn't be willing to die for a woman like that. She was a real Allan. But as he looked after them, riding off, he saw only a blur and felt very much like the little boy his Aunt Blaze had called him.

A sudden, unseasonal wind and rainstorm, with flashes of lightening, and along dark growls of thunder rolling down from the peaks, came in the night. It was still raining hard at daybreak, and made the long ride to Big Sur through overgrown trails seemed as cold and wet as a long swim in a cold river. Greub fought the wet brush, cursed as the cold trickled down his back. Zan was just as wet, cold and uncomfortable, but still he was glad for the storm. First, because he was a Coast man and a cattleman, he was always willing to trade discomfort for a good stand of early grass on the dry ranges. Also, storms kept people indoors. He had no wish to face the eyes of outsiders. He even hoped the storm was heavy enough to keep his Uncle Stephen in Monterey. There was nothing for either of them to gain by having a talk together. Nothing could make him change his story now. He would never risk saying one word that could bring Lara into court.

The horses' hoofs made no sound on the wet, dark earth of the Coast Trail. When they turned down into a Canyon to make the crossing, both horses and riders became alert. The round stones were wet and slippery with the new wash. Stray rocks, washed loose from their slight hold on the steep cliff faces above the trail, came thundering down at terrific speed. If they struck a hollow tree, they echoed and re-echoed like a wild tribal drum. If they struck a big redwood limb, it broke off, then came plunging down to block the trail. If the rocks chanced to hit a man, Zan thought, that was one man who would not have to stand trial. He smiled wryly to himself. It looked like life, even in prison, was still dear to a man. He found himself watching out for stray rocks and branches falling warily as did Misty and Mr. Greub.

Little streams, which yesterday afternoon were a faint voiced trickle, now roared with their own noisy importance and carried a full cargo of small logs, large limbs and every sort of debris as it swept down from the steep Canyons, clearing out the needles and leaves, the dead growth branches and limbs fallen since spring.

Already they had traveled past May Creek, Olay Creek and were almost even with the trail to Grandfather Allan's ranch. Zan half hoped that a slide, a rock—something…anything, would get them past the Home Trail without time to even glance at the ranch. He felt that otherwise, no matter how much it pained him, he would give in and take a long look, as far as his eyes could follow the deep-worn thread of the ancient Allan lifeline.

But he was not to pass the home trail without notice.

Misty's ears came forward, he nickered. Through a curtain of gray rain, Gramp's red Ranger answered. The old man rode forward, blocked the trail facing him.

Although he looked shrunken from the rain, Old Zande's eyes and voice seemed as bold as a young mountain lion.

"I thought to leave my grandson, my namesake, to the just of the court," he said. "It was like age had made me soft and I felt shame to face a man of our family who had wantoned with the harlot; whose hands were black with murder. But the voice of God came to me in the thunder of this night and I knew my own fault. The burden of your guilt is heavy on me. I saw you straying from our ways even when you were a small boy. But I was old, and foolish fond of you. I told myself you were Zande Allan. Would live up to your name."

Zan looked at his grandfather, tightened his lips, and said nothing.

Ranger was crowding closer to Misty and the old man reined in the restless horse with a gnarled old hand, saying bitterly, "I warned you. When you were no more than ten years, I warned you that the wages of sin are death. I told you that the trail to the saloon and the brothel led straight to hell. What more could I do? I couldn't take you to hell and show you the harvest of sin. Did you heed me? No. You thought I was an old fool!"

Zan said, "I always heeded you. Never said a thing against your wishes till I was of a man's age. I told you I was going to get a job on the road. I was twenty-one and had the right."

"Oh, merciful God," old Zande muttered. "You had the right! So you were twenty-one and you built road. How long you been twenty-one? About three months! Making a new road for men to travel a new way of

life, he tells me. And look where your new road has took you! Had you stayed with your land, lived like an Allan, you could look for an honorable death in your old age. But you say you gotta follow a new road. In three months of your new way, you've dishonored a young girl—your own cousin. You and the Williams boy were both after her like dogs in heat. And, now, murder! Your hands are blood guilty. You've made a byword of the name of Zande Allan."

Mr. Greub had been quietly backing away. Neither of the Zande Allans paid any attention to him. This clash of wills over a way of life was a thing of such intensity, that to both men it was as though they were the only men on earth.

Zan answered his grandfather. "It's the way you're taking what's happened that'll make a byword of us Allans. Nothing's going to break me, Gramp. Not sorrow for your shame. Not my term in jail. I'll be planning on coming out to build road. And if they hang me, by God, they can only hang a man's body. That thing that makes me want to build for tomorrow comes out of somewhere deeper than breathing. No one can hang that urge dead. No matter who builds it, I know this road is goin' to be a buildin' till it's done."

"Road, hell! It's the devil's advocate. It didn't even start gettin' built and it brought us ruin."

Zan looked startled. Then his eyes, his voice softened. He said slowly, "You're not looking at it straight, Gramp. Not a thing that's happened now but could have happened right here fifty years ago. Tilli is mountain born. So's Merve. Me, too. What's wrong's been done, didn't come in to us from the outside."

The old man glared at him. "Three months from home, and who of us knows what you been up to."

Zan said, "Once Grandmother said you was afraid of the road, or you wouldn't hate it so much. I say you're really afraid for us Allans."

The old man shrank back. He said, "You miscall my words. But mark me. This machine-made road you're trying to build, to run out and meet, that's the Great Beast, coming to destroy the worlds. Idleness, corruption, the scattering of our seed to the ends of the earth, till no man's got a home place; that's what I'm afeared of."

Zan said fiercely, "You're afraid for us? Afraid the Allan ain't strong enough for life outside these mountains? I'm not afraid. When machines come, Allans will use 'em. Hang one of us—hang ten of us Allans, and what's left is still good people. I believe in us, if you don't."

Old Zande muttered, "Lost. Lost. Lost."

He shrank down into his saddle, pulled Ranger around, faced into the cold and headed for the hills.

By the time they reached the coast settlement called Big Sur, both Mr. Greub and Zan were so wet, cold and saddle-weary they dismounted like two old men. The motor stage came down the hill as they were unsaddling in the open shed.

Stephen Janson got out of the stage and was followed by a stout, frightened looking man in gray gloves, gray overcoat and a light gray hat. He carried an umbrella that he promptly opened. Zan hurried forward before that umbrella could come bobbing toward Misty.

Stephen reached for Zan's hand, held onto it as he said, "This is Mr. Kemp, Zan. He's head of the law firm of Kemp and Kemp, and he's here to help you."

Zan bowed to Mr. Kemp. Please to meet you, sir." Then he turned to

172

his uncle, saying, "I got to go out on this stage with Mr. Greub, Uncle Stephen. Looks like not much time for talk."

While Greub and Mr. Kemp were greeting each other as old friends, Stephen called, "Come along, Mr. Greub. You and Zan need to get dried off. We'll have coffee right away, and order dinner. I know there's time. The stage driver has to eat before he starts back."

Zan followed slowly, feeling small that he was uncomfortable at the possibility of meeting someone who had heard of the Allan affair.

A broad, competent looking woman in a large white apron bustled in from the kitchen, calling loudly as she came, "I brought the soup and coffee straight off. Seems like anyone's been out in this weather would want something hot about as quick as they could get it."

Stephen said, "I didn't notice any of the family around. Not sick, I hope."

She laughed boomingly. "Oh, no. Just gone to the city. Slack season, you know. They need a change, same as I did. I like filling in here. But there's no choice in ordering. You have to take the family dinner or—" She smiled.

Stephen said, "Family dinner, eh? Well, let's have four of them."

She loaded the table with what the country afforded at that season. Crisp trout, buttery ears of sweet golden corn, saucer-sized slices of fresh tomatoes, fried potatoes, hot biscuits and wild pigeon pie crowded the table.

Both Zan and Stephen lacked appetite but Mr. Greub and the lawyer were eating like real Coast men. But when apple dumplings flanked by a milk pitcher of cream too thick to pour, came in with another pot of coffee, even the city men groaned. But they both dug out liberal helpings of cream with the long-handled spoon that stood straight up in the center of the cream. Mr. Kemp said, "I haven't seen anything like this since the last time I had dinner on my grandparent's homestead."

Stephen nodded. "This is a good country," he said. Honest food, honest people. Not one of them that wouldn't give you their best."

Mr. Greub pushed back from the table, saying something about wanting to leave a note for Martin Allan, and took himself away.

The others settled themselves on benches around the large fireplace.

Mr. Kemp turned to Zan. "Well, young fellow, let's have the straight out story of this unfortunate affair and we'll see what we can do."

Zan said carefully, "The Coroner got the whole thing. It's all written down. I got nothing I can add to what I already said."

Mr. Kemp pressed his lips together, patted his fingertips against each other as he rested his arms on his knees. "That so?" He asked pleasantly.

"Well now, we better go over it all very, very carefully, just the same. You see, Mr. Allan, there's quite a difference between me and the Coroner. He wants to find someone guilty. But I'm here to find something that will prove you're innocent. From what your uncle tells me, you're in a rather tight corner just now. He feels that you're holding something back. That doesn't sound reasonable to me, not when your life can be at stake, your very life, on this charge. It's only that you don't know the law, have no idea how important seemingly small things can turn out to be." He looked up, his eyes smiling, his eyebrows taking a sort of humorous lift. He said, "Strange things clutter up truth, the real facts—especially when violent death and a pretty young girl come into the same picture. Perhaps you'd rather your uncle left us?"

Stephen stood up quickly, but Zan jumped to his feet, put his hand on his uncle's arm. "I got nothing to say that the whole world can't hear," Zan said. "I told how it was, at the Coroner's inquiry. The man took it down in writing."

"Yes. I know. But I want to listen while you tell it once more. Tell me what you said then, and what you have been thinking about the whole business, since the hearing."

Zan said, "I been thinking to tell the judge just how it was, let him do his judging. I've had all the trial I want. That's what I been thinking, and that's what I'll do."

He eyed the lawyer steadily, his face telling nothing of what was in his heart. He was thinking so many things. At whatever the cost, Lara must be kept safe at home, safe in school. He was thinking of freedom with an ache that hurt like cold winter's rain. But the thought of saving himself at the cost of such hurt as Tilli's being tried for murder and as what it would bring to all the Allans, never once entered his mind. He did think that he'd grown up wanting to do something for more people than himself. "Greater love—lay down his life—" Yes, he could do that, and quietly, if it came to that.

The lawyer was looking at Stephen. Stephen was looking at Zan and both of the older men looked exasperated. At last Stephen said, stiffly, "That's no way to act, Zan. You've got to think of the family. You don't know the law—"

"That's so," interrupted Zan. "But I know one law: 'Thou shalt not kill.' I don't doubt that I could be primed to tell a better sounding story. But when they got to cross questioning me, I'm no lawyer. I'd trip myself up, be made to look like a liar in court. I'll tell it all to the judge again if I have to, but I won't have no trial. I know you want to help me, Uncle Stephen, but it wouldn't work out like that. I'm sorry, but that's how it is."

Mr. Kemp said impatiently, "Nonsense. We're not living in the Old Testament, young man. This is the twentieth century."

"Should be. Maybe it is, in San Francisco. But I spent the first twenty-one years of my life living in the Old Testament. Guess that sort of marks a man."

It was a new idea to Zan and it pleased him. For a minute he forgot his troubles and a slow-growing grin lightened his eyes, made him look like a boy.

Stephen's arm came across his shoulder, and he said huskily, "You're just a lad, Zan. Think of Blaze—"

"Yes sir. I have. And Gramp, too. All of us Allans. But—"

The driver put his head through the door, called, "Ready for the stage, please. The motor stage is leaving."

Mr. Kemp shook hands with Stephen, and whispered, "I'll work on him. Don't worry. We'll fix it up."

Stephen looked dubious but he put both hands on Zan's shoulders, and urged, "Let Mr. Kemp do what he can to help you. There is a time to be stubborn, and a time to compromise. But this is the time to think of your family, remember them."

Zan said, "I can't think of anything else."

The motor stage was warming up, making a fearful clatter. Greub opened the door from the post office, calling "Hurry. They're waiting for us."

Calling good-by to Stephen, the three men ran through slashing rain, climbed into the old automobile and it started moving. The wheels were spinning and sliding on the wet clay road as it moved off toward the first hill.

Greub and Kemp fell into easy talk of San Francisco, of restaurants, parks, theaters and people they both knew.

Zan rubbed the rear window on the right side to clear the rain so he could see outside. It did not occur to him at the time that, for the first time in his life, he was riding in an automobile.

As slow, slippery miles slid away behind them, he kept a spot on the window clear, looking out through a heavy rain at all he could see of the harsh Santa Lucia peaks.

The only thing he knew beyond a doubt is that a man in the fix had better take a long, long look at the hills home.

X

It was a February morning in 1936 when Zan Allan walked out, and heard the prison gates shut behind him. He couldn't quite grasp the passing of time. Seven years had gone by, at times feeling as slow as the passing of his whole twenty-eight years, and others as quickly as a single season, from beginning to end.

It startled him to find that a sense of freedom did not burst upon him with the sudden joyousness of Christmas morning in childhood. He didn't feel free. He felt shy and lonely. The people on the street look strange, foreign. The steady stream of automobiles roaring along the wet street was confusing, frightening.

The streams he was longing to hear were roaring their wild winter song in the deep canyons of the Santa Lucias. Without a minute's pause to look at a great city, he headed for home.

A bus brought him to Monterey in time to get into the bank where his Aunt Blaze had said she would leave his papers in a safe deposit box. When he had identified himself and got the box open, he found his papers, and fourteen Christmas letters from his Aunt Blaze.

There was a ten-dollar bill in each of them. There was money for cattle, money for rent, which his ranch had earned. He had felt numb. Now he learned that the joy of being still dearly remembered was like a sharp pain. It was light, a light in the window of a cabin high on the mountain. It was the home hunger, and it was wonderful.

He bought a used truck. He bought new Levis, a pair of stout boots. He bought a stock of groceries, but he didn't remember to eat anything. He remembered to buy a shovel. No winter-blocked roads and trail could hold him away as long as he had a shovel. He was jealous of every minute that still lay between him and his own country.

He found snow, very wet snow, lying at the top of Rocky Creek grade. He shoveled snow and tied rope around the truck wheels to make traction before he got through the soggy mess at the summit of the Serra Grade.

He worked at the shoveling and he drove with the nervous intensity of a man pursued. He could not feel really free until he was among his own mountains. No matter what else had changed, the mountains would be there—not waiting for him, not missing him, just tending to their own business of being mountains. A man with a mountain at his back had something he could depend on.

Zan had not asked how far the road was open. It had not seemed to matter. He could drive as far as there was a road, leave the car and pack on into his cabin.

After he passed Eagle's point the road became very rough, and so narrow it seemed little more than a trail. But his headlights showed tire tracks still ahead.

The hubs of his truck began to scrape against the solid rock cliffs on the inside track, although he had already edged over so close to the shore side of the road that he knew part of his tire was hanging out over space. But ahead of him, other tire tracks looked like bicycle tracks. He shifted into low and crept along until the road widened a bit, then narrowed again at the next canyon.

The road cut deep into a deep canyon and crossed the creek where a thirty-foot waterfall used to flow through the redwoods and feed the rich green ferns that flourished on both sides of the steep slopes.

Then he began picking his way among great boulders, thankful for his years of truck driving in prison, until reaching the next canyon.

Crossing the south side of Partington Canyon and Landing, he heard a small trickle of sound that almost instantly grew into a great, tearing roar. He stopped his truck abruptly, and waited while an avalanche of rock hurtled down the mountain at such speed that it jumped the road, landing clear and falling directly into the sea far below. The sky was clear and thick with bright stars, but he knew there must have been a mighty rain recently to have left the slush on the high passes and so loosened the soil that all those rocks, mud and debris just let go. As his truck made a minute's swing to the north, getting around a large slide, he looked back and saw lights back in Partington Canyon, apparently from several houses. There was another cluster of lights at what he judged to be McWay Canyon. The lights made him feel as a stranger in his own land. People were living now where no one had ever lived before.

At Anderson Landing he could make out cars, trucks, all sorts of machinery, parked off the road on the west side. This must be the prison road camp.

He drove past the buildings, all dark and silent, into the canyon and was about to drive out onto a low bridge that hung barely above the swollen stream.

He had not seen the little shelter house until an old man, holding up a lantern, stepped out of it, and stopped him by waving the lantern.

"Live down this way?" The old man asked.

Zan leaned out of his truck window, answering, "I'm going down to my ranch."

"Your ranch? What name did you say?"

"I didn't say. You didn't ask. My name is Allan.

"Allan? Oh, sure, Mr. Allan. I ain't got all you Allans straight yet; seems these mountains are thick with Allans. You go right ahead. Guess you been warned not to talk to the convicts, have you?"

"Yes. I know about that," Zan answered. He drove off before the old man could ask any more questions.

At Clay Creek he could make out what looked like a smaller camp on the flat above the road and he wondered about it. There seemed no point in crowding the country with camps.

The road had been better for the last few miles, level and fairly straight. He wondered how it would seem when he had a road on his place and he could drive right up to his own cabin.

As he neared his own place he found he was driving more slowly. He had dreamed of this minute for so long that he was almost afraid to go out of the dream and into the reality. Everything was so changed. He had gotten here so quickly, so easily, in his own truck, and over a road he had had no part in building.

There were still years of work to be done before the highway could be called finished, but he could never have any share in that building. That had been made clear to him, long ago, in prison. Even though the prison sentence was finished and he was considered a free man, he would never be permitted to work on any project where convict labor was doing part of the job. The prison officials had been friendly, but they told him it was out of the question. He would be considered an ideal contact man in helping prisoners escape. They had tried to cheer him up by telling him that they didn't think he'd do that, but they told him because it was a rule that applied to all freed prisoners.

He shrugged his shoulders. Well, he could build a private road on the Coast if he felt like it—a road up to his own house. But his first real job would be the one Dariel Beeson had offered him at Boulder Dam in Colorado. Dariel had sent him a letter, at least twice a year, each and every one for all seven years he was in prison. The letters had come from Alaska, from the Canal Zone, from strange states and far places. Dariel, too, had written him that prison law would not allow him to work on the Coast road, even when he was free. But he had offered Zan a long-time job at Boulder, saying that by the time it was done, Zan would have had plenty of experience at building something for many more people than just himself.

Thinking of this, Zan grinned, thought, "Guess I'll build a bit for myself, first. Tomorrow I'll start cutting a road up to my cabin.

Watching ahead, for he was very close now, he saw how the road just ahead was wide enough for a feeder road to take off from it. There was a gate across the road. The little road went up the draw to his own cabin.

Stunned for a minute, he sat unmoving in his car. Then he shook his head with no feeling of bitterness, and laughed out loud. He drove up to the gate and climbed out of the car. As he swung open the heavy, split rail gate and propped it, he told himself, "Looks like something's again' me doing any road building on this Coast, even to my own cabin."

Then he stood there uncertain as to whether he should drive in or not. His Aunt Blaze had written as though the place had been rented. Maybe it was still rented.

He lit a cigarette and leaned against the truck, wondering if renters would take a shot at a strange fellow who barged in near midnight.

He knew he was stalling for time. He admitted to himself that he was plain scared. The Coast people would look at him as though he were a kangaroo, or a giraffe. Any ex-convict who belonged to the Allan family would be a stranger sight than any freak looking beast.

In prison he had knowed this would be the way of it, but in prison he had also knowed exactly how he would face it. In prison it had been easy to say he'd act as though nothing had ever happened. But now it didn't seem so easy.

The first few years in prison he always figured on going off to some far place when he was free. But this was his place. He belonged here. He wanted to live here. He wanted to die here, when his time came.

"Well, make up your mind, Allan, make up your mind. You going in or aren't you?"

He didn't answer himself. He climbed into the cab, drove up the curve of the draw, was over the rise and in front of the cabin before he saw the house was lighted.

A woman's voice was singing softly, "—*longing for the sweetheart I left in old Monterey…*"

The singing stopped, the door opened and a woman stood in the doorway—a dark, slender silhouette against the light behind her. She called out, "Who is it, please?"

His scalp prickled. Her voice sounded so young, so un-frightened. What could he say that would explain his being at her door at midnight? That wouldn't alarm her, and that would let him get away quickly?

"I'm a stranger to this road," he said. "I guess I've lost my way."

He heard a sharply indrawn breath. Then she said, "Zan! You've come home."

She ran and was beside him in seconds, her hands holding his shoulders, half laughing, half crying as she said, "Come in quickly so I can look at you. Oh, Zan. You are here. The years are gone!"

He found he was stammering, "Lara? No. You can't be little Lara. But you are."

She laughed shakily, "Am I? I wonder! I can hear you, but I can't see the Zan I remember, either. I'll make coffee, right away. We'll drink it, and look at each other."

She turned and he followed her to the door, but stood on the porch looking in at the room he had never seen.

Lara walked into the kitchen, stopped beside a sink on the far wall, turned on a faucet and measured four cups of cold water into a squat brown enameled coffee pot. She put it on the shining blacktopped cook stove. The stove was trimmed in green enamel, had a warming oven over it. He could see a hanging lamp, and linoleum on the kitchen floor.

She walked back into the large room, asked, "Why don't you come in, Zan? Does the house look strange to you?"

He answered, "I feel out of place here."

Some of the brightness went out of Lara's look. She said, "I guess I've turned it into a woman's house."

He stepped in and closed the door but stayed beside it, looking at the room. The whole south wall had been lighted by windows. The corner at the north and east was taken up with two couches back against a built in box that served as a table. It held a lamp, some books, ashtrays and a box laid over with chips of abalone shell, filled with cigarettes. The couches were covered with bright Indian blankets and a regular litter of black silk pillows leaned against the redwood wall.

Above the old hewed mantle, a mirror hanging along its full length reflected shelves lined with books on the opposite wall. The floor was covered with a gray and black Indian rug. Low, polished chests of drawers held branched candlesticks and bowls of flowers.

There was a door at the north end of the room where no door had been.

He took another step into the room, and said, "The fireplace didn't get changed much. Used to draw good and didn't smoke."

As though she were making small talk with a stranger, Lara said brightly, "No, that's right. And though it draws well, it really uses very little wood."

Turning away abruptly, she went over to the table between the couches, picked up the abalone box and walked back, saying, "I smoke, even if the fireplace doesn't, so that's taken care of."

She stood close to him, offering the box, "Have one?"

He picked a cigarette out awkwardly, lit it, and turned to toss the match into the fireplace. Lara stopped him. "Light, please?"

He stood looking at her, the match burning down until it burnt his fingers. He threw the match behind him, in the direction of the fire, but he did not take his eyes from her.

Her skin was delicate and fine, but too white. Her brow was broad and square. Her hair, swept back and falling to her shoulders, was alive and black as her eyes. He thought, "She's pretty. Her mouth and eyes perfectly suited her narrow face."

Lara said, "I'm still waiting for a light, Zan."

He looked at her. "Must you, Lara? I can't believe you mean to smoke it."

She lifted her chin, made a nose at him. "Light it and find out," she said. "All women smoke now, except school teachers. They're not allowed to smoke. That's why I do."

He shut his eyes, tried to blot out the years, see the little Lara in this girl. He opened his eyes. The young woman with a cigarette in her hand was still waiting for the light. She said, "Well, you've been looking at me. Don't you think I look like a school teacher—or something?"

You don't look like you'd be smoking cigarettes like a toughy," he said. "I don't want to see you do it, Lara."

She put the cigarette back in the box. She smiled. That's to please you now." She shrugged. "But I'll have one with my coffee." She thrust the cigarette box at him. "Take it, Zan. I smell the coffee. If it boils, it's ruined!"

She dashed for the kitchen and he shut his eyes again, trying to bring back the look of this room as it used to be. It was no use. He saw only her fresh white blouse with a bow of the same thin, crisp stuff tied under her chin; the full blue skirt with straps of the same blue crossed over the blouse like suspenders. He could still smell a delicate scent of flowers, where she had been standing. This Lara was no more like the long-legged, pale child of his prison memories than this room was like the room he had planned to return to.

He shook his head, walked curiously over to the bookshelves to see if all these books were schoolbooks. He read two titles and stopped, bewildered by a feeling that he was in a strange dream. Crime and Punishment. Green Mansions. They stood side by side here in the same order that he had read them in prison. They were the first two books he had taken from the prison library, the first two books he had ever read. He had read and re-read them in prison until he was as familiar with these two books as he was with the Santa Lucias. How heart-broken he had been when the chaplain told him they were not histories of real people. He touched Green Mansions lovingly. He had loved Rima so terribly. The chaplain had killed her with a word, and it still hurt to remember his emptiness when he had to admit she was just made up, not real at all.

He backed away from the shelves, sat on a low wooden stool by the fireplace and looked at the bookshelves. Part of his plan had been to build a book shelf and, one by one, buy the books that, in prison, had taken him to new places, given him new ideas about all life; books became friends that were more real to him than prison guards or chaplains.

The two books he had meant to buy first were already here, looking perfectly at home, while he remained feeling like an outsider.

He made up his mind to say nothing about the books. This girl with her strange beauty, her cigarettes, living alone and making coffee at midnight made him feel out of place. The shy, awkward, sweet shadow of a little girl who had followed him everywhere in his youth had gone away with the years. There'd be no picking up that old relationship. She was a woman now.

Lara brought in a tray with coffee, small cakes, and a dish of raisins and nuts. She put it on the low table in front of the fire, added her cigarette box to the other things, and sat down on a little cross-legged stool she pulled forward from the wall.

Picking up the coffee pot, she poured a cup full, smiled as she passed it to him, saying, "It's hot, strong, and black. Do you want it sweet, too?"

"Hot, strong and black suits me."

He tasted the coffee, meaning to keep silent, but the words seemed to slip out in spite of his will. "It's good, too. So are you, Lara. To make me so welcome, go to all this trouble to make coffee when it's so late."

She raised her head as though startled, a look of hurt in her eyes. "If you had stayed free, and I'd been in prison for seven years, would it be a lot of trouble for you to make me a cup of coffee when I got back?"

"That's a woman's sort of question, Lara. You couldn't do anything that you'd be put in prison for."

She sipped her coffee, nibbled at a raisin and reached for a cigarette. She tapped it on the table, turned it in her fingers for a minute; a smile appeared quickly, then vanished from her face.

"I've often thought of mass murder of school boards," she said jokingly. "But let's not go into that." She held up the cigarette, and looked at him.

Zan reached into his pocket for a match, scratched it on the hearth behind him, and then held the flame toward her. She drew a deep breath and the tip of the cigarette glowed brightly. She was not just putting on a show, Zan thought. She was used to smoking cigarettes, no question about that.

But he couldn't think of anything to say. There was too much to say. His eyes kept coming to rest on the bookshelves. Finally he blurted out, "Looks like you do a lot of reading."

She said, "Yes. You taught me that. I've got a couple of your books here, Zan.

He said, "Not my books. Only two books I ever owned in my life went to prison with me, still are, out in my bag now."

"The *Bible* and *Emerson's Essays*," she said with an air of triumph. "I know."

"You know too goldarn much, begging your pardon, Lara. But you do. Have you turned into a witch?

"Naturally," she smiled. "That's the children's favorite word for a school teacher. Me a witch? Could be. I've got a broom in the kitchen and I don't use it very much for sweeping."

For the first minute since he came into the house he felt at ease. He laughed, reached out, touched the tip end of the bow under her chin with an odd delicacy before he said, "That's witchery; but it feels real. Feels like cloth, but it looks like mist. You're starting to seem real, too, Lara.

She blinked her eyes rapidly, turned her head away, and got up. She came back from the bookcase with two books in her hand. She said, in a shy, little-girl voice, "Yours, Zan. One a birthday, the other a Christmas gift. I got them for you before I left the Bishop's house."

He drew his eyebrows together, thinking. "Bishop's house? I don't seem to—" his face cleared, "Sure, the Bishop that was a minister. Where you lived and worked and went to town school."

He looked at the fire, trying to figure by what chance she had picked out, of all the books there were, these two books for him, *Crime and Punishment* and *Green Mansions*. He gave up. "How come you picked these, Lara?"

Now she was smiling happily, pushed the books into his hand and sat down by the coffee table. She had to struggle with laughter as she said, solemnly, "It cost me a quart of tomato juice and six crystal glasses to find out which books to get you that you were reading in prison, but it was worth it."

He didn't know what to say. All the trouble she'd gone to, just to find out what books he was reading in prison, then to go fetch copies and put them in her shelf, just waiting for me to come pick them up.

She wouldn't look at him, picked up her cigarette, which was still burning, and sat holding it, looking at the fire.

He blinked. Then he asked, "My blankets still here, and my cooking gear?"

She looked at him, bit her lip, and then said smoothly, "Yes, they are. Pots all scoured clean and the blankets put down in cedar shavings."

Her voice gathered an edge as she went on rapidly, "And I was going to turn the house over to you as soon as you came, but I don't think I will. I've got it rented to the last of May, Mr. Zan Allan, and I think I'll keep it. Houses are not so easy to find down here. You go hunt yourself one."

"All right," he said, "all right. I was trying to be polite and not pry. That don't suit you, does it? You want to do all the teasing, I guess."

She reached over, tweaked his ear. "I'll tell you—even if you won't ask, you stubborn old Allan! I was bringing in a tray with tomato juice, strictly temperance, you know how minister's families are. Well, a chaplain was visiting. I heard him say your name—and there went the tray, clattering to the floor! But it was worth it. He told me about you, how he was so interested in what you were reading. Mrs. Bishop didn't want me to pay for the things I'd dropped. But I wanted to."

Zan thought of her wages as a schoolgirl helper back in 1929. She had been so proud that not only was she going to school, but also she was going to earn two dollars a week, every week. He didn't know how much six crystal glasses cost, but they sounded pretty important.

He swallowed twice before he managed to say, "Two books of my own. That's pretty nice, Chicken."

At hearing him call her his favorite name, Chicken, she smiled, then looked away, and finally said, "The fire needs a stick, don't you think, Zan?"

He went over, raked and poked at the fire, putting a stick on it with great care. He straightened up, said casually, "How's Gramp."

"Furious. And wonderful. Thin as a string, now, and still bold as a blue jay. He's suing, or trying to sue, road contractors, the county, the state. I think he means to sue the President. He intends to live to see this road dumped back into the ocean."

Zan said, "But the road's already around Buzzard Point. How come

Gramp let that to happen?"

Lara shrugged. "What could he do? It was condemned, appraised, taken by the government. Gramp took the money for it, too. Scared me when I heard that. I think now he's up to something worse than shooting too close to the road builders."

Zan's eyebrows shot up, but he broke into a slow grin as he said, "Well, the old buzzard. Did he really shoot at them?"

Lara made a rueful face. "Of course, he did. Twice. The first time was passed off as an accident; no one wants to fight a man that's nearly a hundred! But he wasn't satisfied with his luck. He nicked a boot the second time, got hauled into justice court. That suited him fine. Gave him another chance to speak his piece about the road. He said plenty, and paid plenty with an extra fine for being contemptuous. But he's been too quiet, ever since. I hope he keeps out of trouble, but his being quiet bothers me."

"He'll be thinking up something, all right. I'll go up and see him soon." He took a quick look around the room, and said, "I'll get my blankets and shove off now, Lara."

She lit a candle, opened the new door to the north and he could see the door opened into a tin-lined storeroom.

"Come hold this lid up, will you Zan?"

He followed her in, braced open the lid of a big tin-lined wooden chest while Lara found the blankets and a box of kitchenware.

"Neat," he said, as he picked up the blankets. "A whole box lined with tin. Keeps out the rats, and mice, too, I guess."

She nodded. When the chest was closed she followed Zan to the door, urging, "Come up for breakfast. I have it at seven, but I'll see that it's earlier tomorrow so we can have a chance to talk before this teacher has to get to work."

"That's kind of you," he said, "but I got stuff along with me and I'll enjoy a campfire again. Been a long time."

"Yes, hasn't it?" She had agreed so charmingly that Zan was completely unprepared for the storm that followed. "I know what I'm doing. I can take care of myself," she said. Her eyes were bright black coals, her body taut with anger as she said, "Don't think you're the first man that's had coffee with me after midnight, or that you'll be the last. I won't have you treat me as though I were a baby. Good night."

She started to close the door but he put his foot on the sill and she couldn't bring herself to shutting the door on his foot.

His face was almost expressionless as he leaned against the door-frame and said, "When I was eleven, and you was four years old, more or less, you were showing me the same fierce, feisty little face I just seen. You're still a baby, Chicken."

She was still furious. "You won't come to breakfast because you think it wouldn't look nice for a teacher to have a man around."

"You got me all wrong, Lara. Sure, a man for breakfast would be fine for you, lucky for him. But how'd it look to all the old jugs that pour gossip all over the Coast?"

She answered, "And do you think I care?" Then she suddenly laughed, said "old jug," as she stepped outside and slipped her arm through his. "I'll walk with you to see your truck. Old jug, that's such a cute way to say 'gossip'. Maybe I'd better be the one to warn you that your sister Maria's a real old jug—a big one filled with lots of gossip. She certainly hopes for the worst about everyone."

"Poor Maria, she never did have much fun." Zan's thoughts went back to the fancy brass bead with brass knobs. Maria must have spent almost as imprisoned a life as he had. "She didn't marry?"

"Maria?" Lara's voice rose in astonishment. "Maria couldn't bring herself to marry anything as common as a man. Now, go on, call me an old jug, I've got it coming."

They were at his car. "Well, suppose I'll say good night, little pitcher, and let it go at that?"

Lara answered gaily, "No, I'll be a jug or nothing! Well, good night, Zan. Come share dinner with me tomorrow night, will you?"

He said slowly, "No. I'll go up and see Pa tomorrow. Maybe Aunt Blaze and Stephen, too. And I got a line on a job. Be staying here only a couple of days. But I'll see you when I'm down on the Coast again. Thanks for the coffee."

As though she had some trouble forming the words, she said slowly, sounding sad, "Yes, of course. Do that, Zan. Good night."

She went rapidly back into the house but she closed the door slowly behind her. Zan got in his truck, started the engine.

As he put the truck in gear, he looked back and had one glimpse of Lara blowing out a lamp.

XI

It was still dark when Zan woke but he knew the time was exactly fifteen minutes of five. For an instant he thought he was still in San Quentin, and he must hurry to make the breakfast food line by five or miss getting any food.

His hair was damp with fog; the tarpaulin over his bed had shed little runnels of water as he sat up. The Creek was chuckling over the dark rocks as he sank back into his warm blankets.

A man should have a lazy five minutes, listening to the talk of his own creek, when he'd been those many years in prison without that privilege. Listening to creek talk, after years of hearing mostly prison talk of filth and hate, seemed like listening to a pretty group of little girls walking to school.

School. Teacher. Lara. No, let it alone. Teachers teach. Preachers preach. Convicts are convicts. Not even the prettiest teacher can find a way to say "convict" so it sounds good.

He was out of his blankets before the time the line-up would be formed back in prison. He wanted to keep busy, stop thinking. Find the matches, gather up some stuff that would burn, and give him enough light to pick some dead wood out of the willows. The dry papers wrapped around things he had bought in Monterey would do right well.

By the time he got a fire going that was large enough to give light to see by, he was thinking of bacon and coffee. And by the time he was turning hot cakes, he was singing, once more happy to be flipping a pan of cakes. He'd hunted out the white enamel plate with its matching cup and was pouring coffee before he heard the words he was singing:

"Eyes like the morning star, cheek like a rose,
Lara was a pretty girl, God Almighty knows—"

He stopped singing. He might as well face it. There was nothing for him to do but to keep away from Lara. She thought she loved him, but she was held to him first by her child's memory, and now by a girl's need for being in love.

Marriage with anyone was not for him. It was no fair deal to any woman to be pointed out as the wife of an ex-convict. Children growing up, going to school, wouldn't get much of a break, having a jailbird father. He'd have to go it alone, remembering that work was a good companion.

His own ranch was another of the things he was going to do without for a long time.

He cleaned up every trace of his having made camp. Packed his stuff back in the truck and drove out onto the road.

Then he stopped his engine. It certainly would be no more than neighborly to go cut some wood for Lara, take her to wherever she had her school, instead of driving off, leaving her to walk.

He spoke to himself angrily, "You damned fool." He said, "you know what you got to do."

The car moved north through a dark and silent world until he came to Anderson Landing. It was a prison, all right. He saw the lights, smelled the coffee, and wondered if they had a line-up, too.

The old man was hurrying toward the bridge with a lantern.

This time he said, "Morning, Mr. Allan. You're out early. Had breakfast?"

"Yes, I did. I'm the early bird, this time. Ought to find some worms today, I guess."

The man laughed. "The salmon's running up the Creeks now," he said. "Don't know if they take worms."

Zan smiled, shifted gears and drove up the hill, off the detour.

As he crept cautiously around the narrow footing that skirted Buzzard Point, he had a deep satisfaction in remembering that his descent on a rope through the fog in 1929, was at least a small part of his being able to drive this stretch of road. That was a long time ago, for him. But only a minute of time for something as big and long lasting as this road would be.

He must keep that in mind on his new job. Nothing that amounts to much gets done in a hurry.

He rounded the point and stopped the car. He'd wait here until there was a bit of daylight. Since there was a road to his cabin, there might be a road up to Uncle Stephen's place. He decided that even if there was a road, he still wanted to make his first trip up home by the Old Trail. A trail changed so little, years made no difference. The same stumps, with the same moss and ferns growing on them, would lean out toward the trail. The redwood would seem completely unchanged. The well-remembered boulders would be the same color and shape.

While he was on the trail, climbing slowly up the mountain, he could forget the years. Everything was the same color and shape as the last time fate led him up this trail. What a simple child he had been, being certain that a twenty-first birthday would magically change him into a man.

When dawn came Zan had trouble in finding the Old Trail. Overcast from the road had so changed the look of the place where the trail used to take off, that Zan passed the entrance a couple of times before he realized that a new entrance would have had to be made farther north than where the old trail used to start.

In good daylight, now, he easily found the new part of the trail. He went back to his truck, drove along the road looking for a place wide enough to park so it would be off the road, out of the way. That done, he locked his truck and hurried to get out on the trail.

A few wild blue irises, a spray of wild pink currant and one early robin greeted his homesick eyes even before he had gotten onto the Old Trail itself. It seemed steeper than he remembered, and he was glad to linger and look at the few yellow violets, and the few white ones growing on sheltered banks a little higher up the mountain. Every step up the trail was one step back toward winter, and a period of late blooming growth. Soon he had left the lush growth of the lower Coast behind as he climbed the steep trail to the high country. Now and again he stopped to rest a spell, and enjoyed the clean smell of the early morning air, now almost winter sharp.

The Creek was roaring full, sometimes spilling over its banks, so he knew it had been a winter of good rain. The high pastures would already be green with new grasses.

Blaze had written of his cattle. He'd like to see them. If it had not been for his complication with Lara—oh, hell, he was making the complication himself. Was no reason why he couldn't go to see her in a friendly way. It would look queer if he didn't go to look at his own stock.

But he knew he wouldn't go, so just forget it.

He sat on a log by the creek, looking sullenly at a little waterfall, bright with white water. All the white water in the world couldn't wash out the filthy things and perverse people he had lived among as part of his daily life in prison. These dark old rocks were dark and old when his great grandfather came into this country, and were no darker and no older than he felt since he had steered his life into darkness in order to keep another darkness away from his own kin. He had made that choice in the young strength of his innocence and ignorance.

He felt better as he started climbing, again certain that with all he knew now of ugliness and misery, he would make the same choice again, if it was between hurt for one Allan, or hurt for the whole Allan tribe.

He paused at his Uncle Martin's gate, stood looking at the few shrubs and trees that remained of Tena's garden. The house looked as thought it had been deserted for a long time, and it seemed much smaller than he remembered.

The gate sagged and part of the pantry roof had blown off. The horse tie under the big oak had fallen and been lying on the ground for a long time.

More than anything else, the Allan tree convinced Zan that his Uncle Martin had not been at this ranch for years. The garden spoke of the absence of Aunt Tena, but the tree, with all its branches still cluttering the house yard, told him Martin Allan had abandoned his ranch. Not even Martin, grown portly and prosperous, could get so far from the pattern of his early years as to let good oak wood firewood lie rotting, not twenty feet from the wood shed.

Zan turned away from the gate, thinking of Tilli in a white dress with blue ribbons fluttering, pouring lemonade on a hot summer afternoon. He walked on slowly, thinking it would be best not to ask about Tilli.

He climbed an open slope slowly, thinking of Rima, the shy, lovely wood-spirit he had read about in *Green Mansions*. Now, there was a girl! Rima had been a living person to him, his first love. How young he had been at twenty-one, brooding over how he could get out of prison, go to South Africa and find Rima!

The sharp barking of a dog brought his thoughts back from his South African romance fantasy. He called softly to an elderly black and white shepherd dog that was coming down the trail a bit stiffly.

"Here, Bottle. Come on, Bottle."

The dog stopped, stood still, watching him; he stopped barking and began to wag his tail slightly. Perhaps his name was "Bottle," but Zan doubted it. Both Maria and his grandfather had been put out by little Lara's choice of Bottle as a name for the shepherd pup Gramp had gotten when she was about three years old.

The dog smelled the hand Zan offered for inspection, then wagged and submitted to a pat on the head. He fell in behind and followed Zan the rest of the way to Zan's old family home.

His father was sitting on his bench by the well house, his back turned, facing the Canyon.

Zan's feet crunched on the gravel of the trail but his father did not look around. Zan wondered if he had become hard of hearing. The dog trotted ahead, shoved his nose under his father's relaxed fingers that were trailing below the bench level. His fingers grasped the dog's ear gently, slipped down on his head, and closed fondly on the thick ruff. "Where you been, Sheppy?"

Zan said, "He walked me home, Pa. But I called him Bottle."

His father got to his feet, stood bracing himself by a cane that had been leaning against his knee, and peered at Zan, his eyes startled, his mouth quivering.

"You ain't Zan," he said. "No. Not my boy. Zan's just a young'n."

Zan answered, "But it's been some time, Father. It's me, Zan. Are you all right? Where's Maria?"

"Zan, eh? You don't mean it." He dropped back on the bench and studied Zan's face intently. "Yes, by God it is! You look too much like my Pa not to be one of us. Maria's gone this morning, thank the Lord. Good thing you come home; that girl's gone potty. Nothing but religion and stinginess out of her from hell to breakfast. Turned me clear against it, that's what she's done. How do you feel about scripture, son?"

Zan laughed, sat down on the bench beside his father. "Well, I'm not sure now of hellfire and eternal damnation, as I was brought up to be. A good sermon is a fine thing. I heard some good ones, as well as a lot of stupid cruel things said under the name of religion while I was in prison."

There, he'd done it; said "prison" straight out and his father hadn't even noticed it. He'd come home.

His father was poking at the toe of his boot with his stick and Zan saw it must be a habit. The toe of the right shoe was a lot more worn than the left one.

His father stopped poking his shoe, gave him his attention again, saying, "High time you come home, Zan. I can use another hand with the chores, and having another man to cook for, might take Maria's mind off tending to too much of God's business. I come to think it's plumb dangerous to get too much religion. Maria ain't speaking to me, right now, 'cause I up an' told her getting drunk on religion was no better'n getting drunk on whiskey."

Zan said, "You're using a cane, Pa. Is it rheumatism, or did you get hurt?"

"You over here to see an Allan with rheumatics? You didn't. No, I got smart. Maria was dingdonging at me all the time, so to plague her I put a saddle on that colt I'd been gentling for quite a spell. Damned if she wasn't still too frisky for me and threw me a good one, broke a leg bone real good."

"Tony come over from Jolon, brought the doctor, and broke the colt, got us the winter's wood. Him and Lola's got quite a family now, five or six, I forgot. Maria's again' 'em all. I guess you know Tony married Lola after she divorced that traveling man? Good thing, too. Not the kind of girl ever shoulda married a man that's gone from home part of the time. Tony's smart. He put the kids with his Aunt Carmen and brought Lola along over here. Guess they'll be having a new one on the way about now."

"So Tony finally got what he wanted. That's good."

"Yup. An' he still wants it. That's even better."

Zan nodded. "Yes. Tony's lucky." He thought for a minute and then said, "I was planning to go up to Stephen's house, see the folks. How you fixed for horses now, Pa? How about you riding up with me? You're too good a company to leave."

His father brightened. "You think so? That's like your mother, boy, saying a thing like that. Maybe Maria's been happier if your mother could have stayed longer with us. I got the horses all right, but I can't ride till the damned leg gets over its crankiness. You stay away from the Janson's today."

Zan looked startled. "What's wrong with them?"

194

The old man sniffed. "Maria's up there. They won't be fit company for an octopus by the time she's through savin' all of 'em. Good God, she's got a face, to go up there after what she did to Kari. Nice little girl young Kari was. She sure was."

Zan wondered about Kari, but his father seemed to be getting tired and excited. He let it go. "Suppose I go in and see what I can scare up to eat, Pa? How's that sound to you?"

"Good idea, fine. Maria left me a snack, covered up on the table, but seems I don't have much relish lately. You was always handy around a stove, yes, that's right. I remember you was."

Inside the house the checker box lay exactly where it was when Zan left. It seemed like a painfully clean kitchen, but not very friendly. The fact that there was no dust on the checker box didn't mean it was being used. There was no speck of dust anywhere. Maria always thought checkers were a waste of time. He doubted that she would play a game with her father. The box had most likely not been opened in the last seven years.

A very worn and mended napkin on the table sheltered one thin sandwich. Zan looked at it angrily, and then made for the pantry. After one look inside the fully laden storehouse, he came back, took the plate to the back porch, scraped the sandwich into the pail that held scraps for the chickens.

He skimmed the top milk from a large milk pan to fill two mugs, and put them on the table. Then he built up a quick fire with small wood, and made toast, scrambled eggs, then opened a jar of mixed quince and applesauce.

He was pouring the sauce out into a squat brown crockery dish when his father came into the kitchen.

The older man said, laughing nervously, "Maria'll start crackling when she finds you been into them eggs." He pulled back the bench, laid his stick across the end of the table, and slowly edged himself into his place at the table.

Zan set the empty glass jar down on the worktable, looked around at his father and asked, "Nothing wrong with the eggs, is there? They're as fresh as today. Or is Maria saving them to set a hen?"

"Hell, no. Maria's gone money crazy since that bunch of road workers come in here. She's selling all the milk, all the butter, and every egg she can shake out of a hen. She's wearing herself cranky packing all the stuff down to the road. She grudges even a bit of skim milk I drink. She even lets the skim clabber, makes pot cheese, and then sells it."

Zan chuckled. "That sounds funny, but it's bad. Say, we're drinking more than half-cream, now. What'll she think of that?"

The old man winked. "Lucky for you she's too Christian to tell you. Boy, these eggs look good. I believe I'm hungry, now."

They were both hungry and ate in easy silence until the food was gone.

"More, Pa?"

The old man shook his head, looked up at the shelf. "How about clearing off dishes and trying a game of checkers. Can't remember when last I had a game; not since young Stephen went to England."

"Cousin Stephen? What's he doing in England?"

Stephen? Say, that boy's got something. Graduated from the University, too; some more chemistry after that. He's got a feel for leather, for tanning. Going on to Russia when he's through in England, over into Persia, too. Seems like they do good leatherwork in a lot of heathen places. Nice boy, Stevie. I miss him. Yes, I do at that."

Zan picked up the dishes, left everything as neat as he'd found it, before he took down the checkerboard.

Zan had learned a bit of chess, during recreation hours in prison, and now found himself awkward at checkers. His father was on his third straight victory, when Maria came in.

Her father said, "Say hello to your brother Zan, girl. He's through at the jail and now he's come home."

Maria looked frightened. "That's not Zan. No one could change that much. How do you know he isn't an escaped convict? I told you it wasn't safe to have those men working without an armed guard." She looked sternly at her brother, and asked, "What you up to, making so free here?"

"It's like Pa says, Maria. I'm free now. I wanted to see you and Pa before I went off to work. You haven't changed in looks one bit, far as I can see."

She glanced at herself in the small round mirror on the kitchen shelf, looked rather pleased as she said, "Well, I've picked up a little weight, I guess, but I've never lost a tooth or found a gray hair yet."

She looked at the empty plate, the napkin folded beside it, "I et with Blaze," she told her father. She hesitated a minute, then asked, "Has he had anything?"

Her father made a triple jump on the checkerboard, grinned at his son, and started to gather up the checkers before he answered Maria.

"Who? Zan? Sure, he et. He got lunch for both of us."

Maria walked into the pantry. When she came out her expression was as black as her skirt. She looked at Zan. "You certainly made yourself to home, I'll say that. Didn't Pa tell you I had customers for my cream and eggs?"

"Yes, he mentioned it; but I knew you wouldn't mind."

Her eyes showed more anger than her voice as she said, "Well, I do mind. I have to. Now my customers will go short. They mightn't mean much to you, being in jail half your life, but the whole Coast, even the strangers that come in to work on the road, feel they can trust me. Now I'll be short on eggs, and I don't know what I'll do."

Her father pushed back the bench, reached for his cane and pointed at Maria saying, "you either go lay an egg, or quit cackling. What you think you're doing, girl? How come you get the idea you own everything around here?"

She looked startled, saying stubbornly, "I feed and take care of the hens. I milk the cows and churn the butter. You want me to work for nothing"?"

Her father answered, "Don't give me that stuff. When the crops are sold, you get your share, same as the rest of us. If you don't want to feed hens or milk cows, get rid of them. Hell, this ranch makes enough so's we can buy our milk and eggs."

He took a deep breath, pushed himself to his feet before he went on, "But as long as anything's feeding on our land, hen, cow, or pig, what they give in the way of food belongs to all of us alike. I'll hear no more about it."

He was trembling. His cane slipped from his hand and it fell on the floor. As he sat down on the bench, he muttered, "Played out, played out. Good for nothin', no more."

Maria picked up the cane, came over and put it in her father's hand, saying anxiously, "You oughtn't to work yourself up like that, Pa. You ain't well, remember that. I'll make you some more sage and parsley herb tea and this time I'll see that you drink it."

The old man said fretfully, "I don't want any of that sort of slop. A

197

good stewed hen, and parsley dumplings will do. If you're bound that parsley's good for a man, I'll take mine with chicken gravy."

Zan said, "I'll go kill a chicken for you, Maria. I'm going to ride up to Uncle Stephen's, but I'll be back for supper, if that's all right with you."

Maria said stiffly, "Well, if Pa's asked you to stay here—"

Zan felt a hot prick of temper but he said only, "I haven't been asked."

Their father put in, "Ask, hell. Why should anyone ask Zan? He belongs here."

Zan felt the same warm rush of love and embarrassment he used to feel when he was a small boy and his father spoke a word of praise for something Zan had done. The family was not given to easy praise, or words of affection. It was taken for granted that a child would do a task well; Allans were not slack or careless. If it was not well done, the child heard about it, and was made to do it over. Any praise was treasured, stored up and remembered.

Zan said, "You better show me which hen you'd rather I killed, Maria."

She said reluctantly, "Yes, I guess so. I got a rooster I was figuring to get rid of."

She followed him out of the room and down to the pens, her voice full of wistful wonder. "You wouldn't believe it, Zan, but them folks working on the road think nothing of paying a dollar for a skinny old white rooster, long as it's plucked and cleaned. They don't want 'em at any price if they have to pick or draw them. A queer lot, these new people are."

"They earn their money easier than we're used to, city people do," he answered, "and they're used to buying everything they need."

"All I know about 'em is, they're a bunch of wasters. Seems like they only work to get money to eat and dance, gamble, and drink hard liquor. They all got more empty bottles in their garbage than anything else, and there used to be a United States law against liquor, too—still is, mind you, for under ager's, least in this county! That road is going to be the ruination of the Coast, that's what it is."

She looked around the chicken run, pointed out a tall, skinny rooster with a deformed leg and said, "I suppose we might as well stew him."

Zan grabbed a plump bird standing beside Maria's choice, wrung its neck before she had time to protest.

Her mouth was a thin line but she kept it closed, followed him to the porch, pointed out an empty pan to put the chicken in.

Zan washed his hands, ran a comb through his hair, and straightened his kerchief before he called to Maria, "I'll be back before six."

Maria didn't answer. He went down to the barn, pick up a halter and went toward the pasture, feeling that time had rolled back, that space and freedom stretched endlessly before him.

It was good to be on a horse, riding the Old Trail winding up through the dark pine trees, along sharp ridges where the madrone trees were already budding. The grass was still small and sparse in this high country and it was good to look down the long ridges so far that the Coast Mountains looked like small hills. It was assuring to see the line of dark green that meant thick grass on the bench lands. Even though the country looked small, way down there, it was a good place to own sixty-four acres. A man could pasture a lot of stock on that rich land.

It was a terrible shock to see that Stephen's great log castle was gone. Where the proudest house on the Coast had once made history because part of it was three stories high, there was now a long, one story log house with a wing facing south, at each end.

He rode forward, looking at the height of the orchard. At the outside edge, the old trees stood tall. Small trees formed the ring close around the new house. By the size of the new orchard trees, Zan judged the fire must have taken out the house about six years ago.

A tall, blond young fellow came out of the saddle room as Zan rode into the barnyard. For a minute Zan stared at him, puzzled. The young fellow stared back in a rather superior way, said distantly, "I'm Allan Janson. Were you looking for my father?"

Zan said, "Yes. And for your mother, too. I'm Zan Allan."

The boy looked up at him for an instant, looked away and said, "They're up at the house."

He went back into the building. Zan got down, tied the horse, loosened the cinch, and walked slowly toward the house. It took him a bit of thinking to figure out that it was not unkindness that made the boy short of speech, but youth and uncertainty of what was the right thing to say.

He felt slightly uncertain of himself as he got near the door. Should he knock? If he did, his Uncle Stephen might think his manners had improved. Stephen always had been a bit overly mannered, to the Coast way of thinking. But Aunt Blaze wasn't born a Janson. She was an Allan through and through.

Zan ran up the two steps, crossed the porch and opened the door. He called, "Aunt Blaze, Uncle Stephen? Are you home? It's Zan."

He heard something drop with a clatter and then the sound of light feet running toward him. Blaze came through the door, stopped.

Her madrone colored hair had streaks of gray, now, and her slenderness had become spare straightness, but he knew he was looking at his Aunt Blaze.

She hesitated, said questioningly, "Zan?"

He nodded, not trusting himself to speak.

"Oh, it is, it is!" She was beside him, her hands warm on his shoulders as she murmured, "What an idiot I am. No sense at all. It's been so long, and I was still looking for a boy! Isn't that crazy of me? You are tall, and broader, but you haven't changed half as much as I have."

He managed a laugh. "Young Allan's the only one that really startled me. He still looks like a youngster. When I rode in, he didn't seem to know who I was, then he seemed not to care."

Blaze looked sad for a minute, her teeth catching at her lip. Then she said, "He is a youngster." She turned her head, said rapidly, "We lost our born Allan the same year you left. We took our second Allan from an orphanage. Oh, Zan, he's such a dear boy, we can't love any of our children more than Allan." She took a deep breath, said, "He's at the shy age now, but he talks a streak when he's around with youngsters. But let's talk about you, forget the problems of children."

"That's what I say, Aunt Blaze, let's forget them." A tall spare man with a thin fringe of gray hair, wearing horn-rimmed glasses, sauntered in, a folded newspaper in his hand.

"Welcome home, Zan. You're looking fine."

His hand was firm, his voice vigorous. Zan made a quick calculation. Uncle Stephen was seventy, Aunt Blaze was sixty-two. It was a frightening thought.

Stephen said, "I heard you come in, Zan, but I thought Blaze ought to have first chance at you. But since she was just chattering, it seemed fair enough to break in."

"Now, Stephen—"

Blaze did manage to get a note of protest into her voice, but Zan saw how her eyes lighted, meeting her husband's glance.

Stephen said, "Let's get some rum. How about some of that smoked salmon and a few kickshaws? Do you suppose Christine will quit if you ask her to fix up a tray for us?"

"Certainly not. I'll help Christine get the things together. You two sit down and get cozy, I'll be right back."

Zan followed his uncle to a wide, low couch that faced a great single pane of glass, stretching from floor to ceiling and giving a wonderful view of the mountains and Coast. The rug was deep, the furniture dark and solid, giving the room an air of both age and comfort.

"I guess this is even a better house than the old one," Zan said. "It was a shock, though, not to see the house I was looking to see."

Stephen shrugged, opened and closed his hands. "A small trash fire, a sudden wind. You know how it goes. It was a hard loss, the children all growing up in it. And I hated to lose most of that first little orchard Blaze and I planted early on. But when a thing happens, well, it's happened."

Zan looked at the view silently. He, too, knew that when a thing happens, it happens.

"Must have been a job packing that window up here," he said.

"Not as much as you'd think." Stephen laughed as he said, "We got a road up to this house, Zan."

"I didn't see a sign of it, coming over."

Blaze came in, set down on the table in front of them a small tray holding a squat stone bottle, sugar cubes, a pitcher with hot water, some cut lemons and glasses. She smiled at Zan and said, "We hid the road from father. Put it down the north Canyon, and the garage on the north side of the barn. And I wouldn't take anything for it, now that we've got it."

"Must have been a big job, wasn't it?" Zan asked.

"Not bad," Stephen answered. "After the fire we had to build a direct trail to the road, to pack in stuff to build with. We kept widening it here and there and, at last, Blaze gave in, said I'd better hire one of what she calls 'The Monsters,' and make a real road."

Blaze was mixing lemon, sugar, and hot water in the thick glasses.

Zan watched her deft hands for a minute before he murmured, "What monster, Aunt Blaze?"

Handing a glass to Stephen, another to Zan, she tipped her head to one side, and said "Those iron bulldozer things that eat mountains. You never saw such monsters. Honestly, they can peel a mile of road off a mountain almost as quickly as I can peel an orange. Times are certainly changing, Zan, even down here. Can you believe we've got an automatic ice box, a gas stove, constant hot water, all sorts of unbelievable things?"

"I saw some of them in the prison, Aunt Blaze. But they run by electricity. You haven't got that, have you?"

She answered, "No, it's bottled gas. I don't know how it works, but it does, and that's what I'm interested in."

Stephen grumbled, "I'm interested in that salmon. Did you tell Christine to bring it in?"

Blaze said soothingly, "Drink your toddy, dear. She'll be along with it. You're not drinking yours, Zan. Don't you like hot rum?"

Zan thought he felt as young and confused as young Allan had been out at the barn, and he was reluctant to tell the simple truth. But he plunged in. "I don't know. I've never tasted any sort of liquor. Remember how Gramp made all us boys promise we'd neither smoke or drink till we were older?"

Stephen chuckled. "That's after he softened up. You should have heard him on that Devil's Brew, when I was a young fellow!"

They all laughed. Zan tasted his punch. "It's good," he said.
Blaze and Stephen picked up their glasses, held them toward him for an instant, murmuring the old Coast toast:

"Kindness."

Zan answered, "Kindness."

Then he said, "I see I shouldn't have tasted it ahead to the rest, should I? They didn't serve wine with meals up in San Quentin. Not that there wasn't some to be had, even up there. But I was the good boy, trying to keep the rules, keep out of trouble, get home."

He raised his shoulder, made a face and said "And I got home!"
"Poor lambie," Blaze murmured. "It was tough. But anyway, you are home, and you're still young."

Zan thanked them for the Christmas letter and gifts, told about buying his truck, what he had learned about the family from Lara and his father.

"I guess I'm about caught up on the folks now, except for Avery and Margaret. How are they?"

The looked amazed, both asking at once, "Didn't anyone tell you about Margaret and Avery?"

Zan set down his glass carefully before he asked, "What happened to them?"

"It's perfectly wonderful," Blaze said, excitedly. "You remember Gramp was so sick when you were leaving to Salinas? He took a bad turn before we could get home. He was out of his head. Well, he tried to get into my old room to find me, and he fell as he opened the door. Avery was out, doing his chores, and there was bedfast Margaret, looking down on the floor at Grampa, at what she thought was a dying man."

Stephen cut in, "And bedfast as she was, Margaret climbed out of bed, and real fast got her smelling salts, had Gramp sitting up, though still on the floor, and when Avery came into the kitchen with an armful of wood, he heard Margaret calling."

Stephen threw back his head, enjoying his own laughter. "No one ever told us, but my guess is that when Avery got Gramp safe back into his own bed, he came back, got Margaret in her bed, and climbed in with her."

"Now, Stephen," Blaze protested.

Stephen grinned. "I'm too old to believe in miracles," he said. "However it came about, their young baby Avery has his birthdays on the first of August, and I can count months. Anyway, he's a swell kid, Zan, and the pride of his old grandfather's life."

Zan shook his head wonderingly, "I can believe in miracles," he said, "when I hear anything so wonderful. How's Margaret now?"

Positively blooming," Blaze answered. "I don't know if you remember, Zan, but even the old doctor used to say that most of what ailed her was shock and fear. Psychiatrists now a days would say it was some deeply hidden guilt sense. You know—Avery shy and awkward, Maria, shy and virginal; and then to have a building tremble from an earthquake and come tumbling into their bridal bed could have caused some of the problem. Women do take a lot of blame to themselves, you know. I wouldn't be surprised if Margaret had felt she and Avery were directly responsible for the quake itself"

Zan found his hand unsteady as he reached for his glass, drained it. He was fascinated by the theory Blaze had advanced, stunned to hear her voice in it. It seemed amazing that she would say such things to anyone,

203

even her husband.

He asked, "Are they still living with Gramp?"

Stephen said, "Sure. And Margaret can have any newfangled gadget she wants—pressure cooker, a fancy washing machine with a gasoline motor—"

"That's nothing," Blaze laughed. "Zan, there's a grand piano at the home place. Gramp got it for Avery's twenty-fifth anniversary, but between us, it's because little Avery was so crazy about the piano at the school."

Zan drew a long breath. "Oh, stop this, it's too much," he protested.

Piano at the home place, piano at the school. Maybe it's this drink, but I feel dizzy. Now I can believe anything. Did Gramp have the piano hauled up on *his* new road?"

Blaze made a nose at him. "You know better than that. He still hates the road, of course. Though I do think he gets some fun out of it when he can find a big, loose rock leaning over the edge, so's he can nudge it and roll it down onto the road."

Zan thought for a minute, and then asked, "Is he still working?"

Stephen answered, "He takes most things easy, now. Does a few chores. And he's still fencing Buzzard pasture. That job is all his, won't let anyone help him. Anyway, it keeps the old boy out of mischief."

"Father's health is wonderful," Blaze said. "I believe he sees and hears better now than he did at seventy, or eighty. Sometimes he seems forgetful. He still asks why Tena and Martin don't come down. Neither of them have been back since they were divorced."

"Divorced? Martin and Tena?"

Blaze nodded. "Yes. I know. They were together for such a long time."

She continued, "Tilli wanted to get into the movies, but not a bit more than Tena wanted her to. Tena went with her to Hollywood, stayed there to look after her. I guess she needed some looking after; so pretty, but not a lick of sense. Anyway, Martin got tired of living alone. He divorced Tena for desertion, and he married again, quite a young woman. Poor Tena. She was so crazy to get Tilli into pictures."

Zan said, "We got to see a few movies, up there in prison, but I'm sure I never saw Tilli in one."

Stephen shrugged, "I'm sure you didn't. Tilli tried, God knows.

Guess she played up to everything but the camera. Got more mink coats than close-ups."

Blaze said, "Now Stephen. Tilli did get a few parts, you know she did. It looked like she was starting to get better ones, until she broke down, lost her child and then lost the movie parts."

Zan asked, "Has she been back here any?"

Stephen answered, "Once. Right after the talking pictures were getting a good start. Had a nervous breakdown—you know, not enough sleep, too much to drink, and trying to keep going on Hollywood pills. She had some sort of row with Gramp."

Blaze said, "I don't see why you go into all that."

Stephen chuckled. "Tilli's getting her third divorce, right now. She's tried American money, Latin charm and a French title so far."

Blaze said gravely, "Well, she's managed all that part of her life very well, considering. No scandals in any of her divorces."

Zan felt they were both watching him. He couldn't think of anything to say and was glad to see a rather vague looking, middle-aged woman come in with a laden tray. She put it down by Blaze, and said, "Pleased to meet you, I'm sure," and hurried away.

Stephen started putting smoked salmon and rye bread sandwiches together, handing them around on plates as Blaze poured coffee.

When everyone finished their sandwiches and Zan's cup was empty, he put it on the tray, stood up, saying, "Those Christmas letters waiting—well, I got no words. You know how it is; I'll never forget it. I'm having supper with Pa and Maria, so I got to shove off. And I guess I'll not be seeing you for a spell. Dariel Beeson's got a job for me on Boulder Dam."

Blaze said, "Oh, that's fine, Zan. I'm so glad for you. You won't stay away too long, will you?"

"No. I belong here. I'm coming back but I got to try myself against some big job first. Was what I always wanted. And I got to find out about people and places, so I'll know this is the place I can't get along without."

Blaze said, "Mr. Beeson's a good friend to you, I know. But you must be sure to see Lara. She's as much our family as any of us. Did you see her?"

Zan fumbled, hoping Aunt Blaze was not going to ask much about his visit with Lara. "I already saw her. I came late, and didn't stay long. It was near midnight. I had no idea she was there."

Blaze said, "Oh dear, men can be so stupid. That child has been counting days for a long time—ever since you left, just waiting for her hero to come home. I suppose you said, "You're looking very well, Miss Ramirez." Would be just like an Allan man, come glowering out of prison and glare at the poor little dear."

Zan blinked his eyes at her. "I never got around to the compliments," he said. We got to jawing at each other too quick. A nice little girl like that shouldn't smoke cigarettes. I don't care how many of them do it."

Stephen stood up, stretched. "It's the fashion now, all the girls smoke. What I think you ought to worry about is your Murtagh. Lara's seeing too much of that guy. He's very popular with the girls, all the girls, but there's something flashing and tricky about him, to my thinking. I don't trust him, especially with Lara."

Zan said, "Murtagh? I don't seem to—wait a minute. He was chasing Lara, the day of the Coroner's inquest. Yes, and she was mad at me because I made him leave her alone. That kid, huh? So he's back here?"

"Very much back here," Blaze said. "He's living in one of that little group of houses close to the school. Lara has been planning to take one of those houses as soon as the married engineer, living in it now, moves out. And Mr. Murtagh has offered his truck to move her in, and was delighted to do it, too."

"I got a truck."

Zan waited for reactions to that bombshell, but none came. Blaze glanced at the clock. "School's out," she said. It's three. I expect Lara is riding down to your place right now in his truck and will probably move out this afternoon."

Zan did not think so, but he kept that to himself. He said, "Well, I'm staying with Pa for a day or so. Too bad if she leaves the house on my account. She's done a lot for it, got herself fixed nice there."

"She was fixing it for your comfort," Blaze said drily. "Lara always had taken a lot of pleasure out of anything she could do for you, Zan."

"I see." Zan hesitated for a minute, and then said, "I'm glad you told me. She was such a little tyke, you know. I forgot this grown woman is Lara, even started thinking about her like I would a stranger."

Zan started to leave, but decided it would seem strange if he didn't ask after Kari. "Pa was telling me Stephen was in England, doing fine. He started to tell me something about the rest, but right then Maria come in, full of business. We never got to Kari. How is she?"

Stephen and Blaze exchanged a quick glance. Then Blaze said, slowly, as though she were choosing her words, "Kari's married, has two children. She's living out in the Mohave, on a desert ranch. She's so busy she hardly ever writes, much less gets home to see us."

Stephen said bitterly, "The whole truth is, Kari married a good-for-nothing. He was a cat skinner, here on the road, got fired. Drunk on the job. He's a drinker."

Blaze walked over to the window, stood close to it, her back turned, as Zan said, feeling he must say something, "Maybe it will work out, Uncle Stephen. Kari must think so."

Blaze turned quickly, wiping tears from her face. "She got into it, and she's as stubborn as her grandfather. She'd rather die than admit a mistake. Roy can be attractive, I know that. But Maria, with her prayers, her lectures on being talked about, her prophesies of evil to come if Kari didn't mend her way—Oh, Zan. Kari was such a sweet youngster. The more Maria howled calamity, the more certain my poor baby daughter was that it was her job in life to save Roy."

Blaze drew a long breath, let it out and shrugged her shoulders. "I know it's Kari's life, and it's her right to make a choice. I wish I didn't feel it was all so hopeless."

Zan said, "She'll make something of it, I bet she will. Isn't like she was the sort that picks up something, sets it down, picks up something else, and then reaches back for the first one. Long as she sticks with her choice, settles things in her own way, she'll come out all right. Time spent on getting what we want never did bother any of us Allans. Long as Kari's got children, she's got something to work with."

Stephen said crossly, "Quite a philosopher. I think I'm one, too, till my own child gets off on the wrong track."

Zan said, "Yes, the other fellow's troubles are always easy to fix up. Didn't work so good for me on my own, either."

He started toward the door and they followed. Zan said, "*Adios*," and left them standing together on the entrance porch.

There was no sound from his adopted cousin Allan anywhere around the barns. Zan saddled the brown horse, rode off toward his home, feeling that Kari and her drunken cat skinner were at least together in their youth. He wondered if, ten years from now, he would still feel as empty and at loose ends as he felt today.

He was very glib with his advice about Kari sticking to her choice, making something of her life. He knew he had done the only thing that was possible for him to do long ago when he protected Tilli, when he made his choice, but right now, even in the face of freedom, it seemed a long, lonely trail he'd put himself on.

He had no youth left. When he was twenty-one he should have done things he could look back on, such as a settled ranch, a comforting wife, children growing…

The fitful wind of the late February afternoon seemed to be striking a chill through him, but buttoning his jacket against it did not make him any warmer.

He couldn't ask any woman to marry him. His sons would never ride beside him, larking and full of spring as young colts.

"You damned fool," he told himself. "How'd you like to be riding toward another prison stretch?"

With a short laugh, he straightened up, tightened his legs against the brown horse's ribs. The horse lengthened his step.

Right this minute he was riding toward a lighted house, a door that would open to him, a father who would welcome him, share food, fire, a game of checkers. A father who would take comfort that a man of his house once more slept in freedom under the home roof.

XII

After three days with his father and Maria, Zan felt restless. He began to think that if Maria stopped the checker game once more to read dire prophecies from the Book of Revelations, tying them all up to the new road, and to the wastrels who had come into the Big Sur to work on the road, he'd say something he'd be sorry for.

It was mid-morning when he followed his father down to the wood lot, cut and stacked several racks of wood, and then sat down on one of the logs to help his father look over the country.

The slide on Stony Peak was another thing that seemed a little smaller than it had looked when he was a boy. Otherwise, the great silent country lay in the same folds it had held since man's eyes first saw it. Along the living streams through every deep valley, the thick stands of darkly green redwoods seen from far away still looked like toy trees.

It was all more lovely than even his most aching memories had pictured it, and yet—

Zan turned to his father. "You remember the last time I had supper with you, Pa? Maria had the furniture new then, and I'd come up from the Coast for the first time after I'd left home. You remember that night?"

His father nodded.

Zan said, "You told me then that there's no going back. I remember your words. You said, 'the place hasn't changed, but you have!' You remember saying that?"

His father nodded again, and his faded eyes brightened as though taking on a bit of color from the grayish blue of the winter sky.

After a minute he said, "It wasn't the country to hold you here, Zan. You got a lot of young life to catch up on, and you'll not do it here. Light out whenever the notion takes you. Don't pay no mind to Maria. If she'd start praying for a widower with a few feisty kids to house break, Maria'd be on the right track of her with her own salvation."

Zan laughed. "I'll go down to the Coast this morning, Pa. I left my truck parked down there, and I'd like to get working again."

His father said, "You got no need to work for wages, Zan. Me and Tony agreed your share ought to be laid by for you each year, so you'd have a stake to get yourself started. It's not much, but a little every year piles up. It's in that tobacco box on the shelf by the checkers."

Zan protested, "I haven't done a thing to earn it."

"That's right," his father agreed cheerfully. "You haven't. You just happened to be borned here, Boy. And what the place makes goes out to each. Share and share alike. Tony isn't earning his, either. He takes it because it's his. Maria and me take our share every month by living here, and take a fair wage ourselves."

Zan swallowed, looked off at the mountain, and nodded his head. After a minute, both men got up, walked back to the house. Zan got his odds and ends together, wrote a little note to Maria, and slipped it into the empty tobacco box with one of the ten-dollar bills he had taken from the box. If she didn't find it soon, she'd find it some day, and he hoped she'd like the note he'd written.

The farewells were brief and casual. Zan strode off down the trail- feeling that now he was moving toward some of that life that his father had been talking about.

Since his truck was pointed the right way, Zan drove the short dis- tance north to where he expected Stephen's private road would come into the main road. He found it, so tucked away and sheltered by a willow growth at the entrance of the Canyon, that a stranger to the Coast would have had a hard time finding it.

Zan backed into the entrance, turn his truck and started driving slowly down toward his own place.

This was his first daylight look at the new road. He admitted to him- self upon seeing the great machine cuts across the face of the mountains, baring hideously raw earth barren, without leaving even a blade of grass, that his horror was stronger in him right now that his amazement and wonder that men, so determined, could really move mountains.

Where Partington Canyon had year 'round been green as spring, there were now great raw cuts, with their loose rocks constantly sliding from the steep mountain slope onto the new road. On the side of the road toward the sea, redwoods that used to tower almost two-hundred feet above the old Trail were half-buried in the welter or rock, earth and giant trees that had been dynamited from the shoulder of the mountain. He knew that with the lower part of the standing trees were covered with so much slough, the giants would quickly die and turn into snags, because they were living things and needed to be able to breathe in the part of the trunk that was close to the ground.

He saw how much mountain had been displaced to make the quarter-mile of the rough, narrow road around Buzzard Point. It was scarcely a one-way road. The whole structure of the Coast would have to shake before man could anchor a full-width road along the cliffs. Much cliff land would need to be dynamited and scraped off the steep mountainsides to make a road wide enough and fit for two cars to pass.

At May Creek there was great activity. On the long flat approach to the Canyon, a fine wide stretch of road that had been built easily across the gentle bench land was filled with steam shovels, bulldozers, trucks and a small army of men with picks and shovels.

All the men and equipment seemed to be heading his way, all urged on by a man in a bright red coat who was carrying a red flag.

Zan pulled off the road, stopped his truck with the idea of watching how modern road building was done.

The men walking were out ahead of the equipment and, at first, to Zan they seemed very much like the men on the old survey gang. Then he noticed that the old man who had twice challenged him at the low bridge over Anderson Creek, was talking with the man. This bunch of men, whether middle-aged or young, either dour-faced or larking like young colts, was all the convict laborers. He had started his car even before he caught a glimpse of Mario Lucca in the middle of the group of convicts. Mario had been a fellow inmate in prison for a few years. Zan did not want Mario to see him while Lucca was still a prisoner and he was now a free man.

The man in the red coat was running now, motioning to Zan to turn into a detour, and shouting, "Step on it unless you want to be caught here for a couple of hours. The blast is going off any time, but you can get through it if you're started before I get a sign to hold the traffic."

Mario Lucca was walking right beside the truck now. He looked in, but his face displayed no more curiosity than one stranger would have for another. Zan bent over his shift lever until Lucca had passed.

The detour followed the Old Trail down to the stream, forded it, and then the steep south slope took all the power in Zan's truck to climb out of the canyon to where he pulled out, looking over the rim. He had not remembered that any of the old trails were that steep. On horseback, the gentle pull out of May Creek was considered an easy bit of trail. Already he was considering the road as needed by cars, not by horses and pack trains.

He stopped at the Canyon's rim and looked back, waiting for the blast.

It seemed so long in coming that Zan felt for his pack of ready-made cigarettes, and looked at it appreciatively before drawing one out and lighting it. The cigarette was almost finished, and he had decided that something had gone wrong with the dynamite charge. He was pinching out the fire from the very short stub when he heard a dull boom

There was not much smoke, not nearly the noise he had expected, but looking across the quarter mile of May Canyon, he saw that the great leaning rock cliff that Allans had ridden out around since Great-grampa's time of 1834, had vanished without smoke or noise.

It was gone. Simply gone.

That particular obstruction around which the trail had been made to accommodate its way to the cliffs way, had never meant anything much to any one of the Allan men but for the occasional rolling of a rock down onto the Trail. The Allan women had loved the point because it's whole craggy side had been covered with maidenhair and print ferns.

Zan wondered at himself. The cliff had suddenly become dear and familiar, now that it had vanished as completely as yesterday had passed. Gone. Forever.

From its place would raise the great pier of a high bridge. Through the years thousands of cars would cross the bridge so swiftly that the people in the cars would scarcely be aware that a bridge was there, much less that men had blasted and toiled to put the pier there so they could cross in safety.

The years had passed so quickly. Once the Coast people of his own generation were gone forever, there would be no one left who would

remember the Coast that was.

In prison he had thought that the noise of the jute mill and the narrowness of the cell, an experience that had endured for years, would forever come between himself and the great silence and space of his own country.

He felt now that the prison years had also gone into the past. He could adjust himself to them more easily than he could to the new world that the road would bring. All the years he had wanted this road, that he had never given a thought to how the country itself would be changed by it. People were to use the road and come easily to the Coast and see the country as he saw it.

He wondered if his grandfather had known how the road would build its own cliffs, create small canyons and even change the mountains into new shapes.

He started the truck. Now he had held his personal burial services for the country as it used to be, and now would set out on his way to live for today instead of yesterday.

The people who would fly by in their cars would never see the small canyons flowered with fresh green ferns. But they would drive back to their crowded cities, taking with them the shapes of the mountains, the picture of a small ranch house etched into a green pocket on the rocky shoulder of a high hill. No part of America now was anything like the country the original Pilgrims had discovered. Only an utter fool would want to put it back the way it was. That's what he'd been lamenting, back there by May Creek. A fine road builder, he was, having such bellyache thoughts.

The flag was down. He drove off, nearing the schoolhouse, noticing as he passed by that the door was shut, school was out, closed. He wondered if he should have stopped, walked up to the Schoolhouse Canyon to see if Lara had moved, if there was anything he could do to help her.

The truck crept ahead slowly, dodging the many rocks, large and small, that had rolled down from the fresh cut slopes above. He thought it was best to keep things behind him, just like the schoolhouse.

He shifted into second as he started down a small draw. The road made a very abrupt turn just before it got to the little spring in the gulch. Zan steered carefully between two boulders that seemed to have very recently rolled down from the new cut that, some day, would be the beginning of a bridge across this canyon. The day the road would be open between Monterey and San Simeon began to seem like a far-off day. It was not only Old Zande Allan against the road. The very country itself: the mountains, the creeks and canyon, and the ever-restless side hills all fought from being disturbed by man and his machines.

He came out of his wondering on the ways of man with mountains, and the way of mountains on man, as he slammed on his brakes.

By the time the car stopped, he was opposite Lara, who had stopped walking, stood by the side of the road, and looking remarkably pretty.

Zan leaned over to unfasten the door on Lara's side, called down, "Jump in, Lara. I'm going the same way you are."

She made a nose at him, but drew herself up onto the high step of the truck, then slid down beside Zan. "You're just about as gallant as you were when I was a child of thirteen."

Zan started the truck, drove along slowly. "Thirteen. That's what you were when I left here. Had to count back and get it right. Remember when I told you I'd be an old man before you would, and how disappointed that made you?"

Lara shook her head. "That's not how I remember it. I was heart-broken because you had always been too old for me to marry."

"Sure. That's how it was. I remember now. You know, you stayed just that age, never grew any older to me all the time I was gone away. I'd be thinking about you, times when I happened to be thinking something that had you in it, and I'd call you 'Chicken,' same as I did when you were two years old."

Lara sounded cross as she said, "Am I supposed to be grateful that sometimes you thought of something that 'had me in it'?"

He looked at her, startled. "I didn't say that to make you mad," Lara. "You're mad because I thought of you as the same little Chicken?"

She shrugged, saying "of course not, silly. I guess I'm out of sorts because my dear little school children were such perfect fiends today. But I'd have regular riots on my hands if they ever got to know that they upset me. I really want to be a good teacher, so I hold my tongue to keep my self-respect, and that way I kept the children's respect."

He said, "So, that's how you do it? Sounds like you are a pretty smart girl—as well as a pretty girl. Bein' growed up's becoming to you, Chicken."

She did not laugh, but he saw the quirk at the corner of her mouth, felt that she was laughing, though she didn't make a sound until she said, seriously "Never mind the pretty speeches, Zan. I'm used to thinking of you as the strong and silent type."

He swung off the curving road that led around the hill and drove up to his house, stopping at the gate. "Here you are," he said.

He stepped out, came around the car and opened the door, but did not offer his hand to help her down. Lara stepped out, started up the trail through the gate, and then turned and asked, "Why don't you come up and stay to supper, Zan, some people are coming over tonight and I'd like you to get to know them. Come along, please do."

He looked uncomfortable, hesitated, and then said, "I'd like to, but the truth is, I'm shy of meeting strangers."

She turned, ran back and slid her arm through his. "I know, Zan. You're like Gramp. Something happened to you, and like a hurt bear you want to hide out and suck a lonely paw to make it heal. But, Zan, you've got a life to live. Meet people. Talk to them. Don't try to hide anything. Just say right out that you've been in prison and then, that's it—there you are. Nothing for them to stare at you about or whisper behind your back."

He said, "Next time, maybe. But not now, Lara. I got to get used to the fact that I can come or go, work or sit and look at work, either way, whatever I feel like doing, 'stead of doing something 'cause the rules make me. Getting used to that is enough for me to catch up on for the next month or so."

She let go of his arm, stepped back and looked at him. "You're not a coward. I know you're not. And don't forget that I know what happened years ago in the cedars. I was there that day, remember, you know I was, even though we've never talked about it. I know you must have loved Tilli very much to allow her not to get punished for what she did—to prevent her from going to prison instead of you. So you took the blame. All by yourself, never told anyone, and you've paid the price with your freedom. But it's over now, it's past and gone. So is Tilli. She's long gone. But you've still got to keep on living, Zan."

When he didn't answer she suddenly turned on him.

"All right. Do whatever you want. It's your life. Goodbye, Zan."

Without pausing or glancing back to soften her words, she strode up the hill toward the house.

Zan stood looking after her. It had never before occurred to him that Lara would think he took the blame for what Tilli had done because she thought he'd loved Tilli.

But he wouldn't say anything now to change Lara's notion that he'd had feelings for Tilli. That would explain everything to everybody: his family, Lara, and any of the neighbors who gave it a thought; it would put his growing into an old bachelor down to a hopeless love for Tilli.

He didn't much like the idea of everyone thinking of him a complete idiot, but after all, what did it matter now?

Nothing he had planned for his life this far had worked out, except that one thing. He had bought into and paid for so dearly—protecting the Allan name, making sure that no scandal had ever touched the name of the Allan women. He had let Tilli get away with murder. He had kept young Lara from being put on the rack of a public trial. And now he'd just been freed from his fear that Lara might ever connect himself with the reason he refused a jury trial and pled guilty to a judge. Yes, give things some time and they worked out!

He looked up at the house and saw the first blue smoke of a new fire coming straight up from the chimney. It looked good.

There was no reason why he shouldn't eat his supper with Lara and her friends. He had served out his time, paid his dues, and had been granted a new start in life.

He sauntered up the trail, knocked softly on the door, calling "Will you let a fellow change his mind, Lara? I'd like to help you get supper, help you eat it, and meet your friends."

She called, "Come on in, you big Oaf. I don't expect you to sing for your supper, but you'll have to earn it."

He opened the door, took off his hat as he stepped inside, and turned instinctively to hang it on the set of deer horns that used to be over the front door for that very purpose.

He felt light-hearted, almost young again, when he saw that the great branching antlers were exactly where he had nailed them up soon after he'd first moved into the house.

"What's the job? I can peel and splice spuds. Do it fast and slice 'em thin, too."

Lara was busy tying on an apron. She made a crisp bow of her apron's wide white organdy strings, then took an apron that was made of blue and white ticking, shaped like a carpenter's apron, from a nail behind the stove and handed it to Zan.

Then she laughed and said, teasingly, "Nice guest you are. Come in and as good as order fried potatoes. The potatoes are not going to be peeled, my fine fellow. They're going to be baked."

"Baked, huh? Well, it's hard to spoil a good potato. I'll try to eat them just the same. But the only reason for planting potatoes and digging them up is so that they can turn up as fried potatoes."

He sighed sadly, and then asked, "Where'll I find some potatoes to wash and pretty up for the oven?"

Lara had a thick madrone cutting board, a knife and a couple of cloves of garlic assembled on the edge of the drain board by the sink. She looked over her shoulder and said, "Large paper sack in a wood box, and to the left of the door as you go in." She picked up the knife, started prying the hard silvery covering off the little garlic clove as Zan, in the pantry, stuck his head back in the door to ask a question.

"How many potatoes, Lara? And how large? There's a lot of small spuds in this sack."

"Keep on digging down and you'll find some large ones. Get six smooth ones, all the same size."

Zan muttered and shifted potatoes around in the bag, picking out six that he thought answered all the directions he'd had.

He piled the potatoes on a thin pie plate and brought them into the kitchen.

Lara looked at them, nodding, "Give them a good bath, use hot water and then use the scrub brush hanging over the sink. Drat this garlic. I don't see why it has to grow a coat so thick it's tough to cut off."

Zan had taken a white enameled kettle from the nail on the wall, filled it with water and let the potatoes soak a spell while he went to see about the trouble with the garlic.

"Give me the knife," Zan said.

He had suspected the knife was dull. Testing the blade with his thumb, he looked horrified. "Knife? This thing? I wouldn't have a dirt hoe with a blade as dull as that. Where's your whet stone?"

Lara glanced at the clock, grumbling, "I haven't got time to have you go into the knife-sharpening side of my life. It's almost five o'clock and I ought to have the sauce cooking already."

Zan said firmly, "Where's that whet stone?"

"Second drawer on the left," Lara answered resignedly.

Zan pulled it open, started poking around in the miscellany, calling out, "Bottle opener, can opener, apple corer, hotcake turner, mixin' spoon, cookie cutters. Say, Lara, you must cook a lot of fancy stuff. But where's the stone?"

"I wish you'd just tend to the potatoes! But if you'll pull out the drawer and stop poking around all that stuff so I'll never find anything, then you'd see the whet stone."

"Sure enough, here it is, and a good stone, too."

Zan came over and took the knife from her hand. He began stroking the blade on the stone, making quick, light strokes along the entire blade, from tip to handle and, after a few seconds, he handed it back.

"There you are. Now I'll fix those potatoes, get 'em in the oven, and then I'll chop up that stuff for you."

He scrubbed the potatoes, piled them on a dish and started toward the oven with them.

Lara looked around, called "Oh, no, Zan. Cut a thick slice off each end. Then dry them on that clean towel and rub some olive oil over

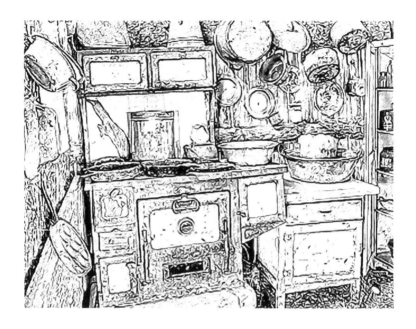

them and sprinkle them good with salt."

He obeyed, but protested as he put them in the oven, "Looks like a waste of salt. It'll all fall off when bakin,' won't it?"

He thought Lara looked like an enchanting child as she told him seriously, "It's the best way to cook potatoes. The skins taste so good. I've learned a lot of new ways of cooking since the men who are working on the road have started bringing their families here to live, that is, when they can find any sort of house for them."

"Looks to me like there were all sorts of new houses on the ridges when I drove out from Monterey."

"Mostly shacks," Lara said. "Not the sort of places where a family should have to live. People need some comfort, some privacy, and a bit of beauty in their lives if they're going to be happy here."

Zan grinned at her. "Is that so?" He asked.

"I always thought all a house was good for was to get out of the weather. There's plenty of beauty right outside if a fellow's got to have it."

Lara laughed. "All right, you old cave man. Suppose you take care of the drinks, next. Get a tray out of the cupboard, and there's a bottle of whiskey, and I guess there's some gin. Anyway, get what there is, and six glasses, and that tall blue glass bottle, that you can fill with water and set the tray over on the table by the bookshelf."

Zan stood still. Why should Lara have hard liquor in a house where she lived alone? Even though prohibition was lifted, it was still illegal to have liquor here. He suddenly remembered that Blaze and Stephen didn't seem to pay any attention to it, either. They had rum. And the bottle had a foreign label on it, Zan remembered. It must have been smuggled into the county as well as bought illegally. But maybe Stephen was still using some liquor he'd stored before the ban, down in his cellar, but that would have been too long ago...

He asked Lara carefully, "How did you get your liquor, from Stephen?"

Lara looked amused, mysterious. "There's ways. Rum-running still goes on in Monterey like it used to everywhere else and—" She shrugged, "You know someone who knows someone, and they tell you how many times to knock on a door so's they'll answer it."

"Good God, Lara! You don't do things like that! You're trying to act smart. I don't like it!"

Lara sighed, closed her eyes for a second. "Zan, this isn't the world you left seven years ago, that world has ended and we're living in a new one."

Zan said, "I've lived with misery and filth in prison, with wrecked lives, and I always kept thinking of the mountains, of the people who had pride in being human. I'm damned if I'll fix up a tray with whiskey and glasses, Lara."

Lara said, "Good heavens! You sound like I felt the day I left the Bishop's house to find my way into the world. Zan, my poor dear, You're so ridiculous, and so sweet. And you make me feel like a decadent old hag—at twenty-one! Shame on you!"

Suddenly she broke into a burst of happy laughter. "Mr. Beeson tells you that you must move along with the world. You tell it to me, and I think you are so wise. Now, here I am telling you to move along with the world, to take the day as it comes."

Zan said angrily, "And you're talking like a half-baked potato. Every man makes his own world. He can go as far as he wants: roads, bridges, telephones and radios, flying machines. But the men that push the new world along come from decency and order."

"And speaking of half-baked potatoes," Lara said smoothly, "You got to put some lilac on the fire. I'll fix the drinks."

Zan went over to the stove, opened the oven door, felt of the potatoes. The he lifted a stove lid, reached in the wood box, filled the firebox with the few pieces left. He went out the back door and filled his arms with redwood limbs, some lilac, and a few chunks of black oak.

By the time he had brought in enough wood to fill the box so the lid would barely shut, Lara was coming out of the storeroom carrying a tray with the liquor, glasses and water pitcher.

Zan said, "Let me take it, Lara. That looks heavy."

Lara kept her hands on it, smiled teasingly at him as she said, "You don't have to drink any of it, but be careful you don't spill it. The kids who are coming to dinner will howl like wolves if they don't get a drink before supper."

"I haven't got anything against a drink," Zan said. "I had a couple of drinks with Uncle Stephen. I just don't like the idea of a young woman, living alone, feeling it's necessary to—Oh, shoot, I don't know what I think. I had a drink with Aunt Blaze, too. Suppose I have one with you?"

Lara said, "A good idea. You pour it, Zan. A light one for me while I get this sauce on the stove."

"What's a light one?"

Lara was already stirring some butter that was bubbling in the frying pan. "A thimbleful of liquor with half a glass of water. That's a light drink."

Zan measured one glass as instructed. Then he considered the bottle and wondered what was a man's drink but didn't want to feel foolish asking Lara so he mixed the opposite proportion of her drink and measured a half glass of whiskey and a quarter glass of water.

He took the glasses over to the stove and waited while Lara finished stirring the chopped garlic in the butter, added some parsley and some finely minced herbs. Zan sniffed appreciatively.

He smelled of the drink as he was about to taste it, wrinkled his nose and handed Lara the 'light drink' glass.

"That stuff you're cookin' smells good, makes me hungry."

He raised his glass to take another sniff. "Your cookin' smells a lot better than this does."

Lara said, "Why not? I made the sauce, and I know what's in it. Heaven only knows who made this liquor, or what's in it, but for sure it's got a bigger kick to it than garlic."

She lifted the glass, looked at him with such sweet innocence that Zan felt dizzy.

"Kindness," she said.

She reached out, made the rim of her glass kiss the rim of his, and he responded huskily, "Kindness, little Chicken."

Lara took a sip, barely tasted her drink, but Zan put his head back and swallowed it down, the entire glass full.

"Hold your breath, Zan. Swallow before you say anything."

Lara's voice was so urgent that Zan obeyed without any question. He took a deep breath, and then suffered.

"Whoof! Ugh! It burns worse'n the swig of kerosene I swallowed at four years old. No wonder you sipped so gingerly. That's as strong as I ever want. The rum up at the Janson's had a good taste, sort of tasted like nutmeg or something."

Lara started to say something but stopped to listen. There was a roaring sound of a motor zooming up the hill, stopping abruptly at the gate, and a loud voice shouting, "Hello, the house! Send out the Saint Bernard, there's a dying man at your gate."

Lara turned to Zan. "That's Johnny," she said. "You meet him at the door with a drink. I've got to keep stirring the sauce right now or it'll burn."

"I'll stir," Zan said.

He took the turner from her hand, started stirring the mixture carefully, but he managed to watch how much whiskey she'd put in the glass.

Lara mixed almost the same amount as he'd poured for himself, saying resignedly, "It's no use trying to give Johnny a gentleman's drink. He can drink a tumbler straight down or take a big swig right out of the bottle and never even blink."

Zan thought that over. Evidently he'd had more than a "gentleman's drink." But it hadn't hurt him, none. In fact, he felt fine, kinda good, even a little happy, and feeling like talking to people.

He looked at the small bit of color from the sunset still touching the edge of the low clouds far out to sea. Pretty. Sure looked pretty. So did Lara. Lara was a very pretty girl, God Almighty knows that she's all right; even he, Zan Allan, knows that much. Spunky little squirrel, too. Pretty house, tasty garlic sauce. Maybe have another bit of drink before she gets back. But where is Lara? Got to stir this stuff or it'll burn. Don't want to get it burned. If a man's got to burn something, let him burn bridges. Sure, all smart people burned their bridges. He put the runner down on the edge of the pan, felt for a cigarette in his pocket, broke off a splinter from the stick of redwood sticks and lit it from the fire in the stove. Then he dropped the charred stick into the garlic and oil mixture in the frying pan.

The heat from the stove seemed to be making him feel dizzy. Funny, the stuff women put up with, and never complain. Never heard a woman grumble because the heat from the cook stove made her feel dizzy. Women were brave. Men were strong. Garlic was strong. Damn hell. The garlic was burning. Where was Lara?

He grabbed the cake turner, dropped it in the wood box, and began to stir the burning garlic with the stick he thought he'd thrown away. Suddenly it occurred to him that it was possible to move the burning pan from the hottest part of the stove. He pulled it back, put the stick in his hand into the firebox of the stove, rescued the turner from the wood box and carried it over to the sink.

Before he washed the turner he drank two large glasses of ice-cold spring water and found them helpful in getting over the dizzy feeling that bothered him when standing over the stove.

The door opened and Lara, smiling, stepped inside, but stopped dramatically, smelling the air. "You wretch," she said. "Zan Allan, I trusted you with a pan of innocent garlic and now it's ruined."

She came over to Zan, leaving a tall, wide-shouldered man with rather small dark eyes and a scar on his jaw, draped against the doorframe.

"What a crime, burning my garlic," Lara said, and took the wood ladle from Zan's hand, saying "go shake hands with Johnny Murtagh. He says he remembers you."

So this was Johnny Murtagh.

Johnny Murtagh detached himself from the doorframe, came across the room, and began to pump Zan's hand with so much vigor that Zan felt embarrassed. He wondered what ailed the man, besides being named Murtagh.

About the time Zan had decided to detach his hand and hide it, Johnny let go abruptly.

"You bet I remember you, guy. You're the fellow that shook the day-lights out of me when I was about thirteen. Only man ever did it. Proud to shake the hand that shook Johnny Murtagh! You remember me?"

"I'm afraid I don't, Zan said. "There was a man here named Murtagh worked for the Greater Western Engineering. But he'd be getting close to sixty by now; yes, he'd be about that. I don't remember that I ever shook him, though."

Lara seemed upset. "Of course you remember Johnny, Zan. You rescued me from the big beast. He was running after me with a rubber snake, out in front of the mess hall, and Aunt Blaze sent you to my rescue. I was awfully mad at you for breaking up my first romance."

Zan said, "Oh, I remember that kid—red-head, with freckles."

He looked at Murtagh, shook his head. "You've gotten to be an awful lot of man in a few years. I'll think twice now before I shake you."

Murtagh grinned. The scar vanished and, for a minute, he looked like an amiable bear. He hooked one big thumb in the little change pocket of his trousers, gestured with the other toward Lara.

"She's the one can do it. Gives a fellow one of those wide-eyed looks and says, "Why Johnny Mur-tak!" Half pint, that's all she is, and she can set a fellow back on his heels with a look."

Lara laughed. "Why, Johnny Murtagh!" She turned to Zan and asked seriously, "I didn't see anything happen to his heels, did you, Zan?"

He said, "I can't spend my time looking at heels."

He felt sober, and out of sorts when Lara and Johnny laughed as though he had told a joke. Lara said, "That will do for both of us; just a pair of heels!"

She was suddenly very busy, flashing in and out of the storeroom, opening the oven, and getting a handful of knives and forks.

Zan stood in the center of the floor feeling useless, out of place. Lara came out of the storeroom with a butcher's paper package and gave it to him.

"Don't you think you could broil a steak over the lilac coals in the cook stove, Zan? It won't take long, the steak is cut paper thin."

"I'll try. Ought to be a thicker cut, though, if you're going to cook it over the coals. It'll be done in five minutes. Better wait till the others get here."

Lara said, "Oh, I forgot to tell you. Johnny said they're not coming.

We'll meet them later at the Mitley's. Annie had to go to town, and Fred drove her in, so they won't be here in time for the dinner, but we'll have fun anyway."

Johnny insisted they have another drink while the steak cooked and the table was set. Zan said, "This time I'll take a light one. I'm new with this stuff.

Lara immediately stopped putting out the silverware and fixed the drinks. She poured two drinks that were smaller than the one he'd fixed for her. The third drink had even less whiskey, which she gave to young Murtagh.

Once more everyone toasted, "Kindness."

Both men helped clear after dinner while Lara disappeared for a few minutes. Murtagh asked about life in the prison and Zan found he didn't resent it. Lara had been right. Admit it, talk about it, and the fear of it became less. But he wondered if the whiskey didn't have something to do with making him talk and laugh about it come easier.

Lara reappeared looking like something a man might dream up

when spring was new and the moon was young. She was wearing the blue skirt, the white blouse with a bow, and a thick sweater embroidered with flowers.

"I'm ready," she said, "Let's go over to the Mitley's."

Johnny walked with Lara and Zan went to his own truck. He kept saying, over their protest, "I might want to leave early. I could, as long as I got my truck."

Johnny said, "That's all right with me. Take anything you want, as long as it isn't Lara! My girl rides with me, see?

Zan said nothing. He was watching Lara. She stood off at one side, her head tipped down, her eyes seeming to see only the white buckle and bow on the slippers she was wearing. But Zan could see that her mouth had an amused quirk at the corner.

Maybe she was waiting to see if he'd make an effort to have her ride in his car. Wondering if all women were like Tilli, he decided that if Lara wanted to play that game, he'd play, but not the card she'd expect."

Murtagh was looking rather belligerent until Zan turned to him, "Well, take good care of my little sister, Johnny, and don't drive too fast. I'll be following you and I'm new at driving."

Without even a glance at Zan, Lara let Johnny help her into his car.

Zan got into his truck, turned on the lights, and saw Lara was leaning against Murtagh's shoulder, lifting her face close to his as he looked down at her, saying something Zan couldn't hear.

Murtagh sped down the narrow road, swung rapidly onto the new highway, and it was all Zan could do to keep up with him. The road was dusty, even though it was still the February wet season. Rocks, turns, dips into unexpected canyons kept Zan's feet and hands busy with the brake and gear levers, but he did not keep his thoughts on the road hazards.

He was wondering if being allowed to vote was what had changed young women so much. It didn't seem to matter if they were six or sixty anymore. They all wore their dresses the same little girl length. And, six or sixty, their hair was cut short. No braids, no pompadours, no twists or puffs. Lara was the only girl he'd seen whose hair touched her shoulders. The rest of them had cut it just below the ear line, and some even chopped it off as short as a man's hair.

This business of living along with the times was not as easy as it used to sound when Mr. Beeson talked about it. A fellow had to do it; he could

226

see that. But, just the same, Zan acknowledged an ache for the days when women's hair was long and men's hair was short, every thing proper and in its place, women and men, the long and short of it.

He recalled the white frills, soft curls and skirts that touched the floor; when he was twenty, these things made women very mysterious creatures to Zan.

It seemed shameless of Lara to be cuddling up to that fellow Murtagh unless that was the only way women nowadays could get men to realize that there was still the softness of women under those short, skimpy skirts. That thought was disturbing. Zan had been sure that Lara all but told him that she loved him, that very first night he saw her when he'd come back to the Coast. If she was trying now to tell Johnny Murtagh the same things. Was she being a deceitful, double-crossing, no-account female and—what was he saying?

He wanted Lara to be married, to be happy, to have children and a real life. So why was he bothered about Lara getting herself a man?

The car ahead of him had stopped. Lara and Murtagh were out of it, standing beside the road by the time Zan pulled to a stop a few feet behind them.

He leaned out his window and called, "This the place?"

The night was dark. He couldn't see a light anywhere. He got out of his car and walked up to the other two.

He said, "The road was so dusty I don't know where we are. Is this where we're going?"

Lara said, "The house is a couple of hundred feet back on a side road and I've been arguing with Johnny. There's hardly any room to park when you drive in, and there'll be a lot of cars.

Johnny picked up a bottle from his car, looked at it, and said, "We ought to kill this one, take in a fresh one."

Lara sounded annoyed. "Why don't you leave one in the car? Take the other down to Mrs. Mitley? Maybe Zan wants another drink now, but I don't."

Zan said, "I've had plenty."

Murtagh put the bottle back into his car, got another one from under the seat and put it into his hip pocked.

"Wait a minute," he said.

He pulled the first bottle back from inside the car and drank till it was empty. He wiped his mouth and said, "Great stuff! Builds a guy up! Now I'm all set to make the girls happy."

Lara tucked her hand under Zan's arm and said, "Then let's go."

Murtagh walked on the other side of Lara and started to take her arm, but she reminded him that they needed a flashlight, so he returned to his car for one.

Zan knew all about flashlights. All prison guards had them.

Flashlights. In prison Zan had thought of himself as better informed than the men around him who took no interest in books. With the help of the prison library, he had explored a lot of strange lands and had learned about times and ways throughout history. Writers sometimes had a way of setting out people so real and alive that, after the lights were put out at nine, he could go right on living in their lives. When the book was finished, if people came to bad things, bad hurts, then a man could go back over the book, figure out how they'd brought those things to themselves by a choice they couldn't help but make. Seeing the whole man, or woman, from the beginning to the end of the book, he could finally figure out how it was that, say, Lord Jim walked out to meet death, or how in *Maria Chapdelaine* she endured her broken heart and chose life.

In the darkness Lara walked silently beside him, lightly touching his arm. Zan realized that he was moving toward an evening as strange to him as any eighteenth century landing on a South Pacific island. He knew how the word "sophistication" looked in print, and knew its written meaning. He had even felt that, sometimes, even he was sophisticated.

In the light of his seven year-old longing to take the guard's flashlight into his own hand, turn it on and off, and see how far the beam would carry. But now, facing to go into a room full of unknown people, he felt like a bashful schoolboy.

The old patterns of the Coast were broken. Coast life was no longer bound by a field and a fence, or a hoe and a bag of potatoes to plant. It had changed forever. Even his own father, back in the hills, sensed the change when he told Zan he had a lot of changes to catch up on.

He tightened his arm against Lara's hand, lengthened his step.

XIII

As Johnny Murtagh opened the cabin door without knocking, Zan's first impressions were of smoke, noise and dim lights. By the time a heavy voice shouted, "Well, come on in if you're coming, and shut the door after you," Zan had things vaguely sorted out.

The smoke came mostly from cigarettes, dim glows winking like fireflies in the dusky log room. A couple of shaded kerosene lamps gave the smoke a blue tinge, and added their odor to the rich, oily smell of meat roasting over an open fire. The noise was a clamor of many voices talking and the sound of a phonograph that was scratching a song with a voice singing, "Ain't we got fun."

Zan murmured in Lara's ear, "The Queen must be playing croquet close by…here comes the Duchess with the pepper."
Lara leaned against him holding her breath, shaking with laughter. She whispered, "Don't Zan. I can't stand it."

A large woman, looking almost square, her red face framed by frizzled brownish-grey hair, waddled toward them with a tin full of red peppers in one hand and basting spoon in the other. She shouted, "Who you got there, Lara?"

It was the same voice that had shouted them to "come in and shut the door."

Lara took her hand affectionately, swung it with a gesture of childlike gaiety as she said, "Mitty, I want you to know Zan Allan," then turned to him and said, "Zan, this is Mrs. Mitley."

Mrs. Mitley extended a thick hand, shook his, saying, "Zan Allan, huh? Never would a guessed it. I was sort of looking for a kid, but you're damn near as old as I am!" laughed, boomingly. Zan thought she was noisy and vulgar but likeable. There was warmth to her, generosity as well

229

as vigor. She was fat, but not lazy. She had muscles like a blacksmith.

"It's good to be here," Zan said.

She was already shuffling away as she shouted, "I guess it's good to be anywhere else, after ten years in the calaboose!"

Zan was startled to hear himself shouting after her, "seven years! And that's plenty long enough."

The voices in the cabin suddenly stopped and the phonograph ending the song and scratched peevishly, but no one bothered to shut it off.

Now Zan could make out about a dozen people sitting around a low table toward the back of the room. He was conscious of heads turning to look at him.

Johnny said, "How's about a drink all around? I'm buying."

A short man with wide shoulders, a full white face and stone gray eyes peering under a low forehead, growled deep in his throat, "Nobody's buying tonight. Throw five bucks into the kitty and the joint's yours. There a turkey on the rack and a whole ham—enough food to feed the whole Coast."

Mrs. Mitley looked up from the turkey she was basting, licked off the spoon and smacked her lips. "We got four cases of real gin. And I mean *real gin*. Ever heard of such a thing? An' Sally's bringin' ice and some pineapple juice to mix up with the gin. How's that for a drink?

Johnny said, "You'd better hide a bottle or two right now, then."

"Sez you." Mom Mitley's grin was friendly as she bore down on him with a lard bucket with a slot in the cover and the word "Kitty" scrawled on top.

There was a soft, rustling noise in the lard pail as she shook it and bent her head to listen. "Feed the poor kitty, Johnny, it's hungry."

Johnny gave her a shove, protesting playfully, "How you think I'm going to get folding money to feed that thing?"

"And wouldn't you be mad if I told you?" She jeered. "But what I know, and don't tell, won't hurt anyone. Feed the kitty."

Zan had been figuring, deciding what to do. Fifteen dollars would buy three feeder calves. But what the hell. Wasn't it spring?

His hand went into his pocket as he stepped over to Mrs. Mitley, reached across Johnny and the money slipped through the slot as he said, "Here's for three of us, Ma'am."

Johnny looked at Zan rather hard but before he could say anything,

Lara had taken Johnny's arm, smiled and said, "That was nice, Zan. We thank you, don't we Johnny?"

He looked down at her and said, "Sure, sure thing. Let's have a drink."

Lara seem restless as she asked Zan to get their drinks. "We'll find a place together at the table."

The last thing Zan wanted was a drink. His head had barely stopped buzzing from the last one, but he made his way through the crowd, back to where Mr. Mitley stood by a rough table filled with open bottles, glasses and a water pitcher. He didn't look up.

Zan asked, "I give that hungry kitty three meals. It's all right if I help myself?

"Sure is," he said. "I need a bartender, but do I get one? No, Sir. They all plant themselves and I do the work. Help yourself, then come help me."

Zan poured a full drink for Johnny, a small one for Lara and a glass of water for himself, then made his way through the room to the table.

He found Lara and Murtagh just sitting down and Zan sat down across from her against the wall, facing them as they sat together. The empty space beside him was his.

He handed Lara and Johnny their drinks, then wondered if he'd given Johnny the glass of water, but Murtagh lifted, then smelled his glass and seemed satisfied. He picked up a knife and rapped it sharply on the table for attention.

"Let's all have a drink to the only Allan boy that ever got jugged."

Laughter broke out as people pushed back their benched, picked up their glasses and stood up.

Lara was getting up and Zan pushed back the box on which he'd been sitting. She whispered, "No, Zan. It's a toast to you, and you don't drink until after. Sit still and look pretty."

Johnny was on his feet calling, "Bottom's up to Zan Allan."

Zan clutched his glass of water, fearful that this ceremony might mean someone else was going to drink it. He relaxed slightly and suddenly remembered that he could be clumsy and drop his glass if he had to.

There was warmth in the laughing shouts of, "Kindness to Zan Allan."

Lara's voice was soft, her smile lovely as she looked at Zan and said, "Welcome home, Zan."

Zan's stomach roiled uneasily as he watched the large men and slim girls drain their glasses and smelled the sweet smell of gin mingled with the aroma of browning turkey.

Lara dropped down beside him, whispering, "Now it's your turn to say something to answer their toast and take a drink. Remember, it's bottom's up, but you can do it"

The other people were back in their places, their glasses refilled. Zan stood up, lifted his glass of water. The warmth these folks—these strangers, had shown him made it hard to say anything.

"Thank you, everyone!" He said, lifting his glass.

He caught the cold glance of Mr. Mitley, still behind his bar table, looking at him curiously and calling out, "Cut out the soft soap stuff and tip your glass, boy, bottom's up!"

Zan was thirsty and the water tasted so cool and fresh that he drained it before he realized it wasn't whisky. He remembered to hold his breath for a second, then faked a shudder and rubbed his mouth with the back of his hand.

Mr. Mitley said, "Well, you toss off gin like it was water. Thought you was just out of jail. For God's sake, watta they drinkin' up there at Quentin?"

Zan blinked for a second, then said, "Oh, potato peelings and swill. But not till they've run it through a couple of times."

Laughter greeted his comment, then in the minute's stillness that followed, a thin elderly woman said, "I've heard that before. What's more, I bet some of it's going on in the road-building convict camps here on the Coast."

Johnny Murtagh said, "Well, Jane, you don't have to believe it even if you see it, do you? Anyway, the poor devils ought to have something to live for after the kind of work they do."

Zan saw the women smiling, nudging each other. One of the young ones with a doll face said, "Quit griping, Aunt Jane, or take the pledge. Let's all have another one."

The bartender picked up a bottle of gin and water, and circled the table, filling the glasses. Then, outside where the cars were parked, someone began playing a strange tune on a horn.

The bartender stopped pouring and Mrs. Mitley stopped basting the turkey.

A handsome boy at the end of the table said, "That's Sally. Maybe she brought the new records." He crossed the room and stood by the door until he heard her approach, then opened the door as the girl outside reached for the handle.

"Hi, Sally," he called. How's your astronomy?"

A wisp of a blond girl with large brown eyes and full pink mouth, said pertly, "And wouldn't you like to know?"

"Wouldn't I" he said.

She winked her eyes at him saying, "Try to act your age, darling. Here—" She shoved an armful of packages at him. "Put that stuff some place and run help Sammy get the rest, will you?"

The boy added Sally's packages to the overburdened bar table, calling back to her, "Did you get the new records?"

She didn't answer, but walked over to Mrs. Mitley, hugged her and said, "I'm starving, simply perishing. Oh, Mom, I've had the most wonderful things happening to me, all day."

Mrs. Mitley turned the turkey, picked up a butcher knife and said,

"Can you fly with one wing, Dearie?"

The girl looked at the wing her mother was cutting off the turkey, wrinkled her nose. "It'll take two wings before I'd struggle with that." She called over her shoulder, "Daddy, bring little Sally a double gin, won't you please?"

"I'll give you a double clout with both fists," he growled.

Zan watched him pick up a tumbler of gin and pour generously, adding very little water. "Well, come and get it," he said. His eyebrows were drawn together, his chin jutted out and his low forehead was deeply creased. He looked dangerous to Zan.

But Sally urged, "Step on it, Papa, I'm perishing," and turned her attention to her mother.

"Dan and I had a beautiful fight, right in front of the Post Office, so I suppose you'll hear all about it.

Her mother shook her head, urging, "Tell me you're through with him, Sally?"

Sally pursed her lips. "He's through with me. Anyway, he says so. And, I hope so, too. He's going to divorce me. Isn't that a joke? And he throwing the book at me, mental cruelty, desertion—oh, I can't remember the half of it.

Mr. Mitley sounded neither disturbed or resentful as he commented, "Cheapskate, that's what he is. Don't want to pay alimony, that's what ails him. You're well rid of him, Dearie."

Her father was beside the girl, thrusting the glass into her hands, scowling as he said "If you can't get nothin' else from him, for God's sake at least get your name back."

"Too much bother," laughed Sally. I'll be changing it again, soon enough. You know me."

Her father faded back into the shadows behind the bar but Zan could still see his white hand moving like some clumsy white bird against the swirling clouds of blue smoke.

The girl picked up the brown, glossy turkey wing. Her hands were small, helpless looking baby hands, but her dark red fingers seemed to have been dipped in blood. He whispered to Lara, "What's the matter with her fingers?"

Lara looked. "Nothing, why?" Then she said, "Oh, the color. That's nothing but nail enamel. Most women paint their nails to match their

234

lips now. I don't happen to care for it, though, myself."

"That's good," said Zan, "I don't care for it, either."

But he continued to take long looks at Sally, attracted by the prettiness of her petulant face, and the beauty of her slim figure. The fact that she ate sloppily, like a child of four, moved him to feel pity.

Sally tossed the tip of the turkey wing in the direction of the bar, never looking to see where it might have fallen, then rubbed her hand on the back of her skirt. Zan thought it too bad that she hadn't been brought up by a woman like Grandma Allan, or with the minister folks, as Lara had.

Lara nudged him with her elbow. He looked around and saw that her eyes had an impish light in them. She said softly, "Watch yourself, Zan. The Coast girls call Sally, 'the man-eating shark.'"

The door banged open and a handsome young boy came in, loaded with more packages. Mario Lucca, the convict worker, followed him.

Sally ran to meet Lucca. "I thought you'd ditched the party, Sammy. Mom, this is Sammy. I picked him up by Grimes Canyon. Seen him heading north and made him come here tonight. He was looking for some fun."

Mrs. Mitley said, "Say, if that's the pineapple sherbet you're carrying, set it over on the bar. Help yourself to the gin and stick around, Sammy."

Zan had pulled back, getting Lara between himself and the convict's roving eyes. Lucca was out of bounds of the convict's road-building camp. It was after hours, too. If he had the sense to take only one drink and rush back to camp, he might get away with it. Otherwise, he'd get picked up and sent back to prison for a longer time and all guards in the camp would be fined.

Even in work-thin dungarees, Mario Lucca was handsome. His hair was a glossy black and curly as when he had first entered San Quentin Prison. He still carried his head arrogantly and his eyes still brightly black as when Zan had first seen him shortly after Zan had been admitted.

Zan heard Murtagh say, "'Scuse me a minute, Lara, I got to see a fellow."

He left the table, joined Mario Lucca at the bar, filling a fresh glass for himself, then began talking quietly, heads close together.

Soon they seemed to be arguing and, although their voices became louder, Zan could not hear the words. He knew he heard Murtagh say, "don't get caught." Then he thought to hear Mario saying, though it didn't make any sense, "Marked the place—same time—I'll find it—"

Prison had been as hard on Mario as it would have been on a humming bird. He only had a three-year stretch; would be out and free in a few months more. As close as Zan could figure, Lucca would be up for parole again by June, so why was he putting himself at risk?

Johnny came back set his half-finished drink down with a bang. "That fool," he said. "I'll take care of him."

Lara looked curious. "Take care of what, of who? I tell you, Johnny, go get us one of those sherbet things Cass is shaking up. Then come back and spill your troubles. Didn't Sally get the record you wanted, or what?"

"Or what!"

Murtagh sounded ugly. But he got up, went over to the bar where Mitley had just put down a large metal shaker full of the mixed drink.

Johnny returned with two glass that looked to be filled with milk but smelling of pineapple.

"Watch that stuff, Lara," he said, as he put one of the glasses in front of her. "It's really dynamite."

Lara tasted it, raising her eyebrows, said, "It's really very good."

Johnny put the other glass down in front of Zan, "Don't feel like you gotta take this," he said. "I'll get you plain gin, if you like."

Zan had his fingers around the glass, enjoying the cool feel of it in contrast to the hot, smoky room. He looked up at Murtagh and told him it was all right.

Murtagh returned to the bar, filling his glass from the bottle and began drinking it straight down. He didn't come back, but leaned against the bar talking to Lucca.

Zan tasted his drink. He thought it did taste slightly of gin, but not enough to spoil the smooth, sweet taste of the cold fruit and ice. He and Lara sat in friendly silence, sipping their drinks, watching what was happening around the room.

Sally was flitting around, taking tastes from glasses offered. She squealed mischievously as she slapped the hands that reached for her under the shelter of tables to pinch her.

Zan got up and made his way to the bar, passing near Mario who, by now, was resisting Murtagh's efforts to push him toward the door.

Nothing seemed to disturb Zan. It seemed a wonderful party, nice folks, and a beautiful room. Lara was so gay. She was laughing at nothing and that was so funny that he laughed with her. He felt so light-hearted that it did not seem at all strange that he felt he was floating—not walking toward the bar.

The phonograph started playing again and Zan tried a few dance steps on his way back to Lara. He was delighted with the spatter of applause; felt bold and sure of himself. He had never known he could dance, but evidently it was easy. He was dancing and people liked it.

Lara was laughing, too, when Zan started to take his place in the corner. "You're funny, Zan, and you're cute," she said, reaching for the nearest drink.

"No, no, no—" He stopped himself with an effort. Mustn't go on saying "no"—there was something else he wanted to tell Lara. What was it?

He left the table and found the floor uneven and crowded as he started back to the bar.

Sally was having a furious argument with Murtagh by the time he was almost to the bar. He stopped and listened, enjoying Sally's tiny flashing eyes, the way she gestured with a clenched fist as though she were pounding an invisible table. "Maybe he has got to go home," she said angrily, "I wouldn't know. But I brought Sammy here and if he's going any place, he's going with me in my car. You just stay out of this, Johnny Murtagh. You think you're smart, you do."

Zan wondered vaguely why she was calling Mario 'Sammy'.

Cass Mitley said, "You're not going out of this door along with that fellow. That's flat. Try it and I'll wallop the hell out of you!"

Sally's lip dropped. "Aw, Pops," she protested, "you're goofy. Sammy's a good guy. Only had to slap him once on the way here, and I picked him up after dark, see. He's all right."

Her father answered, "Nothing doing," and started around the table.

Mario was mumbling something, weaving slightly from left to right.

Sally took hold of his arm coaxing, "Come on, Sammy, we'll go places. Better places than this. You don't have to do nothing you don't like. I don't either. We'll go away from this old place and you and me—." She looked around and her glance met Zan's.

Sammy was looking at the floor, his head drooped, and his eyes almost shut. Sally's eyes implored Zan to help; her hand motioned him toward the outside door.

Zan stared at her in confusion for a minute and then, through a fog, he decided that Sally wanted him to help her. He caught the door handle as it whirled past, managed to find out how it worked, and opened the door a crack. The outside air seemed to clear his head and he took a deep breath, opened the door and stepped out into the darkness.

The creek rushed noisily through the canyon but no wind stirred and the wedge of ocean at the canyon's mouth was so smooth that the big stars made narrow tracks of reflected light across the surface of the sea. Zan looked at it, remembering it, loving it, but puzzled that every star had three tracks of light and none of them seemed to stay put. He wondered vaguely if he ought to open the door and tell everyone about this strange thing, but he was saved from the task of deciding when the door opened behind him and Sally, her father, and Mario were blocking the light. Cass Mitley pushed Mario to one side, leaned his head out and looked, calling, "Hey, you. Where are you?"

Zan didn't remember anyone else had come outside. He thought this over, then asked, "Me, Zan, I'm here. Looking for me?"

Mitley growled, "Yes, you. Get rid of that drunk and get my girl back here quick. It's a white car." He slammed the door and was gone.

The night was so black, there were so many cars parked along the road. None of them seemed white. Then he remembered that Sally was the last one to drive in and hers must be the last car parked. He felt his way around the car, a large car, felt for the running board and sat down, striking a match to shield the glow from the cabin. Yes, it was a white car.

Zan felt for the handle to the rear door, opened it, climbed in, shoved some things onto the floor and sagged down on the seat. He felt disgusted with himself for having lit the match. The car had felt white. He'd known it all along.

There was a murmur of voices growing louder and Zan shrank down out of sight. If the guards were looking for him, they must not find him hiding in someone's car. They had him for murder, for which he had confessed. They had him for his cellmate's jailbreak because all he could say was he didn't know anything about it. Being in a strange car would be stealing a car, and he'd get life for that. If he needed a car to sleep in, he should have got into his own truck.

The front door of the car was suddenly jerked open and Zan heard Sally's voice, coaxing Sammy. He heard a scuffle as she shoved him inside the car. "No, you ride with me and I'll drive. I'm learning to drive, see, and I'll show you how good I've learned."

Sammy said, "You go drive. I wanna stay here. There's a party and girls and drink."

Sally laughed. "I'm a girl, and stuff. We'll go for a little ride first."

He was mumbling, pulling at the door, trying to get out as Sally started driving. It roared down the narrow rough road, skidding as it turned onto the narrow Coast road above the cliff.

Zan suddenly found himself cold all over, his stomach in a wild turmoil of sherbet and gin. He wiped the sweat off his forehead, did his best to hold out, but it was no use. He reached over, touched Sally on the shoulder, and muttered thickly, "Stop, quick. I'm going to be sick."

"Not in my car! My new clothes are back there."

She slammed on the brake so hard that Zan was flung violently forward against the front seat and, for a minute, thought he was about to lose his stomach, but Sally was on her knees in the front seat, reaching over for the back door handle and managed to unlatch it, saying, "Now get out, quick, and hurry up!"

Zan was shivering so violently that he thought he was about to die, but he got his legs outside and managed to stand. He fell against the bumper, clutched it, and braced himself though the spasms that followed. He'd never in his life been sick this way. He found it painful, slightly frightening and completely disgusting. He felt he couldn't face Sally.

Her voice sounded urgent, but still cheerful and friendly as she called, "Get done with it, fellow, fast, this Indian is getting out of hand. Let's go."

Zan hesitated. He life seemed to come flowing back into him. His shivering has passed and his stomach was settling down, then he became aware he was thinking.

He walked around the car and said sheepishly, "I'm ashamed, I'm sorry."

She said urgently, "Get in quick, or we'll have a job of chasing Sammy. He's so squirrely we could lose him any second.

Zan got in, slamming the door shut behind him, and said, "I apologize to you, Ma'am."

She laughed. "You're a funny drunk. Where you been since prohibition?"

She shifted gears and the car moved on toward the prison camp.

Mario shouted, "The sonofabitch has been taking it easy in San Quentin, that's where he's been. I saw you, Allan. Don't think I didn't. I'll pull your guts out with my bare hands."

Sally said, "Now, Sammy. That's no way to talk."

"You shut up. This is between me and Allan. Let me at him. That's all I want. Just one chance."

Zan said, "Better stop the car, Miss. We got to get Mario back safe to camp. We can't do it until we get things figured out between us."

Sally asked, "What you got to figure about? All we got to do is take him where he's going, isn't it?"

"Nobody's taking me back to camp. I left. I won't go back."

Zan said, "Stop the car! We got to get this settled before we get so close they'll hear us. Funny they aren't beating the road looking for Mario right now."

Sally stopped, sighing as she said, "Oh, dear."

Zan leaned forward. "Look, Mario. You can stick out these few months. My God, man, think. You'll be free to go anywhere by summer, if you stay put now."

Mario turned with his knees in the seat, facing Zan. He swung his fist in a wide arc, hit Zan in the mouth and his head snapped back from the force of the blow. He could feel that his lip was bleeding and his first impulse was to swing right back at Lucca.

He held himself in, said, "Come on, Mario. I'm not going to get this girl's car all messed up. Get out of the car."

Zan stepped out, walked a few steps behind the car, and waited. Mario slid out, lurched back along the car, bracing himself by a hand on the car.

"Where you hiding, Allan?"

Zan went back a few more steps before he answered, "Here."

The convict left the side of the car, rushed forward and fell with a noisy grunt.

Zan tried persuasion again as soon as Lucca got back on his feet. "Listen, Mario. The only way you can get back to the camp safe is if the guards got a reason, mebbe think you been hit by a car. That's it! Remember that. You were struck by a car."

"You're a damned liar, Allan. I never got hit by a car in my life."

"You're going to get hit by one. Remember that when you wake up, Mario. Remember: a car hit you. You were taking a walk on the road and a car hit you."

The drunken man sounded almost convinced. "What car?"

"It was a truck."

Zan moved forward swiftly, drew back his fist. In the split second before the blow, he thought there was every reason for him to stay out of this. Every reason but one—somehow he couldn't stay out of it.

His fist missed Lucca's chin in the dark and struck him in the chest, and Mario fell forward against Zan, who fell with him.

He was crawling out from the tangle when Sally leaned out of the car, calling, "What's going on out there?"

Zan, on his feet now, went to her quickly. "We got it figured out. A truck him. We'll put him out of the car close to camp where they'll find him easy. He can't be blamed escapin' camp for being hit by a car."

Sally sounded confused. "I didn't hear a car. Is he bad hurt?"

"No. I told him a truck hit him then knocked him out."

She was angry, asking sharply, "What made you do that to Sammy? Why? The poor guy's drunk. It's not fair. He's goofy."

Zan decided that the whole Coast was goofy: this girl, himself, and everyone. Patiently, and speaking very slowly, he explained. "This boy you're calling Sammy is a convict road worker named Mario Lucca. He was running away from the road camp—escaping when you picked him up. If he's caught, he could get life imprisonment. Remember that. I'm trying to help get him back to camp without being caught."

"Yeah? So what you going to do with him now?"

Zan sat down heavily on the running board. "Women are smart. You figure it out, or anyway, try to help me figure out what's best for him."

He looked up at her hopefully, trying to make out how she felt about this, but her face was in the shadow of the glow from the instrument board. He didn't know that she could see him until she said, "Say, you're cute. Your face is all bloody."

"That's nothing. Mario took a poke at me. Do you know how close we are to the prison camp?"

"Hmm, let's see. That must have been McWay Canyon we crossed last. The camp is pretty close, I think."

"About a quarter of a mile. Almost too close. What time is it, do you think?"

Sally held up her watch to the dash light. "Eight twenty, but it doesn't keep very good time."

Zan said excitedly, "We musn't be foolin' around here. They'll be out looking, by now, since he didn't come in for supper. Where did you pick him up?"

"By Grimes Point, I think. Just around there, anyway."

Zan urged, "It cost the camp guards two hundred dollars apiece if one of these fellows gets away. They'll be men posted on the hills, every place, looking for him."

Sally said, "That sounds bad. Say, wait a minute. I've got an idea."

He said doubtfully, "Well, let's have it. Be quick. Can't you start turning the car while you're telling it?"

"That's it," Sally said excitedly. "You pull off his pants. Get him out of his coat, too. Hurry up. I'm going to run over them."

Zan's heart flopped. Drink must've got her, too.

"Let's get out of here quick," he said. "I'll drive if you'd rather, I mean, if you don't feel well."

"Do as I tell you. Get his suit clothes off him. I'll back the car over 'em, see. Then you shove him in the back while I drive down to the prison place and tell them I hit him, see? Tell 'em to come help get him."

"You can't go down there, or say that. They'll hold you for hitting him."

She sniffed scornfully. "You ain't very smart. They'll be so sorry for me they'll all try their best to comfort me, and then date me up. Get those pants off Sammy."

It was a good idea. Might even work. Zan went back to Mario, found him coming to his senses and much too active to submit tamely to losing his trousers. He said, softly, "This will hurt, but it's good for you, and he hit the convict in the face.

Mario was very limp, hard to undress, but Zan had his coat and trousers in hand when he went back to Sally. She said, "Where'd you hit him?"

"Somewhere close to his stomach the first time, but had to pop him on the chin this time."

243

"That's good," She said. "He got to be marked up some, have some bruises. Listen. Soon as I've marked the tire on his clothes, you get him back into 'em, else they mightn't think I was not on the up and up with Sammy, see. Then you take some brush and scratch his face. He'd be scratched if a car knocked him down. Soon as that's done, you get off the road, walk back toward Pop's until you see my lights coming. If I blink 'em once, that means It's all right for you to ride back with me. But say, how'll I know when to blink?"

Zan thought for a minute. "I'll be across McWay canyon, to the right, up there amongst the eucalyptus trees. No one could see you blink the lights, except someone right down in the canyon."

"Sure," she said, "that's good. Get his clothes out in front. I'll roll over it once, then brake so I'll slide, and then pick them up. Then I won't have to turn, see? I'll be on my way toward the convict camp."

A few seconds later, after struggling to dress Mario, Zan watched the car lights fade out of sight and become a dim glow as she left the main road and dipped down the steep pitch toward the main camp buildings.

His fingers were clumsy. He was in too much of a hurry. Mario made feeble groans and added to Zan's nervous hurry. But it was done before there was any light coming his way from the camp.

He felt around until he found a bristly dead lilac, broke off a small branch. He dragged the twigs harshly enough across Mario's face to scratch him up.

All the time he had been thinking about getting away to the canyon where he was to wait for Sally. He was counting on taking the Old Trail until he should have crossed the McWay Creek at a point close to the old barbecue ground among the eucalyptus trees.

It took his so long to make those couple of hundred feet up, some of it almost straight up, and all blocked by thick undergrowth, that he began to fear Sally would be back before he could reach the appointed spot.

Crawling on his hands and knees, just when he thought his breath was spent and too tired to crawl another foot, he suddenly reached the trail. Now on the well-trodden track, he regained his strength, stood up and moved as quickly as he could in the dark.

The Old Coast Trail was the main highway of the Coast before the new road. It had already returned its ownership from horses, deer and cattle back to the coyote, mountain lion and wildcat, and to the raccoon and fox, where all could travel undisturbed far above the new road. More than anything that had happened since leaving prison and returning to the land of his youth, this trail spoke of how life on the Coast had been changed by the new road.

He found that the little bridge at the creek was gone, and the water was still high and cold. He took off his shoes, pulled up his trouser legs, and felt his way against the rushing current, over slippery round boulders beneath his feet.

One false step dunked him to his thighs, but he was soon on the opposite bank, shod again, and ready to join Sally the instant he saw her lights.

There was no sign of a car so he made his way up through the eucalyptus grove high enough where he could catch even the faint gleam of light from far off.

He waited, feeling warm from his climb and lucky that he was waiting instead of being waited for. After a long time he began to feel cold, conscious of his clammy wet trouser legs, and wondered if it would be seen anywhere if struck a match to light a cigarette.

The matches were out of his pocket and a cigarette in hand when he saw, to the north, a group of lights.

Two cars, but they were coming in the wrong direction. As they drew nearer, he could see how the headlights flooded both sides of the road, and he knew that if Mario had not yet been moved, that these two cars would find him.

The cars were coming on steadily, traveling fast. Zan could see their lights sweeping out strongly as they made turns where the road curved out to the west.

There was complete darkness for a minute as the high mountain blocked off their lights. By this time Zan was so tense that he took a chance, sheltered the match with his coat, and lit the cigarette that he'd never before wanted so badly.

It was cupped in his hand, and he could see no farther than a firefly's glow, as the cars, closely following each other, came around the last curve before the short, steep incline into McWay canyon.

To the south now, he could see a glow in the sky that meant a car, or cars.

Zan felt limp with relief. Sally would meet these cars somewhere on the flat stretched before they got to the prison camp.

The cars heading south sped by, far below where he watched. As soon as they made the turn onto the flat, Zan took a few tokes from his smoke, then crushed the stub and prepared for a long wait.

He could tell when the lights of Sally's car met the lights of the southbound ones, and all cars stopped. The lights merged into one big glow, burned steadily for a few seconds, and then they all went dark.

The small wind that always touches the canyons with light cold fingers even on the warmest days found his wet trouser legs and turned them into clammy coverings, cold as icicles. The ground on which he sat was damp and cold as any February. Up the canyon an owl hooted for rain and from the high ridges the mournful howling of coyotes from peak to peak went on as they always had.

The owl moved to a closer tree, went on with his hooting. The coyote chorus changed into a fierce yappin,' then faded out to a couple of soloists as if wailing for all the sorrow, the cold and the hunger of the world.

Zan lit another cigarette, got up and paced a prison beat of twelve steps east, twelve steps west. It was warming, but the short nervous steps were too reminiscent of years of restless nights in prison. He went back to the place where he had been sitting.

Something must have gone wrong.

Then there was a glow to the south. It grew. It separated. The larger light moved on south, but the smaller one grew brighter as the other faded, and Zan was waiting to see what happened after the north bound car came into the canyon.

It dipped, came down the grade steadily, crossed the creek, and he began to feel that it was not going to stop. When the car had reached the upgrade on the north side of the canyon, suddenly the lights blinked once, the car rolled a few more feet, and the lights went out.

Zan went crashing down the hillside, all caution forgotten.

XIV

As Sally's car got closer to her father's house and turned up the canyon road, Zan could hear music with hands clapping and feet stamping in time to it.

Sally shrieked with delight. "The music came! Pop got 'em from Watsonville. What do you know about that! Listen to that guitar. I could dance all night!"

Zan remembered her favorite word, and said it, "Sounds wonderful."

He walked beside her to the door and opened it. She jumped inside, calling gaily, "Hi! Here I am, Pops, Music's wonderful. What a party!"

Her mother, busy loading plates with ham, turkey, red beans and all the barbecue trimmings, heard above the din and looked around, "About time you showed up," she said. "Want to eat now?"

Like a cold, gray battleship, her father moved down on them. He threw his arms around Sally, kissed her loudly, and yelled, "Where you been, Wench? Up to no good, I bet." He turned her around, pretending to spank her, as he brushed a few strands of dry foxtail grass off the back of her skirt. He gave her a slight shake, saying reproachfully, "And everyone here yellin' for you to come back, dance the Charleston for 'em."

He yelled over his shoulder at the musicians, "Charleston! Play the Charleston," and shoved Sally forward, urging, "Get along, kid. They'll clear a place for you."

Zan had stood back and Cass Mitley paid no attention to him until Sally was in the center of the room and the four musicians started a lively tune.

Then her father said, with great seriousness, "Watch this now, Allan. She's good, the pumpkin is, even if she is my own kid."

She was good. Zan could see that it was savage, exciting and done

247

with great skill.

He told Sally's father, "She's a dancer, all right. I guess any dancer would have to hurry to keep ahead of your girl."

Her father said, "She'll do in a pinch." He went back to the bar, calling, "Well, make yourself to home. Come get a drink whenever you want one."

Zan didn't answer. He was looking through the smoke, trying to see if Lara and Johnny Murtagh were still sitting in the same corner.

The table was nearly deserted. They were not there.

Thinking they must have gone home, he started edging his way through the crowd of dancers with the idea of thanking the Mitleys, saying good night and leaving.

Suddenly there was a great crash as one of the dancing truck drivers picked up a slight fellow who was standing, watching the musicians, and threw him smack into the middle of the large base drum. The head of the drum split, the small man was tucked into the hollow shell. The crowd roared with delight, but the drummer was furious.

He leapt across his broken drum, charged the crowd, yelling, "So you want to fight? You want to fight, do you?"

Sally called, "Don't do me like that, Charlie. I was just getting good and hot. Music. Make the music."

Clapping, whistling, shouts of "Charleston! Come on, Charlie. Slap that hog barrel!"

The other musicians pulled the drummer free, stood him up, and went he back growling, "Some bastard broke my drum," then shrug his shoulders, turned over the drum, and the dance went on.

Despite their protests that he must eat and drink, stay and dance, Zan said good night to the Mitleys.

Sally took note of his going with a wave of her hand.

Zan shut the heavy door behind him, feeling that between his first closing of this door, and this second closing, he had lived a whole lifetime.

One night, shared with others, out in this bootleg world had taught him more than his years of book reading about life in prison. He was no longer like Mr. Kipling's Tomlinson: "I have seen, I have heard, I have read—but the Devil asked, "What have you done?"

Outside, he stood still, listening to the far-off, pulsing rhythm of the sea, feeling it closer to him than the wild one-step music right behind him. He felt fine that he had been drunk, but he never wanted to be drunk again. He was now free of his fear of drink. A man could take it, or leave it alone.

He went toward his truck, planning to sleep in the truck tonight. In the morning, he would go up the mountain to the old Home Place, go to see Gramp.

He opened the door of the truck and Lara's voice said, "Zan?"

"Yes. Anything wrong, Lara. Where's Murtagh?"

She sounded forlorn as she said, "I don't know. He had to go someplace."

He slid beside her, put his hands on the steering wheel and asked, "Would you like to go home, Lara?"

She drew as far away in the corner as she could get, as though she were withdrawing from him, from everything. He could scarcely hear the small voice when she said, "Yes."

Zan felt shame for having neglected Lara, even though she had come to the party with Murtagh. He should have looked out for her.

He hoped the car moving along might make her feel more cheerful, but she stayed so still in her corner that she scarcely seemed to be breathing.

Lara had always been a happy, though quiet child. And now had always seemed to be a gay, self-possessed young woman. Her silence made him uncomfortable. It filled the car more than any amount of talking and the longer the silence held, the harder it seemed to say anything.

They were past the prison camp, getting close to his own place, before he managed to ask, "Did you have fun, Lara?"

She didn't answer.

His road gate was still open, just as they had left it, and the car went silently up the grassy lane. When he had stopped, opened the door for Lara, he asked, "Would you like me to come in, light the lamps, start a fire for you, Lara?"

She said, "Don't bother."

She also stood there as though she were waiting for him. He decided she must have been waiting. She didn't say good by, or anything else. Just stood there. He started to walk toward the house and she walked along, keeping pace with him, but walking clear across the road from him.

He found the door unlocked and went in first, leaving the door open for Lara. He found a lamp and lit it.

Lara was still standing outside. He could see her in the lamp light, slim, and as withdrawn as the porch post beside her.

He put kindling and wood in the fireplace, lit it, and crouched down, holding out his hands to the blaze. Instinct told him that if he left her alone, the fire would draw her to its warmth.

The kindling had burned down and he put a larger log on the fire before he heard her enter the room.

As though ready for instant flight, she hesitated half way between the door and the fire. He stood up, said, "Ill get more wood in a minute. How about some coffee?"

"No."

Zan began to feel impatient. There was no reason why she should treat him this way. She didn't act as though she was feeling bad from drinking that pineapple stuff. And if she'd had a quarrel with Murtagh, why should she take it out on him? Well, he had a lot to learn about women.

Zan yawned, smiled apologetically and said, "I bet you're sleepy, too. I'll put the screen in front of the fireplace, and get along. Good night, Lara. Sleep well."

"I hate you," she said. She went over to the fireplace, sat down on the floor and hid her face in her hands. "I hate you so much, I could kill you. But I can't, I can't. I can't bear to hurt you."

He was beside her in two steps, bending over her, urging, "But why, Lara? I wouldn't do anything to hurt you for the world."

Between sobs, she gasped brokenly, "Go way. I wish I was dead. I hate myself."

He walked the length of the room, then back again to the fire. This was terrible. How had she gotten into such a state?

She was crying again and he couldn't stand it. He asked, "Where's Johnny?"

She jumped to her feet, her large eyes reflecting the firelight, the only live thing in her white face. "You did something to him, too. Johnny's in trouble and you did it. I know you did. I was happier when you were in prison."

Zan said harshly, "I'm glad you were happy. I wasn't. But I can get out of here damn quick if that's what you want."

He didn't know if it was the play of firelight on her, or if she really was swaying like a grass stem in the wind. His anger left him as he looked at her.

"Should I go get Aunt Blaze to stay with you for awhile? I can't bear to see you like this, Lara."

She took a step toward him, her hand drawn back as though about to strike him. "Get out of my sight," she said in a low, terrible voice. "I drew every breath of my life for you. I tried to be someone you'd be proud to have when you came home. All right. I learned tonight what you want. A coast hussy. Go on back to her!"

"Go back, Lara?" He asked. "There's nothing for me to go back to out there but work."

For the first time her face looked alive.

She said, "Why do you say that to me? Have you forgotten that I know what happened in the cedars that day with Tilli?"

"Almost," he said. "God knows, I've tried hard enough to forget it.

It's not easy for me to think of what I put you through, making you promise to lie."

She shook her head. "Do you think I'm that stupid, Zan? You can't. You know I've loved you as though you were a God since before I learned to walk. How else could I hate you so much for taking off with that cheap girl tonight?"

His hand shot out and closed roughly on her shoulder, shaking her furiously. "Stop that. You talk like a cheap book. If I could have a wife and children, I wouldn't want one who was willing to have her children pointed out as convict's kids."

"All right. Maybe you can fool yourself. But you don't fool me. Any man that will take seven years in prison to protect Tilli Allan, and love her enough to keep silent about what she did, no matter what she does to them, then come back to the Coast and snatch up the first little trollop that's enough like her to be her twin, knows what he wants and isn't going to change. I'd never fit into that picture frame."

Zan started to say something, to defend himself, to tell her he had never felt anything but pity for Tilli and had no interest in the filly tonight, Sally, then thought better of it. Sometimes the more you trying to untangle a rope the worse it got messed up. He said, "Don't leave here, Lara. Not on account of me. I'm leaving the Coast tomorrow."

She reached behind her, tightened her fingers on the mantle and said, "Maybe that's the best. Who knows? I've been in prison with you for all those years, Zan, and I've got to break out somehow." She shut her eyes, thinking.

She opened them and tears spilled out on her cheeks, splashing onto her hands. "I'll find a new road for my life, too, Zan. It's a sin to waste, to wither away by waiting for you, to deny living life. Johnny loves me, and he needs someone. I'll make a life without you."

He picked up her hand, felt her tears on it as he laid it against his cheek and said, "Go with God, little Chicken."

She held on to his hand, leaned toward him and said, "I've earned the right to kiss you once."

Her arms seemed scarcely to touch him, her body to brush his as fleetingly as though she were a bird flying in the forest. Her brief kiss seemed more like a child's than a woman's.

Zan couldn't see as he stumbled out of the house, past his truck and down the road, his heart calling to himself, "Rima, Rima, Rima." He had found her at last in Lara. But now he had lost her forever.

He had walked almost to the highway before he noticed what he was doing. He went back up the hill with slow, heavy steps, got in his truck and drove to Buzzard's Point.

Toward morning he slept a little, leaning against the inside door of the truck. He didn't want to sleep. As soon as he did, in his dreams Rima spun him a cobweb, cast it playfully toward him and instantly Lara appeared, clothed in gauzy brilliance, smiling radiantly, holding out her hands.

He shook himself awake stepped out of the cab and walked along Buzzard Point in the half-light, in which a boulder seemed as unsubstantial as fog and a pebble might look suddenly large and menacing. The wind was cold. He couldn't seem to walk fast enough to warm himself, so he began gathering up dried greasewood roots, bits of sticks, anything he could find to start a small fire so that the light of it would help locate more wood nearby.

Soon he had a good fire burning. He rummaged around in the back of the truck, wishing he had a flashlight. He finally found coffee, a small bucket with pail. He piled on more wood and went north, searching for the spring that ought to be there. He found it, held his pail under the trickle until he judged he had enough water for coffee.

It seemed best to keep doing something, and he hustled around, found the right sort of branched stick to make a crane over some coals, hung his coffee bucket as soon as he found a rock that would balance the weight of the water in the pail.

He drank his coffee in the same pail he'd cooked it in and smoked a cigarette by the time dawn was lighting up the eastern sky.

His truck was blocking the road and he thought he should move it before someone came along. He backed it into a place by the spring that was wide enough, then went back to the fire, built it up, and sat down to watch the sunrise.

As the morning sun was touching everything with soft colors—gold, rose, violet and pink—Zan looked at the sky gloomily for a while, then got up and cleaned up after his breakfast. Soon everything was packed back in his truck, ashes from the fire drowned by water and covered with loose stones and gravel so that no mark of a fire ever having been there was left.

The quiet was broken by a sound of a rock rolling down the cliff. Zan turned and saw a tall, thin old man coming down the deer trail that led up the mountain between the spring and the edge of Buzzard Point. The old man was carrying a walking stick but did not use it to help himself come down the zigzag trail.

Excitement stirred throughout Zan as the man walked slowly toward him. He was almost at the spring where the trail touched the road when the old man hailed him. "Thought I saw smoke from a fire down here," he called.

Zan's face rose up to meet the other man's glance. He couldn't speak. It was Gramp. It couldn't be! But it was.

Gramp thumped his stick against a rock, raised his voice. "Guess you didn't hear me. Said I thought there was a fire down here some place."

Zan steadied his voice, saying, "I cooked breakfast here, Gramp. Then I put out the fire."

The old man put both hands on his stick, leaned forward on it, peering down with his head turned sideways as though listening. He said, "Well. So it's you, Zan. Changed, though. Awful changed. Yes. Was you coming up to the house?"

Zan said, "I'd aimed to."

The old man stood looking out over the country, his stick planted between his feet, both his gnarled hands clasping the top knot a mountain mahogany stick. The stick seemed to Zan no more gnarled and indestructible than the man leaning on it. Gramp's hair was still thick on his head, but now it was a flat white, no shine left to it.

But his eyes were bright, there was a touch of color on his lean check bones. Except that his head, carried forward like an inquisitive eagle's, seemed carried a bit closer to his shoulders than once it was, but Gramp stood as straight as ever.

The head cocked sideways, the bright eyes blinked rapidly as the old man said, "Remember now, it wasn't me that asked you to come up. I asked if you was meaning to."

Zan grinned, but said gravely, "And I said I'd aimed to come."

He was, and always would be, his Gramp's man. He knew Gramp was as proud of him this minute as he had been when he was eight years old.

Gramp was his mountain. A man with a mountain at his back had something he could trust.

The old man thumped his stick again. He said, "Well, if you're a comin' up, come on. I never go any further than this spot." He pointed his stick down at the road. "I never put a foot on that snake of a road. Never will till I've figured how to step square on its head. I'll do it, too. Don't fool yourself that because I'm getting old, I've got soft."

Zan said, "Never saw you look better, never did." He started up the cliff, paused on the edge of the small flat place where his grandfather stood. The two men looked at each other closely for a minute, saying nothing. Then Zan said, "You haven't changed about the road, Gramp. Neither have I."

The eagle-beak nose wrinkled, the old claws tightened around the head of the stick as Gramp said, "You going to work on this here serpent road? You going to do that again?"

"You know I would if I could," Zan said, "but the prison laws won't let me."

One hand left the stick, rested on his grandson's shoulder as Gramp said, "You should thank God for that. I do. Well, you've had a long hard time, Boy. Even as Jacob served seven years for Rachel, you served yours. I know."

Zan moistened his lips nervously. He said, "What do you mean? You know—. Know what?"

"Talk straight. You know what I mean. That Tilli—Augh—such an Allan, never has been afore. I told her what I thought of her wanton, evil life. Five years ago, that was. So she wanted to hurt me for that. She told me what you done, how you lied for her, saved her, for what she done herself by shooting that boy who bred her with child... And she called you a fool, a damned fool for what you did for her. So what have you got to say for yourself now?"

Zan looked square at him, "Nothing, Sir."

The old man looked out to sea, back at the mountains behind him. Then he said, "A good answer. Yes sir, that'll do fine."

The old Allan man and the young Allan man stood together silently with the mountains at their backs and their eyes peering far out at the sea's horizon. Then Gramp said briskly, "We better get started. Say, you won't believe it till you come take a listen at the wireless set Avery's got. I

255

tell you it talks as plain as I do and knows a damn sight more. Can preach a sermon like you never hoped to hear in your life, and without taking a breath, then start singing soprano. You'll have to turn it on, hear it for yourself before you can believe it."

"I got a job, Gramp. Ought to be there now. Aunt Blaze, Pop, Lara—they all said you was fine. But I had to see for myself. I'm glad I did, not only for seeing you well, Gramp, but it's a load lifted, you knowing about that Tilli shot Mervin. Tilli won't tell no one else. She'd know the story was safe with you, so we don't need worry about her reputation as an Allan woman, bad as it is, it's still a good kept secret."

The old man nodded. "Rocks got sense," he said. "They sit quiet. We can, too."

The two men sat in silence for a while, peering out to sea.

"What's the job you got," asked Gramp.

"With Dariel Beeson. He's working on Boulder Dam now. He's offered me a good job there."

Gramp rubbed his hand over his jaw and chin, thinking. "Sure. Boulder Dam. Heard about it on the wireless. Hear things that way. Seems like they don't get enough rain for the crops down in that country. Well, Boy, if you're going to get 'em water by plantin' time, you better get started."

Zan said, "That's right. I'll have to make the dirt fly." He put both hands over the old man's hands that were firmly clasping the stick. But as he saw the faded old eyes blink, become over-bright and watered a bit, he lifted his hands quickly and hurried away.

Gramp raised his voice as Zan walked away, "Remember Moses. Got water from a rock for a thirsty land. God be with you, Zan."

Zan kept walking straight ahead but before he stepped into his truck, he had to turn and look once more at Gramp.

With head up and back straight, the old patriarch was climbing steadily up his straight rock mountain toward the Home Place.

Zan got in and reached for the shift, then started north on the road that seemed to lead to his long held dream of building something for the world of men yet to come. His grandfather's Old Testament blessing had made that seem so clear; water for flocks and herds, for gardens of dates and oranges drawing their life from Boulder's water dam. He would be helping bring a promised land to generations. The waters would pour

timelessly, bring food and light to a multitude, long after his work had been done.

Zan drove slowly, looking at the road. There were some stretches where the roadwork seemed almost finished. There was plenty of miles left where the road was not much more than a wide trail. He could see old scars on the mountains where the first, hand-made roads had once been cut. All but a few patches of that early road had long since slid into the ocean. But the road now being built with new road machinery looked as though it could defy even the Santa Lucias to shrug it off their shoulders.

When he left the valley of the Big Sur River and turned up the Old County Road by the flats, it was exactly as steep and narrow as that rainy day seven years ago when he'd first ridden over it in the old auto stage on the way to the judge, then prison.

He drove on, wondering why cars continued to climb over all these mountain grades when the new road along the Coast could cut off hours of driving time. Climbing out of the valley, reaching the summit above Bixby Creek he had his answer. He sat spellbound, looking at a bridge whose center span reached higher than the tallest redwood on the Coast. The bridge was something far beyond his wildest imaginings. He thought of his boyhood fancies of cobweb cables and steel lace swinging airily over space. But this bridge had a graceful form, a powerful beauty and a solid structure.

It took his breath away.

Zan longed to drive over to the bridge and walk out on the part of it that was finished. Men with wheelbarrows swarmed over it. Concrete mixers were churning away at either end of it. All sorts of fascinating things were happening all at once. There was even a thread of road connecting up with the old road, but it was marked with a hand-painted sign, "Keep Out."

Someday he could drive across Bixby Creek on this bridge as freely as any man. He was used to waiting for "somedays." Perhaps a someday would never come for a togetherness between himself and Lara, but anyway a life held only so many days and no man could know when they would suddenly end. Life was to be lived. Lara said that. He knew it. Granpa Allan said always that it wasn't what happened to a person that counted. Was how they took it.

He recalled that Lara thought if a body couldn't find something good in a dull day, they wouldn't know how to see something good in a bright one.

Already today he had more than he had ever hoped for in his life. It was a great relief knowing that Lara knew why he had gone to prison, though she'd misjudged that he had feelings for Tilli. And today he learned that his grandfather also knew what he'd done and why he'd gone to prison.

The road along the Coast, as he reached it after coming down the tricky Rocky Creek grade, seemed a marvel of width and safety. He

258

watched his speedometer climb up to forty-five miles, and remembered the old stage driver trying to make his auto stage get up to twenty miles an hour.

The road was not surfaced, so Zan slowed down to thirty and sped along smoothly, still able to look at the slopes covered with wild lilac, the patches of poppies and the small bays and inlets with tiny beaches of golden sand.

He had crossed Mal Paso Bridge when a car came thundering past him, making at least fifty. The dust boiled up behind it and blew great clouds over a car that was closely following. He peered through the dust, curious about such hurry, and very dimly made out a woman's face looking back through the window of the first car. His heart leaped. For a fleeting instant he thought he saw Lara. He knew he would seem to see her constantly, all the time. For years, every half-seen face would always seem to be the face of Lara.

The second car held four men. His eyes followed that car with curiosity. Something about all four of the men, something alert and wary, took his thoughts back to prison and the watchful way of the guards. He puzzled about the men for a few minutes, and then found his foot pushing down on the gas, racing to pass that car. He knew now who those men in the following car were. They were the alcohol prohibition officers who had been on the Coast last night. The car they were chasing was Johnny Murtagh's car. The girl in the car was Lara.

Zan was using every bit of power in his truck as he passed the prohibition officer's car, then edged up to Johnny's car. He managed to hold his speed, draw a short distance ahead before Zan signaled them he was stopping.

Johnny wasn't stopping. Zan honked, kept on trying to flag him down. Johnny drove faster.

Zan saw that if he were going to stop Johnny, he'd have to block the road. He sped up his truck again and raced at top speed for another mile, then swung his car corner-wise across the road, blocking it, but keeping his engine running. It looked like a bad crash coming, but he'd have to risk everything, even if Lara got hurt. She'd be worse hurt if she were hauled into court. Whatever mess she was in, he'd have to get her clear of it.

Johnny did his best to break Zan's nerve. He drove straight at him and was almost upon him before the brakes started shrieking. Johnny's car swung like a stepped-on snake. Zan threw in his clutch and sent his car forward a few yards, then again swung across the road to block it.

The cars crashed together. Zan's truck spun halfway around. The back end of Johnny's car turned halfway around and plowed trunk first into the oncoming prohibition officers' car. None of the cars turned over.

The four officers, guns pulled and ready, leaped out. Johnny and Zan hit the road at the same time.

Lara cried out, "No, Johnny! Don't!"

All of Zan's weight went into the blind swing as he swung around. His arm went smashing against Johnny's face. Johnny's gun went off as Murtagh fell, the bullet splintering a road railing.

Lara was out of the car. One of the officers grabbed her while two of them picked up Johnny. The fourth turned on Zan.

"What's this? Both you fellows runners?" He asked.

Zan said, "No. I wanted to get the girl out of his car—and out of this. She's my sister and has nothing to do with this."

"That right?" The man asked Lara.

"I'm not his sister," Lara said.

Zan put in. "Same thing. We were raised in the same family." He turned, pleading to the officer, "She's a school teacher down the Coast and doesn't know anything about rum-running."

Lara said sharply, "If I could learn to teach school, I could for sure learn running rum."

The officer pulled a face, raised his eyebrows. "Spunky little kitten, are you? But you're in bad company, Miss. We had our eyes on this Murtagh fellow ever since he was running it at Silver City. Now we know we got him—and with the goods on him. Guess we got you, too."

Lara leaned over Johnny, put her hand on his forehead, then felt for his pulse. She turned a white face toward Zan. "You might have killed him," she said. "Can't you ever learn to keep out of other people's doings?"

Without answering her, Zan turned back to the officer. "I been away for a long time. Just got back and don't know what's going on here. My sister and I went to a party with Murtagh last night. I'm sure she knows nothing about this bootleg business, no more'n I did. I'm takin' her out

of this, taking her home."

Lara said, "Johnny's in trouble. He needs someone. I'm staying here."

Zan didn't look around. He said to the man, "Would you want your sister mixed into anything like this?"

"My sister?" The man asked, smiling. "Surely not! But she's about ten. And this little filly's of age, isn't she? I guess it's her headache if she wants it that way."

Zan got into his truck, backed it around so that it was headed back down the Coast. He pulled up beside the men who were lifting John, heard them say a deputy should drive Johnny's car, and that Lara and Johnny should go into the Federal car.

Leaving the engine running, Zan got out, leaving the door open. He stepped close to the man he had been talking with before and said in a low voice, "I'm taking her home where she belongs."

The man's shoulders shook with amusement. "Maybe you can. Myself? I wouldn't want that job!" He turned to take a look at Johnny, who was struggling against being put into the car. Then he looked at Zan and nodded. "We know where to find her if we want her."

Lara was beside the Federal car, anxiously watching Johnny. Zan walked up behind her, wrapped one arm around her, slid the other under he knees, and then lifted her off the ground and into his car with one quick boost. She tried to push him back as he squeezed into the truck after her but he moved in as though nothing opposed him, slammed the door shut, started the truck and began driving south.

Lara jerked her door open, but he pulled her back, and held onto her with one arm, drawing her so close to him that she had no room to fight him off as the truck picked up speed.

Lara twisted her head around, looked back over her shoulder, and then said in a flat voice, "They've gone. Now Johnny won't have a friend there to do anything to help him and you're playing God again. You don't want me. But you're trying to live my life for me."

His foot came down harder on the gas until he had to shift into low gear for the steep Rocky Creek grade past Palo Colorado Canyon.

After a few miles, he took his arm away and Lara turned her back, slid over to the other side and put her forehead against the window.

Zan remembered leaning his forehead against the auto stage window when he was taken to town for trial, a journey he did not want to make. After a time he took a quick glance at the back of her head, found her drying tears off the window with the edge of her sleeve. He said, "I didn't want to hurt you, Lara. Anything but that."

She said slowly, "You choose such strange ways to prove that. It was like you killed me last night. But I still go on living. At least let me alone to live my own way. I'll live my own life. You go live yours."

"I can't," he said. "You can't either. Nobody can. You're a part of all us Allans, Lara. One Allan in prison is bad enough. Right now you're hurt and don't care what happens to you. But how about the family?"

She didn't answer. She turned back to the window and they drove in complete silence down the Coast and up the short road to Zan's gate.

He stopped the truck, got out and opened the gate, came back and opened the door for Lara.

She walked up to the porch and he followed her. He said, "I don't want to interfere, Lara. But I can wait over, and if you still think you ought to go to Salinas and be with Johnny tomorrow, I'll take you. I only wanted you to have time to think it out."

She drew a deep breath. "You go wherever you're going," she said. "I can get wherever I want to go all by myself. I'll go to Johnny and I want you to know why. He thinks women are people, able to face life, make choices and share trouble. You think you're modern, planning for tomorrow. But it's a man's world you plan for. You think women are property...to be protected. I don't want any of your protection, so go away. Now. Quick."

He was outside the yard; closing the gate before he looked up, saw her hand on the door. He called, "You, or the folks, can always reach me at Boulder, care of Dariel Beeson."

She made no answers. He watched her step into the house, close the door behind her.

Trying not to think, not to feel, he backed up his truck as though he himself were a machine, turned his car around, and once more headed north on the road, leaving the Coast.

XV

Throughout the spring of 1937, across the entire country, newspapers had been carrying stories and photographs about the nearly completed Big Sur Coast highway.

There were stories of the eighteen-year project with photos of the blasting of the sheer cliffs, the state of the art, earth moving steam shovels and the caravans of dump trucks that hauled the blasted rock to nearby dump sites. There were interviews of the surveyors, including Mr. Beeson, engineers and even two convicts from the labor camps. Several national newspapers printed photographs of the Bixby Creek Bridge during its construction, then almost near completion, featuring its graceful arch and heralding the fact that it was the longest, single-span concrete bridge in all the United States.

Zan knew he had to be there on the very day in July when the great road-opening event occurred that launched the entire highway with a formal ceremony announcing the Big Sur Coast and country was open for public travel.

Early in the afternoon of July 2nd, he pulled over and stopped his new, heavy-duty truck as he approached the impressive new bridge at Bixby Creek Canyon.

He parked his truck with extra caution, for it was loaded with his brand new bulldozer. The new truck and trail blazer, or bull dozer, represented most of his savings from his job working on and around Boulder Dam. He stopped an instant to look with delight and some modest pride at the new 'dozer. Owning that piece of equipment was like commanding an army of workers. It could build road, level mountains, and plow land—almost anything. It was all he needed to make a good living, to be completely independent while living on his ranch on the Big Sur Coast.

He snuck one more look at the machine, and then walked out onto the bridge, still unofficially open to automobile traffic.

The bridge had a beauty as strong and enduring as the mountains that framed it; a grandeur that matched the deep canyon out of which it seemed to grow naturally. For a long time he stood there thinking of how the bridge grew upwards from the deep canyon floor far below and of the men with the genius to design such a bridge. He also thought of how it grew, of how many men it took with blistered hands and aching arms to assemble the enormous redwood beams and scaffolding, construct the complex forms, and pour the tons of cement—all of that to create a monumental work of engineering beauty that would bring thousands of people to this otherwise unknown and unspoiled Coast—perhaps the last such place in the country where rugged homesteaders had lived with horses and mules for a century before being opened up to the modern times.

He thought about the many men who had each done their part, the hard work, all of the unspectacular things; the kind of labor pains that brings birth to every man-made work that endures the test of time.

He felt proud of his share in building Boulder Dam, he was thinking, as he walked back to his truck, and drove for the first time across the bridge, slowly, making his first crossing take as long a time as possible.

He recalled one night at the boulder camp in Mr. Beeson's office reading an article in the engineering journal telling about the amount of concrete and steel used to span 700 feet some 260 feet above the canyon. The magazine said it was this highest single-span arch bridge in the entire world. Now that was something, and he was driving over it and the new road to his own Home Place.

He had passed Hurricane Point before it occurred to him that he was not having to haul his heavy new load over the Old Coast Road, the original pass from Bixby Creek beyond the Little Sur River to Andrew Molera's Ranch on the flat south of Point Sur Lighthouse. No Sir, now he was traveling on a smooth level highway beneath his new tires.

When he stopped at the gate to his house, the house looked empty. Half a dozen young steers were grazing in Misty and Buster's old pasture. Part of the fence was down, gave itself up to the storms and time. One of the steer, frightened by the large truck and load, hightailed it for the

ravine, and Zan chuckled to himself. He'd caught a glimpse of Gramp's brand on one of the steers.

His feet went lightly past the little house as though not to awaken old memories. By the spring box he lifted one of the flat stones and found the key where he'd always left it. Although rusty, as was the lock, the door opened, but with an awful creaking sound.

He stepped in, looked startled. Everything looked just as it had been the night he had said goodbye to Lara. Nothing had been taken from the kitchen. He walked forward, listening for steps other than his own. In the main room, the books, lamps, pillows—everything that Lara had used to make a home out of his old house were still right where she had put them. That was queer and he felt a gnawing feeling in his stomach. Aunt Blaze had written that Lara had left the Coast before her school term had ended, right after Zan had gone to Boulder Dam.

He called out, but no one answered. Then he went over and opened the corner closet. Zan began to feel something almost frightening about this quiet house. He couldn't think what had happened.

The dress she'd worn to Mitley's party hung in her closet, the soft white sweater with the tiny flowers he remembered was folded on the narrow shelf. The sweater lay as though it had just been placed there, but the small blue and pink forget-me-nots had been eaten off in patches. Moths fluttered up as he opened the door. He shut the closet door, stood before it, his head bent.

He went across the room to the windows, raising their shades. In this light he could see that, while the room looked as neat and orderly as though Lara lived in it daily, but a film of thick dust lay over everything.

There was a book lying open on the low table before the fireplace. A piece of paper and a pencil lay across the page. He blew away the dust. Written on the paper were a few words that had been copied from the page on which the paper rested. It read:

> *"And when I went on further, and called again and again,*
> *there was no reply, and I knew that she had indeed gone on*
> *that long journey alone."*

Lara and Rima were so much the same one in his thoughts that the message seemed to be addressed to him. Lara, his Rima, had gone on to that inescapable burning of her tree. He had sent her there. She had offered him love and life, and he had been too frightened to take it.

He put down the pencil, hurried out of the house and threw himself into a fury of unloading his truck, building a stand to hold the truck and tractor supplies. His hands shook, his knees felt brittle and his mouth was dry. But he could not stop trying to make the place seem normal by doing the things he would have done if he'd come back to the sort of empty house he had expected to find—without all of Lara's things inside, just as they were, frozen in time.

He rolled the last barrel of Diesel oil off the truck, went over to the low chopping block, and sat down to stare unseeingly at the weathered chips lying around the block.

He could only see the years he had spent trying to get used to the world that was so different from his youth in the mountains. Yet, that new world had been shut off from him during those seven years he had spent in prison. He had learned to work with men, live with them, drink and play poker, and not feel that the Devil was entering it into his book. He had even learned something about women. Somewhere along the way he had come to feel that men and women were not made because of things that were said about them. They made and shaped themselves by their own thoughts put into actions. He had tried to play God for the whole Allan family, when every one of them was just as capable of facing things as he was.

Now he acknowledged to himself that he had come expecting to find Lara waiting for him because she loved him, and at long last, he had come to know that he loved her.

There was a noise on the mountain behind him. He couldn't see anything of the steers, but he heard a vigorous young voice shouting, "Hi ya! Hay ya! Get going there, you ornery bastards!"

He stood up, stepped on the block and then he saw a wide head bobbing along just above the brush. It disappeared and he heard crashing in the bush around on the side of the draw coming closer.

A boyish face under a broad hat came into view. Zan had seen the long legs of the boy, the outgrown saddle perched on a bright blanket, and the white star on the roan's forehead before the boy noticed him.

The boy checked his horse, looked suspiciously at Zan. "What you doing here?" He asked.

"I live here."

The boy looked at his scornfully. "The hell you do. I know better. This place belongs to my cousin."

"The steers belong to your cousin?" Zan asked mildly. He was delighted to see that young Avery had none of his father's shyness. He looked like Avery, but he was of different stuff. He was as brash and as full of his own importance as the truck drivers down around Boulder City and as he had been as a young Allan man.

The book looked at him for a minute before he answered, "What's it to you? They don't belong to you!"

"That's so," Zan agreed. "But where I come from, cattle rustlers don't live long."

"Bull! That's movie stuff. I come for 'em, and I'm takin' 'em away, see." He paused, his eye-catching sight of Zan's machine.

"What's the oil and dozer for?"

For me to use. This is my place, Avery. I'm your cousin Zan, and I've come home to live."

"Gee, are you? And you own a bulldozer? Want to hire a cat skinner? I want a vacation job."

Zan said, "Maybe you could give me a hand at that. But I won't be

269

able to hire much help. At least for a while. Took most of my money to buy the truck and the dozer."

The boy spit thoughtfully, hitched up his pants, and Zan recognized the gesture of a famous movie bad man.

Avery said, "Well, I guess it's all right. Allans always trade work." He laughed with young joyfulness. "But unless you're pretty good at running piano scales, I don't see how I'd trade back even with you."

Before Zan could think up an answer, the boy asked, "You ever hear anything from Lara since she got arrested?"

Zan felt as though he had been dropped into an icy spring, but he managed to say, "No. When I...when was it...when did that happen?"

"Oh, gosh, I don't know. I was a kid and didn't pay much attention."

He looked up at the boy who was slouched lazily in the saddle.

"You mean the police arrested Lara?"

"Oh, sure. And Johnny Murtagh, too. Jesus, didn't that guy think he was something, though? Had fifty cases in the company truck with just some loose dirt shoveled over it, driving along as biggity as all get out. I guess he had Aunt Lara for a front. He never knew the prohbi's had been watching him till, bingo, they closed in on him. I'd like to 'a seen that."

Zan said, "Where's Lara now?

The boy looked surprised, slightly affronted. "That's what I asked you."

"Was Lara in jail?"

"Well, it wasn't my fault! You mad at me?"

Zan said, controlling himself to an effect of steadiness, "No, of course not. I'm sorry. I hadn't heard. Was worried about Lara. Awful worried."

"There's nothin' to worry about. She only had to stay in jail a little while. Gee, that's not much. You had to stay forever almost, didn't you? And you look all right."

"Didn't she come back?"

The boy shrugged. "Maybe. I forget. Guess it seemed pretty slow to her down here, after things like that. Maybe she went in the movies. I got a cousin that's in 'em."

Zan said, "I think I'll drive up and see Aunt Blaze."

The boy said, "Well, I got to round up that damn stock. Gramp's waiting' for me to bring 'em in. I moved all the stock off Buzzard this

270

morning. Gramps goin' to summer fallow it, I guess."

"Is the road up to the Janson's open, do you know?"

"Oh, sure. Uncle Stephen never rides any more. Don't drive much, either. But he got a license again, spite of his eyes."

"Then I guess I'll be seeing you later, Avery. I want to go up and see Aunt Blaze as soon as I can get there."

Avery leaned forward in his saddle. "Save your gas," he advised. "Everyone's out to town. Guess most of 'em went clear up to the city. I knows Mom and Aunt Blaze was setting out to get all fixed up in San Francisco, and I guess the rest'll string along. Getting' new duds and getting' their hair fixed for Pioneer Day, you know."

The cold horror of Lara's empty house, her being arrested, having vanished, was making Zan sweat. He felt impelled to keep Avery talking. There was a possibility the boy knew something he had forgotten, something he might remember if he went on talking.

"What's Pioneer Day?" Zan asked.

"Say, you didn't come back for it? I thought you must of, when you said you was my cousin. It was in the papers. Didn't you see about it?'

Zan shook his head.

The boy looked thoughtful. "Well, you got to be born here, or anyway, been here for twenty-five years, and when you're an old pioneer, you get to go to the barbecue after Gramp cuts the ribbon they're gonna tie across the north side of Clay Creek.

He paused, and then said, "People's coming to take moving pictures and newspaper fellows to write about it and take pictures of Gramp. It was even on the radio. He's old, more'n a hundred, and they'll snap him cutting the ribbon. He's real tickled about it."

Zan sat down on the block heavily. "Gramp is? He's really going to cut it?"

"Oh, sure. Say, he just shelled out money for the Allan women to get fixed up. He's glad to have 'em out of the place for a spell, I guess, so's he can finish his fence at Buzzard without Mom or someone picking on him for workin' so hard. They're going to have the barbecue at Buzzard pasture and he wants it fixed up just right. And we'll get another party when Big Creek Bridge is finished and the governor and all will come to open the whole road."

"What does Gramp think about Lara being gone?"

"I guess he doesn't think about it. Don't think anyone ever told him. He's pretty old, you know, and old men worry. That's what Mom said. A whole gang's working at Big Creek. Cat-skinners and everything. Guess that big party's coming up real quick."

Zan could not keep on talking. His mind was whirling like a windmill on a gusty day, racing madly one minute, then slowed down to nothing the next.

Avery waited a few seconds, and then said, "Well, so long. I'll be seeing you."

Zan stood up, asked, "When will the folks be back, do you know?"

The boy said indifferently, "Maybe tonight, maybe tomorrow. Pop said I didn't have to practice while they were gone, so....he grinned charmingly, his blue eyes full of the same mischief Zan remembered seeing in Granma Allan's eyes, "I worked up a Chopin nocturne for a surprise. Funny how a fellow likes to do things when he don't have to, ain't it?"

"I guess that's the way it is," Zan answered.

The boy touched his horse lightly and the roan moved off. Suddenly Zan remembered something, and called out, "I forgot to ask, when is Pioneer Day?"

"Oh, didn't you know? Fourth of July, of course, and there's going to be fireworks. Uncle Stephen's looking out for that, and I bet they're really something!"

"Fourth of July? That's day after tomorrow. They'll surely be back tonight. I'll go see Blaze tomorrow."

The boy pulled up his horse. "Be a waste of time," he called back. "They're all coming up to our place to help fix things for the party. Barbecue's up there, remember? And the fireworks are, too."

Zan answered, "so long, then. See you tomorrow."

The boy rode out of sight and Zan sank down on the chopping block, his chin against his fists.

How could the family let such a thing happen to Lara? They would not go to her aid, stand by her, when she was in need of a family in back of her? It seemed as hard to believe as that Gramp was acting pleased to cut a ribbon to open the road.

He tried to tell himself that just because young Avery didn't know where Lara was, that was no sight that the older ones did not know. But the dust that lay so thickly on Lara's bright cushions seemed to be settling heavy on his heart, filling his nose and throat, so that it was hard for him to breathe or swallow.

Going back into the house, where the full blue skirt with the gay suspenders pathetically drooped down from the hanger, where the moths had gathered the bright wool forget-me-nots, was like standing inside an open coffin.

Zan got up slowly, moved toward the job of getting his bulldozer off the truck. He looked around for a possible place and decided that he could back up to the low cut that had washed out on the mountain side of the small draw beyond the spring.

It was a slow, tedious job to back the truck across the rank grass. He had to fetch a shovel from the tool shed and scrape a track part of the way. Once against the bank, he found he didn't even need to look for boards. He made a small excavation so the rear wheels of the truck fit nearly into the wall of the cut, and made it easy to drive the dozer out onto his land.

Any other time he would have been glowing with pride, and would have used the trailblazer to make a road across the grass and back to the gate. But now he left his clean, unscarred caterpillar dozer in all its brave new paint sit right where it was, once it had cleared the truck. He parked his truck beside the gate, then gathered up a handful of chips from beside the chopping block and went into the house.

By the time the fire was roaring and the water in the kettle on the stove was boiling, he began washing windows.

Before it was lamp lighting time, the pillows had been brushed and shaken clean of dust, and put out on the porch to air. The moth-ridden clothes were pinned to the clothesline in the back yard so the sun could burn them clean. The closet, curtains, everything that was cloth in the house was cleaned and taken out in the light of the day.

It was midnight before the last book, dusted and fresh smelling once more, was back on the shelves. Zan had lit the lamps as soon as fading light made them necessary to see to go on with the work. Everything seemed done, until he suddenly remembered the washed dishes, still stacked on the kitchen table. He hung the thin cups on their hooks, sorted the dishes so that they would fill the shelf beside the kitchen window. Then he walked through the little house twice, checking to see that it was all as Lara had kept it. But he was not through yet. A fire in the fireplace with candles lit on either side of the mantle mirror was still needed to finish the picture that Lara had made of the house.

Zan laid a fire in the cold empty grate, touched a match to it, and as the flames leaped up he lit the candles. Yes, that did it. If Lara walked in the next minute, she would find herself at home.

He dropped into the comfortable chair beside the fire and suddenly became conscious of how tired he was. He had eaten nothing since breakfast, but he wasn't hungry. His head dropped back against the softness of the upholstered chair, his eyes watching the door.

The more he had cleaned the house, and the closer he came to getting everything looking as he had last seen it, the more reasonable it seemed to him to expect Lara to appear. It was completely ridiculous to think, just because a twenty-two-year old boy didn't know where she was, that the rest of the family had not kept in touch with her. Aunt Blaze would know. And Blaze would write Lara to come to the family celebration. Lara would come. Yes. He could believe that. He would believe it.

He shut his eyes and made a picture of Lara coming in through the door, going over to sit on the floor on one of her black cushions, and seem like a slender-stemmed canyon flower in the reflected light.

His head nodded and it seemed he should get up and make coffee. It was better to have it fresh, though, and make it after she arrived.

He struggled out of the chair, went into the kitchen and built up the fire. Then he emptied the water from the teakettle, filled it with fresh cold water, and put it back on the stove. He felt more alert after moving around, but the chair was certainly comfortable.

Yes. Lara would drive down from Monterey with the family. It could easily be that she and Avery and Maria would think it sensible to stay here over night, not go up the trail so late. Pa and Maria would drive up with Stephen. It seemed more reasonable to feel sure that Lara would come to this house that was waiting for her, than it seemed his grandfather would have consented to cut the ribbon that symbolically opened the road. He'd have to see Gramp actually cut it before he would believe it had happened.

But he couldn't shake off a feeling that, even at one hundred and one, Gramp was up to something.

The candles burned down and the fire became a few glowing coals, when Zan's head dropped forward, finding a comfortable brace between his shoulder and the back of the chair.

The kettle stopped smelling of fresh coffee in the kitchen. The candles blinked signals of distress then went down for the last time, drowned in their own pool of melted wax.

The lamps were still burning steadily and their heat, and the hot ashes in the fireplace, the cook stove, had kept the room from chill when Zan woke at last.

His neck and shoulders were stiff as he yawned, stretched and stood up. The clock on the mantle, that he had wound and set, said it was half after six. He checked it against his watch and the clock was right.

He went into the kitchen, feeling rested and vaguely excited, not even disappointed that none of his family had come as he had visualized. It was wish thinking that had made him expect them. Of course none of them would come to a house that had stood empty for so long.

He decided they must have all gone up to Stephen's place; he would ride across to the home place this morning.

He made a fire, ate a good breakfast, and then stowed all his provisions neatly in the cupboards and storeroom. He put his own clothes into a hastily improved closet in the shed.

A hot shower still seemed a miracle of convenience in a Coast house, but Zan had to laugh at himself for also feeling for an electric light switch every time he opened a door. The years of feeling for switches had made a city pattern in his hand.

The morning lagged in spite of his keeping busy every minute. He cleaned Misty's and Buster's saddles, oiled the bridles, repaired the broken fence section, and still it was only ten o'clock. He filled both truck and tractor with oil, gas and water. Then he decided to try out the cat and drove grandly down his own road smoothing and grading as he went. When he turned and drove back, the road was as smooth as a city street.

Time still dragged, and he decided to shave, get dressed in his new Levi's, and have a bit of lunch before taking the old trail up the mountain. He'd get there too fast if he drove his truck around Buzzard and parked at the spring to take the short cut. Zan had no wish to get up to his grandfather's house before all the family would be there. And he spent much more time and care over the tying of his gay silk scarf, the exact angle of his hat, that he ordinarily found necessary.

The day was clear and bright, the brushes were swaying from the finches, wrens, thrushes and quail that were singing out excitedly. The wren seemed to call, "Lara, Lara, Lara!" The quail sounded like they were cooing, "Come see this. Come see this."

But Lara did not answer. Yet, Zan felt certain she was no farther away than one mountain.

He shut the door and cut across the pasture until he came across the Old Trail, then held himself to a leisurely pace that would bring him to his grandfather's house in about an hour.

The trail angled back at the last canyon and came out above the old house that crouched on its small round hill, looking to Zan like an old hen hovering over a flock of chicks to keep them warm.

Young voices were calling and he could hear the slam of doors, but the walnut trees out back had grown broad and full enough to hide the back door and his grandmother's flower garden.

It was a good ranch to look down on. Not a gap in any of the fencing, no board loose or missing from any of the barns or sheds, not even a hand-split shake that needed replacing on any roof. The orchard was groomed, trimmed to precision. The grain and hay fields were still in their stage of soft greenness, and the shoots moved off in orderly rows across the mountain like a pigmy army waving silvery green banners.

Zan felt a mounting excitement. The beauty, the permanence of what Allan blood had created in a land seemingly set to repel man and his puny endeavors, filled him with a fierce pride.

He went down the Allan Trail, in through the gate where as a boy he had his first sharp cleavage from his grandfather's way. Looking at how everything on the ranch had been held to the pattern set by Gramp in his youth, it seemed to Zan more than ever unbelievable that Gramp could change so much as to cut a ribbon to open a road he so detested. He said to himself again, "When I see Gramp cut that ribbon, then I'll believe it!"

No one else was in the back garden as Zan opened the gate and went up the trail made of crushed abalone shell. Grandma Allan's lilac had green leaves and a few late purple flowers.

The back door was shut, but the house was full of sound. For a minute he hesitated. Then he opened the door and stepped into the kitchen just as a chord of music was struck on a piano in the front room.

Zan stayed where he was, listening to voices, and young and old, singing together as they worked in the kitchen, *"The Last Rose of Summer."*

The Kitchen was changed. A modern white enameled gas stove stood beside the old woodstove, and even that stove was changed. The big copper reservoir that Granma Allan had been so proud of was gone. A white sink with shiny nickel faucets had replaced the pump and copper boiler. The old steeple clock with its wood scallop trimming was still on the same shelf, and the row of kerosene lamps gleamed in their old corner. The long table and benches that had served generations of Allans was still in use, but stood on a floor snugly covered with waxed linoleum.

Granma's favorite song was unchanged. He could see her so clearly as he listened to the words.

> 'Tis the last rose of summer
> Left blooming alone;
> All her lovely companions
> Are faded and gone;
>
> No flower of her kindred,
> No rosebud is nigh,
> To reflect back her blushes,
> To give sigh for sigh.
> I'll not leave thee, thou lone one!

He remembered her as he listened to the family voices sing the song, and sing it well, as they had for generations. So often, along about four o'clock, before supper and chores got everyone busy, Granma would put down her mending. She would sit in her low chair, holding little Lara, and Gram would go over, open the organ and start to pump. Her voice was so true, so sweet with the words, words that made a fellow think could smell the rose flowers as he listened to them. But the best was the way Granma cross her hands on the organ keys, making strange chords and trills that fitted in just right with the words:

> To pine on the stem;

Since the lovely are sleeping,
Go, sleep thou with them.

Thus kindly I scatter,
Thy leaves o'er the bed,
Where thy mates of the garden
Lie scentless and dead.

So soon may I follow,
When friendships decay,
From Love's shining circle
The gems drop away.

When true hearts lie withered
And fond ones are flown,
Oh! Who would inhabit,
This bleak world alone?

If there was still a little time before supper chores, Granma would always sing *Gypsy's Warning*, a song Zan always felt was sad, but Gram always had a funny secret sort of smile on her face when she finished that one. There was something between her and Gramp about that song. He could tell. There was a look that passed between them, if Gramp happened to come in when she was singing about Gypsies.

He used to feel put-on that he had to hold the baby, Lara. Now his head was bent, he was listening intently to the singing, straining to catch a note of Lara's voice. There were too many voices for him to name any one of them with confidence.

The song finished. Zan still hesitated, waiting. Lara might be the one to come into the kitchen for something. He heard a shuffle, as if chairs were being moved, and then he heard young Avery's voice, clear and confident. "You can all listen if you feel like it, but this is special for Mom."

The house was suddenly filled with an amazing, intricate sound, an undertone that was steady as a heartbeat, a wild wandering rush of sound that no Santa Lucia winter storm could have bested. The speed, the strength, the authority and maturity of this music was a marvel to Zan. It seemed impossible that the glib, fifteen-year old Avery could be playing this music.

But the music stopped as dramatically as it had started, and for an instant there was complete silence in the house. Then Gramp's voice, lower than it used to be but still full of strength and confidence, said, "That's my brother Mel all over, yes sir. Mel could of done that if he'd had a pianner. All he was good for was a tune. Avery's all right; a good hand with the stock he has, too."

Avery said, "Gee, thanks, Gramp." Then he asked, almost timidly, "You like it, Mom? I had to work it out in my head, till I got the family off the ranch so's I could practice. I'm going to call it *"Mountain Winter."*

A deep warm voice said, "Oh Avery, my dear—"

"Well, by gosh. What's to cry about, Mom?"

Zan opened the door, stepped in, and answered, "Maybe it's the best way for someone to show you they like nice things, Kid."

Blaze called out, "Oh, Zan! How wonderful—"

He smiled across the room at her, his eyes anxiously searching it for an instant before he turned to his grandfather, then to his own father who was sitting next to the old man.

"Hello, all," Zan said. "I'm home again, this time to stay!"

His father jumped up and grabbed Zan's hand, but Gramp growled, "And who asked you to come?"

Gramp Allan put his hand on the arm of his chair, and stood up, frowning forbiddingly. Zan put one hand on his father's shoulder, the other on his grandfather's, drew them both close to him and grinned at the crowd, "Don't we look pretty? Three Zande Allans!" He looked down from his two inches of height advantage, shook the old man fondly. "Never trust a runt, Gramp. By golly, I'm taller than you are."

"Bah," said the old man. "No credit to you that I'm shrinkin', is it?"

Gramp looked over at the enlargement of the group picture that Mr. Randall had made, then back at his grandson. His old hand felt the muscle of Zan's arm, slid up over his shoulder and down his back appraisingly. "Pretty good," he said, "thought you'd be living on cigarettes, drinkin' liquor and staying up all night, like the rest of your generation. But you'll do, you'll do."

The family had waited until Zan had received his grandfather's welcome, then they all surged toward him at once.

He kissed Maria, Blaze kissed him, and then he reached for Margaret,

"Thanks for bringing little Avery into the family, Aunt Margaret. You look swell, Uncle Avery."

Blaze was plucking his sleeve, urging, "Look, Zan. Our big Stephy is home from Russia. Think of his having five sons! And here's Kari. She brought here three little ones, aren't they darlings?"

They were. Two small girls and a tiny boy, still unsteady on his feet. Young Stephen was eagerly showing the pictures he had with him. "My wife, Sonia. You can see she's beautiful, but the picture doesn't do her justice. Look, here's the boys. This is our country place. Do you like it?"

Zan kept nodding, managing to smile while streams of talk rushed at him from all sides. But Lara was not there. And no one mentioned her.

Zan's eyes sought anxiously for a minute alone with his Aunt Blaze, but it didn't look as though anyone was going to be alone today, with this crowd of the family on the ranch.

Finally he caught her glance, motioned with his head.

Blaze looked around, saying, "I'm so happy that my head's spinning with all this excitement. Let's you and I go look at mother's garden, and have a quiet moment, shall we?"

She slipped her arm through his and they went out the side door, passing the place where the children's table had been set on the day of the family picture taking.

As soon as they were down in the garden, Blaze stopped.

Zan asked, "Where's Lara? Why didn't she come?"

Blaze said in a very flat voice, "Why, don't you know where Lara is?"

Zan felt like he was choking, smothering. Aunt Blaze sounded so stern. Was Lara dead? In prison? Where was she?

He asked accusingly, "How could I know? I haven't been here. No one wrote me a thing about Lara."

Blaze said, "We had a few notes from you. I don't remember in even one of them that you asked about Lara."

Zan felt a quick heat burn down the back of his neck. He looked completely miserable as he said in a low voice, "I didn't, Aunt Blaze. I couldn't."

Her face brightened. "Well," she said. "That sounds better. But you knew Lara was in Murtagh's truck. You brought her back to your place. Then you left her alone there, and went away. How could you do that, and never ask how she had fared?"

Zan sighed deeply, and then said, "I was a fool. An ignorant fool.

Only tell me, is she all right? Do you know where she is?"

Blaze answered, "No, not exactly. She couldn't get a school teaching job again after she'd gone to Salinas and was held for questioning. The fact that she was released, with no charges against her, didn't mean a thing. She couldn't get a school anywhere to take her. And Johnny Murtagh turned on her, blamed her for his being caught. He wouldn't even see her, and she had tried so hard to help him as a friend. Well, that's how things go sometimes, you know that. He's doing ten years in McNeil Prison. They proved he really was a key man for a large bootlegging ring."

"Never mind him. Where's Lara," Zan implored.

Blaze said indignantly, "Well, why all the hurry so sudden? You had years in which you didn't even give her a thought."

He said, "I never stopped thinking of Lara. I—well, damn it, I thought I couldn't—being a convict and all. You know how I'd feel, with other folks talking about her and our kids if'en we'd ever had any. I pushed myself away…I had to stay away from her for her own good."

Blaze looked at him, her eyes bright with happiness. "So, you do love the child," she said frankly.

She drew Zan to her, patting him fondly. "It will work out, Zan. Lara's a private teacher, traveling with a very nice family right now. But I sent her word, long ago, about the Pioneer Day, and about Gramp. I think she'll try to get home for it."

He said, "I got to find her. I've been waiting too long now. Someone else will get Lara to love 'em before I can tell her. Could happen anytime, any minute. Then what?"

Blaze said teasingly, "No one will get Lara. She intends to be an old maid. She said so. But you must stay here for the road opening. You simply can't leave until your grandfather's had his big day of opening the new road."

She laughed shakily, "Dear father. Oldest man in the county, you know. He's terribly proud of it."

Zan shook his head, still not relieved from the news about Lara. "I know Gramp. He's stubborn, not changeable. I bet he's up to something."

"Could be," Zan, "but what are you up to?"

Flustered, Zan said, "I come back to be with…nothin' I guess, just kinda hopin', waitin' for Lara I 'spect."

Blaze pounced. "There, that proves it. You changed your mind about not being good enough for Lara, didn't you?"

Zan looked confused. Damn women, anyway. They had no business figurin' things out, being so smart and all.

He said, "That's nothing to do with Gramp. I been out among people, had a few things knocked into my mule head. Gramp's been right here lording over his mountains. He's old and stringly, but I'd bet my last cent he's got something up his sleeve. He's no soft, doddering old man, not matter if he's two hundred years old!"

Blaze said, "But you'll stay and tell him how fine it was for him to cut the ribbon, won't you, Zan? Yes, you will. That's settled, then. You'll see it through to the last fire works, and on July 5th, if Lara doesn't come, you go bring her home."

"If I could, I'd do anything. Yes, I'll stay. I won't have to pretend that I'm proud of Gramp. He always was my man, Aunt Blaze. And I'll go fetch Lara, if she ain't come home, wherever she is."

She said, "Well, I've got to go help get supper for this crowd. You visit around, Zan. I'll cook, and I'll pray. You might try that yourself, praying I mean."

He turned and walked out toward the barn and Blaze walked off briskly toward the kitchen.

The large harvest table, split long from a downed redwood long ago, was a full twelve-foot plank four inches thick. The three Zande Allans sat at one end, with Gramps at the head, while the other eleven adults sat closely together on the other benches, but here they were, all together. Because Lola had six children, she got the place of honor at old Zande's right side, and she also had the job of seeing that the nine children crowded around the kitchen worktable were given second helpings.

The room hummed like a newly moved swarm of bees. The women reliving their exciting shopping days in the city, commented admiringly on each others new hair dos, planning for the big doings today and barbecue tomorrow.

The men spoke little, ate with relish, except for old Zande, who ate slowly, sparingly, and now and again spoke in a very low voice, more to himself than to the others, something about his generation increasing and his seed multiplying.

When the dessert came on, he refused any, but suddenly looked over at his grandson Stephen and said, "Pass over those pictures of your children, Stephy."

"It's a pleasure, Granpa."

He took the small case with the group of five children from his pocket with evident pride, passed it along until it reached their great grandfather. The old man took his magnifying glass from his pocket, studied the chubby smiling faces for quite a time. Then he put the glass back in his pocket, started the picture passing back to his grandson.

He nodded his head thoughtfully, pursed his lips, and finally said, "And you says those little young ones speak Russian?"

Stephen laughed. "They certainly do. You ought to hear the chatter they can make."

The old man shook his head doubtfully. "Seems a strange thing to me. Little children like that able to talk such a foreign tongue as Russian. Don't understand how they can do it. I couldn't."

Stephen said soothingly, "They speak English, too, Gramp. We don't hire any nurse that can't speak English well."

Gramp was a bit cantankerous. "You'll addle the poor children with strange languages, Boy. Bring 'em home and let 'em learn plain American talk. You do that."

Stephen answered respectfully, "Yes'r. I'll do that, and soon. Sonia wants the children to know and love their father's homeland."

"Increase and multiply," Gramp said, "increase and multiply. That's good."

The old man had been looking at the clock, and when the first of the smaller ones from the children's table began to whimper and be held by their mothers, he stood up.

"'Scuse me," he said. "I'm going out back."

Blaze looked outside, got up and began lighting lamps. "It's getting dark, Pa," she said, "don't you think one of the boys better walk along with you?"

"Fiddlesticks." The old man paused at the door and looked back angrily. "I walk alone, know what I'm doing. Remember that. I ain't wearin' didies yet by a long shot!"

He closed the door behind him, shutting out his mutter, repeating, "long shot."

Zan too had eaten very little. He picked at his dessert, waiting for the dinner to be over. He hoped his absent-mindedness would pass for shyness in being among his family after being away for so long.

During the course of dinner, Zan was unable to keep his mind on anything but plans for Lara, for seeing her, for being with her, this time forever. He planned to get the ribbon cut at Clay Creek, watch the last Roman candle, then quick good by's and down to his truck, then find Lara, she was somewhere, he'd find her for sure…

Time droned on over coffee. The darkness began crowding in at the windows, and Zan felt too restless to sit any longer. He turned to his father, saying "I got things I still want finished tonight down to my place, Pa. I'll say goodnight," he looked around at the rest of the family, "good night to all of you for now, and I'll have a word with Gramp outside. Thanks for the fine supper, girls. The Allan women sure know their kettles."

Blaze urged, "You can wait just a few more minutes, Zan. There's no Boulder Dam factory whistle going to blow for you down on your ranch, or a time clock to punch. Gramp's wonderfully well, but he's a bit fussy and childish over some things. You better tell him good night here, instead of shouting at the outhouse as you go past,"

She colored a bit as the others laughed with childish abandon. Stephen laughed until he choked and coughed, trying to say, "I thought you had plumbing now, haven't you?"

Maria raised her eyebrows, and said primly, "Yes. Certainly we have. But Gramp doesn't trust it."

Young Stephen struggled for a minute, stifling his laughter, but remembering that Maria has no sense of humor, he lost the fight with his restraint and starting laughing, a laughter that seized the entire family with contagion, and they were leaning against each other, shaking and dabbing laughter-tears out of their eyes.

There was a sudden fierce but muffled sound that seemed to shake the entire house. Stephen said, "Sounds like we got a revolution starting pretty darn close."

Kari's little girl, Hannah, looked around from fussing over her baby brother's bib and said calmly, "There's blasting on the road, Mama."

Blaze looked at her grandchild fondly and said, "Yes, dear," but he looked troubled as she turned to the others.

"It sounded too close to be the Big Creek crew, though they've been working night and day so the whole road can be opened this month."

Avery said, "Gee, I wonder—" and got up, went down the hall to his room.

Then two more explosions, both larger than the last, one following right after the other, rattled the windows and a clay cup fell from the children's table and fell to the floor, smashing it into small pieces.

Zan was on his feet. "Dynamite—and close! Comin' from Buzzard pasture!"

There was another blast and Zan yelled, "It's Gramp! That's what he's been up to! He'll kill himself!"

He was out the door as feet running down the hall were followed by the sight of Avery, flashlight in hand. "Gramp?" He asked, his face worried. "We got to find him."

He pushed the flashlight into Zan's hand and they ran ahead of the others to the outhouse. It was empty.

Zan said, "It's Buzzard Point, for sure. He's blown it!"

Tony and young Stephen were chugging along behind, trying to catch up. They also had flashlights and, far behind them, he saw the bobbing lanterns lighting the way for the rest of the grown ups.

Avery saw the old man first. "There's Gramp! Look, over there. He's flat. He's dead!"

Zan reached his grandfather and bent over, turned the light onto his face, then felt his pulse. "A rock caught him, cut his head. He's breathing. Get a cot, or something for a stretcher."

Avery started to run back with the other men, but Zan called him. "Stay with Gramp, kid. He'll be all right. I want to see what happened."

Zan took the flash light, got as close as he could to the great broken slice that had taken the fence and all the front of Buzzard Point down to smother the narrow track of highway cut along the cliff, almost seven hundred feet below. "A sweet mess," he muttered. "The old hellion, the grand old fool!"

Gramp was groaning when Zan came back. He felt his pulse again. It was stronger. Tony and Stephen ran up with an improvised stretcher and blanket. The old man groaned harder as he was lifted on to it. He was entirely lucid as he looked up into Zan's face, whispering "I told Beeson they'd not try to best me while I held Buzzard. And, by God, I proved it."

285

His head rolled back limply and Maria started to cry. Gramp's eyes were shut but he said sharply, "Stop snivellin', girl. We'll have the barbecue. The trail—the Home Trail's still open. Like it always has been and always will be."

By the time the stretcher-bearers were at the house, old Zande was brisk and full of orders. He waved away bandages and town remedies with distain. "A dab of Hannah's herb salve, if you got to fuss over me. It's on the clock shelf. I'm tuckered now. Get away so's I can get some rest."

Zan said again, "Gramp's all right. Watch him a bit. I got to try to open the road."

Hearing Zan, the old man jerked up in bed, shook a crooked finger at him. "Poor boy," he said. "You're more'n half Martin, stubborn as your Granma. I've bested you, Zan. Admit it like a man."

Zan's head went forward, his jaw clamped. Then he took a deep breath and said calmly, "Gramp, I'll make you an offer. If the road's open tomorrow so's cars can drive down to Clay Creek for the doings, are you man enough to come out and cut that ribbon like you promised?"

The old man lay back and closed his eyes. Zan stood waiting and, slowly, a grand sardonic smile spread across the old man's mouth. His eyes fluttered open and he said, "You're crazy, but you got the Allan fight in you. You're licked, boy. But if'n you can pull off a miracle, and I can get down there to see it, I'll cut the damn ribbon. If'n you can pull that off, Boy, I'll even eat the scissors if you like."

Maria said, "You're talking too much, Father. And, anyway, there's only one pair of scissors."

Zan yelled, "Goodnight, all of you, I got an offer to win and I best get to it!"

He still had Avery's flashlight and hung on to it. He'll need it for his wild race down the mountain trail to his place.

As he ran, stumbling here and there, his clothes became torn, his face scratched and, from one overhanging branch that caught him, one eye was swelling. His breath had been left somewhere on one of the short cuts, but he made it down the darkened trail to his place, where he stopped, leaning against his truck, his heart hitting like a sledge hammer, his lungs gasping for breath. He held onto the door for a minute to gather himself before he could even open it to climb in and head toward his cabin to get his dozer.

He made his way back to his cabin and backed the truck across the yard and loaded the bulldozer.

He felt small and puny standing beside the large machine. But the caterpillar tractor looked like a small toy when compared to what Gramp had been able to dynamite down onto the road.

Once on the road he began to feel better. It seemed no time at all before he was at the slide beneath Buzzard Point. The minute he shut off his engine, he could hear loose rock, slides from the dynamite still running strong enough to sound bad.

He climbed down, leaving the lights burning, and walked out into the beginning of the rubble covering the new road. A boulder zinged past his head, missing him, while others clattered all around. He remembered the flashlight, took it from his pocket, and crossed the slide with rocks falling all around. He stumbled over rolling boulders, floundered into soft places, but waded on through the flowing rubble, bound to see how deeply the road was covered in the worst places.

He judged that at the point itself, the rocks and debris were fifteen feet high, and for quite a stretch. He could see a few places beyond, where it looked even deeper, but those places were shorter. It looked like an impossible job to do. But he had to do it.

He got the machine into action, starting to buck huge boulders, stones and small rock, all mixed together in a mountain of rubble covering the road for a long distance.

He kept at it steadily, his progress seemingly slight against the mountain of material needing to be moved. It was such a short time before eleven o'clock tomorrow morning when folks would start drivin' in for the ceremony, confident of a road to be dedicated. The road had to be open. He vowed to himself it would be.

He felt feverishly hopeful until he uncovered a rock too large for his cat. He lit a cigarette, damned his lack of dynamite.

As he crushed out his smoke, threw it away, his eye caught a beam of light that stood sharply out across the sea, and then disappeared from sight. It was a car, not far off, and traveling fast, judging by the speed at which the light had swung.

Zan thought of the blind curve as the car would come onto the slide. At the rate the car was traveling, it could easily plow into another rock to bounce it off the road and send it hurtling down six hundred feet, straight to the ocean.

He grabbed the flashlight, started to run north across the slide. He had to get there before the car was too close to pull up in time. Zan, breathless, beat the car by the length of a city block, was out in the clear on the other side of the slide, blinking a warning. The brakes screeched, the car swung a bit, but it stopped safely.

Zan had a plan. He ran forward, put his head in a the open window and said urgently, "Say, could you drive a truck?"

A woman's voice said coolly, "Yes. If I had to."

It was Lara!

He clutched at the door, caught his breath and said, "You have to, Lara, Gramp's dynamited Buzzard Point."

He opened the door, grabbed her and pulled her out, saying, "Thank God you're here, Lara. There's some cat skinners working on a slide at Big Creek. You must go after them. Come on. Come on."

He pulled her across the slide, rocks still clacking past them in the darkness, ignoring her protests that she couldn't run so fast. He didn't

tell her why. He was too busy telling himself that no rock could fall with Lara's name on it as he pulled her safely over the slide so she would not be under those falling rocks one second longer than she had to be.

She managed to gasp, "You got a lot of it cleared," as he thrust herself into the truck and showed her the shift.

"Tell 'em I need a big cat, a heavy one. Tell 'em—no, never mind. Just tell 'em Buzzard Point's down. Remind them the road's to be opened at eleven tomorrow. They'll know what I need." She got the large truck started as he ran after it, shouting, "And dynamite, tell 'em dynamite!"

The truck picked up speed as it pulled away. Zan started back to his work. He walked rapidly back to the dozer, kept repeating brokenly, "Jesus, it's her! It is! It's Lara!"

As he backed up the cat for another go at the slide, Zan suddenly felt like a giant. He could do anything; get the slide cleared with a shovel if he had to. He drove the cat where he'd cleared the first pass, and started widening that area. He worked with nervous intensity, but caught himself, far too soon, starting to watch for a truck light from the south.

Nothing mattered now. Lara was here. She was safe, home.

He didn't feel tired, but ever so eager by the time the lights appeared coming from the south. He backed clear of the rockslide, and then edged over toward the bank so the larger cat could take the lead.

The truck hauling the huge bulldozer stopped, a man jumped down, came over, holding out his hand as he said, "So, you got something your cheese box can't buck, is it? I'm Joe Russell. I know you're Zan Allan, so let's get to work!"

Zan rung his hands. "Suits me. Get your sixty horse to show up my thirty, and I'll buy the beer."

"Hold you to it," Russell yelled as the work started.

The blasting had been done before Lara returned in Zan's truck, bringing coffee and sandwiches.

Over sandwiches Zan told Russell of his wager with his grandfather, watching Lara's eyes darken with fear as he told of the blasts, then crinkle with amusement as she learned Gramp was still fighting, still full of beans.

Russell drained his coffee, saying, "He'll cut that damn ribbon if he can get down here. Maybe there's a big 'if' in that, my lad. Tell you what, Zan. We'll wipe up this mess, neat and pretty, by about seven, way we're going. What you say if we roll up a bit of this mountain, surprise your grandpa with a road to his gate? Make it easy for him to get down to Clay Creek, understand?"

Zan said, "It could be done. You first, roughing it out. Me, following, to smooth it out." He turned to Lara with the first word he had spoken to her since he told her to go to Big Creek camp to get help.

Want to drive your car up to Gramp's, Lara?"

She looked thoughtful. "He won't like it," she said.

Russell shook with laughter. "He can throw it over Buzzard Point if he don't want it up there, can't he?"

Lara said with grave dignity, "There's nothing funny about our grandfather, Mr. Russell. He's a great man, and he's tamed this whole coast country."

"That's right, he is," Russell agreed.

The men got up and started working again. It was seven-thirty when at last Zan and Russell agreed it was a job done.

The road was open.

They took the entrance for the new road to the Home Place off at the deer trail just south of the spring. Zan felt it was one of his life's great moments when he swung the cat up the mountain, was on high above the level of the new road, and climbing steadily. The broken ravine gave them some trouble, but the two large machines were in sight of the house by ten o'clock.

The children came tearing down the mountain to meet them, followed the large dozer in front, as though it was the Pied Piper. They had no eyes for Zan's smaller outfit, or for Lara's little coupe.

If the hubbub of Zan's first arrival at the Home Place after an absence of so many years was tremendous, this reunion was complete bedlam. Too many wonders were all happening at once. Lara was home. Zan had cleared the road so it would be open for the ceremony as planned. And now the Home Place itself had at last been invaded by what Gramps called the serpent, a road right to his place!

The old man Zande leaned against the fence, looking. Zan said nothing to him. He had caught a glimpse of the old face working hard to keep the control that Gramp always felt was a man's duty.

The women flew into the house to get dressed for the ceremony. Somebody provided a simple breakfast, quickly eaten by the family and the bulldozer operators.

Russell turned the dozer around and headed down the new road, promising that cars would be sent up in time for all of them to ride down to the ceremony.

Gramp stayed erect and silent until Russell, the stranger, had gone, and after the women and children had returned inside the house, then he let go of the picket fence and went into the house without a word.

Zan went over to the fence where Gramp had been standing, leaned against it, and was fully aware of Lara, who was moving like a flower among his grandmother's garden. He wondered what he would say to her, once she was ready to let him talk. He knew enough about women now to know that Lara was holding off, doing some thinking.

But he didn't want to go without at least a word to her. He said, "I'm goin' down to the place, Lara, to clean up. Do you want to come with me, now?"

She looked at him across from the lilac bush, shook her heard. "No," she said.

He looked at her, his breath stuck in his chest.

Then she looked at him, squarely, and said, ""Not now...not yet."

His breath broke free; the answer more than pleased him.

He drove down Gramp's new road in his cat and was clear of it just as a string of cars came along, turning up the mountain as though a road had always been there.

Cleaned up and fresh, Zan arrived a Clay Creek just as his grandfather was being approached by old Doc Roberts, who steadied himself with a cane in his right hand and his arm around a young man on his left. As he approached Zande, he said excitedly, "Well hello, old friend, I see you've made it for this historic occasion."

"Don't be saying you got the best of me 'cause you didn't. I'd a had the damn thing shut down if'en my grandson hadn't challenged me and cleared off old Buzzard's beak from where I'd blasted it off the upside. If anyone bested me, it was him, an Allan to the bone."

"There, there, Mr. Allan, I heard you've been a bit mischievous, but that didn't stop the road, nothing has and nothing will, and you must own up that it's rather ironic it was your own blood who helped make this day possible."

"Well, Doctor, jus' 'cause you can't stop something, don't make it right to happen. The water gate's open and you can't stop water from flowin' downstream, jus' like now you can't stop the flow of outlanders into the Big Sur."

"As you know," Mr. Allan, "I have nothing but respect for you and the Allan family, and it is my sincere hope that everything that comes to you from this road will be a blessing."

"And that'll come from above, not from you or this road. I'm not at peace with it yet, Doctor, may never be, but it's here and so am I, so let's get on with it before the day's spent jabberin' away."

Just then a distinguished looking man in a clothes suit made of three pieces started urging Gramp to pick up the scissors and get ready for the photographers. Zan dashed over as Gramp was roaring, "The hell with pictures. What do I care about getting my picture took? Nothing! And that's just what I told Hannah!

"Now where is that boy?" He bellowed.

Zan stood beside him and asked, "Me, Sir?"

Old Zande looked sidewise like a cross parrot, snapped "Yes'r, you, Sir. Where in tarnation you been, boy. Where's them blasted scissors?"

Blaze, her eyes laughing but full of tears, handed her father the scissors. He gave her a smile, asking, "Is that Hannah there behind you, Daughter?"

Blaze looked around, then back to him sand said, "No, Father. That's Lara. You remember our Lara. Mother raised her."

"Yes, yes. Of course, that's right. But she favors Hannah some. Yes, she does, more'n some, more'n mebbe anyone."

Zan glanced at Lara who, to his surprise, returned his glance so full on at him that he wanted to look away, but he held fast, keeping his gaze steady, and it seemed for a spell they were locked in time. From only a few steps apart they looked deeply into each other's eyes as if nobody else was there.

Zan suddenly began to feel at ease, taking each breath more easily than the last, and feeling to home looking in her eyes. Then Lara began to smile, just slightly at first, but when he returned it, her smile broadened, then became full faced, and her eyes seemed to brighten with a happiness Zan hadn't seen since she was a small girl on his knee. Zan's heart was pumping strongly, and he finally felt comfort with the woman he had loved for so long, yet for so long denied it to himself and her. He now knew, strongly and for the first time, after the ceremony and fixings were done, that they'd be going to their Home Place together and living on their ranch till the end of their time.

Zan and Lara stood there, frozen with their shared feelings, as if alone together in time, and then Blaze nudged Zan with her elbow, nodding toward Grampa Allan.

The old man's first son, Zande Junior and the grandson Zan each took the old man by one arm and moved forward into a battery of cameras poised in front of what was probably the largest crowd of folks ever to gather on the Big Sur at any one time.

Within touching distance of the ribbon, Old Zande halted.

"I'll cut this here ribbon, but I'll say you a few things, first."

There was clapping and hearty calls of "hear, hear, speech, Mr. Allan!"

"I'm talking to my children," he said, "and my generations. I was young in this land. In 1850 we had hopes and plans. They were new in our day as anything is new in this day. Our job was to fill this hard land with fertile fields, with sons whose sons would have sons. I think Almighty God put a charge on men that they should live in their own time. But he's real patient, God is, and He let me stay on way past my time, so's I could see a miracle. I knocked down a mountain and I lived to see a man of his time pick it up with the help of God with the new ways of this time."

"Here, Boy," He said, you cut this thing. It's your time, your day, your road."

Zan shook his head, steadied his voice."

"I wouldn't make the pretty picture you'll make, Gramp. And you got to cut it, or eat the scissor, remember?"

Old Zande hung back for a moment, reluctant to face all these people, as he give in to the new times, to the new road. He shook his head, wet his lips, and then said in a strong but quavering voice, "So help me God, I'll do it!"

The scissors trembled in his hand as he walked three steps forward. Cheers echoed from the crowd, bouncing back from the hills, then waning out to sea, and hats sailed high in the air as he made one quick, firm slash and the ribbon parted in two pieces.

His children, grandchildren and great-grandchildren, as well as his friends, neighbors and total strangers, crowded around, but the first Zande Allan turned away from them all.

"I've overstayed my time," he said, I'll be goin' to home now, to be with Hannah, and take some rest."

THE END

ABOUT THE AUTHORS

Lillian Bos Ross and her husband Harry Dicken Ross first backpacked into Big Sur in the summer of 1923. They were down from Telegraph Hill in San Francisco where they were booksellers and part of a bohemian writers group. Inspired by Big Sur's beauty and its residents' pioneer lifestyle, they decided to free themselves from their regulated life and moved to Big Sur.

After opening the first art gallery in Salinas, then spent a stint at the Hearst Castle where Dicken worked as a tile setter and wood carver, after which they hitched a 22-mile ride into the south coast of Big Sur with a man who earned $4.00 a day mining gold at Salmon Creek.

The magnificent and rugged coastal land enchanted them and in 1939 they settled into Livermore Ledge, a Big Sur homestead house. They lived on salmon, abalone, wild berries and bought coffee, eggs and honey for $1.00 from their friendly neighboring Big Sur homesteader families. Dicken sold a few carved sculptures and Lillian wrote stories for area publications.

The Stranger became a best seller and received the National Book Award in 1942, to which the *New York Times* exclaimed, "So long as America has a stock of Zande and Hannah Allans…it can face any tomorrow unafraid" and Eleanor Roosevelt wrote, "…it carries a thread of inspiration all through it, which should be good news for us in these days."

World War II was in full battle during the writing of *The Stranger.* In her diaries Lillian wrote on December 11, 1941, that "a Japanese submarine fired 12 shots at a lumber schooner off Pfeiffer Point" and three days later "the tanker *Larry Doheny* was bombed a few miles south of us and another tanker was sunk at San Simeon." These were nervous times for all Americans.

The second novel, *Blaze Allan,* named after Zande and Hannah's daughter, reveals the raw individualism, rugged character and strength

295

of the American Pioneers whose last survivors flourished on the remote Big Sur Coast long before the automobile road, which took eighteen years to carve from the Big Sur cliffs, and opened up this inaccessible and sparsely populated land to the travelers of the world. When Lillian passed in 1959 she left behind the skeleton of the third book of the *Big Sur Trilogy*, an unfinished manuscript that was destined to be completed some fifty years later by Gary M. Koeppel.

Lillian Bos Ross and Harry Dicken Ross

From the Pat Hathaway Collection

Gary M. Koeppel   After studying writing at Oregon State University under Bernard Malamud, author of *The Natural* and other novels, he abandoned dental school to become a graduate fellow at the Iowa Writer's Workshop where he wrote several short stories and a novel, *Harehound*. Upon graduation, he became a professor of English and Creative Writing at Iowa, Puerto Rico and Portland State University in Oregon.

While teaching writing at Portland State University in 1967, Koeppel developed a new method of teaching writing to university students and was invited by Esalen founder Dick Price and Gestalt psychologist Fritz Perles to move to Big Sur and teach his "Experiential Composition" to their seminarians. But in the late 1960's Esalen suffered from everything excessive, which created an environment of paranoia and psychosis, so Koeppel resigned and moved to Malibu where, by chance and circumstance, he developed a new type of candle that involved sculpting sand castings in public at malls throughout California, then at Universal Studios and Disneyland.

In 1971 Koeppel returned to Big Sur, bought the Coast Gallery and wrote a book about his candle sculpting titled *"Sculptured Sandcast Candles."* In 1973 a 100-year storm inundated the gallery, which he rebuilt in 1974 out of large, municipal redwood water tanks, creating what has become a major architectural landmark on the Big Sur Coast.

For the next forty years Koeppel and his wife, Emma, opened four more Coast Galleries and produced 30 art events around the world. After co-founding the Big Sur Chamber of Commerce and founding the Big Sur Volunteer Fire Brigade, from 1978 to 1981 Koeppel published the Big Sur Gazette newspaper that successfully thwarted an attempt to seize private property and federalize Big Sur as a national park.

In 2012 Koeppel returned to writing full time with his first project to fulfill the promise he made in 1985 to Lillian's husband, Dicken, who asked him to complete her unfinished manuscript of *The Road,* the third novel of the *Big Sur Trilogy.*

The Road completes the 100-year saga of three generations of the Zande Allan family who homesteaded their remote South Coast property from the 1830's through 1937. Called the saga of the last American pioneer family, the third novel is a mixture of history and fiction that tells the story of the building of Highway One and ends with the opening of a road that changed forever the lives of the Big Sur pioneer families while also opening up the Big Sur Coast to the visitors of the world who will forever be awed by its majestic beauty.

ACKNOWLEDGMENTS

Delia Bradford, a plein air painter born in Big Sur to artist parents, painted the covers of the three books of the *Big Sur Trilogy*. (www.deliabradford.com)

Roger Rybkowski of Adpartner graphic design, edited, designed and prepared the *Big Sur Trilogy* for publication. (www.myadpartner.biz).

Gary M. Koeppel, educator, artist and entrepreneur, resurrected the first two novels and rewrote the third unpublished manuscript to create the *Big Sur Trilogy*.

Robin Coventry, now passed, many of whose illustrations of Big Sur homesteads populate and embellish the written storytelling in the *Big Sur Trilogy*.

Photo archivist Pat Hathaway provided numerous historic photographs that were converted into black & white sketches to embellish the *Big Sur Trilogy*. (www.caviews.com)

Coast Publishing in Carmel, California publishes art books, novels and limited edition art prints and sculpture. (www.cstpub.com)

Made in the USA
San Bernardino, CA
02 October 2013